Vendetta

Also by Stanley Salmons

ALEXEI'S TREE AND OTHER STORIES

A BIT OF IRISH MIST

THE TOMB

THE CANTERPURRY TALES

FOOTPRINTS IN THE ASH

NH_3

THE MAN IN TWO BODIES

The Planetary Trilogy:

BOOK 1: SATURN RUN

BOOK 2: MARS RUN

BOOK 3: JUPITER RUN

Jim Slater Series:

THE DOMINO MAN

COUNTERFEIT

THE REICH LEGACY

VENDETTA

Stanley Salmons

Copyright © 2018 Stanley Salmons
All rights reserved.
The right of Stanley Salmons to be identified as author of this work has been asserted by him in accordance with the Copyright, Designs and Patents Act 1988

ISBN: 1724531166

ISBN-13: 978-1724531162

This novel is a work of fiction. Any resemblance between the characters and actual persons, living or dead, is entirely coincidental.

Stanley Salmons was born in London. He is internationally known for his work in the fields of biomedical engineering and muscle physiology, published in over two hundred scientific articles and twelve scientific books. Although still contributing to the real world of research, he maintains a parallel existence as a fiction writer, in which he can draw from his broad scientific experience. He has published over forty short stories in various magazines and anthologies. This is his eleventh novel.

GLOSSARY

Camo	Camouflage
claymore	An antipersonnel mine
CENTCOM	United States Central Command
CID	US Criminal Investigation Command
DoD	United States Department of Defense
FAA	Federal Aviation Administration of the US
frag	Kill an unpopular man with a grenade
good-nite	A (fictional) grenade that disperses a short-acting anaesthetic gas
Incoming	Incoming fire
Infil/exfil	Infiltration/exfiltration
JSOC	Joint Special Operations Command
KPA	Korean People's Army
NCIC	The National Crime Information Center
NK	North Korea
NSA	National Security Agency
ORs	Other ranks
RA	Resolution Advisory
RPG	Rocket-propelled grenade
SAD/SOG	Special Activities Division Special Operations Group
SAF	Special Assignment Force (fictional Special Operations Force of the US Army)
SAS	Special Air Service (Special Forces unit of the British army)
SEALS	United States Navy Sea, Air and Land Forces (Special Operations Force of the US Navy)
Sim	Flight simulator, used in training and evaluating pilots

GLOSSARY (contd)

SOCOM	United States Special Operations Command
tab	March or jog with heavy equipment over difficult terrain
TCAS	Traffic Collision Avoidance System
USCYBERCOM	United States Cyber Command
USDB	United States Disciplinary Barracks ('Leavenworth') Leavenworth, Kansas
USP	United States Penitentiary, Leavenworth, Kansas
XO	Second-in-Command

WASHINGTON

Bob Cressington, Secretary of Defense

Tony Grieg, Senior Special Agent, FBI

John Abadi, Director of Digital Innovation, CIA

Joseph Templeton, Director of CIA and Commander of JSOC

Admiral Mike Randall, Director of NSA and Commander of USCYBERCOM

Chester Hardman, Secretary of State for Homeland Security

Major-General Seaman, Commander of 24th Air Force

Laura Gianni, Director of the Department of Energy

For Paula, Graham, Daniel, and Debby

1

Colonel Jim Slater made a habit of being in his office at six in the morning. That way he could clear his desk of outstanding tasks and still be in time to join the daily 10k tab with full pack. New recruits were probably surprised to find their CO on the exercise with them, but they'd assume he did it to keep fit. Actually there was an even better reason. When you shut yourself away in an office all sorts of issues could pass you by. On a tab you could keep in touch. By the time they'd completed the hill climb everyone would be sweating freely and ready for a short rest. It was a moment when someone would often sit down next to him for a quiet word about a general problem or a personal one that would never have made it across his desk in the normal way. Even when conversations around him were limited to the normal banter he got the chance to gauge what they used to refer to back in the 22 SAS as 'atmospherics'. Right now he had no need to ask why the overall mood on the ground was subdued. The Special Assignment Force trained intensively for every conceivable kind of scenario but they hadn't been given a real mission for months and it was having a bad effect on morale. Unfortunately it was out of his hands. He had to respond to orders from Washington, and they normally came via General Wendell Harken.

He'd been at his desk for barely half an hour when a message came up on his screen. Evidently the working day started early in Washington, too. The message was brief:

'Holoconference at 10 am. Confirm. Wendell.'

Jim felt a small surge of energy. A holoconference could mean action and it couldn't some soon enough. He spoke his confirmation into the messaging service and tried, not all that successfully, to return his attention to the jobs in hand. Frequent glances at his watch seemed only to make the time pass more slowly. Finally, with ten minutes to go, he heaved a sigh of relief and walked the short distance to the holoconference suite.

By now all the officers and ORs who didn't have other duties were out on the tab, so the base was quiet. Although they weren't yet into April, here in North Carolina it was already sultry. Even his footsteps on the magnacrete path seemed to be muffled by a dense blanket of warm and humid air. The tab would be harder in a spell like this, but it was good practice. A mission could be in a tropical or subtropical region and they needed to be fully operational in conditions as tough – and tougher – than this.

He unlocked the door to the windowless room, went in, and closed it behind him. It took just a few moments for his eyes to adjust to the subdued red illumination. The room acquired shape: the single chair, the console, the floor-mounted projector in the centre. He sat down, powered up the console, switched to receiving mode, and waited. You didn't use this means of communication just so you could see each other – you could do that on a phone. But holoconferencing involved the transmission of large amounts of encrypted data and for that it used an intranet. To his knowledge the system had never been hacked.

As he waited Jim could picture Wendell at the Pentagon, leaving his office on the D-ring for the holoconference suite on the same floor. He would be striding along the corridor at this moment, his shirt immaculately pressed, the tie knotted precisely, the trousers creased to a knife-edge.

If – as he hoped – this was an assignment he'd have to decide who to send. Brian Murdoch came instantly to mind. Chubby and good-natured, the man could ass around with the best of them when he was at Fort Piper, but once in the field he led with absolute authority. Brian had missed out on the last two missions, and Jim knew what it felt like when that kept happening. Of course the decision would be easier if this was a bigger action; he could send two squads, even three—

Harken's image stuttered in blue and white above the projector, then consolidated in full colour, head and shoulders only. The familiar face looked like it was carved from granite and the hair, greying now, was still cropped short. It was ten o'clock on the dot.

'Jim,' he said.

'Wendell,' Jim replied. 'What's up?'

'Job for you. Cameroon.'

'Cameroon?' In his head Jim was already running through the problems encountered in that region. It was generally trafficking of some kind – drugs, arms, or people – usually run by local militias.

'The US Army has a detachment out there,' Harken continued. 'They're in a purely advisory role, helping the Cameroonian regular army to cope with insurgents coming down from Nigeria. The detachment is under the command of a Major Leadenthall. He's requested assistance.'

'Assistance with what?'

'There've been reports of whole villages being wiped out,' Harken said. 'When the Cameroonian regulars go in all they find is bodies: men, older women and children. Some are hacked to pieces; for the others it's bullets or grenades. They never find any girls or young women. That almost certainly points to a sex trafficking operation. The regulars asked Leadenthall for some sort of help, but it was outside his terms of reference. He's passed it up the line. SOCOM saw a potential risk to US relations with both Nigeria and Cameroon, so they want it done quietly. That's why they gave it to us.'

'Is that all we've got to go on?' Jim said. 'What size of force do we need? How do we equip them?'

'The bare minimum. From what I've been told they just want tactical help. It's delicate because the operation's so close to the border.'

'Just one squad, then, with multirifles?'

'That should do it. Major Leadenthall will give them a full briefing when they get there.'

It remained only to get the contact information and the location of the field unit and they terminated the call. Jim sat back and sighed. It was a bit disappointing but at least it was a mission. He shut things down and returned to his office. After a few minutes he buzzed the intercom.

'Bagley.'

'Yes, Colonel?'

'When Captain Murdoch gets back from the tab ask him to drop by, would you?'

2

Jim settled down to organizing the logistics for the operation, starting with military transport from Raleigh-Durham airfield. Brian Murdoch had been jubilant at getting the mission. He'd left the office with a spring in his stride and went off to pick his team, brief them, and draw equipment from the armoury. Jim envied him; he'd have relished the action himself but that was seldom possible now. He turned back to his task. He'd got the squad as far as Garoua International Airport, but the US Army detachment was further north. It would be quickest if they could send a Rotofan to pick the guys up from Garoua…

There was a light knock at the door. He looked up. His aide-de-camp rarely made a complete entrance but the face that had appeared around the door was enough. It used to remind Jim of a hurt spaniel but these days it was more like a disappointed bloodhound. Sergeant Bagley had honed the expression and the put-upon voice to the pitch of an art form. Perhaps it reflected some kind of struggle in the man's private life – if indeed he had a private life. Jim had never enquired. Theirs was a professional relationship. He preferred to keep it that way and he suspected Bagley felt the same way.

'Yes, Bagley?'

'Lieutenant Holly Cressington's here for her interview, sir.'

'Okay, give me a couple of minutes, then show her in.'

The Special Assignment Force never advertised vacancies, but from time to time an application would be received from a serving soldier in the US Army and these would be looked at. Few made it past that stage; those who did were invited for interview. If they were considered suitable they'd be put through an induction course that had been devised by Wendell Harken when he was CO. It was tough – very tough – and not many passed. It called for more than strength and endurance: there were psychological assessments, tests of intelligence and judgement in stressful situations, survival skills, unarmed combat, handling of weapons, and more. In theory the SAF was open to women as well as men and separate accommodation was provided for them. Many did well in the technical and intellectual tasks but couldn't meet the physical challenges. Those who did get through ranked with the best they had. Soldiers like Sally Kent, who'd stopped a bullet in the leg during the Tanzanian mission. The round had shattered her femur, putting her in hospital and rehab for some time. Now she was back on base. She wasn't fit for active duty – he knew that and she knew that – but she was working on it, spending an hour or more in the gym every day to restore the strength in her wasted leg muscles.

He reached into a drawer, took out Lieutenant Holly Cressington's service record, and leafed quickly through it to refresh his memory. She was seeking a transfer from the

101st Airborne. During officer training she'd ranked top in both marksmanship and unarmed combat, and in every other respect her qualifications and record were outstanding. It seemed like she was as good as Sally, and if so she'd be a real asset. There was one problem: her father was Bob Cressington, US Secretary of Defense. It shouldn't have made a difference but it did; SAF operations were challenging and they were dangerous. It wasn't only death or injury the soldiers faced; there was always the possibility of capture, which could be particularly bad for a woman. If she joined the Force the ultimate responsibility for her safety would rest with him, and in her case that responsibility would be particularly hard to bear, because he and Bob were on very good terms.

He had no time to dwell on it further. There was another light knock, Bagley opened the door, and Lieutenant Cressington took two steps inside. She was smaller than he'd anticipated, and lightly built. Her hair was dark and cut regulation length. She gave him a crisp salute.

'Lieutenant Holly Cressington, sir!'

'At ease, Lieutenant,' Jim said. 'Have a seat.' He pointed to a chair in front of the desk. She took it and sat up, neat and straight. It was natural for him to look for a family resemblance and indeed it was there in the lean, squarish face, but his attention was riveted to her eyes. Bob's eyes were grey, but hers were a light grey, pale enough to be startling. They were framed with long, dark eyelashes that only heightened the contrast.

Strange, he thought, how his gaze was always drawn to the eyes. He remembered the physician who'd been assigned to euthanase him back in 2052. She'd had nice eyes, too...

The memory sent a chill draught through him and he hastily returned to present business.

He was about to open the interview when Holly Cressington pre-empted him.

'Permission to speak, sir.'

'No need to be formal, Lieutenant. Go ahead.'

'Sir, I'm aware that you know my father. I'd like to make it clear before we start that I have never used his government role to gain favourable treatment before and I'm not trying to use it now. If I'm good enough I'd like to join the SAF but if I'm accepted I want it to be on my own merits.'

Jim raised his eyebrows and smiled. 'I assure you, Lieutenant, that if you are accepted it won't be on any other basis.' He tapped her resumé. 'But you have an excellent record and a good prospect of going up the ranks where you are. Why apply to us?'

'It's the elite force. I've known that for years, and it's always been my goal to be part of it. But I knew I had to prove my worth in the regulars first. I'm ready now.'

Jim regarded her thoughtfully. 'Your father's been conspicuously successful in his career. We can't ignore that. Has it left you feeling that you, personally, have something to prove?'

The glint in those electric eyes showed she'd seen through the question. 'I just want to be as good as any other soldier, sir, male or female.'

As good as, not better, Jim noted with approval. 'All right, let me ask you this. Suppose you're on a mission and you find yourself with people who aren't working as a team. What do you do?'

The answer came promptly. 'That situation wouldn't arise, sir. We conduct exercises all the time and any behaviour like that would be rooted out right away. I assume the SAF would do the same, probably even more so.'

Jim nodded. It was a good answer. He consulted her resumé. 'You mention spoken Arabic. Region?'

'Gulf. I also have a little Spanish.'

'So I see. South American dialects?'

'No, I haven't had the opportunity, but I'm a quick learner.'

The interview continued. He was looking for reasons to reject her but found none. More than that, he was impressed. Finally he drew matters to a close.

'All right, Lieutenant. We'll take you onto induction and see how it works out. The course starts next week. In the meantime you can use all the facilities on the base. You'll be assigned accommodation here and I'll get Lieutenant Sally Kent to show you around. Good luck.'

He rose and extended a hand, and she was on her feet instantly, taking his own in a firm grip.

'Thank you, sir.'

There was a pretty flush in her cheeks as she saluted. Then she turned smartly and left the office.

He remained standing for a few moments, looking wistfully at the door. She was unlikely to meet the physical challenges of the induction course. Pity. She'd have been a lively addition to their ranks.

3

Two days later Jim received a peremptory summons to appear before a subcommittee from the Defense Finance and Accounting Service. He was to report to the Pentagon in the late morning.

He got there early and went straight to Wendell Harken's office. It was unusual to see Wendell's desk strewn with papers – legal papers, in all probability, which were still circulated and archived as hard copy. Apart from the desk the room was as uncluttered and as minimally furnished as ever. Behind the desk was a large wall screen where there would have been a window if there had been windows on D-ring. Wendell's be-ribboned tunic was carefully draped on a hangar next to the door.

Jim felt a pang of guilt at interrupting the man in the middle of something, but he was still indignant at being dragged away from Fort Piper when there was a mission in progress.

'Wendell, I've been summoned by the DFAS. Why? Bagley and I keep a close eye on finances and there's no way we've exceeded budget.'

Wendell cleared some of the papers to one side and rested his arms on the desk. 'The SAF may not be, Jim, but as an entity the Department of Defense is. We're coming to the end of the second quarter, and the accountants down in Indianapolis are clearly concerned about the overspend. They've sent a delegation here. Their brief is to review allocations to subordinate departments, services, and agencies for the next two quarters.'

This is what it does to you, Jim thought. *When Wendell was my CO at Fort Piper he talked to me like a soldier. These days he sounds more and more like a politician.*

'You weren't singled out, Jim,' Wendell added. 'None of us had much notice.'

Jim frowned. 'Let me understand this. Are you saying they could cut our budget for the second half?'

'I can't rule it out, but it's more likely they're looking ahead to allocations in the next fiscal year. It's unlikely this administration will increase the Department's appropriation, and costs are rising all the time, so they'll need to make economies.'

'And the SAF's in the firing line?'

Wendell sighed. 'It always is. And it's always the same question: why do we need another, highly expensive Special Force? Why can't the SAF's assignments be handled by Delta Force or the SEALS?'

'They could have put that question to you. No one knows the SAF better.'

'They'll speak to me, of course, but they insist on having someone closer to the action, as they put it. What we both have to do is convince them that the SAF represents good value for money.'

'I never think about my people in those terms.'

'For the purposes of this exercise that's precisely what you have to do.'

*

The meeting was held in a windowless conference room on the third floor. On the other side of a table four men and one woman stood up as he was shown in. The man in the centre extended a delicate hand and Jim shook it lightly. He took in at a glance the well-tailored suits and shirts. Three of the suits were in a glossy fabric that Jim didn't recognize, although it looked costly. The woman wore the jacket of her trouser suit over a silk blouse, with a silk scarf at the neck. They all sat down and Jim took the single chair facing them. The man who'd shaken his hand thanked him for coming – as if he'd a choice. They didn't introduce themselves.

Jim worked it out quickly. The one in the centre was the senior member of the committee and he'd be the one asking the questions. The others were already leafing through paperwork or looking at tablets. One man stared fixedly at two sheets of paper, placed side by side in front of him, no doubt making some sort of comparison. The senior man glanced at some notes, then clasped those pale hands and leaned forward. He had grey hair, which was thinning, and wore gold-rimmed glasses. To Jim's jaundiced eye he was the epitome of somebody who would examine a military operation in which men and women put their lives on the line and reduce it to figures on a spreadsheet.

'Colonel,' he began. 'We're looking into the way the Defense Department's budget is spent. This is a very large department with many subdivisions, so it's only fair to compare like with like. In this instance we're looking at the allocations to Special Forces. Your command, the SAF, is not large but compared to other Special Forces the payroll costs are disproportionately high.'

Jim waited. He hadn't been asked a question yet.

After an expectant pause the man grimaced slightly and asked the question. 'Can you explain that?'

'We're very light on administration and infrastructure at Fort Piper,' Jim said. 'The vast bulk of those costs go on operational staff.'

'Yes, Colonel, but the cost per head seems particularly high. Can you say why that is?'

Jim looked along the line of expensive suits and the question raised a tingle of resentment. He remained calm.

'Sir, our soldiers aren't grunts off the street. Most have degrees, usually in a branch of engineering, and all are fluent in at least one foreign language. They're ambitious, highly committed, experienced and highly trained. It's quite natural to find individuals like that higher up the pay scale.'

'And you need personnel of that calibre for your operations?'

'Absolutely.'

'Are you saying the SAF is better than the SEALS or Delta Force?'

Jim saw the trap door opening up. 'Not better, sir, but we have different skills. I'm sure this committee's aware that we're often asked to undertake challenging missions deep in other sovereign territories. There are invariably issues of both national security and international relations at stake, so we work covertly and deniably. We go in, we do the job, we come out, and we leave not a trace behind. The fact that our operations have created no major international incidents speaks for itself.'

He was glossing over the hoo-ha created by their mission in the Honduras, but it was three years ago and he hoped they'd forgotten about it – if they ever knew.

'Yes, yes, but can you be a bit more specific than that?'

'Sir, I'm not at liberty to discuss specifics. All our missions are classified, but it's not just that: I have to protect the safety and anonymity of my soldiers. All I can do is give you examples of the types of mission we undertake.'

'Very well, then, go on.'

He did go on. He described hostage extractions, a foiled assassination, and the breaking up of a drug trafficking network, putting it all in general terms. He could provide more detail on one operation because it had received so much media attention already. It was, of course, the Africa mission he'd planned and led himself when he was a Lieutenant-Colonel, although that one had really passed its sell-by date by now.

Eventually they excused him from further questioning. Out in the corridor he took a deep breath. He thought he'd survived the interrogation reasonably well. Still, he was glad it was over. He checked his watch. He didn't like to be away from base when he had a team in the field, but there was time for a quick word with Bob Cressington if Bob was free. It was important to phone ahead; security was especially tight up on the fifth floor.

Bob's PA picked him up from the E-ring check point and showed him in.

'Jim!' Bob said, rising from his chair to shake hands. 'How're you doing?'

'Pretty good, Bob. Yourself?'

'Same old battles. Everyone scrambling for a bigger slice of the cake when there's less cake to go round.'

'As long as there are a few crumbs left for my outfit.'

Bob laughed. 'Come and sit down.' They took armchairs by the window. Outside, the sky was an uninterrupted grey, but at least it wasn't raining.

Despite the burdens of office Bob still managed to look youthful and fit. 'Can't spend long, I'm afraid,' he said. 'I've got Chiefs of Staff in fifteen minutes. What's on your mind?'

'I assume you know we accepted Holly onto the induction course to see if she makes the grade.'

'Yes, she told me.'

'I wasn't sure how you'd feel about it.'

He nodded. 'Good of you to ask, Jim, but she's her own person. Whether you decide to accept her or reject her, it's your decision. I wouldn't want to influence you one way or the other.'

'That's the way she wanted it, too.' He hesitated, then added, 'Are you worried about her?'

'Sure I'm worried about her, I'm her father. That's what it is to be a parent, you worry about them all the time.' He sighed. 'I love my daughter but if that's what she's set her heart on…'

'Okay. That's really all I wanted to know. Look, I won't keep you any longer. You have a meeting and I need to get back to Fort Piper.'

They stood up and Bob walked Jim to the door. Jim held it open, but turned before leaving.

'The course calls for incredible resilience and fitness, Bob. The success rate is never high, and it's a lot lower for women. She probably won't get through.'

Bob smiled. 'I wouldn't bet on that.'

4

He reached the base in time for dinner in the mess hall and sat down next to Sergeant Ted Nichols. They didn't specify a minimum height for the SAF and Ted was one of the shortest men on the base. When he was out on manoeuvres, fully loaded, he looked as wide as he was tall. But anyone who thought he was fat would be making a serious mistake. Fat had no place in the fitness regime they maintained here.

'Bagley said you were in Washington, Jim. Been chatting up the great and the good?'

Jim snorted. 'I'd have sooner been on the morning tab with you guys.'

'You must be joking. Damned pack gets heavier every time I do it. I thought this kind of thing was supposed to get easier.'

'Maybe it's you getting heavier, Ted, not the pack.'

'Hey, could be.'

Jim didn't enquire about Holly – he knew he wouldn't have to. Word got around quickly if there was someone new on the base, especially if that someone was a striking young woman. The subject came up soon enough. Ned Howells, sitting opposite them, was responsible for the gym and he brought it up first.

'New girl was in today,' he said. 'Introduced herself then did some circuit training. Three circuits without stopping.'

'Three?' Ted said.

He nodded. 'Had a word with me afterwards. She was breathing lightly.'

'Breathing lightly. Jesus!' Ted folded his arms on the table and sank his head into them.

The others laughed.

'Yeah, she said she'd like to do some unarmed combat too,' Ned continued. 'There was no one else around, so I took her on the mat myself. She knows the moves and she's fast. Hasn't got a man's strength but with speed like that she may not need it.'

Coming from Ned that was high praise. Jim normally shared instruction duties in unarmed combat with him, so it was quite possible he'd be taking the young woman on himself at some stage. It should be interesting.

'Where is she, anyway?' Jim asked, looking around. He spotted Sally, got up, and went over to her. 'Lieutenant Cressington not with you?' he asked.

'No. I said I'd call for her but she didn't want to come.' Sally screwed up her face. 'She's a private sort of person, Jim. I don't think she's ready to fraternize just yet.'

'Well try to encourage her. Sounds like she's burning calories hand over fist and she needs to take some on board. Is she going on the run tomorrow?'

'You bet. I suggested she did it without full pack but she wouldn't hear of it.' She shrugged. 'Determined young lady.'

'All right, we won't push it. Thanks, Sally.'

'No problem.'

*

As Lieutenant Cressington progressed through the induction course Jim started to take an increasing interest in reports of her progress. To his surprise she'd already passed tests of endurance, speed and accuracy on the firing range, survival in the jungle, combat training, and resistance to interrogation. She'd done well so far – very well – but that was no reason to change his prediction. Now would come the toughest part of all. In case she was taken prisoner she'd be required to know who her captors were and where she was being taken. She'd be expected to recognize a variety of languages, and for languages such as Spanish and Arabic that were associated with the usual trouble spots she'd need to spot local variations. She'd be hooded and taken on a circuitous route then asked to trace it on a map. Finally she'd be taken abroad to an unidentified destination and the two exercises would be put together. More candidates dropped out at this stage than at any other.

In the end it was Bob Cressington who was the better judge of his daughter's capabilities. She returned to base having put in a very creditable performance and the final report was one of the most impressive he'd ever seen. There were no grounds whatever to deny her admission to the SAF.

She evidently knew that, too, when she arrived at his office. Her cheeks were flushed and those eyes lit up the room.

He smiled. 'Welcome to the SAF, Captain Cressington.'

She blinked. 'Er, Lieutenant, sir.'

'Captain. You could hardly make a move like this without a promotion. Congratulations.'

'Thank you, sir.'

They shook hands and she left the office. Jim bit his lip. He could see some hard decisions on the horizon. It wasn't a problem yet; she'd still have to undergo more training and take part in operational exercises. But after that she'd be champing at the bit to lead a squad on a real assignment. Security was tight at Fort Piper, and the convention was not to discuss their assignments, either before or after completion. All the same, she'd see other teams going out and coming back and she'd be wondering when the hell her turn was coming. Sooner or later he'd have to give her a chance; it was a matter of picking the right mission. He couldn't give her a non-risky assignment and she wouldn't appreciate it if he did. At the same time it would be a disaster if she was a casualty and not only because her father was Bob Cressington. He faced an uncomfortable reality: he felt protective of her, too.

5

Jim was always restless when he had men in the field. He felt disconnected, out of it. He wanted to be there, with them, not behind a desk. At this moment Brian's squad was the only team on operational duty and he was waiting for the call. When the secure phone began its insistent beeping he hit the button right away.

'Yes, Brian?'

The familiar voice came down the line, slow and cheerful.

'We're with the US Army detachment now, Jim. This guy Major Leadenthall just briefed me. It's a trafficking operation, right enough, but all they know for sure is the insurgents have set up way stations in the jungle. It looks like they take the girls and young women there, not back to Nigeria. These guys may be good at snatching the girls but I reckon they're not smart enough to figure out how to shift them. Most likely they trade them with criminal gangs from Cameroon or Chad. Those people'd know where to ship them and how.'

'So what do they want from you?'

'Situation's different to what we were told, Jim. The Cameroonian regulars here think they've located one of these here way stations. They asked the US Army to move in and take it.'

'Why don't they take it themselves?' Jim asked.

'Good question. They say there may be captives in there with a few insurgents guarding them. They'd like to free the girls and capture the insurgents – could give them a lot of intel about the rest of the operation. They think the US Army is better equipped and trained to do it.'

'And Major Leadenthall has no intention of doing so.'

'Damn right. He says there's a formal agreement with the government: they're there in a purely advisory capacity and this is outside their remit. He put the request in because we could do it quietly and not upset anyone.'

Jim gave a short, ironic laugh. 'This doesn't sound like *tactical help* to me.'

'Me neither.'

'What's your reading of the situation, Brian?'

'Me? I think he's got it wrong. Insurgents aren't going to take captives and then be stuck with them for God-knows-how-long while they negotiate the deals – they're not that stupid. They'll have it all set up in advance and they'll move the girls out quick as they can. I wouldn't rate our chances of finding anyone in that way station. That's what I think. But Leadenthall seems to be taking it all at face value, so he's landed it on our doorstep. What do you say, Jim? Do we go ahead or not?'

Jim thought quickly. Without question the operation was something the Cameroonian ground forces should have handled themselves. Major Leadenthall was within his rights to refuse cooperation – his detachment was there in a strictly non-combatant role – but he should have thrown the request right back at them. Instead it had landed in SOCOM's lap, and now the SAF was involved. Leadenthall was going to get his ass kicked over this, and the cost of the operation wouldn't be coming from the SAF's budget, either. But all that could be sorted out afterwards. Right now he had a decision to make.

It was an experienced team out there. Brian was first-class, of course, and so was Sergeant Eddie Mayer, his second-in-command. Both had numerous missions under their belt, and they'd worked together on many of them. He ran through a quick mental roll call of the rest: Darren, Charlie, Javid, Bruno, Ken, Fernando. The objective should be well within their capabilities and they'd be very disappointed if they were pulled out now.

'Jim, you still there?'

'Yeah. Okay, look Brian, situation's different, but it's the kind of thing we do. Go for it.'

'Thought you'd say that. No problem. I'll tell the others.'

'Take care, Brian.'

'You too, Jim.'

He clicked off.

It was a straightforward decision and he returned to his work without giving it a second thought.

6

To get to the suspected way station the SAF team had to penetrate some distance into Cameroonian rainforest. A young soldier from the national army had been detailed to take them to the spot. He guided them quickly along a broad path where the undergrowth had been thinned by the passage of animals or men or both.

Like the rest of the squad Captain Brian Murdoch was wearing a helmet and body armour and carrying a pack as well as his multirifle. He felt enveloped by the heat and humidity. He knew it was the same for the others; their shirt collars were dark and their camo'd faces were streaked with sweat.

The path narrowed. He saw something, frowned, and held up a hand. Sergeant Eddie Mayer wandered over to see what it was about. Eddie was a big guy – six-foot-six and broad across the shoulders – and his long jaw gave him a lugubrious look. He peered over Brian's shoulder.

Brian was examining some branches on one side of the path, the tips of which were broken. Then he went to the trees on the other side and found the same thing. 'Something big passed this way,' he said quietly.

'Do they have elephants here?' Eddie asked.

'Not that I know of.' He bent to brush some leaf litter away and pointed. 'But if they do, they run on tyres.'

Eddie looked more closely. 'Wide tread. Not a car. Deep, too. Must have been carrying a load. How long ago?'

'Hard to say, but not that long.' He turned to the rest of the squad. 'Okay, look sharp.'

They spaced themselves out, walking in single file, rifles fanning to the rear, both sides, and the front.

The rainforest was heavy with silence, which made the sudden noises the more startling: hoots and answering hoots of birds or monkeys, an insect fizzing past, rustles in the undergrowth as birds, reptiles, or small mammals fled in alarm at their passage. Rifles jerked up at every sound.

The Cameroonian soldier who was guiding them was particularly jumpy, eyes darting around, tongue travelling over his lips. When he held up a hand for them to halt and pointed ahead his finger was trembling and his dark eyes were wide with fear.

Brian said to him, *'Quel âge avez-vous?'*

'Dix-huit ans, m'sieu.'

Brian sighed. An eighteen-year-old kid. He pointed to the ground. *'Attendez-nous ici, comprenez?'*

The youngster nodded gratefully.

He beckoned to Eddie and the two crept forward. After a couple of hundred yards a clearing opened up to the left and they saw their target. It looked like a small warehouse. The walls were of cinder block and it had a pitched roof bearing a box-like construction at one end. Despite Eddie's size neither he nor Brian made a sound as they circled the building at a safe distance and came back to the starting point.

Brian kept his voice low. 'Quite a job to build this in the jungle.'

Eddie said, 'Whatever made those tyre tracks probably had the blocks and cement on it.'

'Or people.'

'Yeah, could be people.'

'Well one thing's for sure – this thing's been here no time at all. We're in a rainforest, for Christ's sake. Plants grow like stink, but the stuff in that clearing has put on hardly anything at all.'

'Maybe they cut it again,' Eddie offered.

'Nah, they might do that round the door but the rest would be good cover.' He looked around, scanning the area. 'I don't like it, Eddie. Something about this place. It's too darned quiet.'

'Chances are there's no one inside by now.'

'If they are in there it's dangerous, and if they aren't it could be booby-trapped, so it's still dangerous. Shame there aren't any windows, I'd have put good-nites through the windows if there were any. Knock any hostiles cold for a short while so we could bust in and make things safe.'

Eddie pointed to the box-like structure. 'Could drop one down that ventilation shaft or chimney or whatever it is.'

'Too big for a chimney. Any case, they wouldn't light a cooking fire here – the smoke would go above the forest canopy and give their position away. No, it's got to be for ventilation. But where does it go to? If it's just a hole in the roof, okay, but maybe it goes into a loft or a basement or something. Then we could rush in and find everyone in there wide awake, rifles cocked.'

'See what you mean.'

'Tell you what, we'll drop a smoke bomb instead. We'll know if it works because you'll see smoke under the door and they'll come running out.'

'Sounds good. With a smoke bomb we'd know for sure.'

'I'll do it.' He pointed to a tree growing a couple of metres behind the building. The trunk was sheer but it was laced with a tangle of thick vines. 'There's a branch up there, almost overhanging the roof – I can use that. Okay, we'll brief the others.'

They returned to the waiting soldiers and Brian signalled them to come round him. He said, 'Okay, it's not much more than a cinder-block shed. No windows, just the one door in the front. Can't tell if anyone's in there but we'll play it safe. I'll drop a smoke bomb down the ventilation shaft on the roof. Eddie, station yourself where you can see me and signal the others when I let it go. Darren, Charlie, Javid, Bruno – take up positions at the front. If people run out carrying weapons, open fire. Fernando, if nobody makes an appearance put a grenade through the door and we'll go in. Any questions?'

Ken held up his multirifle. 'We got smart grenades in the under-barrels, Brian. I'm setting twenty metres. Okay?'

'Should be about right.' Brian looked around. 'Okay, let's do it.'

Five minutes later everyone was in position, and Brian began to climb the tree.

7

Eddie watched Brian move out onto the branch and swing down onto the roof.

It was over in seconds, yet whenever Eddie looked back on it every instant seemed to stretch into minutes. Starting with the man who stood up inside that ventilation shaft and stitched Brian with a continuous burst from a machine pistol.

The impact sent Brian flying backwards off the roof. At the same time a hail of fire came down from the trees opposite the front of the building. He saw Bruno go down before switching his gaze quickly back to that ventilation shaft. The man there was swivelling around, looking for a new target. Eddie raised his multirifle and fired a burst of three that hurled him against the opposite side of the shaft. He bounced off it and flopped over the near edge. The machine pistol slid over the roof.

Eddie brought the rifle round swiftly, searching for a fresh target, waiting for muzzle flashes among the trees. Before he could fire, the others launched smart grenades. The ranging was good; the grenades exploded and the firing stopped abruptly. Bodies dropped from the trees – one… two… three… four… five – followed by an avalanche of leaves that covered them almost completely. Leaves continued to float down during the silence that followed. Then two more men came running out of the forest, shouting and firing like lunatics. Ken lifted his rifle and took both of them down.

Eddie shouted, 'Fernando, put a grenade through that door. There may be more inside.'

'What about the hostages?'

'There are no fucking hostages! Just do it!'

Fernando nodded and fired the grenade. Eddie slung his rifle over his shoulder and hurried over to the back of the building. When he saw Brian lying there he closed his eyes and his shoulders slumped. The body armour had stopped a few rounds but one had smashed through Brian's visor, exiting through the back of his head. Eddie's big hands clenched and unclenched. Then he went back to see what had happened to the others.

Javid and Ken were seeing to Bruno with pressure dressings and morphine. One trouser leg was soaked in blood. Javid took a marker and drew a large 'M' on Bruno's forehead.

He said, 'Hang in, there, Bruno. We'll get you to a hospital real soon.'

Bruno's eyes were half closed – he was already in a haze of morphine. He mumbled something like 'Yeah.'

Darren and Fernando were attending to Charlie, who was propped up against a tree. Eddie went over. They were bandaging his hand and fixing up a sling.

'How bad, Charlie?'

Charlie was trembling all over. He moistened his lips. 'Hurts like fuck.'

'Can you walk back?'

He nodded shakily. 'I guess.'

'Anyone else hit?'

'No.'

Darren took Eddie's arm, drew him to one side, 'What happened to Brian?'

Eddie shook his head.

'Oh, Christ.'

Eddie straightened up. With Brian gone he was now in command. 'Okay, guys. Rig a couple of stretchers out of tree branches. I'm going to talk to that kid.'

He ran back. The young soldier was still standing there, shaking like a leaf. Eddie gathered the boy's shirt in his left hand, lifted him off his feet at arm's length, and slapped him, forehand then backhand. From a woman the slaps would have been hard; from someone as big and powerful as Eddie they almost knocked him senseless. Eddie didn't speak French but he didn't need to. He just jerked his thumb over his shoulder.

The youngster sobbed. *'Je ne sais rien, m'sieu! Je ne sais rien!'*

He lifted his open palm and the soldier shook his head and repeated it again and again.

Eddie dropped him back on his feet, took him by the scruff of his neck, and led him to the clearing. He pointed to the stretchers, which the others were already putting together, and indicated with gestures that he should help to carry them. The youngster nodded vigorously. He seemed only too keen to make himself useful.

Fernando had evidently done what he could for Charlie's hand. Eddie beckoned to him and jerked his head towards the warehouse. The door was hanging on its hinges and now only a wisp of smoke was curling from the open doorway. They went in, rifles at the ready.

The warehouse was empty. The walls were pocked with cavities made by the grenade. Smoke and dust hung in the air, and the floor was littered with pieces of cinderblock. There was nothing else. He turned to Fernando, their eyes met, and Fernando grimaced. Then Eddie looked up and frowned. The ceiling where that ventilation shaft should have entered continued right to the walls without uninterruption. Light came through a line of air bricks placed just under the eaves. They were there for ventilation. So what was the shaft for?

'Fernando, take a couple of guys and get Brian's...' His throat closed; he couldn't say it. He swallowed. 'Put Brian on one of those stretchers. Something I need to check.'

'Okay.'

Eddie went round the back, climbed the tree and went out on the branch that put him on the roof. He walked up the shallow slope of the roof to the body slumped over the shaft. He picked the body up like a sack of potatoes and threw it over the side of the warehouse. Then he looked down into the shaft.

It didn't go anywhere. The base was solid planking.

8

Jim never initiated contact with a squad when a mission was in progress because it smacked too much of nannying; he left it to them to contact him. It was still too early to expect a report from Brian. The target may have been deep in the jungle. They had to reach it, do a recce, carry out the mission, and get back, possibly with prisoners or hostages, or both, who would hold them up. They wouldn't have a satellite connection until they were at the US army base again. He'd just have to be patient.

Bagley looked in. His expression was even more sorrowful than usual.

'Excuse me, sir, but there's a man at gate security. Been there all morning asking to see you.'

'I don't see anyone without an appointment, you know that.'

'Yes, sir, guard detail told him that but he's very insistent. Says he's driven down from Baltimore. And,' he paused, 'they think he's getting seriously dehydrated. He's sweating a lot.'

Jim scowled. 'Who is he and what does he want?'

'Says he's a publisher. Wants to talk something over with you. Says he only needs ten minutes of your time.'

'All right,' Jim sighed. 'Have them do a thorough security search and send him up. Give him exactly ten minutes, then come and tell me I'm due for my next appointment.'

'Sir.'

As he reached the door, Jim said, 'And you'd better give him some water before you show him in here.'

Some minutes later Bagley opened the door again and announced, 'Mr Denton Brice.'

The man who entered looked more like a salesman than Jim's idea of a publisher. He was wearing an ill-fitting blue suit and his pale blue shirt, open at the neck, was stained darkly down the front, no doubt from the water he'd been drinking too fast. His face was brick red. He extended a smooth, very damp, hand. Jim took it as briefly as he could and pointed to a chair. He flopped into it.

'Thank you for the water, Colonel. Boy, it's close. I don't know how you people survive this weather.'

'We dress for it,' Jim said pointedly. 'I'm told you've been waiting for some time. Why didn't you make an appointment?'

Brice leaned forward in a manner he no doubt judged suitable for imparting confidences, and Jim caught a whiff of peppermint-laden breath. 'To be perfectly honest with you, Colonel, I thought you'd turn me down, so I came in person.'

'It's that important?'

'To me, yes. I hope you'll find it of interest, too.'

He dipped into a briefcase and withdrew a slim paperback. 'We're a small publishing house, Colonel. Just a handful of books a year, produced as ebooks and paperbacks like this,' he held up the one in his hand. 'To be honest with you our sales are not that good as a rule. But this here was an exception. It's a memoir from a Special Forces soldier about his combat experiences. Four hundred copies sold so far and it's still moving well. There's a market out there – you can see that. People are keen to read about Special Forces operations. I guess they've had their share of fiction and they're hungry for the real McCoy.'

He placed it on Jim's desk. Jim ignored it, waiting.

'I read about your exploits in Africa, Colonel. If that guy,' he pointed at the book, 'could sell four hundred plus, someone with your career and experience should be able to sell ten times that – a hundred times even.'

Jim narrowed his eyes. 'You're asking me to write a book?'

'Like you to consider it, yes. Of course, you wouldn't exactly have to write it. We can use ghost writers if we give them the material.'

'Mr Brice, our operations are not intended for general consumption.'

'Yes, well, I understand that but maybe you could write about the older ones, or ones already known to the public – like the Africa business. We can offer you a very favourable package and the royalties on sales like that would be very handsome. Very handsome indeed.'

Jim was about to protest again but Brice forestalled him. 'Look, I don't need an answer now and I don't want to take up any more of your valuable time. Please accept this copy with my compliments. Take a look at it when you've got a moment and have a think about my offer – you sure won't get a better one.' He filched in a pocket, took out a billfold, and extracted a card, which he placed on the book. 'Don't hesitate to contact me if you need any more information or if you'd like to discuss it further. So that's it – for the moment. Thank you for seeing me.'

He got to his feet just as Bagley opened the door and announced that Jim's next appointment was waiting.

'Thank you, Bagley. Mr Brice is just leaving. Have him escorted out, would you?'

When the door closed Jim sat there for a few moments, shaking his head. Then he picked up the book, thrust the card inside the cover, and tossed it into a bottom desk drawer.

He looked at his watch and clicked his tongue in irritation. He'd missed the morning tab now. Still, he could get an hour in at the gym.

9

Major Todd Harper hummed along with the radio as he drove. He loved the way the light spread across the Nevada desert this early in the morning. Soon enough the landscape would be shimmering in the heat of the day, but right now the air had a translucent quality. Ahead of him the blacktop cut a straight line through the sagebrush, heading past a horseshoe-shaped mountain formation, its outline just visible against an indigo sky. He turned off the road and followed a rough, unsigned road towards the foothills of those mountains. After a couple of miles the road ran into a gap between towering cliffs and the sky disappeared from view.

He drove on down the tunnel. At the barrier he showed his ID to the sensor and spoke his name for the voiceprint check.

The barrier lifted and he cruised forward under the sign that said 'ELECTRIC VEHICLES ONLY' and into the underground car park. One or two cars were there already. He switched off the motor, got out, and heard the vehicle self-lock as he walked away. It wasn't necessary: everyone here had a high security clearance and there was no way a thief could get in or out. The metal staircase rang under his boots as he descended to the floor below.

He felt good, as he always did these days when he reported for work. It was the best job in the world. He'd done tours of duty in F38s and F42s, reconnaissance and ground attack. Those stealth designs were good but they weren't foolproof. Every time he flew into a war zone his pulse would race, his palms would tingle, and his body would stiffen with tension. He'd be half-expecting the fierce buzz-buzz of the alarm, the red 'INCOMING' warning flashing on the panel, and the ground-to-air missiles that appeared out of nowhere. Like on his last mission. Two good buddies never made it back from that one, and it had set him thinking. The way things were going he couldn't see manned flights continuing to be any part of a modern Air Force; the future lay with drones. He applied for retraining at Holloman Air Force Base in New Mexico. The transfer was approved and for over a year now he'd been operational in Nevada.

Donna was happy here, too. He was still in a combat role but for the first time in their married life they had a house of their own instead of temporary accommodation at Air Force bases around the world. The kids went to school, they could plan and do things as a family and, as Donna put it, she wasn't in constant fear that one day what was left of her husband would be returned to her in a body bag.

Hank Allshaw was in the changing room, already zipping up his khaki flight suit. Hank was about ten years his junior. They invariably flew together.

'You're early, Hank,' Todd commented, as he took his own one-piece suit off the hangar.

'Baxter chewed me out last week for being late. Last warning, he said. Old buzzard. You know what I think? People like him, when they stop flying it makes 'em bitter.'

'Don't know about that. I heard he keeps a P51 on a heritage airfield not far from here.'

'A P51? Jesus, that'd be more fun than a barrel full of monkeys!'

Todd shrugged. 'It's only what I heard.'

He zipped the suit up and they entered the control room. Colonel Baxter was waiting for them. He evidently couldn't resist a glance at his watch but since it wasn't quite six o'clock all he did was grunt and look up at them.

'You're on reconnaissance. Quick as you can now. High altitude observation – I don't want 'em to know they've been spotted.'

'Operating out of…?' Todd asked.

'Djibouti. Camp Lemmonier.'

Todd thought quickly. Camp Lemmonier managed the US military presence in the Horn of Africa. It also supported aerial operations in the Gulf.

'What's this about, sir?'

'A US citizen's been kidnapped in Sana'a. Your job is to track him and the people who snatched him. You've got a Global Condor all fuelled up and waiting out there. Coordinates are on your screens. Tell me when you're airborne.'

Todd nodded 'Sir'. Baxter returned to his office and he and Hank went over to their flight seats.

Todd said. 'Your turn to fly,' and he pointed to the seat on the left.

Hank made the connection to the ground team in Djibouti. Then the two pilots ran the system checks. A screen in front of them now displayed the view from the

drone's forward camera. He transmitted the one-word message:
Ready
The response came back quickly:
Ready
Hank sent:
Yours
They responded:
Ours

Thousands of miles away the drone's engines started. The camera view shimmied, then settled. The unmanned craft had no cockpit, of course, but it wasn't hard for Todd to imagine himself in one, listening to the high-pitched whine of turbines running up to speed. The key to flying these things was to become an extension of the craft. In that respect it was no different to flying F42s – or even driving an automobile.

A light extinguished on his instrument panel: brakes off. Now the screen showed the runway reeling in with increasing speed, then dropping away as the Condor took off into a clear blue sky. Visibility would be excellent today. But then, barring the occasional dust storm, it usually was in that part of the world.

He'd grown accustomed to the curious sensation of being in two places at once and it took no effort to bring his mind back into the Control Center. On the panel in front of him the altimeters continued to wind rapidly as the drone gained height. To his right a couple more pilots had taken their seats. They'd be on another mission, maybe in an entirely different part of the world. He flicked a switch to open the line to the Director's office and said, 'Airborne now, Colonel.'

Baxter emerged from his office and came up behind them. For a moment he studied the gigantic wall screen above their heads, which displayed a map of the entire area. On that map the drone was an icon at the end of a lengthening white line that traced its flight path and current position. Altimeters in front of each pilot were still spinning as the aircraft continued to gain height.

'When did this happen?' Todd asked.

'Just over an hour ago. We got early warning on this one.'

Todd sucked at his lip. 'Still, they could be anywhere by now.'

'No, a satellite spotted a black SUV leaving the city and speeding north-west along the Mareb Road. It's lost contact now but you should be able to pick it up again. My guess is they'll go off road sooner or later. When you've sighted it, stay on it like glue.'

'Will do.'

Baxter glanced up again at the wall screen, nodded, and went back to his office. Todd exchanged pained glances with Hank. Reconnaissance missions could go on for hours, the most boring assignments they ever had. They were important, all the same, especially in circumstances like this, with a US citizen at risk. And, as he always told himself, it was a whole lot better than being shot at.

He turned back to the screens in front of him. The drone was crossing the Bab al-Mandeb Strait, well on the way to the southern Yemen coast.

There was nothing to be done until control was returned to them. It was one of the first things he'd learned at the Remotely Piloted Aircraft Formal Training Unit at Holloman. The instructor conducted a conversation while feeding Todd's own voice back to him through

39

headphones. Initially it was simply like speaking into a tunnel. Then the instructor increased the delay by one or two seconds and, to Todd's dismay, his own speech became slurred and degenerated into rubbish.

'So what was the point of that?' the instructor asked, briskly removing the headphones. 'I'll tell you. You'll be controlling a drone by sending signals along several miles of buried fibre optic cable to a satellite dish on a neighbouring mountain top, and that signal has to go up to a net of geosynchronous satellites and down again to the drone. The signal latency is something like the one you just experienced and if you handle that craft the way you were just speaking to me you will crash on take-off. And if you don't crash on take-off you'll sure as hell crash big-time on landing. Understand? So you do not control that craft on take-off or landing. You pass control to the people on the ground and they pass control back to you when they're good and ready. Reverse procedure for landing.'

So they waited. Thirty minutes later the message came up:

Yours

Hank responded:

Ours

The craft was flying straight and level at 350 mph and an altitude of 30,000 feet. He leaned forward and set the automatic pilot to the coordinates where the black SUV was last seen.

On the camera view they watched the coast pass under them and the desert terrain began to roll by.

10

Jim was in his office towards lunch time when there was a brief knock at the door and Tommy Geiger came in. Tommy's promising career had hit a wall when a grenade exploded too close to him during an attack, and he still needed hospital attention from time to time to dig out pieces of shrapnel that had worked their way to the surface. He was in his late forties now but he kept himself fit, and led the occasional mission. He also took a load off Jim by running the operational exercises that simulated all the possible scenarios, and monitoring how the soldiers coped with them, both as a team and individually. When Jim wasn't at Fort Piper, Tommy took over as XO, so he was one of Jim's most useful officers. On Jim's recommendation he'd been promoted from Major to Lieutenant-Colonel some months before. He'd earned it.

'Seen the footage on that snatch, Jim?'

'Saw a newsread item about an hour ago. It was pretty sketchy.'

Tommy held up a memory tile. 'Want to see the whole sequence? I recorded it.'

'Sure.'

Jim took the tile and fed it into the reader on his desk. 'Did they name the kidnap victim yet?'

'Guy called William Lampeter. They said he was an IT consultant, in Yemen to advise the government on security measures. He'd just come out of a restaurant with two other guys when it happened.'

'Anyone claim responsibility yet?'

'No, but they sure looked like jihadis to me.'

The video came up on Jim's desk screen.

The footage was evidently a compilation from several colour CCTV cameras placed along the street. That was no surprise: Yemen had been a war zone for many years and the peace settlement had never been recognized by the Sons of the Caliphate, the jihadi militants who held territory in the east of the country. Terrorist attacks were not infrequent, and the capital Sana'a was therefore well kitted out for surveillance.

Three men, Caucasian in appearance, emerged onto the pavement and walked towards the first camera. Two were tall and well-built. They wore dark suits and wrap-around sunglasses, and their hair was cropped short, military style. The third man, walking between them, was a skinny-looking individual. He wore a rumpled lightweight jacket over a T-shirt and slacks. The camera angle switched to show a black SUV coming up behind them. It slowed and two men leapt out. They were dressed in loose-fitting black robes, and the black scarves wrapped around their heads and faces concealed all but their eyes. Both carried machine pistols. One of the dark-suited men whirled but the jihadis opened fire immediately and he and his companion flew back onto the pavement. The SUV drew level with the smaller man, another assailant jumped out and all three bundled him into the back of the vehicle. The two with the machine pistols paused to shout something to the street, then they got in, the doors slammed shut, and the SUV took off fast, spewing dust and grit in its wake. It had all happened in broad daylight and the whole thing was over in seconds.

'Who were the bodyguards?' Jim asked.

'How do you know...?' Geiger read Jim's expression, 'Yeah, 'course they were. Don't know. Haven't been identified.'

'Any idea what they were shouting?'

'Arabic slogans. Translated as something like *Down with America! Death to Americans!* according to the news item I heard. The usual garbage.'

Jim wound back to the moment the jihadis opened fire, forward a few frames, paused it, and zoomed in on the smaller man. The resolution was surprisingly good; maybe the footage had already been enhanced. The still image caught him staring at the two bodyguards, his mouth open in disbelief. He was young, maybe in his early thirties, although his hair was receding prematurely. Jim stepped back a few frames to a point before the shooting, when the young man was looking up. He had watery grey eyes, and pallid skin that looked like it had never been entirely free of acne.

'Very professional job, wouldn't you say, Jim?' Tommy said.

'Yeah,' Jim replied slowly. 'If we'd been assigned to snatch him I guess we'd have done it the same way. Except we might have tasered the two with him instead of killing them. I wonder where these guys got their training.'

He ejected the tile. Tommy took it from him, then said, 'Any word from Brian yet?'

Jim shook his head. 'Not yet. He should have come through by now. It's beginning to bug me.'

'May have taken longer than expected to reach the target. I wouldn't worry, Jim. Brian can handle it.'

Jim sighed. 'That's what I keep telling myself.'

'You want some lunch?'

'Yeah, okay.'

They walked over to the mess hall and drew their meals from the counter. Jim became aware of something in the atmosphere, although it was hardly more than a murmur of excited conversation. Tommy had caught it, too, because as they sat down at a table with some of the non-comms he said to the sergeant opposite him:

'Ray, what's all the buzz about?'

'We just got the latest on that kidnapping.'

'And…?'

'Sons of the Caliphate have claimed responsibility.'

'That figures.'

'They'll probably issue demands and execute him if they aren't met in 72 hours.'

Tommy nodded. 'That's the usual pattern.'

'Think we'll get a rescue mission?'

Tommy looked at Jim, who shrugged. 'Maybe. Depends on the intel. Right now we have no idea where they've taken him. My guess is, nothing's going to happen until we do.'

Across the room one of the conversations swelled, and a woman's voice was clearly audible. Captain Holly Cressington. Despite her initial reticence she seemed to be mixing well enough now.

Tommy said, 'She's hungry for a real mission, Jim.'

'Yeah, but she's not ready for it yet.'

'I wouldn't say that. She had a deal of experience with the 101st Airborne. I've watched her on operational exercises during induction and in the last week or so. It's like she was born to it.'

'What about hostage extractions?'

'Yeah, those too. Your call, Jim, but from where I stand she's good to go. Believe it.'

*

A message came from Harken later that afternoon and they set up a holoconference right away.

'You've heard about this kidnap in the Yemen, Jim?'

'Yes.'

'JSOC's been observing the SUV with reconnaissance drones. It drove into an abandoned village about thirty ks from Sana'a. Looks like they've gone to ground for the moment. SOCOM wants us to initiate a rescue mission. We'll have to be quick, though, or we'll be watching film of that man's execution. I'll send the coordinates and the aerial photos through the data channel.'

'How many hostiles, Wendell?'

'Four, so far as we know: the three assailants caught on camera and the driver. There's no record of a base at the village where they stopped, so there probably aren't more than that.'

'Okay, we'll handle it.'

'Who are you going to put on it, Jim?'

'I don't know. I'll think about it.'

'Well don't take too long. Good luck.'

The holoimage faded. Jim continued to sit there. It was often this way: nothing much happening for months then two missions ordered inside a week. Captain Cressington to lead this one? She was clearly impatient for action, but was she ready for it? According to Tommy she was, and if anyone should know whether she was up to scratch it was him.

What are the risks? It doesn't look too bad. Low-grade target, four hostiles. They look pretty well-trained but then so are we.

He collected the target data Wendell had transmitted, left the holoconference suite and headed back to his office deep in thought. By the time he got there he'd made up his mind.

'Bagley, tell Captain Cressington I want to see her.'

*

She sat opposite him, eyes shining in anticipation.

'The US citizen kidnapped in Sana'a,' Jim said. 'We've been ordered to mount a rescue mission and I'm putting you in charge of it.'

'Thank you, sir.'

'Pick your team: I want eight on this, including you. Standard operating procedures, you'll have to decide the details on the ground. The provisional government in Yemen is cooperative – they've already got some US Army personnel out there. I'll arrange transport. Take your team to draw the armaments you need, then assemble in the briefing room in one hour and I'll put you all in the picture.'

'Yes, sir. Thank you, sir.'

She got up and went to the door, then paused and turned.

'I won't let you down, sir.'

He sighed. 'Captain, if there was the remotest possibility of that, you wouldn't be in this outfit.'

*

After she'd left the office Jim sat for a few moments, drumming his fingers on the desk. Should he have left the selection of the squad to her? He grimaced. Of course he shouldn't. She hadn't been here long enough. How could she be expected to know all the personnel and their individual capabilities? The more he thought about it the more he saw his mistake. For one thing he would have put someone really reliable with her, someone like Ted Nichols. Ted had been on a lot of operations and if it looked like she was making a bad decision he had the experience – and the tact – to advise against it. It was too late now, she'd be busy making her selection and if he sailed in and made changes it would undermine her authority and wreck the morale of her team. Maybe he was worrying too much. All the men and women in the force were competent and versatile. He'd just have to hope she'd put together a good blend of skills.

He took a deep breath and got down to the logistics of transporting whatever team she'd cobbled together over to Yemen. An hour after she'd left his office he went to the briefing room, weighed down by the expectation of what he was going to find. They were waiting for him.

He looked at the expectant faces gathered there and felt a burden lift from his shoulders. He needn't have worried: Ted was one of those selected and he couldn't fault her choice of the others, either: demolitions, medical expertise, signals – all well covered. It was extraordinary. She must have been doing her homework, probably chatting while they were on tabs or exercises and getting more information from Sally Kent or the other officers. Once again she'd surprised him.

They knew as much as he did about the purpose of the mission, so he didn't dwell on it. He activated the large screen on one wall of the briefing room and displayed the target information Wendell had sent. First there was a map with a cross for the target. This was followed with aerial footage taken by a high-altitude reconnaissance drone. It showed what looked like a deserted village with a lot of collapsed stone walls. The SUV wasn't visible but two of the houses had at least the remains of roofs, and it may have been tucked away under one of those.

'That's all we have right now,' he said. 'You'll find out more when you're on site doing your recon. Obviously this is time-critical so you'll be leaving from Raleigh-Durham airfield in fifty minutes. Transport's waiting. Good luck.'

The meeting broke up. He checked that Cressington had the right codes for emergency transmissions, but again she was ahead of him. Finally he passed close to Ted. The grin on the man's face said he was looking forward to action, too.

'Stay close to her, won't you, Ted?'

Their eyes met in a moment of complete understanding. 'You bet, boss. You bet.'

11

Jim sat at his desk, pushing a few papers around, unable to concentrate on anything. Was there anything else he should have done to support the people in the field? Holly Cressington and her team would be airborne by now and on their way, and he'd have to leave the hostage extraction in their hands. If they were successful there'd be a lot of media interest, but they wouldn't have to handle any of that. If luck was against them and the jihadis executed the guy before they could get there, the mission would never become public knowledge – anything like this was classified. What about the other team? Brian Murdoch still hadn't made contact, and that was really bothering him now. He went over the possible scenarios once again, and decided the delay was just about feasible.

Finally he concluded that actually there was nothing more he could do. It was a good moment to look over some equipment specifications he'd been given as a print-out. He'd put them in a drawer somewhere... He opened one drawer after another – and came across the paperback left by the publisher. After a moment's hesitation he lifted it out and placed it on the desk.

The title was *A Special Forces Diary* and the author was 'A. Soldier', a not very ingenious pen name. He opened it at random, began to read, then jerked forward and read some more. He flicked over pages, reading passages here and there, feeling the heat rise to his face. With a growl of rage he slammed it down, got to his feet, and paced the room. Several minutes later he returned to his desk and sent a message to General Wendell Harken. Next he messaged Tommy Geiger and told him to take over from him while he was in Washington, possibly for several days. Then he exhaled a long breath through his nose, picked up a fibre pen, opened the book at the first page, and began to read systematically, making notes and consulting the SAF database on his desk screen as he went along.

The window behind him darkened as dusk fell and the glow panels on the ceiling brightened to compensate. He barely noticed.

12

Jim placed the paperback on Wendell Harken's desk and Wendell drew it towards him. It was nine o'clock. Jim had got a member of the motor pool to drive him to Raleigh-Durham for the early flight to Washington. He'd taken a cab to the Concourse entrance of the Pentagon, gone through all the layers of security, and still managed to arrive in Wendell's office in time for this meeting.

'That book,' Jim said, pointing to it, 'blows the SAF's operations wide open. I don't know who the author is or was, but there's no question they had access to our assignments – I was on more than half of them myself. They're thinly disguised, with names and places altered a little, but the methods are there for anyone to read. It's the perfect manual for terrorists and criminals – just the kind of people we're normally up against.'

'And you want the Army to take out an injunction to prevent further publication.'

'Damn right I do.'

'Look, Jim, not that I don't trust your judgement, but if I'm going to involve the legal boys I really need to examine the book for myself. You do understand that, don't you?'

Jim took a deep breath and said, 'Yeah, I guess so.' He blinked eyes that were gritty with fatigue.

Wendell frowned. 'You look exhausted. Have you had any sleep?'

'Not much. I was busy trying to align our own records with what was in the book, assembling lists of personnel, that kind of thing.'

Wendell tapped the cover. 'Look, leave this with me and get a few hours in. There's an overnight room on D-ring you can use. I'll take you down there now.'

Jim sighed. 'It's not a bad idea. I can't think straight at the moment.' They stood up.

'Just a couple of things about the book,' Jim said. 'It's not that long, just fifteen chapters, one mission to each chapter. That's the first thing. The second is that the chapters look to me like they're in chronological order, which is helpful. There were some I couldn't identify. We could talk about that later.'

'I may recognize them if they're detailed enough.'

'Oh they'll be detailed enough – that's the problem. Whoever wrote this either had a very retentive memory or kept records.'

'Which is against regulations.'

'That, Wendell, is the least of it.'

Wendell came round the desk and put a hand on Jim's shoulder.

'Come on. I'll take you to that room. Reveille at 1400 hours, all right?'

Jim gave him a rueful smile. This was more like the old Wendell.

'Okay, thanks.'

*

Soldiers learn how to snatch sleep whenever the opportunity presents itself, and Jim hadn't lost the knack. Normally he also had the knack of waking up on time. If it was 'Reveille at 0600' he'd be awake on the dot. Not this time. He was sound asleep when Wendell woke him at 2 pm. He swung his legs over the side of the bunk, rubbed his eyes with the heels of both hands, and shook his head.

'Wow. Went out like a light.'

'I'm sure you'll feel better for it. There's an en suite through there. Freshen up and come along as soon as you're ready.'

When they were settled in the office again Wendell held up the book. His face was flushed.

'I agree with you entirely, Jim. This is an absolutely scurrilous piece of work. In fact it's the worst breach of security I've experienced in my association with the SAF and probably the worst in its history.' He slapped it back on the desk between them. 'God knows, the success of our covert operations depends on absolute secrecy, so a leak on this scale is extremely serious. The question is, how do we plug it?'

Jim recognized the rhetorical nature of the question and waited.

'From what you say the book has already sold in large numbers.'

'The publisher said it had sold more than four hundred copies already. Mostly as ebooks, I imagine: those could be downloaded anywhere in the world. Maybe he was exaggerating. But maybe he's underestimated. People could have made illegal copies and circulated those, too.'

'That's the problem. Of course members of the armed forces have a lifetime obligation to present anything like this for prepublication review. If that had been done, there'd have been a distant chance of placing it under prior restraint.'

'Only a distant chance?' Jim exclaimed.

'I'm afraid so, Jim. Freedom of speech is strongly protected by the First Amendment. There'd be a heavy burden on the Department to prove that this book endangered our personnel.'

'But it's blindingly obvious these were actual operations—'

'To us, Jim, to us. The places and dates are disguised, as you've indicated, so others would have to decide whether the average man in the street would see them as actual operations or fictional accounts. You'd have the same problem if you sought an injunction.' He shook his head. 'Look, the legal process is too cumbersome for my liking. I'm wondering if there's a quicker way. If the content of the book was in breach of security, what would the position of the publisher be?'

Jim said, 'I should think he'd be guilty of treason.'

'Not necessarily. It would depend on the contract he signed with the author. That could shift responsibility from the publisher to the author.'

Jim's shoulders sagged but Wendell hadn't finished.

'On the other hand legal proceedings are expensive and you say this is a small company.'

'That's what he said, yes.'

'Which means he may not be disposed to defend a suit if one was threatened. In other words it may be possible to bring some pressure on him to withdraw the book voluntarily. So Step One: we see how the publisher reacts to the possibility of a law suit, costs and heavy fines, and a long spell in jail.'

'I should have thought of that,' Jim said quietly. He was being transported back ten years to his time as a Captain. There was more grey in Wendell's hair now, and the jaw line was a little less firm, but otherwise he looked as fit as he'd done back then and he had the same lucid, analytical mind. Whatever other issues Wendell had to deal with at the moment – and there were probably many – he'd focused on this problem and he was taking it apart, piece by piece. Jim was painfully aware of the contrast as he struggled under the weight of his own responsibilities. In addition to running Fort Piper he had a team in Cameroon he hadn't heard from in days, he'd just reluctantly sent a young captain out on her first SAF mission, and now he was trying to deal with a massive breach of security. He wondered how he'd ever become a CO, and if somehow he'd overshot his career grade.

Wendell seemed to have read his body language. He waved a hand dismissively. 'Jim, you were angry and upset and tired. I don't mind telling you, reading it made me angry too, and I'd had prior warning. So don't be too hard on yourself, okay?'

Jim closed his eyes and nodded. 'Okay.'

'Now, Step Two. The man who wrote this book is dangerous – we'll assume it's a man, statistically that's far more likely. It may be that he just did it for the money, and he was either unaware of the security implications or happy to overlook them. I think that's a generous interpretation. We have to deal with the worst scenario, which is that this individual didn't do it for the money; he purposely set out to do harm to the SAF and the men and women who serve in it. So we need to find out who it is.''

'Right, that's something I *have* thought about. I take it you'd agree this is the work of someone who served with the SAF?'

'With that amount of detail? I think it's got to be.'

'And is no longer with the SAF, because if he was he'd be putting *himself* in harm's way.'

'Yes.'

'So that gives us a clue.' Jim laid a hand on the book. 'There were several missions in here I couldn't identify, six in fact. Three of them were at the beginning of the book. What that says to me is that this was someone who was in the SAF when I joined, someone I probably knew.'

'Go on.'

'The other thing is when the book stops, because that's when the writer left the service.'

'Unless he was planning a second volume.'

Jim picked up the thin paperback and held it edge on to Wendell. 'If he'd had more material do you think he'd have left it at this?'

'Okay, good. Point taken.'

'Well,' Jim continued, 'the last chapter was another one I didn't recognize. It seems to have been a joint assignment with the Iraqi Army. Do you recall it?'

'I certainly do, in every damned detail. That and the other thing were both in 2052.'

'2052? Jesus. No wonder I wasn't aware of it. That was when—'

'Yes, Jim. It would have been during the time you were, er, out of the picture.'[1]

---

[1] See *The Domino Man* by this author.

'According to the book the mission was a success. They took out the commander of a jihadi group operating in that area...' Jim frowned. 'What did you mean "the other thing"?'

'The mission itself was a success,' Wendell said slowly, 'but most people will only remember what happened afterwards. The US Regular Army had a small presence out there in Baghdad as well. They were due for rotation but there was some sort of delay with the replacement unit, so we left four of our SAF squad there to bridge the gap. The jihadis must have been really sore about the loss of their commander. They launched a revenge attack in a market square, killed a lot of people. The timing of the attack suggested the jihadis had been tipped off. We helped the Iraqi Army round up suspected sympathizers and a man died during a particularly brutal interrogation. One of our men was present during that interrogation. His name was Sergeant Laverne Dacey.'

'Laverne Dacey? I remember him.'

'Laverne was court-martialled. He was accused of taking part in the violence, or at least aiding and abetting it.'

Jim shook his head. 'Were you at the court martial?'

'Of course – I was his CO, so I was there to testify to the man's character. Which I was happy to do. He was a fine soldier.'

'But was he guilty?'

'He said he took no part in the interrogation. On the other hand he admitted he didn't try to stop it.'

'So what happened to him?'

'The incident was a major embarrassment to the Army and the US government,' Wendell said. 'There was a good deal of pressure on the court to come down hard on those involved. Laverne Dacey got a dishonourable discharge and a prison sentence. So his career was finished and he went to jail.'

Jim whistled softly. 'And at that point the book stops. It's our man, Wendell, it has to be.'

Wendell sighed and nodded. 'It certainly looks that way.'

'You know what's so hard to understand?' Jim said. 'We live and train together, go into action together, face the same dangers, cover each other's backs – the SAF's like a band of brothers. Something like that doesn't just vanish when a guy leaves the service. All the time I was going through the book I was asking myself the same question: what could happen to someone, what did they experience that was so life-changing it broke that bond of loyalty? You just provided the answer. Prison changes people. Rightly or wrongly Laverne would be bitter as hell and resentful about the way he was treated. And he was already in the SAF when I joined. It all fits. He's the obvious candidate. Do you remember how long the prison sentence was?'

'No, but this was seven years ago. It wouldn't have been as long as that, even if he served the full term. He's certainly out by now, as a civilian.'

'We need the FBI in on this, then,' Jim said. 'They'll help us track him down. They can help with the publisher, too.'

Wendell got to his feet. 'There's someone along the corridor I can speak to. He goes over to the Hoover Building all the time and I'm sure he can recommend a good man. I'll go and have a word with him now.'

Jim half-rose in his seat. 'You want me to—?'

Wendell held up a hand. 'No, you're all right here. I won't be a moment.'

Wendell left the office and the door closed behind him. Jim's thoughts drifted to Laverne Dacey. A wiry guy, late thirties, confident, reliable. They'd been in the same squad on a number of assignments – South America, Africa, the Middle East – in fact all the ones in the book that Jim recognized. Dacey never seemed to be fatigued or overheated, just did the job in a calm and resourceful way. Yet this was someone who, by his own admission, stood by while a man was beaten to death. And, it seemed, went on to write a book that endangered his fellow soldiers. It was beyond belief.

The door of the office opened and Wendell came in.

'All settled. They're sending a Senior Special Agent over. He should be here in half an hour.'

'Do we have a name for this guy?'

'Yes. Tony Grieg.'

13

Tony Grieg looked like he'd reached peak fitness at least ten years ago. His grey suit wasn't pressed, his collar was open at the neck, and the slight swelling at his waistline stretched the creases out of his shirt. But he was brisk and alert, his handshake was firm, and his blue eyes flashed quickly from one to the other. They sat down together at Wendell's desk.

'I'll kick off,' Wendell said to Grieg, 'and after that it will be up to you and Colonel Slater. All right?'

'Okay, go ahead.'

Wendell held up the book. 'This was written by a US Army soldier under a pen name. It describes the missions he was engaged on in considerable detail. Although names and places have been altered Colonel Slater and I had no difficulty in recognizing those missions as ones undertaken by the Special Assignment Force. Missions like that are classified, and this is a serious breach of national security. We want to pressure the publisher to withdraw the book and nail the man who wrote it.'

Grieg nodded slowly. 'Okay, that don't sound too hard. If the publisher won't cooperate we threaten legal action.

And the publisher should know the author's real name. But look, if the author's a soldier this is a job for the CID.'

Grieg was referring to the United States Army Criminal Investigation Command. Jim said, 'If the author is who we think it is, the guy was court-martialled, given a dishonourable discharge and a prison sentence. So far as the CID's concerned he's a civilian now.'

'What's this guy's name?'

'Laverne Dacey.'

'He still in prison?'

Wendell said, 'You could check, but I'd say no.'

'You think it's him. How solid is that?'

'The evidence is circumstantial,' Wendell said. 'The last mission in the book took place seven years ago. That suggests the author left the service at that point. And that's when Dacey was court-martialled. Which could well give him a motive for turning his back on his colleagues.'

'That's all you have?'

Jim said, 'He was on at least nine of the missions in the book. I know that because I served with him.'

Grieg's mouth twisted and he rocked his head from side to side. 'Okay, look, here's what we do. Like I say, we go after the publisher first. Get him to pull the book. Ask him who the author is, then go after him. That way we're not saying whether this Dacey guy is your man or not. Where's the publisher?'

Jim turned to Wendell. 'He left a card. I didn't think I'd be using it so I tucked it inside the front cover.'

Wendell opened the cover. The card was still there, wedged up against the spine. He handed it over and Grieg examined it.

'Denton Brice, Managing Director, Maryland Publishing Company, Baltimore.' He looked up. 'It's not that far. I got a car with me. You wanna go up there now?'

Jim blinked, glanced at Wendell, then back to Grieg. Then, 'Sure. Why not?'

Wendell said, 'Good. Here, Jim, you'd better take this with you.' He held out the book.

Jim put it in his document case. 'Okay, Wendell, thanks. We'll take it from here.'

'Good luck. Keep me informed, won't you?'

'Will do.'

*

Tony Grieg pulled up outside an old multi-storey faced with dark red brick, and cancelled the NavAid. They got out and walked up to the building's entrance, which was recessed, with a panel of buttons on the right. Tony ran his finger down them and stopped.

'There y'go,' he said. 'Maryland Publishing Company, third floor. Shall we do this the soft man/hard man way? Best if I'm the hard man.'

Jim said, 'Fine with me.'

'Okay, go ahead.'

Jim pressed the button. There was a pause, then a tinny voice said, 'Who is it?'

'Colonel James Slater, from Fort Piper.'

'Colonel Slater! How nice! Come up.'

He sounds delighted, Jim thought. *That'll change soon enough.*

A low buzz sounded and a lock clicked. They opened the street door, went in, and climbed the stairs.

The Maryland Publishing Company resembled a cheap private detective agency, complete with the name on a wire-reinforced glass window. Brice opened it before they could knock. He recoiled a little when he saw Tony but quickly switched back to Jim.

'Come in, come in, er, gentlemen, welcome.'

The room they entered was no larger than Jim's office at Fort Piper. It contained a desk sitting on a threadbare rug, two filing cabinets, and piles of paper on most of the available surfaces. The single window, clouded with grime, gave no hint of what was outside. Beneath it an air conditioner laboured without noticeable effect. What seemed to be missing was a half-full bottle of bourbon, and that could well be in a drawer somewhere. The one thing that pointed to the nature of the business was a bookshelf carrying a couple of rows of paperbacks, two or three copies of each title. They looked fresh, probably never opened. Presumably the company's publications.

Brice must have noticed the way they were looking around the office. 'This is the tip of the iceberg,' he explained hurriedly, opening his hands. 'Everything is outsourced: editing, layout, cover design, printing, and packaging. More efficient that way. Please, come and sit down.' He shifted some papers and dragged a couple of injection-moulded plastic chairs up to the desk. Then he returned to his own chair. The air conditioner restored its presence by singing metallically for a few seconds, then returned to its background drone.

When they were seated he leaned forward on the desk, a look of eager anticipation on his chubby face. 'So, you're interested in my proposition, Colonel?'

'You could say that, yes. This is my colleague, Mr Anthony Grieg of the Federal Bureau of Investigation.'

The expectant expression faded and he looked at Tony and then to the wallet badge being held out to him.

'Mr Brice,' Tony said. 'Your company published a book titled *A Special Forces Diary*. I'm here to inform you that the content of this book is deeply prejudicial to the national security of the United States, and in particular its military personnel. This is a felony under the Espionage Act of 1917 and you, sir, are guilty of it.'

Brice's face blanched. For a few moments his mouth opened and shut without any sound emerging. Then he spluttered:

'Whoa, whoa, wait a minute here. I'm not aware of any prejudicial material in that book. But if there is any the author's responsible for it, not me. It's in the contract: the author indemnifies the publisher from claims or suits resulting from the content of the book.'

'Well, that's as may be, Mr Brice, but that depends on knowing who the author is. And I don't think his name is "A. Soldier". Who is he?'

'I… I don't know.'

Tony closed and opened his eyes and sighed patiently. 'Mr Brice, I don't think you fully appreciate what very deep shit you're in.'

Brice passed the tip of his tongue over his lips. 'I don't know who it is. Really I don't. I never even met him.'

'In that case the law says the responsibility rests with you, and you'll have to suffer the consequences.'

Jim wasn't sure whether the last statement was correct but the heavy assurance with which it was delivered didn't invite disagreement.

Brice blinked rapidly, licked his lips, and swallowed. The air conditioner sang its periodic tune, ending with a small clatter. It was time for the soft man approach.

'Mr Brice,' he said. 'You may not have met the author but you must have had some contact with him. How was that managed?'

Brice took a deep breath. 'He sent an email, a proposal. He attached a sample chapter, said he'd written fourteen more like it. It was exciting stuff, lots of action, the sort of thing our readers like. The writing was a bit rough but that could be ironed out – there are good editors I can use. I asked for the whole manuscript and he sent it. It looked good. So I offered him a contract and he accepted it.'

'He signed the contract?' Jim asked.

'Yes. All done by email, of course.'

Tony said, 'Show me.'

Brice turned to a laptop on his desk and clicked keys. Then he turned it around.

Jim and Tony bent closer to look at the screen. The signature was an illegible scrawl, it would tell them nothing. Without asking, Tony drew the lap top closer and typed into the search box. A list of emails came up and he opened several in turn. He turned to Jim.

'Different email addresses, different routes each time. He covered his tracks pretty carefully.' He said to Brice, 'You pay this guy royalties?'

'Of course, we have a generous arrangement—'

'How? How d'you get the funds to him?'

'By bank transfer. I send it to an account in the Cayman Islands.'

Tony slapped the lid of the lap top down. 'Okay, I'm taking this with me for analysis. You'll get a receipt.'

Brice's mouth dropped open. 'You can't do that! This is a business I'm running! All my records, all my correspondence, are on that computer.'

Tony's voice went hard. 'You still don't get it, do you? You don't have a business, Mr Brice. By the time you've paid the legal costs and a big fine you'll be bankrupt, and you won't be here sifting through the wreckage either, you'll be in jail.'

Brice began to rock backwards and forwards. 'Oh my God, this is not my fault, really it's not. I had no idea.' He took a tissue from his pocket and began to dab at his forehead.

Soft man again. Jim said to Tony, 'I'm sure Mr Brice would like to cooperate. I have a suggestion. Suppose he undertakes to take the book off the market with immediate effect, paperback and all electronic versions. And we don't really need the whole lap top for analysis, do we? Couldn't we take away a complete copy of the memory? I'm sure you have some high-capacity memory tiles in the office, haven't you, Mr Brice?'

Brice's eyes were wide with hope. He nodded rapidly. 'Yes, yes.'

Jim looked at Tony, who appeared to be weighing the suggestion carefully. 'I don't know... well, okay.' He looked at Brice. 'But if this doesn't lead us to the author you're still on the spot, so don't even think about leaving the country.'

'Is that agreed, Mr Brice?' Jim asked.

The voice was hoarse. 'Yes.'

'You understand that we'll be checking that the book is no longer in circulation.'

'Yes, don't worry. I'll see to it right away.'

Tony held out a palm. 'Memory tile.'

Brice opened a drawer, fumbled around, and took out several, still in their original packaging. In his haste he dropped two but managed to hand one over. Tony extracted the small square tile, plugged it into the lap top, and started the download. Every move he made was leisurely and weighted with quiet authority. When the download was complete he stood up, put a hand into one of the misshapen pockets of his suit jacket, withdrew a plastic evidence bag, and dropped the tile into it. He scrawled something on the label and handed the bag and pen to Brice.

'Sign here. It's to say you authorize the removal of this tile and the data that's on it.'

Brice signed, and Tony sealed the bag.

Jim got to his feet. 'We'll leave it there for the moment, then,' he said.

Brice saw them to the door and closed it quickly as soon as they were outside. Jim had a mental image of the man leaning on it with one hand.

Back on the pavement Jim asked, 'What are you going to do with the data on that tile, Tony?'

'First I give this to the boys in US Cyber Command, see if they can trace the emails and the funds. Second – you have any reports written by this guy Laverne Dacey?'

Jim thought for a moment. 'There should be something on file. Why?'

'I can get a linguist to analyze his writing for syntax, spelling errors, word frequencies, and so on. The book doesn't help us any because Brice had it edited before publication, but we have the raw manuscript on this tile. We can compare it with your reports, see if they're by the same writer. Once we have the evidence I can find out where he lives and we can pay him a visit.'

'I'll look forward to that.'

They got back in the car. Tony reached for the starter button, then paused and looked at Jim. He jerked his head. 'Great job in there. You done this before?'

'No, and I'm not anxious to do it again.'

'You sounded pretty sorry for the guy.'

'Really? I don't know how I kept my hands off his throat.'

'Should have told me, I'd have come down harder on him. Where to now?'

'I should get back to base.'

'Okay, I'll drop you off at the airport.'

*

For the moment the investigation was in Tony's hands and Jim's lack of sleep was catching up with him, so he dozed for a while on the flight back to Raleigh-Durham. At some stage he became aware of a change and blinked his eyes open. They must be on the descent. He yawned and his mind drifted to Laverne Dacey.

Dacey's record with the regular army must have been clean or the SAF would never have taken him on. He'd served well and he should have had a good career ahead of him. The Baghdad incident had snuffed that out like a candle. He'd been on at least nine missions, the ones Jim had identified. That wasn't bad going. The SAF was only called upon when their special expertise was required, and even then it was rare for the whole force to be deployed – it had never happened in Jim's experience. That meant a guy couldn't expect to be on every mission that came up, yet Dacey had clearly been selected for a high proportion of them. He would have spent the rest of the time honing his skills on exercises in practice scenarios – operations like the ones in the book, raiding the warehouses of drug cartels or illegal arms dealers, kidnapping terrorists, extracting hostages…

A cold current travelled down Jim's spine. Brian Murdoch and Holly Cressington were out on typical SAF assignments, pretty much carbon copies of ones in that book. If it had reached the people involved at those targets they'd know precisely what the standard operating procedures were. Both squads were in serious danger.

He was wide awake now. He reached for his phone but they were on final approach and calls couldn't be made at this stage of the flight. In any case it was essential for any such call to go out on one of the secure lines, which he could only access from his office.

He bit his lip with impatience as the aircraft made its unhurried approach, his fingers already hooked around the seat belt release. The whine of the engines dropped to a lower note, the wheels hit the runway and rolled without a bounce, reverse thrust roared and died, and the plane taxied to the stand. As soon as he heard everything spooling down he uncoupled the seat belt and rushed to the forward exit. The moment the door opened he was out, racing along the jetway and into and through the airport. He spotted the waiting sedan from the motor pool and jumped in next to the driver.

'Thanks, Chris. Step on it, will you? I need to be back at base in record time.'

'Sure thing, Colonel.' The car took off with a squeal of tyres.

Chris drove like the wind. Jim said nothing, just sat there, breathing fast and counting the seconds.

14

The all-wheel-drive people carrier drove Holly Cressington and her team north-west out of Sana'a, along the Mareb Road. It was the way the kidnappers had gone and now Youssef, the driver they'd recruited, was following the same route. Youssef was a local man who'd been used several times by UN peacekeepers. He was regarded as a trustworthy guide, but Holly's team searched him and swept his vehicle anyway to make sure there wasn't a phone or transmitter tucked away somewhere.

In Sana'a earlier that evening Holly had studied the photographs yet again, this time with Sergeant Ted Nichols, the most senior and experienced of the NCOs.

'We ought to bivvy out there,' Ted said. 'Somewhere not too far away. Do a recon tomorrow in daylight.'

Holly nodded. 'That would be ideal, Ted, but we don't know how long they're going to hang around. The Colonel would have made contact if there'd been any change, so they're still in there at the moment. But they could decide to make a move any time now and that'd leave us trailing after them across the desert. This may be our best chance.'

'I guess you're right.'

Now all eight of them were in the people carrier, faces streaked with black camo, each holding a multirifle. Holly was in the front passenger seat, following the vehicle's progress on the NavAid, and glancing up from time to time at the ribbon of road illuminated by their headlights. After about thirty kilometres they reached the coordinates where the reconnaissance drone had shown the kidnappers going off-road.

She tapped Youssef on the shoulder and pointed. 'Go off-road here. And dip your headlights.'

He nodded. For ten minutes the vehicle jolted and plunged over the rough terrain; then it descended into a wadi. The ground behind them was now high enough to screen them from the road.

She said, 'Stop here.'

It was 5 ks short of the target but Youssef couldn't know that. The squad disembarked. Holly turned back to speak to Youssef, again using her Arabic.

'Wait here, you understand?'

He nodded, and that was enough. He would wait because he would only get paid on their safe return to Sana'a. They set off on foot.

The usual banter had ceased as if a switch had been thrown; they were in operational mode, walking quickly and silently. The moon wouldn't be up for several hours and the darkness was almost complete, even though the sky was full of stars. Temperatures here dropped quickly at night, and the air was clean and cold. They barely noticed it; they were carrying a lot of kit, and were warm from the exertion.

Holly used her portable GPS to navigate in the darkness. An hour later she called a halt. They crouched down and she examined the terrain ahead with night-vision binoculars. Ted Nichols was at her side. Ahead of them she could see what the aerial photographs had shown: a small cluster of what looked like derelict buildings. An abandoned village. The walls glowed faintly with residual heat from the day, but there was a stronger glow coming from a broken window in the nearest building. She turned to the others and spoke in a low voice.

'Looks like our target's in the nearest house but I don't want any surprises. Jonah, Charlie, circle round to the other side and see what kind of infra-red signature you get from the other houses. Quiet as you can, and don't engage.'

They moved off and the rest waited. Fifteen minutes later they were back.

'Nothing at the other end,' Charlie said, 'it's just ruins. This end's in better shape. They put the SUV in the second house – that one's got a roof but the front wall's gone.'

'What about the first house?'

'Yeah, it's near enough whole. Plenty of infra-red coming from inside.'

'It figures. Two men behind, one in front, and a driver. Add the victim and that makes five – that's your infra-red signature right there. Good, we'll deploy.'

*

Jim burst through the door of his office, slung his document case onto the desk, and opened the secure line. Who to contact first? Brian had a lot of missions under his belt. He could probably handle the unexpected better than Holly. So Holly first.

They'd changed the secure codes. What was it? Damn, he could only remember the old one. The new code would be on the computer, encrypted. He booted up the desk screen.

*

Holly spoke quietly and quickly. 'Ken and Casey, round the back. Charlie, wait till they're in position, then toss in the flash-bangs. Jonah, Neil, Ted, and me'll go in from the front. Any questions?' A low buzz sounded and she held up a hand. 'Wait a moment.'

*

'Captain Cressington?' Jim said, leaning forward across his desk.

'Yes.'

Some of the tension seeped out of him. He was in time. 'Pull your people out, now.'

'What did you say?'

'I said pull out. Abort. Right now.'

'Colonel, there's a hostage in there and we're all in position—'

'Goddamn it, do I have to spell it out? Withdraw to your vehicle and return to base immediately. That's an order. Is that clear?'

There was a pause, the faint sound of someone swallowing. Then a low, 'Affirmative, sir.'

He clicked off and shook his head. The woman was too damned independent for her own good.

He was still on edge but there was another call to make. The new code for the connection to Brian Murdoch was already on the screen. He deep-clicked it to make the connection.

No response.

He dropped back into his chair and tapped his fingers lightly on the desk.

It's standard operating procedure to cut all communication when you go in. No noise, no outside distractions. But they must have made their move by now. If it's over why haven't they got in touch? Maybe they're tracking the insurgents through the jungle.

He bit his lip.

Chances are no one in that neck of the woods ever heard about the book anyway. If the worst comes to the worst Brian can look after himself, and there's a heap of experience in that squad. They should be okay.

He jumped as the phone buzzed, reached out a hand quickly to answer. 'Slater.'

'Jim?'

It wasn't Brian, it was Tony Grieg.

'Yes, Tony.'

'Thought you'd be back by now. Got some news for you.'

'That was quick work. Go ahead.'

'Laverne Dacey served his time at the Manley Correctional Center, North Carolina.'

'Manley, not Leavenworth?'

'Leavenworth's for the more serious stuff. They need to be serving ten years or more. This guy had a four-year sentence. He did three years, then he was released on parole back in March 2055. Okay? That's the good part.'

Jim frowned. 'What's the bad part?'

'He's dead.'

15

Raleigh's Police Department was on Six Forks Road in the north part of the city. Jim drew a car from the pool and drove there the following morning. Tony was already waiting outside in a rectangle of shadow.

Jim parked the car and walked over to him. He said, 'Give it to me again.'

'Whole business just got more interesting, Jim. Like I said, Dacey did three years inside, and they released him four years ago. July last year he was killed in a drive-by shooting. They didn't find the shooter.'

'Why did you want to meet here?'

He shrugged. 'You want to know if he really was the guy who wrote that book. The cops want to know who killed him and why. So maybe we can get something from the investigating officer.'

Jim nodded. 'Okay, let's go.'

A heavily built woman cop was seated at the reception desk. Tony showed her his badge. 'Name's Tony Grieg. I have an appointment with Lieutenant Mirski.'

'Moment.' She spoke quietly into a handset, then put it down. 'Lieutenant Mirski will be right with you.'

Mirski appeared within a minute. He was similar in age and build to Tony but his face was tanned and lined, and where Tony's hair was thick and dark, Mirski's was blond and thinning badly.

'Mirski,' he said. 'Come on up.'

They followed him to a small first floor office, which looked clean and well organized. It was dominated by a large desk, which was striped with sunlight from a louvred blind over the window. He pulled a couple of chairs off a stack and set them in front of the desk. Then he went behind the desk and they all sat down.

'I believe you are lookin' for information on a drive-by shootin',' Mirski said. 'One Laverne Dacey. What's your interest?'

'He may have been involved in a felony we're investigating. Reason Colonel Slater's here,' Tony indicated Jim on his left, 'is the man was formerly with his unit.'

'A felony?' Mirski frowned. 'The victim already did time at Manley.'

'We know that,' Tony said. 'This came after.'

'Well now you do surprise me. And what felony, I'm wonderin', would be important enough for the two of you to be spending time on it after the man's dead.'

Tony grimaced. 'It's an issue of national security, Lieutenant, so I'd sooner not go into it at this point in time. The evidence is strong but it's not cast-iron, so we were hoping you could give us a bit more background.'

Mirski pursed his lips, then said, 'Well, I can tell you what we know. Case is still open.' He tapped on the touch screen that occupied half the desk top. 'Laverne Dacey, 39-

year-old male Caucasian. One previous conviction. Shot July 2058 walkin' home from work.'

'He had a job?' Jim asked.

Mirski looked up. 'Yes he did. In a warehouse, stackin' boxes mainly. He also did nights at another place as a security guard. Occupied a rented apartment. No car, he walked to work and back. Shall I go on?'

'Please.'

'Died at the scene. Street CCTV recordings showed a silver SUV hydro, darkened windows. It stopped th'other side of the street as he was approachin'. Window on the driver's side rolled down, two shots fired, and it drove off. North Carolina number plate, vehicle matched one found outside the city a day later, all burned out.'

'What did the medical examiner say?' Tony asked.

Mirski leafed through a couple of pages on the screen. 'Here we are. *Two entry wounds: one at the top of the chest, the other in the back, above the left hip.*'

'The one in the chest dropped him,' Tony said without hesitation, 'and the shooter put another one in after he went down, just to make sure.'

'Correct. *Numerous small fragments of plastic and the absence of exit wounds point to the use of frangible copolymer ammunition.*' He looked at Jim. 'You'd be familiar with that, Colonel.'

'Yes indeed, we use it in hostage extractions and crowded places to avoid collateral damage. No wonder the guy dropped. A bullet like that dumps all its energy in the target. The shock-wave alone would be enough to rupture vital organs. And you're sure the victim was Laverne Dacey?'

'One hunnert per cent. You want to see the forensic photos?'

'No thanks – I know what those rounds can do. Do you have a photo from an ID card or something?'

Merski did some searching on the screen, then said, 'Here, I'll invert it for you.'

Jim stood to look at the image. The face he saw was more gaunt than he remembered but he recognized it right away, the thin nose, high cheekbones, hazel eyes. 'That's Dacey all right,' he said. He sat down again.

Mirski switched off the screen. He leaned back, picked up a fibre pen and began to turn it expertly end-over-end between his fingers. 'So now you have to ask yourself, why did the shooter use frangible copolymer ammunition? Seems to me there are three possibilities. One, he was a considerate kind of gentleman and he would have just hated to see anyone else injured by shoot-through.'

'Oh yeah,' Tony said.

Jim smiled. 'What's next?'

'Two, he wanted to be damn sure the guy died *wherever* he was hit.'

'Yes.'

'Three, because a bullet like that breaks up so much there's no risk of ballistics identifyin' the weapon.'

'That, too. I guess the cartridge cases were ejected inside the vehicle.'

'Correct. So nothing from those either.'

They sat in silence for a few moments. Then Tony asked, 'Lieutenant, do you have many drive-by shootings in Raleigh?'

Mirski stopped twiddling the pen and tapped the blunt end on the desk. 'No,' he said. 'I'm mighty glad to say we don't. But I have served in other jurisdictions where they do. Guys high on drink or drugs doing it for kicks, or a lone guy who's kind of off his head and goes on a killin' spree, maybe shoots hisself at the end. None o' that fits, 'cause this guy did not fire bursts and rake the entire area; he fired two single shots and brought down just one victim. Then there's the gang or crime syndicate aimin' to take out a rival, maybe usin' a professional hit man. That's a better fit. Two shots, two entry wounds. No debris around from a third bullet and witnesses say they heard just two shots, so no misses. Like I say, it's a better fit, or it would be, except everythin' we learned about Laverne Dacey pointed to him being a decent, peace-lovin', hard-workin', law-abidin' citizen. I'll tell you, Agent Grieg, this talk of a felony makes no sense to me, and neither does this shootin'.'

Tony took a deep breath. 'You have anything else?' he asked.

Mirski nodded. 'Dacey did time at Manley, so I went and spoke to the prison warden there.'

'Because...?' Jim asked.

Mirski put the fibre pen down and his face hardened. The change was barely noticeable except for a deepening in the lines on either side of his mouth. 'This was no random killin', no motiveless crime. Dacey was targeted, that's for damned sure. So he must have made a real bad enemy somewheres. From what his employers tell us, there were no problems at work, none whatever. The manager at that warehouse said he was quiet, reliable, punctual, got on with his job. He was real sorry to lose him. No one could say much at the place he worked nights, but he was there all the hours he should have been. So if he didn't make enemies at work and didn't play hooky from the night job maybe it was someone he came up against in prison.'

'That happens, does it?' Jim asked.

Mirski shook his head. 'Not often. For a whole bunch of reasons, the main one being: when the would-be killer gets out of jail hisself he has not the slightest idea where to find the other guy. Still, we spoke to the warden. He had nothing but good things to say about Dacey. The prison folk gave him no trouble, and he gave the prison folk no trouble, none at all. He was a model prisoner.'

'What did he do in his spare time?' Jim asked. He was thinking about the book.

'Well, they keep 'em pretty busy at Manley, but the warden said he spent what leisure time he had in the library.'

Jim felt a rush of hope. Dacey could well have spent that time writing.

Mirski rested his arms on the desk and leaned forward. 'I just hate to have cases open, especially a cold-blooded killin'' like this one. But this was a very professional job, and they're real hard to crack. So I've cooperated with you, but if you find anythin' that could help I'd be greatly obliged if you'd share it with me.'

Tony said, 'We appreciate what you've given us, Lieutenant. We have nothing for you right now, but if we do get something we'll be sure to let you know.' He got to his feet and Jim did the same.

'Fine. I'll show you gentlemen out.'

Downstairs they shook hands and Jim and Tony left the building.

Tony said, 'Coffee?'

'Coffee would be good.'

They found a bar that had a coffee machine. Tony collected two coffees at the counter and they went over to a table at the end, near a television. The only other customers were by the window and the sound from the television would mask their conversation.

'So what we got here, Jim? A sniper?'

'I don't think so. Snipers like to use long rifles – they're more accurate. So if it was a sniper he'd choose a good viewpoint – a high window or a roof. Sticking a weapon like that out of a car window would be clumsy as hell, and Dacey would see it before the shooter could get the sight to his eye. Remember, part of this guy's training included counter-surveillance. No, it would be a short weapon, something like an assault rifle. From that range it would be accurate enough. Any infantryman could manage it.'

'A soldier, then.'

'Not necessarily. But a civilian would need to know what he was doing, loading a rifle with ammunition like that.'

'Well,' Tony said, 'whoever the perp was he did a damned good job of tracking Dacey down. He even knew the route the guy would take when he walked home from work.'

'Mmm. He must have researched it very carefully.'

'But why? Why go to all that trouble?'

'That's what I don't understand. I guess something in Dacey's past life caught up with him, but what the hell was it? It didn't look like it was from his time in Manley, so it must have been before that.'

Tony's cell phone buzzed and he took it out. 'Grieg.' He listened, nodding, while Jim sipped his coffee. Then he said, 'Thanks, Doc. Great job,' and clicked off. He tucked the phone into a pocket and looked at Jim. 'That was my linguistics expert. He's compared the samples of Dacey's writing you gave me with the raw manuscript we got off Brice's laptop. They weren't a match.'

Jim blinked. 'What?'

'This guy's a good analyst, Jim. He says he's used stylometry, punctuation, collocation analysis, and a bunch of other stuff. Don't ask me what all that means. The bottom line is this: the chance of those passages coming from the same author is less than ten per cent.'

'Dacey didn't write them?' Jim put his fingers to his temples. 'I can't believe we got the wrong guy! I need to go back, maybe take another look at the book. There must be something I missed.'

Tony pushed his empty cup away and stood up. 'Guess we're all done here.'

'I have a car, Tony, I left it at the police department. My turn to give you a ride to the airport.'

16

Jim had been back at his desk for barely an hour when Bagley put his head around the door.

'The personnel carrier just arrived at the gate, sir. That'll be Captain Murdoch's squad coming in. Do you want to see them?'

Jim leapt to his feet. 'You bet I do. Thanks, Bagley.'

He was outside as the personnel carrier rolled up. Five men got out: Eddie, Javid, Ken, Fernando, and Darren. They looked tired and dispirited.

Jim hurried over, frowning. 'Where are the others?'

Eddie Mayer towered in front of him. 'Got them to a hospital.' His mouth twitched. 'One killed, two wounded.'

Jim felt his face go slack. He glanced quickly at the four soldiers standing uneasily in the background. 'Brian?'

Eddie shook his head.

It was like a blow in the chest. When he could speak again he said. 'You took command.'

'Yeah.'

'Eddie, I need to know what happened.'

Eddie turned to the others and jerked his head. 'Go on, guys, get some sleep.'

Jim led Eddie to his office and pulled out a chair for him before taking his own chair behind the desk. The big man sat down heavily.

Jim waited.

Eddie took a deep breath. 'Target was a kind of cinder block warehouse in a clearing. One door, no windows, a ventilation shaft sticking up out the roof. We didn't know where that went, so Brian said he'd drop a smoke bomb instead of a good-nite.'

Jim nodded. *Good decision.*

'He briefed the others and we took up positions. I stood where I could see Brian and they could all see me. He climbed a tree and dropped onto the roof.' He swallowed. 'There was a guy hiding inside that ventilation shaft. He stood up and blew Brian away with an automatic rifle.'

'Jesus.'

'I took the guy out but there were hostiles hidden up in the trees as well, and by that time the boys out front were taking a lot of incoming. Bruno was hit in the leg and Charlie got one in the hand. The others fired smart grenades up into the trees. It worked real well. The hostiles dropped out of the trees like coconuts, five of them. Then two more ran out of the jungle, firing. Ken dropped both of them with bursts of three. Nicely grouped, too. Fernando put a grenade through the door of the warehouse in case there were any inside. And that was it. I went over to Brian. Must have been dead before he hit the ground, Jim. A round had gone through his visor.'

Jim closed his eyes.

'So I went to see what happened to the others. Javid and Ken were seeing to Bruno with dressings and morphine;

Darren and Fernando were bandaging up Charlie. Ken and Fernando took hits, too, but the armour stopped them. I told them to rig a couple of stretchers and ran back a ways. We'd left a kid soldier there who led us in, and I figured he knew more'n he was saying. I slapped him around some but he swore blind he didn't know a thing. So I dragged him back to help with the stretchers.'

'How are Bruno and Charlie?'

'They'll be okay. Bruno lost a lot of blood but they'll fix him up.'

Jim breathed out. 'Did you go into the warehouse?'

'Sure did. And you know what? It was empty.'

Jim said quietly, 'They were expecting you.'

'For sure. Anyway I put two more grenades into it before we left. It's a pile of rubble now.'

'Good.'

Eddie sighed. 'They were tipped off all right. But you know, Jim, there's more to it than that. That box on the roof we thought was a ventilation shaft? It wasn't. It didn't go anywhere. The floor was boarded over.'

'Purpose-built as a defensive position,' Jim breathed.

'Yep. It was like they knew we were coming and they knew in advance just how we'd tackle it.' His shoulders slumped.

'Listen, Eddie, no one could have known this would happen. And you did well, all of you. If you hadn't responded so fast it would have been eight body bags coming back here instead of one.'

Eddie rocked his head from side to side and massaged one big hand over the other. 'I couldn't contact you out there, Jim – we had to get Bruno and Charlie to a hospital fast. I tried later on but you weren't answering.'

Jim grimaced. Eddie would have used the secure line to his office, and he was probably in Raleigh. 'Don't worry about it.' Then, to his dismay, he saw that Eddie's eyes were filling with tears. 'Eddie...?'

'It's Brian...' he burst out. 'Can't believe it, Jim. I loved that guy.'

Jim stood up and went round the desk. Poor Eddie. He'd managed to keep it together all this time, knowing the rest of the team would be looking to him for leadership. Now that he'd shed that responsibility his grief had broken its bounds. The sight of that huge man with tears streaming down his face was almost more than Jim could bear. He laid a hand on Eddie's shoulder and gave it a sympathetic squeeze. He was so choked up himself he could barely speak.

'We all did, Eddie. We all did.'

Eddie exhaled a long sigh. Then he got to his feet, brushed the tears away with his shirt sleeve, and walked clumsily from the office.

Jim sat down at his desk. He pressed an icon on the desk screen and voiced a message that would go directly to Wendell Harken, requesting a holoconference in thirty minutes. The timing was a signal between them that the matter was urgent. Then he put his head in his hands.

No one could have known this would happen? Bullshit! I should have known. I should have looked at that damned book earlier. And when I did I should have woken up to the threat right away. But I didn't. And because of me two of my guys are in hospital and Brian's dead.

He thumped a fist down on the desk and stared at it for a while. Then he slowly raised his head, his mind clearing.

Whether or not someone had been using that warehouse for captives, it was empty when the squad went in. The whole place should have been deserted, but it wasn't, was it? No, they left a reception committee. And they weren't expecting the Cameroonian Army or even the US Army, because either one would have put a couple of RPGs into that warehouse and counted the casualties afterwards, and that wouldn't have played out too well for the man hiding in the ventilation shaft. So they knew it would be the SAF. They could have got the standard operating procedure from the book, but someone had to set the rest up, someone who knew the type of operation the SAF was almost obliged to take on. It was presented in precisely those terms, and Major Leadenthall fell for it and passed it up the line.

First that book and now this. The more he thought about it the more convinced he was. Someone was engaged in a vendetta against the SAF. And whoever it was knew just how to go about it.

*

Thirty minutes later Jim was giving Wendell Harken a complete account of the debacle in Cameroon. By the time he'd finished Wendell's face was burning with anger. He said:

'Major Leadenthall has a great deal to answer for.'

'He certainly does. That's why I contacted you.'

'It was completely improper to pass this one onto us. Worse than that, he allowed himself to become party to a trap. Well, he's going to get a severe reprimand on both counts. And if he doesn't want to be stripped down to Lieutenant he will find out where this request came from and who originated it.'

'The culprit's probably taken off by now.'

'We have to try, Jim, we have to try. What a sorry business this is! I remember Brian Murdoch so well. A fine soldier but also a thoroughly likeable character. It's a grievous loss. What about the casualties?'

'In the nearest hospital at the moment. As soon as they're well enough I'll have them transferred to a military hospital here. Right now I've no idea when they'll be operationally fit again.'

Wendell sighed. 'Leave this with me, Jim. I'll go to the top of Leadenthall's chain of command and I'm in the mood to make some very big waves.'

'Thanks, Wendell.' He paused. 'You know, this wasn't just bad luck. Because of that damned book we're up against people who know exactly how we operate. The risks are unacceptable. I'd like to call a moratorium on any new assignments until we've got it sorted.'

Wendell nodded slowly. 'You're right. We can't afford any more catastrophes like this one. Apart from the terrible loss of life it'll lower morale in the Force and our reputation in the entire Army as well as here in the Department. Do what you have to.'

The holoconference over, Jim made his way back. He walked less briskly than usual, weighed down once more by the dreadful human cost of this mission. The SAF's operations weren't battles in which the expected casualty figures were mere statistics. Each man or woman was trained and equipped to the point where a CO could expect the same number to return as had embarked. Not this time. Eight individuals he'd known well and valued highly had gone out, and thanks to him two were now in a hospital and one was lying in a morgue. That hurt. It hurt a lot.

Bagley was in the outer office and Jim stopped at his ADC's desk. The usual note of authority in his voice had gone, replaced by a profound weariness.

'Bagley, Captain Murdoch's been killed.'

Bagley stood. 'I heard, sir. Sad news, very sad.'

'We'll need to make arrangements to repatriate his body. Then we'll organize a funeral at Arlington. I want the whole Force there.'

'I know the procedure, sir. I've had to do it a couple of times before.'

'Let's get the ball rolling, then.'

'Sir.'

Jim crossed to the inner door to his office, but turned as he got there.

'You're a good man, Bagley.'

17

At six o'clock the following morning Jim was in his office with the book in front of him on the desk.

It was a relief to know that Wendell would initiate an investigation into the Cameroon disaster. Unfortunately it was unlikely to lead anywhere – it was too far from the real source of the problem. The book was surely the best clue they had. Who'd written it? Not Laverne Dacey, according to the language analysis. Even so, Jim wasn't ready to rule the guy out, because there was still a ten percent chance that the passages used in the comparison were from him. The one he'd given Tony had come early in Dacey's service. Several years went by before the book was written, years in which the man had seen more action. He'd then faced a court martial and spent time in jail, during which time – according to the prison warden – he'd spent a lot of time in the library. All that could have influenced his writing style. Furthermore the crucial issue had never been examined: Dacey would have to have been on all the missions described in the book. The trouble was, Jim could only identify nine of them. He needed to try again.

He turned to the first chapter. There was an immediate surprise. Jim had made no marks in the book, but Wendell had. He'd evidently recognized the mission and, next to the chapter heading, he'd neatly pencilled a note naming both the location and the objective. Breathing faster, Jim flicked over the pages to Chapter 2. Again Wendell had identified it. He flicked quickly to the next chapter and the next; Wendell had identified those as well. Then he turned back to the beginning and noted down each mission in turn. Fifteen chapters, fifteen missions, and Wendell had identified all but two, which had question marks against them. The man had an impressive memory. Jim brought his own notes up on the desk screen and compared his interpretation with Wendell's. They coincided for the thirteen he'd recognized, and he could remove Wendell's two question marks. He closed the book and slapped it in triumph. Now he had all of them.

The personnel involved in each mission would still be in the database but they had to be dug out separately for each mission. It took an hour before he had a list of personnel for every mission. Dacey's name appeared on only eleven of the missions. There were four in which he'd played no part.

He sagged in his chair. The language analyst was right. Dacey could not have been the author of the book. It was worse than that: none of the SAF soldiers he'd listed were present on all of the missions, so none of them could have written it. So who the hell did? Who was 'A. Soldier'?

He picked up the book and held it in both hands, staring at it.

There must be something here, something I'm missing.

He started again from Chapter 1. This described a dangerous assignment in which the SAF had intercepted an exchange of drugs for arms between a Mexican cartel and a Los Angeles crime syndicate. He read it carefully, putting himself there at every stage of the mission, paying attention to how it was observed, seeking anything that might yield a clue. He found nothing. He turned the page. Chapter 2: nothing there either. Nothing in Chapter 3. He found it in Chapter 4.

The missions always started with a careful evaluation of the target, the surroundings, access, security measures, and so on. It would be referred to in phrases like 'Recon showed that…' or 'Based on a careful reconnaissance…' But in Chapter 4 it said, 'The recon team reported that…' It was the first reference to a recon team. He leafed ahead, scanning the pages for the words 'recon' or 'reconnaissance'. He got to the end of the book, and nowhere else did he see any reference to a recon team.

He sat back, staring beyond the wall and into the past. He was trying to recall the missions he'd been on when he first joined the SAF more than ten years ago. He could remember the missions themselves – no problem there because the action burned itself into his memory – but was a reconnaissance team involved, too? Now he thought about it, there usually was. They were sometimes there for a while before the SAF arrived and the two groups didn't fraternize that much. He knew they brought the reports back to the team leader, and no doubt they discussed tactics. Is that why the author was careful not to refer to a recon team? Had he dropped his guard, just that once, in Chapter 4?

He checked the time: six o'clock. Wendell could still be there. He pressed a desk screen icon to phone the number at the Pentagon. Wendell answered. He must have seen the origin of the call on his display because he sounded irritated.

'Jim, I'm still working on it—'

'No, this is different. It won't take a moment. When you were CO here at Fort Piper how much use did we make of reconnaissance teams from other battalions?'

Wendell paused a beat, then said, 'A lot. We took them on pretty well every mission.'

'Why?'

'Why? They had expertise and they had specialized equipment: thermal imaging, acoustic dishes, laser vibration-detectors that could pick up conversations from behind closed windows, all kinds of gear. They were very useful. They could tell us how many hostages or the size of the opposition we were up against, points of entry, what security was in place – mission-critical information of that sort.'

'When did we stop using them?'

'After that Baghdad business. In my view Dacey was scape-goated. He didn't take part in that beating; he was convicted because he failed to stop it. The real culprits were a couple of soldiers from the recon team. I wanted to distance the SAF from it as much as possible. Since then we've put more emphasis on reconnaissance techniques in our own training schedule. We only make use of an outside team in specific missions – like the one you led in the Honduras.'

'Thanks, Wendell.'

'Why do you want to know?'

'I'm filling out my picture of the missions in that book. Thanks for annotating the chapters, by the way. You did a great job.'

'Glad it was helpful. I must go.'

The line went dead, but Jim continued to look at the phone. It wasn't just the SAF on those missions; recon teams were involved, too. Why the hell hadn't he thought of that?

He could picture a typical mission. The recon team goes out, sizes up the target, the security, entry points, opposition – all the relevant intel. They report back to the SAF squad leader and discuss the options. The SAF goes in and does the job. Afterwards they go over it again. Normally SAF men don't discuss these things outside of the mission, but this is still within the mission and the squad leader's a little high from the action and ready to talk about it. And one recon man is listening carefully. He has an exceptionally good memory, so retentive that later on he can call upon it to write a chapter on each and every mission. And in that chapter he comments on the standard operating procedures and any departures from them.

He got up and began to pace the room. So who was this guy? Did he simply write the book for profit, or was it part of a deliberate effort to attack the SAF? If it was part of a larger plan, who had such a colossal grudge against the Force. And why?

There was one obvious place to start: the two men taken into custody and brought before a general court martial for mistreating a prisoner. Why hadn't Wendell said something before about the guilty parties in that incident being recon soldiers? He closed his eyes. The answer was simple. They'd both assumed the author could only be someone who'd served with the SAF. After that they'd shut their minds to other possibilities. So strong was his own conviction that he even clung to the ten per cent chance offered by the language analyst. He shook his head.

How stupid can you get?

He knew what he needed now. He was reaching for the phone when his filtered headline newsfeed flashed. He tapped a fingertip on the icon.

Late breaking news:
US citizen kidnapped in the Yemen executed by his captors. Sons of the Caliphate post video of the beheading. President condemns terrorists, and warns that no effort will be spared...

Jim clicked off the newsfeed and took a deep breath.
Another man dies, and I'm responsible for this one, too.

*

Todd Harper and Hank Allshaw continued with the tedious task of flying the Global Condor on its surveillance pattern, and the screens in front of them displayed the moving image from the downward-pointing camera.

Colonel Baxter came up behind them. 'Did you see the newsfeed about the kidnap victim?'

'Yeah,' Todd said. 'Tough break. I thought we'd seen the rescue.'

Hank said, 'The people carrier stopped about five ks from that village and they went right up to it on foot. Then they came away. Sure looked like a rescue.'

Baxter shrugged. 'Maybe it went wrong. I suppose they'll tell us in good time.'

'Sir,' Todd said, 'this bird's getting low on fuel. You want to send up another replacement?'

Baxter paused to think about it. Then he said, 'No point now. Might as well call it off. Return to base.'

'Roger.'

Todd looked to his left but Hank was already setting the autopilot for Camp Lemmonier.

*

Jim was still going over Holly's operation in his head. With the death of a hostage now weighing on his conscience it looked like pulling her out was a bad decision. But was it? Try as he might, he couldn't fault the reasoning behind it. With what he knew—

There was a light knock at the door. He knew that knock well enough. He said 'Yes, Bagley?' even before the man's head appeared around the door.

'Captain Cressington's squad landed at the airport half an hour ago, sir. They're on their way. I expect she'll want to report in. Do you want to see her?'

'Yes, when she comes show her in here.'

The door closed.

He took a deep breath, then phoned Tony Grieg.

'Hi Jim, any progress?'

'Some. I was able to confirm that Laverne Dacey didn't write the book. Not just a ten per cent chance. Zero chance.'

'How come?'

'Wendell and I identified the missions in every chapter between us. Dacey was on eleven of them – eleven, not fifteen. He couldn't have written in that detail about four missions he was never on.'

He heard what sounded like the click of a tongue. 'Leaves us without a suspect, Jim.'

'I'm looking into another possibility right now. Listen, could you get me a transcript of that general court martial?'

'The one that convicted Dacey?'

'Yes, but there were others involved. I want the whole of it.'

There was a pause. Then, 'Shouldn't be too hard. I may have to go to the CID, give reasons.' He grunted. 'One of the defendants was shot dead. That's a pretty good reason.'

'Thanks. It'll be a big file, so best to send it securely via the holoconference data channel. Let me know when you have it and I'll set it up.'

'Will do. Say did you see the news about that American hostage? They executed the poor guy.'

'Yeah, I saw it. I was kind of hoping for a better outcome.'

'Nasty bastards. Curious, though.'

Jim frowned and leaned forward. 'What's curious?'

'Going to all that trouble to capture him, and then just executing him. Why didn't they shoot him at the same time as the other two?'

'I suppose there's more propaganda value doing it this way.'

'Yeah, but as a rule they hang on to them longer than this – you know, milk the situation for all it's worth. They get people all stirred up, plea for mercy, that kind of stuff. And that's when they do it. This ain't one thing or the other, know what I mean? Oh well, I'll be in touch.'

Jim was still thinking about it as he terminated the call.

Was William Lampeter the bait in another trap? Did they deliberately stop in that ruined village to lure the hostage rescue team in, knowing they'd be Special Forces? It would explain why they'd executed Lampeter so soon. When Holly pulled her team out they knew the plan had failed.

Perhaps he was just being paranoid. Or perhaps he'd made the right call after all.

18

There were voices in the outer office: Bagley's familiar care-worn tones, and another, a little lower in pitch, crisp and decisive. A brief knock on his door and Holly Cressington came in. Jim waved her to a chair. She hesitated, then took it. Her body was rigid, her lips tight. He knew what was going on. She was so angry she could barely speak.

'Did you see what they did to that hostage, Colonel?'

'Yes, I saw.'

'We were all ready to go in. We could have saved that man's life.'

'I know that.'

'May I speak freely, sir?'

'Go on.'

'I think you're still worried about exposing me to danger because my father's Defense Secretary. If you can't handle that then I request a transfer.'

Jim was taken aback. He'd said she could speak freely but this was way off base. He focused on the wall behind her, fighting the impulse to explode, ready to match her anger with his for questioning an order and having the impudence to suggest a reason for it. Then he moved his gaze and contemplated her for a moment. He couldn't help but admire her guts, speaking to her Commanding Officer like that. He took a deep breath and counted off several seconds before he responded.

'Captain, you've been through a lengthy induction, including a trip to foreign parts, intensive further training, daily exercises. Have you any idea what all that costs?'

She blinked, no doubt caught off guard by the apparent change of subject. 'I don't know,' she snapped. 'A lot, I imagine.'

'Yes, it is a lot. We don't have an unlimited budget in this outfit, far from it. If I thought I couldn't handle the fact that you're Bob Cressington's daughter I would have saved us a lot of money and not taken you on in the first place. Now you can request a transfer if that's what you want, but you should do it for the right reasons. I have every confidence in your ability to carry out missions assigned to you. But each mission involves a risk/benefit analysis. If the balance of risk changes – at any stage – it's my job to abort the mission. It changed in this case, and that's why I pulled you out.'

'But there was a US citizen in that house in imminent danger! And now those bastards have executed him.'

'I know, and don't think it was an easy decision. But if it's a question of one US citizen or an entire squad of my highly-trained personnel I have no choice.'

She frowned. 'We did a thorough recce. There was nothing else for miles. Your drone reconnaissance report said they were still in that village and we knew which house they were in. The other houses were mostly ruins, nothing in them except for that SUV. We could have done it.'

Jim looked at her, weighing in his mind how much to say.

'What was the plan, Captain? Standard operating procedure: toss in good-nites or flashbangs – probably flashbangs, because the house was open to the night air – then rush in. Secure the captors, pick up the hostage, job done.'

'Yes, that was pretty much it.'

'Okay, a plan like that is fine, but it depends on surprise. Suppose it wasn't a surprise? Suppose those guys were wearing gas masks, ear protectors, and sun visors, so they wouldn't be affected by anything you tossed in? Suppose they were waiting for you in there, standing on either side of the entrance, alert and ready, with automatic weapons cocked and levelled?'

Her face fell. 'They knew we were coming?'

'I couldn't say for sure, but there was a clear and present risk.'

'What risk?'

'I'm not at liberty to tell you that.'

He couldn't give her so much as a hint about what was going on because she was smart enough to start working things out. And she'd get it wrong. She couldn't know when the missions in the book stopped, she couldn't know about the recon teams, she couldn't know about the way they were being targeted. So she – and maybe others, too – would start suspecting each other and that would be disastrous for morale.

Her mouth tightened and she looked away.

Now a flash of annoyance surged through him. Sometimes a senior officer had to make tough decisions and it would help if they weren't held to account by a captain who couldn't possibly have the bigger picture. And then he remembered that there was a time when he was that captain and Wendell Harken was his CO, saying something very similar to him. He leaned forward.

'Look, Cressington, you're a good soldier and I'm glad to have you in this outfit. But there's one thing you have to learn. We have different jobs, you and me. You need to focus on yours and let me do mine.' He stood up. 'That'll be all.'

She was on her feet already, her face flushed, the grey eyes wide. 'Sir.'

She turned briskly and left the office.

He sat down again, wearily this time. Things had been so much easier when he'd embarked on this career. He'd train hard and he'd be exposed to the risk of death or injury on every mission, but that was all part of the adrenaline rush of action. The orders came down the line and he followed them. When the mission was over he could relax, not sit with his brain buzzing with recriminations.

He tried to pick up his train of thought again. The court martial. It would give him information about the two recon men who were on trial. That might be helpful but it wouldn't establish whether either one could be responsible for the book. For that he needed to repeat the process he'd just carried out. He had to find out if any of the recon personnel were on the missions in every single chapter. Trouble was, he had no access to those records. Where could he get hold of them? Then he remembered the Honduras.

The operation Wendell had referred to was a hostage extraction in the Republic's capital, Tegucigalpa, three years ago. He'd led that one himself, and he'd used a recon team. He brought up the internal directory on the desk screen and deep clicked the number for Special Forces Reconnaissance Detachment Alpha. It was answered promptly. He responded:

'This is Colonel James Slater. I'd like to speak to Major Ferenczi.'

Pause. 'Sorry, sir, do you mean Lieutenant-Colonel Ferenczi?'

Lieutenant-Colonel? Better still.

'Yes, that's who I mean.'

'Please hold and I'll connect you.'

He waited.

'Ferenczi. Is this Colonel Slater?'

'It is. Haven't seen you since the Honduras. How are things?'

'Pretty good, pretty good. That was a very successful mission. High profile, too. But I heard the shit hit the fan afterwards.'

'Yeah, I'm glad we got your people out before that happened. Seems like you've had a promotion. Light Colonel. Congratulations.'

'Yes. The commendation you arranged to send down didn't do any harm, either. Thanks for that.'

Jim said, 'You deserved it.'

'So do you have another job for us?'

'Not right now, but I'd like to ask a favour.'

'Go on.'

'I'd like you to send me a copy of your operational records. I need to know which of your personnel took part in missions between 2045 and 2052.'

He could sense the hesitation. 'Access to those records is restricted.'

'I wouldn't ask you if it wasn't important.'

'You don't want to tell me what this is about?'

'For security reasons the fewer people who know, the better. Look, I understand the problem. Perhaps one of your people could courier the records over – that way you'd know they were going straight from your hands into mine. Then all I need is a couple of days with them and when I'm finished I'll destroy what you've given me.'

A long pause. Then, 'Okay.'

'Great.'

'Is that it?'

'Yes, that's it. I really appreciate this, Major— ' he laughed, 'I mean Colonel.'

A short laugh echoed his own. 'I guess one good turn deserves another.'

Now that the call was finished, Jim realized that neither of them had used first names. He didn't even know Ferenczi's – it was a hangover from the formal relationship they'd had with that detachment in the Honduras. Still, it had achieved the desired result. He couldn't do anything now until Tony came up with the transcript and Ferenczi sent him those records.

He sat there for a few moments more, wondering whether there was something he hadn't thought of, but his mind kept going round in circles. He was tired. He'd make an early night of it and do the tab with the guys in the morning. The exercise would be good and it would clear his mind.

There was a knock on the door. Bagley stood there. All of him. That made a change.

'Will you be needing me any more now, Colonel?'

'No, we're all done for today. Thanks, Bagley.' Bagley turned to go. 'Oh, Bagley. An FBI man called Tony Grieg is getting some information for me. If he calls tomorrow morning can you set up a holoconference? I'll be going on the tab, so not before 1000 hours.'

'Tony Grieg. Yes, sir, I'll make a note.' The door clicked shut behind him.

Jim closed everything down and tidied a few documents away. He picked up the book and dropped it back in the drawer. Then he wandered through the empty outer office and headed towards the accommodation blocks. On the way he paused and looked around him. The base was quiet. The sun, now low in the sky, bathed the scene with orange light. From somewhere beyond the parade ground a mockingbird floated a varied sequence of chirps and trills to him over the warm evening air. It was a soothing sound on which to end a difficult day. He heaved a sigh, then made for his quarters.

*

The tab the following morning seemed harder than usual. No one complained, but everyone struggled on the hill climb and Jim was as glad as any of them to rest at the top. Holly Cressington had already got there with a pack almost as large as she was. She said nothing, just settled down at a distance. It looked like she was avoiding him.

Jim leaned against his pack and watched the rest come in. Below him the instantly recognizable figure of Sergeant Ted Nichols appeared, planting his hands alternately on his knees as he laboured up the final rise. He flopped down next to Jim. The sleeve he swiped across his forehead was already dark with sweat.

'All right, Ted?' Jim asked, with a rueful smile.

'Piece of cake – ten years ago.'

Jim laughed.

They rested in silence, getting their breath back. Then Ted leaned closer.

'Jim, you asked me to stay close to Captain Cressington on that Yemen mission. Something I thought you should know. I was on her shoulder the whole time, and she never put a foot wrong.'

Jim said, 'I'm glad to hear it.'

'Yeah, well, you know she was pretty pissed off at you pulling us out last minute like that. I guess we all were. Especially now the guy's been topped.'

'Ted, I said this to her, and I'll say it to you. There's a risk/benefit analysis in every mission. If that changes I have to revise the strategy.'

Ted nodded slowly. 'This has to do with that thing in Cameroon, don't it? Poor Brian and his people getting jumped. But that was Africa, this was Middle East. I mean, there couldn't be a connection, could there?'

Jim took a deep breath. 'We need to go on.' He stood, extended a hand to Nichols, and helped him up. Without letting go of the hand he bent forward and said quietly, 'Things have changed, Ted. I'm still working on it.'

19

On his return from the tab Jim showered, dressed, and had a proper breakfast – as opposed to the quick snack and fruit juice he'd grabbed at 6.30 am and the energy bars he'd chewed on the way. When he entered the office he was still glowing from the recent exertion. Bagley was waiting with the news. Tony Grieg had been in touch and he'd set up a holoconference for ten o'clock.

Jim glanced at his watch: 9.30. He said 'Thanks, Bagley' and went into his office. At 9.55 he opened a drawer, took out a memory tile, and walked down to the holoconference suite to set things up.

Tony's head and shoulders appeared above the projector.

'Hi, Jim. Got what you wanted. Took me a while.'

'Thanks. Have you looked at it?'

'Only the sentencing. Reduced to Private, dishonourable discharge, ten years in Leavenworth – both of them. Not life. The court must've decided they meant to inflict harm but not actually murder the guy. See what you make of it.

By the way, the people at NSA drew a blank on where those emails came from.'

'The ones the author sent to the publisher?'

'Yeah, those. Seems they were sent via the Philippines and North Korea, maybe Russia and China, too. Things run into treacle when they're routed like that, so they still haven't got the source. Whoever sent them was pretty damn good at hiding his tracks. Same with the funds. That starts with the Cayman Islands but then it bounces to Nevis, Cyprus, and God-knows-where-all. Kind of surprised me. I wouldn't have thought the average grunt could manage stuff like that.'

'Me neither. Well, let's see what the transcript gives me. You ready to send?'

'Ready when you are.'

'I'll have to close the vision channel for the transmission, so I'll say goodbye for now. I'll be in touch. Thanks.'

'Sure thing.'

Tony's holoimage collapsed as Jim switched channels from vision to data. The console displayed a new screen. Soon a filename appeared and a black progress bar crept slowly across an empty rectangle. By 10.10 am he'd shut down the suite and was back in his office, feeding the tile into a reader.

First to come up were pictures of the three defendants. There was Laverne Dacey as he remembered him, fuller in the face than the ID photo Mirski had shown them at the Raleigh Police Department, with light brown hair cropped to regulation length. It was a police mugshot and he looked slightly startled. The second defendant was one of the two from the reconnaissance detachment. His name was Conrad Lazar. The photo showed a powerful-looking man with a heavy jaw and bushy black eyebrows. Jim recognized him; he'd been in the recon team on several of his own missions. He'd never actually spoken to him but he was hardly alone in that: the man didn't interact much even with members of his own team. Jim recalled there was one exception. Joseph Kabaki was a big, gentle-mannered Kenyan as taciturn as Lazar himself. It was a wordless companionship but they seemed to do everything together. That was as much as he could remember about Lazar. The third image was of the other recon man, Rod Clayton. Jim recognized him, too. It was a thin, foxy sort of face, topped by mousey hair that had a slight curl to it, despite the regulation cut. Unlike Lazar, who was glaring defiantly at the camera, Clayton's expression was as close to a sneer as the police cameraman would have permitted. Jim had never had any real contact with him either.

He turned to the trial. The defending counsel had argued successfully that the defendants' actions could only be interpreted in the light of what had gone before. There followed accounts from two SAF soldiers and Jim began to build a picture of the preceding events.

An extremist militia was active in the area, and their local commander had been spotted in a housing complex on the outskirts of Baghdad. The eight-man SAF team had been sent to take him out. They were joined by an eight-man team from Special Forces Reconnaissance Detachment Alpha. The mission had been highly successful: the commander and several of his lieutenants had been killed and there had been no civilian casualties. The two squads were ready to exfil when new orders arrived. A US regular army unit had been there, providing support to the Iraqi Army, and there'd been a delay in dispatching their replacements. Four of the recon team and four of the SAF soldiers were asked to stay on until the relief contingent arrived.

A few days later they were on a joint routine patrol around the perimeter of an open market when two children wandered into the centre and blew themselves up. In the ensuing chaos a dozen heavily armed insurgents ran in and let loose a torrent of fire directed at the soldiers, the market stall holders, and the customers. Two of the recon soldiers were killed instantly and the Iraqi soldiers took even heavier casualties. True to their training, the SAF men were quicker to respond, dropping into firing positions and picking targets. The remaining two recon soldiers, Lazar and Clayton, ran to cover and returned fire from there. Nine of the terror squad were killed and the rest ran off. It was not an unfamiliar occurrence in that area and emergency services were set up for it; ambulances were quickly on the scene.

The attack had probably been mounted in revenge for the loss of the commander, and it had clearly been timed to coincide with the passage of the patrol through the market. As the patrols deliberately avoided adhering to a regular timetable it meant someone had contacted them the moment they'd entered the square. While the SAF soldiers busied themselves assisting with front-line medical aid, Lazar and Clayton, with some Iraqi soldiers in tow, rounded up the likely suspects. One was a market trader widely believed to have extremist sympathies. His stall was completely untouched. He was the man who would become the victim of the brutal interrogation by Lazar and Clayton that had brought the matter to court martial.

The charges were read out to Lazar and Clayton. They pleaded not guilty.

Jim read on. A pathologist presented the results of a post mortem, which showed that the victim had died of internal injuries. A number of witnesses had seen the victim when he was detained or in his cell, and testified that he appeared to be uninjured at that stage. Two said they knew Lazar and Clayton were going to interrogate him. Several saw the man after he was dead. None had actually witnessed the beating. Their testimony was inconclusive.

Then Dacey agreed to give evidence from the witness stand. He was sworn in and stated his name. Jim read the verbatim account.

'Sergeant Dacey,' the prosecuting counsel began. 'Were you acquainted with the defendants Sergeant Lazar and Corporal Clayton prior to the attack on the Baghdad market?'

'Yes, sir, we were in different battalions but we'd served together on several missions.'

'Were you friendly with them?'

'We were comrades-in-arms.'

'But not friends.'

'Soldiers under fire look out for each other. Most people would call that friendship.'

'Yet you have volunteered to give evidence against them, Sergeant.'

'Yes, sir. I feel obliged to.'

'You appreciate that in giving evidence you could be incriminating yourself?'

'Yes, sir.'

'Have you been threatened or offered inducements?'

'Sir, it has been suggested that my own case might be dealt with more leniently.'

'And that is why you are taking the stand.'

'No, sir, I'd have done it anyway. I didn't like what I saw, and it would be on my conscience if I failed to report it.'

'Very well. Describe, Sergeant, what you did see.'

'I was present when the suspect was moved from his prison cell to an interrogation room. Sergeant Lazar shouted questions at him. He shrugged and shook his head.'

'Were these questions addressed to the suspect in his own language?'

'Yes, they were. Lazar was a fluent Arabic speaker. I understand the Mesopotamian variety myself, so I knew what he was asking him.'

'Which was?'

'Well, at first they were asking him where his cell phone was. Everyone in that market uses a cell phone but there was nothing on his person or in his stall. They wanted to get a record of his conversation, or at least his contact, from it. They were sure it was his tip-off that led to the attack, and after that he'd probably handed the phone to some kid to carry it off. But the suspect just said he'd never owned a cell phone, which was obviously a lie. Like I said, everyone in that market has one.

'Then they started to ask him who his contact was in the local jihadi group. Corporal Clayton was yelling questions in English as well, and Lazar was translating them into Arabic. The suspect was obviously confused and he was looking from one to the other. Finally they lost patience and Lazar slapped him across the face, first with one hand, then the other. The questioning went on and when they still didn't get a response Lazar punched him very hard in the gut. He went down but Clayton dragged him up and punched him again. Then it was Lazar's turn. It was like a contest to see who could hit him hardest. I didn't like it, so I walked away.'

'Sergeant Dacey, are you aware that walking away could have been taken as demonstrating your tacit approval for what they were doing?'

'I sure hope it wasn't. It was just the opposite. I was disgusted.'

'Thank you, Sergeant. No more questions.'

Defense counsel: 'Sergeant Dacey, you were in a different battalion to the defendants. There is – is there not? – serious rivalry between those battalions?'

'Not at all, sir. Recon do their job and we do ours. We cooperate fully.'

'But you've already said you weren't friends.'

'No, we weren't friends exactly but we certainly weren't enemies.'

'But Sergeant, isn't it true that you are giving this evidence today in an attempt to shift blame from yourself onto Sergeant Lazar and Corporal Clayton?'

'No, sir.'

'Perhaps, then, you'd like to tell us why you were present at the interrogation at all.'

'A lot of people were killed in that market and I could easily have been one of them. I was as interested as anyone to know who'd tipped the insurgents off. The man they were interrogating was the principal suspect.'

'But it turned out that he was innocent, Sergeant, just an ordinary family man with a stall in the market.'

'Actually I don't think he was innocent at all. The Iraqi soldiers have been there a lot longer than us and they collect a lot of intelligence. This guy was high on their list as one to watch.'

'Now, Sergeant, you say you walked away during the suspect's interrogation. Did you see the defendants kill the suspect?'

'No sir, at least I don't think so. They hit him pretty hard but I couldn't say whether the blows were fatal.'

'You made no attempt to stop it.'

'No, sir.'

'Why not?'

'Sir, like I said, the attack that day left a lot of people dead. Two of them were recon soldiers, Bill Seaford and Joseph Kabaki. The defendants had lost friends. They were real angry. I don't think I could have stopped them if I'd tried.'

'But you didn't try?'

'No, I didn't try because I understood their anger.'

'You feel, then, Sergeant, that in those circumstances mistreatment of prisoners can be justified?'

'No. No, of course not. All I'm saying is, I understand what can drive people to do something like that.'

'Do you ever get angry, Sergeant?'

'Sure I do. When you're in the field you see some real bad things. Men, women, children killed, maimed or disfigured for life. Young girls who've been gang-raped until they're unconscious. Fellow soldiers blown up by IEDs. Things like that make us angry, all of us, all the time. I'm no exception. If I didn't get angry about those things I wouldn't be human.'

'Thank you, Sergeant. No more questions.'

After that, Lazar and Clayton must have known their position was untenable. When Clayton took the stand he said:

'When I denied the charges I meant the murder charges. It wasn't like we meant to kill the guy. Sure we roughed him up a bit, but that's 'cos we knew he was lying. He was the one brought those jihadis in to kill our friends and all those people, no question. But he stonewalled. That's why we hit him.'

'You hit him hard?' the Prosecuting counsel asked.

'Not that hard. But he must have had some kind of weakness we didn't know nothin' about. First thing we knew he was dead. But we never meant to kill him.'

Lazar made a similar statement but in fewer words. After that their guilt was not in doubt; it was only a question of how severe the sentence would be.

Jim straightened up. There it was, as clear as day. The motive. He could almost see the faces of those two recon men as the damning evidence unfolded, Lazar's beetling eyebrows knotted, his eyes narrowed, his gaze drilling into his accuser, Clayton's foxy features drawn into a mask of hatred and contempt. Dacey's eyewitness account had convicted both of them. That he'd given evidence at all must have been, in their eyes, a betrayal of the comradeship between soldiers, the unspoken loyalty that bound them to support one another in adversity. And in broader terms, the Special Assignment Force had betrayed Reconnaissance Detachment Alpha.

Over the years of incarceration those feelings would have festered like an open sore, then hardened into resolve. The SAF had to learn what it was like to be hurt, the way they were hurt. And Dacey must die.

But which of them killed Dacey? Which of them wrote the book? And which of them was the present threat?

20

A heavy overcast lent an even more sombre note to the funeral at Arlington. Brian wasn't married, but his mother and father and sister were present. Five members of that ill-fated mission – Eddie, Javid, Ken, Darren, and Fernando – bore the coffin, with Ted Nichols making up the six. Charlie was there too, standing behind the family, his arm in a sling. Bruno couldn't walk yet and was still in hospital. The body bearers placed the casket, then held the flag that was covering it as the chaplain recited the prayer. The casket was lowered. Sixty men in dress blues snapped to attention and saluted. The firing party, in perfect synchrony, fired a three-rifle volley. A single bugler played taps. When the last notes had died on the damp air the body bearers folded the flag and gave it to Jim. He accepted it with a heavy heart, his failure to pull Brian's mission in time haunting him more than ever. As he presented it to the parents he could barely meet their eyes. Struggling to keep his voice steady, he said the words:

'On behalf of the President of the United States and a grateful nation, please accept this flag as a token of the honourable and faithful service of your loved one.'

Brian's father took the flag, his face pale and taut with the effort of self-control. He mouthed 'Thank you', clasped it under his left arm, then reached for his wife's hand. His daughter held onto the other arm, and slowly the chaplain led them back. The soldiers parted to either side and stood to attention as they passed through.

Jim watched them go, saw the daughter lay her head on her father's shoulder.

If this was your doing, Conrad Lazar, or yours, Rodney Clayton, then by God you're going to pay for it.

*

A gloom had settled on the entire force and lingered after their return to Fort Piper. Jim knew he had to get them busy again and he had just the thing to do it. He mustered them in the mess.

'We laid a fine man to rest today,' he said, 'and I know how much that meant to every one of you. But it meant even more to me, because I'm personally responsible.' There was a murmur of protest but he raised a palm to quell it. 'No, it's my job to look after the safety of every man and woman in this Force, and in Brian Murdoch's case I failed. His death could have been prevented.'

The men shifted uneasily. They weren't used to a CO saying things like this. He continued:

'We've been complacent, and I've allowed it to happen. I'm referring to our standard operating procedures. We've been following the same ones for years. They worked well, so we didn't see any need to change them. That was a mistake, and Brian paid the price. In various ways people –

the kind of people we're normally up against – have got wind of how we do things. That represents a serious threat. If we ignore it there'll be more trips to Arlington, something none of us want. So what can we do about it?'

He paused, looking around, giving them a little time to experience the discomfort raised by the question. Then he went on.

'We're going back to the drawing-board, that's what. You all know the type of scenarios we deal with – you've done enough exercises on every one of them.'

There was a low grumble.

'Well I want you, all of you, to criticize how we've done things up to now and think of ways we can do them differently. Captains and Majors: starting as of now I want each of you to get together a small group, six or ten, maybe less but not more. Take one scenario at a time and bat ideas around. Doesn't matter how crazy they seem to be at this stage. Remember, the keynote is speed and surprise.'

'Excuse me Colonel,' Eddie said, 'but what's new about that? We always go for speed and surprise.'

'Sure, you're right, Eddie, because speed and surprise gave us success before. But now the surprise has to be even more complete and the action over so fast that no one on the other side has a chance to reach for a transmitter or a mobile phone to tell their lousy friends how we did it. And it's not just speed and surprise, I want fresh tactics. If we need new kinds of weapon I'll do my damnedest to get them. The hostiles aren't the rabble we used to be up against; they're technologically savvy and better equipped. We've got to stay ahead of them.

'Okay? We'll bring all the suggestions together and make an initial selection. After that we'll try out each one in an exercise, see if it works. If it doesn't work we'll try a different suggestion. This isn't going to happen overnight, we may be doing it for weeks, even months. That's okay, we'll give it as long as it takes. I've spoken to General Harken about this and he's in full agreement. During this time we will not be undertaking any real-life missions. None whatever.'

There were gasps of surprise and groans of disappointment. He raised his voice. 'Get used to it! We move out only after we've moved on. I'm not having any more of you coming back in body bags.'

And he left the mess.

He was striding back to his office when he heard quick footsteps behind him. He stopped and turned. It was Holly Cressington.

'Sir?'

'Yes?'

She took a deep breath. 'I owe you an apology.'

For a moment he was taken aback. Then he said, 'No you don't. If I'd been in your shoes I'd have felt exactly the same way.'

He walked on, but he was thinking how much it took for someone as spirited as Holly to come out with an apology like that.

21

In the afternoon a soldier arrived at the front gate. He told the sentries at the gate he was from Special Forces Reconnaissance Detachment Alpha, and he had a delivery to make in person to Colonel James Slater. He was subjected to the usual security checks, then conducted to Bagley's office. Bagley showed him in.

He saluted. 'Colonel Ferenczi's compliments, sir. He asked me to give you this.'

He removed a memory tile from a pouch on his belt and handed it to Jim.

'Thank you, corporal. Please convey my thanks to Colonel Ferenczi.'

'Yes, sir. Er, the Colonel asked me to remind you of the sensitive nature of the material. He'd be glad if you could tell him when it's been destroyed.'

'I understand. I'll do that.'

'Sir.' He saluted again and turned smartly.

'Corporal...'

The man turned back.

'Please make use of our mess if you'd like some refreshment before you leave. I'll get one of our people to take you down there.'

The soldier's face brightened. 'Thank you, sir.'

As soon as that was arranged Jim loaded the memory tile, muttering to himself, 'Lazar or Clayton, Clayton or Lazar.' Just as he'd hoped, the tile contained the composition of recon teams used in various missions. Unfortunately the records were organized differently – and to his mind less logically – than the SAF's. Moreover, not all the missions were ones conducted with the SAF, so identifying the relevant ones would be more difficult. He arranged the data on a spreadsheet, missions in the book across the top, names down the side, and got to work. It took two hours to complete the same exercise he'd conducted in half the time for the SAF. Finally he destroyed the memory tile.

Three names cropped up on every mission: Lazar, Clayton, and Silva.

He sat back in his chair.

Damn. After all that I'm no further on. So what's the next move? I'll see what Tony thinks.

*

Tony listened without interruption.

'Well done, Jim. This Silva chap is a distraction – Lazar and Clayton are the ones with motive. Give me half an hour. I'll look 'em up.'

Twenty minutes later the phone rang.

'Jim?'

'Yes, Tony.'

'Okay. First, they both served their time at Leavenworth. Second, Clayton died last year. He was still in custody.'

'Really? Looks like Lazar's our man, then. When was he released?'

'That's the part I don't understand. They were sent down in April, 2052, both of them with a ten-year sentence. So when Laverne Dacey was shot dead last year Lazar should have been in Leavenworth. But he wasn't.'

'He wasn't? Why?'

'Because Conrad Lazar was released after only five years. The court recommended he served the full tariff, so it would take some pretty high-level intervention to get him released that soon.'

'We need to find out what that was.'

'You bet we do. Everything else fits. It even makes sense Lazar being a recon soldier.'

'How do you mean?'

'Well, like Mirski said, when you've just come out of prison the difficulty is locating your target. Recon soldiers are trained in intelligence gathering. He'd know how to start looking.'

Jim said, 'What, on the outside? He wouldn't have access to the sort of databases he'd need.'

'Oh, he probably found a way. Maybe he's still got buddies in the service who were willing to help.'

'So what's next?'

'Leavenworth. We need to have a chat with the Commandant. Okay for tomorrow morning?'

*

They met up in the arrivals area of Kansas City International's Central Terminal. Tony rented a Ford sedan, which he drove north-west, then west. They crossed the Missouri River on the double suspension bridge, leaving Missouri for Kansas, and reached the United States Disciplinary Barracks with just ten miles on the clock.

The entrance guard at the gate asked for IDs. Tony passed him the leather folder with his badge and Jim held out his US Army ID. The guard used a handheld device to scan each in turn, then returned them.

'Same procedure when you leave, gennulmen,' he said. 'We-all like to check, jest in case yew take a fancy to the place and feel like stayin'.'

They smiled dutifully at what had to be the man's standard joke.

'I have an appointment to see the Commandant at eleven o'clock,' Tony said. 'How do we get there?'

'Turn right and follow it all the way around. Entrance is right opposite the parking lot. They'll direct you when you go in.'

'Thanks.'

'No problem. Enjoy your visit.'

Their timing was perfect. At eleven o'clock they were waiting in the anteroom to the Commandant's office. Five minutes later the door opened and the Commandant came out.

'Charles Robinson,' he said, and as he shook hands, 'Colonel Slater, Agent Grieg, sorry to keep you waiting. Come on in.'

It was a spacious office: plain white walls, large windows partially shaded by louvred blinds, and a short bookshelf loaded with heavy volumes. The room could have belonged to a lawyer except for a bench with two computer terminals and six closed-circuit television screens. The desk was plain, with no inset screen, just a console. The Commandant sat down in his chair behind the desk and Jim and Tony took the chairs that had been placed in front of it.

Charles Robinson was solidly built, late fifties, clean-shaven, and with silver-grey hair cut short. Colonel was probably his career grade, Jim guessed. He'd serve his time to the best of his ability and retire on a good pension. It didn't sound like a bad deal.

He looked from Jim to Tony. 'Now gentlemen, how can I help you?'

Tony said, 'We're interested in two of your inmates, Conrad Lazar and Rodney Clayton.'

'Oh? Well I would have thought someone in your line of work would be able to search the records.'

'I have. I need more detailed information than I can get that way. Do you remember them?'

Robinson gave a slight chuckle. 'Mr Grieg, there are two thousand inmates in this facility. It's impossible to know all of them.'

Tony's eyes narrowed and his voice hardened. 'All the same I think you might recall those two.'

Robinson inclined his head. 'Yes, actually I do. May I ask the reason for your interest?'

Jim looked at Tony. Tony said, 'In July 2058 an ex-Special Forces soldier, name of Laverne Dacey, was shot dead in Raleigh, North Carolina. He had no known enemies, and the shooter was never found. But we happen to know that his evidence at court martial put Lazar and Clayton in Leavenworth. In my book that's motive, so we're following it up.'

'I see. Let me refresh my memory.'

He took a chair at one of the computers and tapped the keyboard unhurriedly for a while. He read from the screen, then turned round.

'Sent here 2052. We had them in the maximum security wing for four months. They didn't appear to pose a risk, so I moved them to medium security. That way they could be usefully employed.'

What Jim wanted to know was: did Lazar write that book while he was incarcerated here? He'd have to work around to it. 'Can you say what they did in their leisure time?'

Robinson raised his eyebrows. 'Well, the prisoners work a 40-hour week. They have leisure time, but they don't always make good use of it.'

'But you have educational and vocational programs,' Tony prompted.

'Certainly. They can enrol on programs like carpentry, dental assistance, graphic design, screen printing, welding—'

'Computing?' Jim asked.

'Yes, but they're not given access to the internet.'

'What did Lazar do?'

'I believe he spent a lot of time in the library. The librarian is in this wing. I can get him in here if you like.'

Jim nodded. 'Thank you, I think that would be helpful.'

Robinson pressed a button on the console. 'Mendes, would you come to my office?' He turned back. 'He'll be here in a moment.'

Tony said, 'While we're waiting, sir, perhaps you could tell us about Clayton.'

'Clayton's dead.'

'I'm aware of that. I was wondering about the circumstances.'

Robinson's mouth twitched. 'We don't get many deaths in custody – it's one of the reasons I remembered the name. He was on a work detail, assisting some contractors who were laying pipes. He fell in front of an excavator.'

'Fell or was pushed?'

He gave Tony a grim smile. 'You want my opinion? I'd say he was pushed, but it was impossible to prove. The driver was one of the contractor's employees. He was very shaken. Said he saw nothing until the inmates shouted and held up their hands to get him to stop. By that time it was way too late – Clayton was under one of the tracks.' He sighed. 'I have to say I wasn't all that surprised.'

'Oh, why's that?'

'There are no ranks for inmates, but as in any correction facility there is a kind of internal hierarchy. Men who've been here longer, or ones who are serving longer sentences, demand respect from newcomers. I interviewed Lazar and Clayton when I transferred them from maximum security. I told them they'd be working alongside other men and it was in their own interests to get along with them. Lazar took it quietly. He never said much at the best of times – if he had feelings he kept them to himself. Clayton just leered at me. He had a lot of attitude, that one. He wasn't big, but he acted like he was. I couldn't see him showing respect to anyone. It could be that he overstepped the mark once too often.'

There was a knock and the librarian entered the office. He was a skinny man and his dark eyes were wide with alarm.

'Ah, Mendes,' Robinson said. 'These gentlemen were asking about Conrad Lazar. You remember him?'

Mendes relaxed visibly. 'Oh sure. A big, quiet guy. He was a lot of time in the library.'

'Writing?' Jim asked.

Mendes blinked. 'Writing? No, reading.'

'What did he read?'

'History, politics, war. But only in the Middle East.'

Tony said, 'How come you remember his preferences so well?'

'Most men, they like titles with a lot of sex,' Mendes said with a shrug. 'They find a good one, word gets around. Or detective stories, maybe: crime, combat, stuff like that. The books Lazar was reading, it was the first time anyone wanted them. He studied them real hard, too. Made notes. He asked me did I have any books in Arabic – he could speak the language, that one. I had a copy of the Qur'an but he wasn't interested in that.'

Robinson looked at Jim, and Jim nodded.

'All right, Mendes. Thank you. That's all.'

'Sir.' He left the office.

'Now, gentlemen,' Robinson said, 'Are we done?'

Tony said, 'Not quite. Why was Lazar released early?'

'Not released. He'd served five years here and at that point he was transferred to a federal prison, the USP – that's the United States Penitentiary, just 4 miles south of here.'

'So he was released from there.'

'I wouldn't know. I don't keep track of inmates who are no longer in my care. It's as much as I can do to keep up with the ones I have here.'

'Well, the records show he was released,' Tony said. 'And as he was sent here to serve ten years I find it mighty hard to understand why he was transferred at all.'

'It was highly unusual, and that's why I recalled Lazar's name when you mentioned it. A man came here to see him. It was the first time Lazar had received any visitors at all.

The man insisted on privacy, so we let him use an interview room. We had a Corrections Officer standing outside – standard practice. That officer told me they spent a long time in there. Over the next couple of months there were two or three repeat visits. On the final occasion the gentleman came to see me. His name was John Abadi. Said he wanted Lazar moved to the federal prison at the earliest possible opportunity. Naturally I consulted our legal advisers, but they confirmed the request had the necessary authority.'

'Whose authority?' Tony asked.

'Mr Abadi was with the CIA.'

22

'Why?' Tony said, as they walked back to the car. After the air-conditioned interior of the prison the air outside was oven-hot. Fierce sunlight bore down on them and came up again from the magnacrete apron. 'What the fuck is the CIA's interest in Lazar?'

'Sounds like he was being groomed as an agent. Fluent in Arabic, special forces training – he'd be a good candidate. And if they offered him early release he might well go for it.'

'What, to serve in the Middle East?'

'Arabic speaker? Would have to be.'

Tony unlocked the car and a gust of even hotter air escaped from the interior. They left both doors open for a moment.

Jim said, 'Robinson keeps things close to his chest, doesn't he? You need a can-opener to get anything out of him.'

Tony shrugged. 'It's the way some people are. They like to make you work for it. At least he told us about this CIA guy and the transfer.'

They got into the car. Jim fidgeted uncomfortably as the heat from the faux leather upholstery penetrated his shirt. Tony started the engine and set the air-con to maximum.

Jim raised his voice over the noise of the fan. 'We need to think about the time frame here. Lazar was transferred to the USP after doing five years, so that would have been 2057. Dacey was shot dead the following year. If Lazar was responsible—'

'Which seems likely.'

'—which, as you say, seems likely, he had to obtain a rifle and the frangible ammunition, locate Dacey and where he worked, and monitor his movements over a period. Only then could he do the shooting. For a man with Lazar's training that wouldn't take more than a month or two, and you can bet he'd start the moment he was released. Means he could only have been in that federal prison for about a year. But that's still enough time for him to write the book.'

Tony engaged gear. 'Okay, let's go there and find out.'

The air-con had begun to cool the car's interior by the time they approached the large block with its central dome.

Tony said, 'That's the old building, the one they called the "Big Top".' Then pointing, 'My guess is the warden will be in the new block over there.'

They stopped at the gate and Tony showed his badge to the entrance guard. The man confirmed that the warden's office was in the new building. He scanned both IDs.

'We're here to see the Warden,' Tony said. 'Could you let him know we're on our way?'

'Yes, sir, I can do that.'

They went in, got directions, and walked down the corridor. The warden's name was on the door: Edward Saffler. He beckoned them in right away.

The office was light and airy. There were no computer monitors or closed-circuit television screens this time, just a desk screen similar to Jim's own.

Tony shook hands with the warden. 'Tony Grieg, FBI.' He indicated Jim. 'Colonel Slater's here to represent the US Army's interests.'

Jim shook hands in his turn.

Saffler was a younger man than Charles Robinson. He had straight dark hair, a smooth, open countenance, and an impressive girth.

Tony said, 'Good of you to see us at short notice, Mr Saffler.'

'Not at all,' the warden said, rocking slightly from side to side as he walked behind his desk. 'Always a pleasure to help the Bureau.' With a courtly gesture he added, 'Please, gentlemen, do sit down. What can I do for you today?'

'We're making enquiries about one of your inmates,' Tony said. 'Name of Conrad Lazar. He was transferred here from the Disciplinary Barracks in 2057.'

'Lazar, Lazar. Yes, I do remember that man. Most unusual transfer – him and the other one.'

Tony frowned. 'There were two?'

'Yes. Please allow me to look up the record.' He hooked on a pair of metal-rimmed spectacles and bent to the desk screen, where he brought up a keyboard image and tapped for a while. They waited patiently as a sequence of pages projected coloured light on his face and he scanned each one. He read aloud, 'Lazar was transferred here in April, 2057. He was released a year later in April, 2058. He spent his time here in minimum security.' Head still dipped, he looked over his spectacles at them. 'Quite a transfer, from medium security at a place like the USDB, to minimum security at a federal prison. And if you think that's unusual, how about the other one, happened around the same time? He came from "The Hill" – that's the Lansing Correctional Facility, no big distance from here. He was moved from maximum security there to minimum security here.' He paused, eyebrows raised at them, before continuing. 'I questioned it, of course. They said there was no mistake.'

'They?' Tony said. 'You're talking about the CIA?'

'Ye-es. Now how would you know a thing like that?'

'It had a familiar ring to it,' Tony said. 'So who was this other guy?'

'His full name was Saleh ibn Haroun. American-born, can you believe? He was suspected of being one of them there home-grown terrorists. They said the evidence waren't that strong, and they were gettin' kind of edgy about a law suit for wrongful imprisonment and inhumane treatment. So they decided to hedge their bets by makin' this transfer to an easier regime. Fact is, he gave us no trouble.'

Jim said, 'We'd like to know a bit about how they spent their time here.'

'Well, o' course they'd have been on work details. Worst thing you can do for folk like that is leavin' them idle – that's when the mischief starts brewin'. So it keeps 'em busy, they can do somethin' useful, and they get some vocational trainin' at the same time. May help 'em when they get out of here.'

'They'd have leisure time, too,' Jim prompted

'Oh sure. If you want to know more about that, I'd say you should speak to the Corrections Officer for that wing. That would be…' he consulted the screen, 'ah yes, that'd be Meg Olsson.' He took off the spectacles. 'I do believe I have another appointment waitin' for me but I can have someone take you down there.'

'Thanks.'

Saffler opened a door to an adjoining office and put his head through. 'Martin, would you take these two gentlemen down to E-wing to see Meg Olsson?'

They heard 'Sure.' A young man emerged and said, 'Please come with me.'

Tony turned to Saffler. 'Thank you, Mr Saffler. You've been real helpful.'

'No problem at all.'

They met Meg Olsson in a corridor. She looked to be in her thirties, blond hair tied in a ponytail, a pale blue utility shirt, black trousers, and a wide webbing belt heavily loaded with keys and pouches.

Again Tony did the introductions. 'Ma'am, we're making some enquiries about an inmate who was in your care: Conrad Lazar.'

'Yes, I remember him. He was released last year. What did you want to know?'

Tony said, 'What was your impression of him?'

'You'd best step in here.'

She opened the door of what looked like office space for several Corrections Officers. There was coffee-making equipment and a sink in one corner. A man dressed similarly to Olsson was just leaving. He gave them a quick nod. There was no one else around. She led them to some chairs.

'Conrad Lazar,' she said. 'Big guy, kind of brooding. He'd speak to you if you asked him a question but he never started up a conversation. Made me uneasy, to tell you the truth. But he gave no trouble, never complained. What else can I say?'

'Did he have any friends?'

'He did, yeah. There was Saleh. He came in around the same time as Conrad. They got to know each other real quick. I guess that was because Conrad spoke Arabic. So they'd go out on work details together, chat in the day room, that kind of thing. I wouldn't know what about.' She laughed. 'I don' speak Arabic myself.'

Jim said, 'Did Lazar do anything else in his spare time?'

'Did some reading in the library. But mainly writin', a whole lot of writin'.'

A thrill ran through Jim's veins. 'What was he writing?'

'It's none too usual round here, so I did ask him. All he'd say was, "It's a thriller." You know, he was a quiet man, in a powerful, calculating kind of way, very self-contained. I didn't think I'd get much out of him, especially 'bout somethin' as private as that.'

'Maybe we could take a look. Did he use one of your network terminals?'

'Oh no, we wouldn't permit that – it'd give him access to the internet. I wanted to encourage him, though. I looked in some cupboards and found an old notebook computer no one ever used. I let him work on that.'

Jim grimaced. 'And I expect he took it with him when he left.'

'I guess so.' She frowned. 'Come to think of it, I don't even remember the last time I saw it.' She shrugged. 'Oh, well.'

Tony asked, 'Did Lazar get any visitors?'

She pursed her lips. 'No... no I don't believe he ever did have a visitor.'

Jim said, 'What about his friend Saleh? Did he get visitors?'

'No, not that I can recall.'

'Did Saleh write, too?'

'Lord, no. He watched a lot of TV, read trashy books, that kind of thing. But like I say, they spent time together when Conrad wasn't writin'. Them and another guy.'

'They had another friend?'

'Yeah… what was his name, now? Kind of small, unhealthy-lookin', watery eyes, bad case of acne. Funny name, too – Cy, that's it. Cy Sloper. But he was only here a short while.'

'What was he in for?'

'I don't remember. Seein' as he was in minimum security it'd most likely be some kind of white-collar crime.'

Jim said, 'Can you tell us exactly when Lazar was released?'

'I could look it up. Moment.' She went to a terminal on a counter top, and Tony took out his phone to make notes. 'It was last year, 12th April 2058.'

'And Saleh?'

'Saleh was moved from here. I'm afraid I don' know where he's at now.'

Tony looked at Jim, and Jim nodded. He turned to Meg Olsson. 'That's all we need right now, ma'am. Thank you. Appreciate it.'

'Sure thing. You folks leavin' now?'

'Yes, we are.'

'Okay, I'll show you out.'

*

They sat in the car, the engine running, the air-con full on again.

Tony raised his voice to compete with the fan. 'Sure looks like Lazar wrote the book.'

'Yes... You know, the CIA has got a lot to answer for. The USP isn't Leavenworth and minimum security isn't medium security. That gave Lazar the leisure and the facilities to write the damn thing.'

Tony reached for the air con control and turned the fan down a couple of notches to make it easier to talk.

'So,' Jim continued, resuming the conversation at a more normal level, 'either the CIA put him up to it, in which case I want to know why, or they have no idea what he's done, in which case someone should enlighten them. Either way I need to have a talk with this John Abadi.'

'If he'll talk to you.'

'Why shouldn't he talk to me?'

Tony said, 'You think Charles Robinson was cagey, you haven't come up against one of those guys. He could even refuse to see you. He could say there are issues of national security involved.'

Jim said, 'That book's cost the lives of one of my best men and put another two in hospital. He'd better not try to lecture me about national security. He's already breached it.'

'Looks like Lazar killed Dacey, too. You can add him to the casualty list.'

They fell silent. Outside, the sun continued to beat down, baking the parking lot and bouncing dazzling reflections from the rear windows of the cars in front of them. Inside, the air-con had lowered the temperature to a comfortable level. Tony turned the fan right down.

Jim said, 'There's still a problem, Tony. Lazar wasn't released until April 2058. That fits with the shooting all right, but the book was published May 2058. How long does it take to publish a book?'

'Longer than a month, that's for sure. And that publisher guy, Brice, said it needed editing, too.'

'Then it couldn't have been Lazar – he was still inside. They're not given access to the internet, and he didn't get any visitors. And there's the routing of those emails and the royalties. That doesn't sound like Lazar, either. Maybe we're dealing with two different people: Dacey's killer and the author of that book. What about Silva? He was a member of the recon team on all the missions in the book, and he returned to the US before the Baghdad business, so he wasn't involved in the court martial. Maybe he wrote it.'

Tony took a deep breath. 'Too many loose ends, Jim. We need to check some of it out and nail this John Abadi. Are you ticketed back to Raleigh?'

'No. You have something in mind?'

'Yeah, why don't you fly back to Washington with me? We can deal with it all there.'

'Okay, sounds good.'

Tony put the car in gear and steered it out of the parking lot.

23

Major Todd Harper made his routine early-morning journey from the family home across the Nevada desert. Another day and, with the reconnaissance detail over, possibly a different kind of mission. He could only hope so. He drove down into the underground car park and made his way to the changing room, arriving at almost the same time as Major Hank Allshaw. They zipped up their one-piece flight suits and looked at each other.

'Okay?'

'Okay.'

Todd opened the door to the control room and they went in. Once again Colonel Baxter was waiting for them.

'You're here, good. JSOC's identified a target in the Yemen and the strike's actioned. You've got a Damocles at the Code 80 airbase, fuelled, armed, and waiting. You'll be carrying six Radius bombs.'

Todd winced. The Radius was one hell of a weapon. It put out a ground-level shockwave so tight and intense that it cut like a scythe, collapsing every building within range. And the attack drone would be carrying six of them.

Baxter said, 'Coordinates and photos of your target are on your screens. Let's get moving.'

Todd nodded 'Sir' and he and Hank strolled over to their flight seats.

Hank murmured, 'What's his ass so tight about this morning? It's only a routine strike.'

'His ass is always tight,' Todd said. 'My turn, I think,' and he went to the seat on the left.

They didn't bother with the coordinates or the photo; time enough for that. They ran the system checks. A screen in front of them showed the view from the drone's forward camera, across the apron to the runway and beyond to the horizon. Todd made the connection to the ground team, located at a secret airfield north of Yemen's capital, Sana'a. He transmitted:

Ready

The response came quickly.

Ready

Todd sent:

Yours

They responded:

Ours

On the engine instrument panel in front of him two needles quivered and began to climb up the dials. The camera view gave a little shiver as the vibration from the twin turbines spread through the hull. For a moment Todd pictured this drone as a living thing, excited, trembling with the anticipation of action. But it was not a living thing; it was an instrument of destruction. Deploying such a weapon could easily result in what they politely called collateral damage. Was that a possibility this time? Bombs dropped off target and hitting a school or a hospital or a place of worship? No real risk of that – he was experienced enough to make sure it didn't happen. Bombs dropped on an incorrectly identified target? That was harder; they had to work with the intel they received. What about bombs dropped on militants who were using innocent men, women, and children as human shields? That was a really tough one. He could scarcely imagine the terror of those families, already fearful enough about being held captive, as bombs fell from the sky. The collapsing buildings, the deaths, the dreadful injuries, the lives that would never again be the same...

'Todd?'

He turned his head.

Hank gave him a quizzical look. 'Update the boss?'

'Er... oh yeah, sure.' The Director liked to monitor attack missions closely. He held down a switch. 'Ready for take-off, Colonel.'

He released the switch. Thoughts like this never used to trouble him, but he was older now and he had family responsibilities. Hank was young and single. For him a mission like this was a duck shoot. He was right about one thing, though: it wasn't for them to question the decision. By the time the strike was actioned it had already gone a long way: from JSOC to Centcom in the Yemen, and up to the Joint Chiefs, the Secretary of Defense – maybe even the President himself – before coming down to the Drone Control Center and Baxter, the Director. All the pros and cons had been weighed up in Washington.

You have your orders. Do your job.

On the instrument panel the brake light went out and they could see from the forward camera that the drone was moving out to the runway. It didn't stop, just turned to line up. The runway began to creep towards them, first slowly, then faster. It was a longer take-off than usual; six Radius bombs amounted to a heavy payload. Finally the runway dropped away as the drone took to the air.

Todd pressed the switch again. 'Airborne now, Colonel.'

Control was still with the ground team in Yemen, so they settled back to examine photos of the target. It was a village, or had been; most of the buildings were in ruins – not an unusual sight in that area. No doubt the jihadis had taken it over during an earlier operation, then been driven out; the original inhabitants had fled at some stage, and now no one could be bothered to reconstruct it. There were reconnaissance photos taken from several angles but they didn't yield anything more. It wasn't an obvious target.

Baxter came up behind them. 'Insurgents were spotted in that village. Three vehicles came in, one of them big, like a motorhome or camper. They've been hidden in some of those buildings, I assume the ones with some walls still standing and a roof on the top. It won't be hard to find; there's nothing else at those coordinates. I'll leave you to it.'

Todd glanced over his shoulder but Baxter had already gone.

Thirty minutes later a message appeared:

Yours

Todd said, 'Here we go', partly to Hank and partly to himself, and transmitted:

Ours

The craft had already reached the correct altitude. He took the controls, flying straight and level, and set the coordinates of the target on the automatic pilot. Hank confirmed the setting.

They watched the desert terrain roll by. This was the boring part, although unlike surveillance it would be short-lived. On the gigantic wall screen above their heads the drone would be a small icon trailing a lengthening white line as it traversed a map of the Yemen.

Todd said 'Attack mode' and he and Hank pulled down the VR goggles on their headsets. Virtual Reality integrated the images from the front, side, rear, and down-facing cameras. They never used it during high-altitude surveillance because the effect was more like being in freefall than a pilot's view, but it could be useful during a bombing run. Todd swivelled his head, watching out for interceptors. He did it as much as anything to keep himself occupied. Although there were stories about the insurgents having long-range drones of their own, none had ever been sighted. They certainly had short-range drones, but those were no threat to a craft like this.

'Target minus five,' Todd said.

Both of them were sharply focused now.

'Target minus four.'

Hank had control of the munitions. He said, 'We doing this in one pass?'

'Let's drop the payload from the inner and outer pylons first. Then we'll do a sweep and see what's still standing.'

'Willco.'

'Target minus three.'

Then, 'Target minus two. I have a visual.'

Todd ran a finger along the side bar of his goggles to zoom in on the ruined village. The buildings rippled in the desert heat but there was no possibility of a false positive: the layout matched the reconnaissance photos precisely.

'Arm weapons,' Todd called.

Hank flicked the switches. 'Weapons armed.'

'Commencing bombing run.'

The buildings grew larger… larger…

Everything went blank.

'What the fuck…?'

He pushed the VR goggles up and looked at his display screens but they were blank, too.

Hank said, 'What happened?'

Todd brought his hands off the controls. 'No comms.' He slammed a fist down on the arm rest of the flight chair. 'It chose one hell of a time.'

Colonel Baxter must have seen something on the big screen because he was out of the office and on his way over to them.

'You've turned away,' he said. 'Did you deliver the payload?'

'No, sir. We lost the link.'

'Nonsense, it's turned south. No airfields there.'

Todd took off the headset, got up, and stepped back to look at the screen. This was still live; the drone's position was transmitted on an independent channel. The screen showed the flight path curling at its end as the drone executed a wide turn to starboard.

The Colonel was right. If they'd lost comms, the drone was programmed to go to the nearest airfield. That wasn't what it was doing.

He looked round. 'Well, it's not responding, sir. Maybe ground took back control.'

Colour rose to Baxter's face. He muttered 'We'll see about that,' and hurried back to his office. He returned a few minutes later.

'They did not assume control,' he said, and added drily, 'and they somewhat resented the suggestion.'

Hank had left his seat and he was watching the wall screen with them now. He frowned. 'Look at that turn,

Colonel. This is no wild bird. It's being controlled from somewhere.'

Todd said, 'Well not from here,' and he reached over and waggled the joystick with two fingers.

'And not from ground,' Baxter breathed.

A cold silence descended on the three. Todd licked his lips. Perhaps it was just a temporary comms drop-out. Maybe in a minute or two the screens would flicker into life and control would be restored.

Maybe.

And maybe not.

They waited, watching the line trace a half-circle on the wall screen. Then it straightened and began to lengthen rapidly. The drone was almost certainly on full throttle. The line got longer.

Hank pointed at the big screen. 'Seems to have settled on one heading now, sir.'

Baxter blinked a couple of times, then said 'With me' and raced towards his office.

They ran after him. Baxter was already at his desk, controlling the wall screen display. He zoomed out and projected the flight path forward.

He said, 'If it maintains this course it'll be over the eastern part of Sana'a in about ten minutes.'

Hank muttered, 'San'a...?'

Todd felt a rush of panic. He said, 'Can we scramble jets?'

Baxter shook his head briskly. 'No time for that.' Then, 'My God...' He threw open the door to the adjacent office and shouted:

'Get me the US Embassy in Sana'a. Now!'

A pause, then his secretary called out, 'On the line now, sir.'

He returned to his desk and pushed the speaker button.

'All our operatives are busy at this time. Please hold. Your call is important to us—'

'Christ Almighty! Not that number. Direct line to the Ambassador!'

'Sorry, sir,' she called out. Another pause. Then, 'Line's engaged.'

'Interrupt the call.'

Todd could picture the poor girl trying to remember the right sequence. On the wall screen the line had already crossed the outskirts of Sana'a.

The Ambassador's voice came on. 'I'm on a call right now. Is this urgent?'

'Code Florida! Get your staff to the bomb shelters immediately!'

'Code Fl... Who is this?'

'This is Colonel Baxter, Director of Drone Operations Center, Nevada. Repeat, this is not a drill. Get your... Hallo? Hallo?'

All three looked up at the wall screen. The line had stopped moving.

Baxter dropped into the chair behind his desk and sank his head in his hands.

Hank said quietly, 'Oh shit.'

Todd closed his eyes. The best job in the world had just become the worst job in the world.

24

After Jim and Tony had landed at Washington they picked up Tony's car from the short-stay parking lot and drove to the new J. Edgar Hoover Building. Tony left the car in a lift for automatic parking and checked the code for retrieval which had arrived on his phone with a ping. Then Jim followed him to the main entrance of the building. As the doors closed behind them Jim wondered if it was always like this. It seemed to be full of people in a hurry, rushing from one place to another. Evidently it wasn't always like this because he heard Tony mutter, 'What the hell…?'

Tony took him through security, then Jim followed him into a large open plan area filled with people seated at monitors. It was like videos he'd seen of trading floors at investment banks and the atmosphere was just as frenetic. Tony went up to one of the operatives.

'What's going on, Chuck?'

Chuck looked up, one eyebrow raised. 'Where you been, Tony? Another planet?'

'Kansas.'

Chuck rolled his eyes. 'Near enough. Watch, there's a news update coming in.'

They moved round to watch the screen. There were pictures of a bombed building, rescue teams scrambling over it, carrying people on stretchers, everything seen through a haze of dust.

'Where is this?' Tony asked.

'Sana'a, capital of Yemen. That used to be the US Embassy.'

Tony's mouth opened.

Chuck turned up the volume.

…bring you late breaking news from the Yemen. A White House spokesman has confirmed that there was a rocket attack on the US Embassy in Sana'a this afternoon. There was no warning and there will be many casualties. The group calling themselves Sons of the Caliphate are believed to be responsible. Rescue teams are at work in the rubble and many local volunteers are helping in the search for survivors. In view of the security situation in the country the building was operating with less than the normal complement of staff. Nevertheless, at this time fifteen US personnel, including the US Ambassador to the Yemen, are confirmed dead. Flags are flying at half mast on the White House and every government building. The President will be making a statement later today. Meanwhile here, once again, is a video recorded at the moment of the attack.

They watched an apparently ordinary scene of the US Embassy building bathed in sunlight. Then something appeared at top left, moved in fast, and there was a huge explosion.

Chuck turned down the sound.

'Holy shit,' Tony said. Then, 'Where'd they get that footage?'

'CCTV camera across the street. Everything on that side was flattened too, but it'd already transmitted.'

Jim said, 'I only caught a glimpse but it looked like it had wings. A cruise missile? Do they have them?'

'I don't know,' Chuck replied. 'Guess CNN will have another update in a while.'

Tony jerked his head at Jim and they went over to the elevators.

*

Tony had an office on the fourth floor. They paused as he placed his palm on a handprint reader. The door clicked open and they went in.

'Make yourself comfortable, Jim. I just want to check some things out.'

The sparse furniture included an easy chair but Jim ignored it and crossed to the single large window. They were at the rear of the building and the window looked out over parkland. The Capital Beltway was two miles from here in the opposite direction, and compared to central Washington this was positively rural. Behind him he could hear the pattering of the keyboard as Tony conducted his search. Then he heard 'Okay' and turned round.

'Lazar's completely off the radar. No social security number, no driving licence, no registered vehicle, no bank account, nothing on NCIC, yada, yada. My guess is he killed Dacey, burnt the vehicle, then left the country. It's going to take a lot longer to trace him.'

'Come on, Tony, we know roughly where he's gone. The CIA inserted him with the jihadis, so he's in the Yemen, Iraq, Syria, some place like that. That's why they transferred Saleh to the same prison. Saleh had the connections. He was the one gave him the route, told him who'd pass him along.'

'Could Saleh do that? Let me check his record.' Tony went back to the keyboard, then started to read off the screen. 'Saleh ibn Haroun, 25-year-old Arab American. Imprisoned for terrorist activities, including attending training camps in Pakistan and Syria, stock-piling of weapons and bomb-making equipment, and listing potential targets.' He looked at Jim. 'Jesus, he belonged in maximum security all right. They should have thrown away the key, not transferred him to a light regime. He had the connections, that's for sure.'

'But Saleh wasn't released any earlier than Lazar, so none of that explains how the book got published. Maybe Silva did write it.'

'Moment.' Tony tapped some more. 'Silva's still in the Army. Special Forces Reconnaissance.'

Jim shook his head. 'Then it can't be him. If he wrote a book like that he'd be putting *himself* in the firing line. In any case he wouldn't be hanging around, waiting for the fallout.' He thought for a moment. 'What about that other guy Lazar hung out with – what was his name – Cy Sloper? He wasn't in for long. Lazar could have given the manuscript to him to take to a publisher.'

'Worth a look.' More furious key-tapping. Then Tony stared at the screen.

'What is it?'

'Cy Sloper, 28-year-old Caucasian. In on a minor count of hacking into a restricted site. Ten months, sentence reduced to five. A computer geek, Jim.'

'Hacking,' Jim breathed. 'If he's good, he could have made the deal with Brice. It would take someone like that to cover his tracks so well.'

'Sounds like a case the CCRSB may have investigated.'

'CCSRB?'

'Yeah, the Bureau's Criminal, Cyber, Response, and Services Branch. I'll see if they have him on record.' Seconds later he said, 'Yes, they have. Picture of him here.'

Jim went over and looked at the monitor. He saw the face Meg Olsson had described: pale, watery eyes, skin peppered with acne. The man's mouth hung slightly open.

Tony frowned. 'I've seen that face somewhere before…' He shook his head. 'Can't place it.'

'Okay,' Jim said. 'Lazar put the manuscript on a memory tile or something similar and gave it to Sloper before he was released. Why would Sloper want to help him?'

'Share of the royalties, maybe? He'd launder those and keep a good bit for himself.'

'They couldn't have known how it would sell. Had to be something else.'

Tony's attention was back on the screen. 'This record finishes with the prison sentence. I wonder if anything's happened since. The investigating agent should know.' He went back to the heading. 'George Walski. He's a buddy of mine, and he's in that Branch. Let's see if he's around.'

They went down a flight of stairs to an office on the third floor. Walski was there, his collar open and shirtsleeves rolled to his elbows, sitting behind a monitor. He was heavily built, his arms massive and hairy, the right forearm inked with an old tattoo depicting some kind of raptor. He looked up.

'Grieg,' he grunted. 'Here to waste my time?'

'Maybe, maybe not. Now be nice, George, this is Colonel Jim Slater, with me on this case.'

Walski gave Jim a guarded nod.

Tony said, 'We're interested in a guy called Cy Sloper.'

Walski's eyes narrowed. 'What about him?'

'You put him away a couple of years back. Served five months out of ten in minor security, US Penitentiary at Leavenworth.'

Walski grunted. 'He must-a been laughing his fucking head off. We were all over him, just couldn't get the evidence to stick. He got off real light.'

'For hacking into a restricted site.'

'Yeah. Little creep. It was all we could get him for at the time. But we could really stick it to him now.'

'For what?' Tony asked.

'Money laundering, big-time. I'm telling you, the funds he was shifting would make your eyes water. We were ready to nail him for that and for what he could tell us about one of his clients, a big crime syndicate in Las Vegas.'

'Big crime syndicates don't dick around with amateurs,' Tony said. 'If they were using Sloper he must be good.'

'Oh he's good all right, much too good. But after he came out of prison he went to ground. We looked high and low. *Nada*. Anyways, what's your interest?'

'We think he made a friend when he was inside. Did a nasty favour for him.'

'Yeah, well now he's doing nasty favours for somebody else.'

'How d'you mean?'

Walski didn't say anything, just made a hooking motion with one finger to indicate that they should come and look at his monitor. They went and stood behind him. Walski was scrolling through news feeds. He stopped at the kidnap in Sana'a and clicked on it.

They watched as the three men stepped onto the pavement and began to walk towards the camera. Walski pointed at the small man in the middle. 'Keep your eyes on this guy.'

The black SUV pulled in behind them. One of the two companions turned, then flew back as he was hit. The other one followed.

Walski paused the video, then enlarged it, centring on the face of the small man. Pale skin, acne, his mouth open in surprise.

'That's him!' Jim said.

'I knew I'd seen that face somewhere before!' Tony said. 'The media got it wrong. They reported it as William Lampeter.'

'That's the story we released,' Walski said. 'William Lampeter was a British soldier killed in 1916 on the first day of the Battle of the Somme. There's no grave because his body was never found. But if you look carefully you'll find his name among about 70,000 others on the Thiepval Memorial.'

Tony and Jim looked at each other, then back to Walski.

'Why?' Jim said. 'Why tell them it was somebody else?'

'Look at the way the snatch was organized,' Walski said. 'The two guys with him were shot dead and only he was taken. This was no random kidnap: he was targeted. But Cy Sloper was a high-value hostage wanted by the Bureau and we reckoned they knew that. So they'd be expecting us to mount a bid to extract him, and real fast. Telling the world it was William Lampeter changed things. *They* knew who they'd got, but they thought *we* didn't know who they'd got.'

'What's the difference? There'd have been a rescue attempt either way.'

'No, if William Lampeter existed, they'd expect negotiations first. Gave us breathing space while we moved. We took it to the Director of National Intelligence. He passed it to SOCOM and they put Special Forces on it. They made some sort of attempt to pull him out but for some reason it didn't work.'

Jim felt the heat in his face.

Tony was still frowning. He said, 'But it *was* Sloper, and they *did* execute him.'

Walski didn't answer. He was scrolling through the news feeds again. He stopped at the execution.

Two men dressed in loose black robes appeared, black scarves concealing their heads and faces except for the eyes. The victim was between them, wearing an orange prison suit. He was hooded, hands tied in front of him. They made him kneel. Then one of them faced the camera. Although his mouth was obscured it was obvious from his posture and the small movements of the scarf on his lower face that he was making some kind of speech. Then the camera switched to the prisoner.

Walski paused the video. 'Okay, you can't see his face – but look at this.' He zoomed in on the hands. The orange suit was over-sized, the sleeves too long, but the vicitm's fingers were visible. Walski glanced round, first at Jim, then at Tony. Their faces were blank.

'The fingernails,' Walski said.

'What about them?' Tony said. 'A bit long, a bit dirty, is all.'

Walski smiled. 'We spent some time with Sloper. He bit his nails. He bit them right down to the quick.'

Jim felt a slight thrill. 'It's not Sloper. They substituted some other poor guy for him. It was staged.'

Walski nodded. 'The whole shooting match: the kidnap and the execution.'

Tony said, 'You know, I was wondering why they executed him so soon afterwards. It wasn't Sloper at all, they just let everyone think it was. They want us to think the guy no longer exists.'

'I still don't get it,' Jim said. 'Why go to all that trouble?'

Walski shrugged. 'Sloper was real clever at moving funds around. The jihadis may want him to do the same for them. Or maybe they're hoping he can siphon money out of that crime syndicate's account into theirs.'

'Will he cooperate?' Jim asked Walski.

'Oh sure. He was probably in on it.'

'You think so?' Tony said. 'He looked pretty shocked when they iced the two bodyguards.'

'Maybe he wasn't expecting that, but it made it look more convincing, didn't it? No he's cooperating all right. They'll find ways of keeping him happy, probably feed him pretty girls to share his bed. This guy's a real nerd, never had a girlfriend in his life. He'll be thrilled to bits.'

'Did you pass this up the line?'

'Nah. What's the evidence? A still shot of fingers, is all. The Director's a real hardnose; it'd take more than that to convince him.'

'What else do you know about Sloper?'

'Background, you mean? We had quite a big team on this, but what they got was pretty thin. No family, or if there is they're not owning up to it. The agents out west interviewed the Principal at his local college. Poor scholar, no interest in sports, used to skip classes. But he had one friend, name of Randolph Walker. They tracked him down. He said all they ever did was play with his computer. Cy wrote a lot of routines, boasted he could hack into any network he liked. Randolph learned a lot from him about programming, but he went legit. He works for a software company somewhere out there. That's about it.'

Tony said, 'Thanks, George. I owe you one.'

'You owe me about ten. You find that little shit for me and we'll call it quits.'

They returned to Tony's office. This time Jim did take the easy chair. Tony went to the chair behind his desk.

Jim said, 'I bet Lazar set the whole thing up. It could have been part of the deal they made. Sloper tells him the Feds are closing in. He knows next time they'll throw the book at him. Lazar says "Keep your head down till I'm out." Then Lazar's released, shoots Dacey, goes over to the jihadis using the route Saleh gave him. The jihadis are suspicious – of Americans especially – so he has to work with them a while before he's ready. Then he tells them how useful Sloper can be, and arranges the fake kidnap.'

'Could be. Lazar's a planner, no question – you can see that from the way he went after Dacey. And he wouldn't have second thoughts about whacking Sloper's bodyguards.'

'So what's the situation? Is Lazar working for the CIA or not?'

Tony pointed a finger at him. 'Good question. Seems to me the only one can answer that is Mr John Abadi of the miraculous fucking CIA.' He frowned and turned his head. 'I wonder which Directorate he's in. I'll take a look at their personnel list.'

'You can do that? I thought they were sealed up pretty tight.'

'I should be able to get access to their subnet. See, in the Bureau we're mainly concerned with stuff inside the country, but we also have stations abroad. The CIA's main focus is outside the country, but they have interests at home, too. There's some overlap so we're supposed to liaise with each other. Don't laugh.' He turned to his monitor and there was some key tapping. 'Yep, here we go. Abadi...' He looked up at Jim, frowning.

'John Abadi is Director of Digital Innovation.'

'So?'

'That's CIA-speak for cyber espionage.'

25

Jim frowned. 'Cyber espionage? But Lazar was Special Forces Recon. Why recruit him?'

Tony said, 'Yeah, doesn't sound like that would be his number one choice. We're missing something, some sort of connection.'

Jim said, 'Hang on, I've got a hunch. Let me make a call.'

Ferenczi's number was still on his phone. He tapped it. 'This is Colonel Slater. Connect me to Colonel Ferenczi… Yes, hallo, Colonel. I wanted to thank you for the data you sent me. I've destroyed the memory tile… Yes, could I ask you something else? Do your people receive any instruction in techniques of cyber-attack and cyber-defence?… Right, that makes sense. When did it start? 2051. And who does that?… Would you happen to know who was on the first intake?… Sure, I'll wait…' He engaged Tony's eyes, then returned his attention to the phone. 'Excellent, thanks very much… Not sure yet, but I'll keep you informed.'

He clicked off and turned back to Tony. 'In 2051 the CIA approached Special Forces Reconnaissance Detachment Alpha. They offered to train a few of their guys each year in basic cyber techniques. Recon goes out to a lot of the usual hot spots. The thinking is that while they're there they can keep their eyes open for the more obvious signs of cyber activity.'

'Like what?'

'I don't know, not without that training. Rooms full of people and computers, antennas, high power transmitters? – no idea. The interesting thing is who they trained in the first year.'

Tony said, 'Let me guess: Conrad Lazar.'

'Correct. Conrad Lazar, among others. So John Abadi knew Conrad Lazar *before* the Baghdad business – he may even have been involved personally in the training they gave him.'

Tony nodded slowly. 'Okay, it explains Abadi's interest in him. But it doesn't get us much further. We already knew Lazar wrote the book and why, and now he's out of reach.'

'I have a long reach, Tony.'

'All right, suppose you did catch up with him? Could you bring him back here? How? Have him extradited? I don't think so. Kidnap him? Maybe. But even if you did it's not certain you could nail him for the book. He disguised the names and places. He could say it was a work of fiction.'

'What about Dacey's murder?'

'No witnesses, no evidence. We have motive, we have opportunity, we have timing, but it's all circumstantial.'

'What are you saying, Tony?'

Tony shrugged. 'My brief was to get that book pulled from circulation and track down the guy who wrote it. The book's pulled, the guy who wrote it is pretty much out of the picture. It's been fun working with you, Jim, but I can't help you get Lazar. I'm prepared to go out on a limb, but not *that* far out.'

Jim pressed his lips together and nodded. 'Okay, Tony, I understand.'

'Look, I'll contact Lieutenant Mirski, update him on who we think Dacey's shooter was. We owe him that much. No need to mention the CIA business: Lazar was released and he took his revenge. That's about it. What are you going to do?'

'I'm going to talk to John Abadi.'

*

The cab dropped Jim at Langley. He walked through to the inner courtyard, past the Kryptos sculpture and into the cafeteria, where he ordered a coffee and a doughnut. Then he headed for a vacant table.

It wasn't the first time he'd been to the CIA headquarters – he was here once for a detailed briefing. His orders normally came down the line from the DoD through General Harken, but from time to time they came from the CIA's Special Activities Division, specifically their Special Operations Group. SAD/SOG could call on a number of units, including Delta Force and SEALs, but when the mission was delicate, as well as deniable, they would use the SAF. He figured that if communication could travel one way it could travel the other, so he'd phoned Wendell, and Wendell had set up the appointment for him.

Although he did feel peckish that wasn't the main reason for the stop. He was about to meet the man whose actions had, indirectly, taken Brian Murdoch's life and put Bruno and Charlie in hospital. He was angry, but his anger had to be contained if he was going to get anywhere. He ate slowly and drank the coffee, using this opportunity to collect his thoughts.

What do I want from this interview? Most of all I want Lazar, but that may be difficult if he's feeding back useful intel. If, on the other hand, he isn't, he'll be an embarrassment to them and they may welcome my intervention. Should I mention Tony? Bearing in mind what Tony said about the guarded relationship between the agencies it may be best to leave him out of it.

He broke off the line of thought to listen to a news flash coming from a television monitor on the wall.

...was initially believed to be a ground-to-ground missile. Analysis of the film now reveals that it was a drone, apparently crashed deliberately into the building. There is no suggestion that Sons of the Caliphate have the resources to build drones. However, it's known that a US drone crash-landed in northern Yemen about a year ago and it seems likely that this has been refurbished and used in this devastating attack. The present priority at the scene of the disaster is to recover the dead and injured, but investigators will be looking for more evidence in the wreckage. Now other news. A Senate Investigative Committee is to look into reports that...

Jim nodded.

That explains the wings. As for the rest I don't buy it — not for one minute. If that drone had simply crash-landed last year JSOC would have moved heaven and earth to get it back, probably dropped us or another Special Forces outfit out there to secure it. But they didn't; they just left it there. Why? It could only be because it crashed big-time. And now they want me to believe the jihadis put the thing back together and made it airworthy. How likely is that? And how the hell did they fly it? Those things aren't bought off the shelf with a nice little handheld radio transmitter. There has to be more to it, much more.

He glanced at his watch. Time for that appointment.

As he'd anticipated, Abadi didn't meet him at reception. Instead it was a PA who came down, greeted him, and took him up to the office on the third floor. Abadi was sitting behind his desk and he made no move to get up. He was slightly built, dark-complexioned, wavy black hair, and he wore a striped shirt, open at the collar. Jim noted a navy suit jacket hanging on the right-hand wall.

Jim didn't wait to be invited. He stepped forward and drew a chair up to the desk

'James Slater. You're expecting me.'

Abadi's dark eyes dwelled suspiciously on him. 'I think you want the Special Activities Division.'

'No, I want you.'

'Why?'

'Does the name Conrad Lazar mean anything to you?'

'Should it?'

'Yeah, I think it should. He was a Sergeant in the US Army, specifically Special Forces Reconnaissance Detachment Alpha. About eight years ago you trained him – or your people did – in cyber techniques.'

Abadi gave a half-smile. 'We train a lot of people.'

Jim went on, 'Two years ago Conrad Lazar was in Leavenworth serving a ten-year sentence for beating an unarmed prisoner to death. You arranged to have him transferred – after only five years – to a minimum security facility at the nearby federal penitentiary. You also arranged a transfer for another man, Saleh ibn Haroun, a dangerous home-grown terrorist with proven jihadi connections. He was being held at Lansing Correctional Facility in maximum security, but you had him transferred to the same minimum security facility as Lazar. Have I jogged your memory now?'

The half-smile had disappeared. Abadi studied Jim with hooded eyes. Then he said, 'All that's classified information.'

Jim looked away then up to the ceiling and back to Abadi. 'Agent Abadi, you do recognize this uniform, don't you?'

'Sure…'

'And you recognise the rank…'

'Yeah, why…?'

'Then please stop treating me like a dumbfuck grunt. The information is not classified. All a person needs to know is where to look and who to see.'

'I think you'd better leave.'

Jim's patience was wearing thin. 'And I think you'd better cooperate. I'm pissed off with you because I'm dealing with the fallout from a disastrous mission. Lieutenant Mirski of the Raleigh Police Department is pissed off with you because Lazar shot and killed someone in his nice quiet jurisdiction. And the FBI is pissed off with you because Lazar has helped a nasty little man get out of the country just when they were getting ready to re-arrest him.'

Abadi waved a hand. 'I don't know what you're talking about.'

'There's a lot you don't know, Agent Abadi. That's why I'm here.'

'But I don't have to listen to you.'

'No, you don't. I can pass all this up the line and you can explain to your superiors what you've done and how wonderfully well it's worked out.'

It was a long shot. The silence seemed to last for minutes on end.

Abadi rested his hands on the table. 'What do you want from me?'

'You groomed Lazar as an undercover agent, didn't you?'

The half-smile reappeared. 'How long did it take you to work that out?'

'Not long. Question is: why?'

Abadi sighed, then said, 'Let me educate you a little.'

Jim smothered the urge to tell this man once again not to be so damned condescending.

Abadi took a deep breath, then put his fingertips together. 'Sons of the Caliphate is one of several jihadi terrorist groups based in the Middle East. They're particularly dangerous because they're well-organized, well-funded and well-equipped. They've got revenue from the oil wells they've captured and from some crazy people who actually approve of what they're doing. They've got arms and vehicles, some bought, some captured. They hate the West, and the US in particular, but they can't take us on in any conventional kinetic war and they know it. Of course they try to hurt us, and they kill some of our citizens when they get the chance. But that's getting harder. Security is tight: we're on the lookout. How can they really damage us? What's our weak point?'

Jim waited and, as he knew he would, Abadi supplied the answer.

'It's our dependence on technology, specifically the internet. Our critical infrastructure is vulnerable: power systems, water supplies, road, rail and air transport, supply chains, medical centres, financial services, defence—'

Jim wasn't unfamiliar with the dangers of cyber warfare. 'We've known about that for years. All that stuff is air-gapped – those services run on separate intranets.'

'Sure they do, but if you keep looking hard enough you can still find nodes where they connect to the internet, and not all of them are monitored by packet sniffers. Or you have a company with 50,000 employees, operating on an intranet. One employee decides to use his computer to look up a birthday present for his wife and there's a bot waiting for just that to happen. Or the same company is using software with fifty million lines of code, some of it written by people on the other side of the globe, and a few lines have been slipped in that shouldn't have been there. It's a trapdoor that'll let people in, or a logic bomb that only needs to be activated for the whole system to go to hell, or a worm that gets propagated through system after system. In an authoritarian regime measures can be imposed, holes can be plugged. But we're not an authoritarian regime. Our infrastructure depends on private industry, and private industry doesn't like federal interference. They don't want to be told what to do, and they don't want outsiders inspecting their traffic. We're a technologically advanced free-enterprise nation and that puts us at a big disadvantage compared to organizations like Sons of the Caliphate.'

'You're saying these jihadis have cyber warriors?'

'That's exactly what I am saying. Nothing very special about that. Many countries have cyber units: we do, and so does the Russia Union, China, North and South Korea, Israel, and others we know about. A lot of it is focused on stealing industrial or military or political intelligence. Those countries also prepare for larger scale attacks, but they generally hold back from initiating them unless they're specifically threatened. For the jihadis it's different. They aren't interested in holding back. Quite the opposite: they want to cause as much damage as possible to our citizens, our property, and our economy.'

Abadi was getting more animated. He went on:

'We – I mean the CIA – know this, but we still don't know enough about their present capabilities, how fast they're advancing, or what they're aiming to do. It occurred to us that we could get some of that information from people who normally operate in the trouble spots, people who could keep their eyes open for us.'

'Like Special Forces Reconnaissance,' Jim said.

'Like Special Forces Reconnaissance. They'd need instruction, of course. The US isn't like some nation-states, which have universities for cyber warfare, so we set up our own training scheme here in the CIA. The first intake was in 2051.'

'And in walks Conrad Lazar.'

'Yes. Lazar was the ideal recruit. He had combat skills, he was fluent in several kinds of Arabic, and he already had a degree in computer technology before he joined the Army.'

That, Jim thought, *is something I didn't know.*

'So,' Abadi continued, 'eight years ago he received instruction here and at Fort Meade with the United States Cyber Command.'

'Go on.'

'Fast forward to 2057. Some of the terrorist groups had been wiped out, and the territory controlled by Sons of the Caliphate had shrunk. The best they could manage was the odd incursion: do some damage, kill some civilians, maybe kidnap a Westerner and get publicity out of the execution. For them that's small beer. Cyber warfare, now that's much more attractive to a small nonstate outfit, and that's where we saw the threat coming from. By that time we knew we'd been wasting our time training reconnaissance soldiers. It hadn't worked out – we got very little information that way. What we really needed was an operative to go undercover with them. Unfortunately you can't just ask someone to do that because they'd know they were running a serious risk of dying in one of several very nasty ways. But if that someone is serving ten years in Leavenworth and you offer him a reduction of sentence and immediate transfer to a lighter regime – well, you've got his attention.'

Jim said, 'So Lazar agreed, and you sent him to the USP to meet Saleh.'

'Saleh didn't know what was behind it. We knew damn well he had links to the Sons of the Caliphate, but we had a lawyer tell him that the evidence had been re-examined and it wasn't secure. They were transferring him from maximum to minimum security pending a possible appeal. But we told Lazar who Saleh was, and it was down to him to make contact. I imagine it wasn't hard with both of them speaking Arabic. So thanks to Saleh he knew how to get inserted with the jihadis. That was the difficult and dangerous part. You get it wrong, those guys crucify you – literally.'

Jim said, 'Where's Saleh now?'

'I don't have to tell you that. But don't worry, he's still in custody.'

So you've levelled with me about Lazar – finally. But you only did it after I threatened to take it to a higher level. Which suggests to me that Lazar's turned and he's no longer an asset: he's an embarrassment. Let's find out.

Jim tapped on Abadi's desk with two fingers. 'All right, here's the bottom line. Lazar's been with the jihadis for nearly a year. Have you been getting useful intel from him or not?'

26

Jim watched Abadi's face closely, the set of the jaw, the lips clamping a little tighter, and he had the answer he was expecting. 'You haven't heard a peep from him, have you?'

Abadi shrugged.

Jim sensed a shift in the balance of power in the room. He intended to exploit it to the full.

'You see, Agent Abadi,' he continued, savouring the opportunity to be condescending in his turn, 'what you didn't discover in whatever inadequate profiling you did on Lazar is: he may hate the jihadis, but he hates the US one hell of a sight more. The Special Assignment Force in particular.'

'Because he was serving time?'

'More than that. He was in Leavenworth because he beat up a prisoner to get information – information he was convinced the man was hiding. You people used so-called enhanced interrogation to do something similar but *you* didn't go to jail for it. He beat him so badly the prisoner died, but for Lazar that was a detail; he overdid it because he was angry at losing his friend Kabaki in the Baghdad incident. He expected that to be understood. He expected support. He didn't get it. What he got was condemnation, dishonourable discharge, and a hefty prison sentence to be served in a tough regime. So from where he's standing the US operates double standards, one for him, one for everybody else.'

'And the Special Assignment Force? Where does that come in?'

'One of our soldiers, name of Laverne Dacey, witnessed the interrogation and didn't like what he saw. He gave evidence, and it was his evidence that put Lazar and his colleague Clayton away. Lazar remembered that – oh, he remembered it all right. Five years later you had Lazar released from prison, and just a couple of months after that Dacey was shot dead on his way home from work. You see, your protégé found time to murder him before he left the country.'

Abadi's eyes narrowed. 'Are you sure of that?'

'The case is overwhelming. It would take someone of Lazar's experience to track the man down and document his movements. He used frangible ammunition, two shots but one would have been enough. And it was a carefully planned and targeted assassination of a man who had no other known enemies. Finally the timing fits.'

Abadi sighed and opened his hands. 'There are good reasons why we do what we do. Sometimes there are unintended consequences.'

'Unintended consequences?' Jim said, his voice rising. 'I haven't even begun to tell you about the unintended consequences!'

The response was weary. 'Go on.'

Jim's blood was pumping now. 'While Lazar was in that minimal security facility, with the leisure and the opportunity which you so generously gave him, he wrote a book. That book, which has sold upwards of four hundred copies, reveals the secret operating procedures of the SAF, of which I'm the CO. One of my best men has been killed as a direct result, and another two are in hospital.'

Abadi took a deep breath. 'Look, Colonel, that's too bad, but I can't take responsibility for it. He could have written the book when he was in the Disciplinary Barracks, too.'

'Maybe, but he wouldn't have met the man who delivered his manuscript to the publisher by an untraceable route, a man called Cy Sloper.' Again he watched Abadi's face, but it remained impassive.

'And Cy Sloper,' Jim continued, 'was wanted by the Bureau because he was providing money-laundering services for a crime syndicate, maybe more than one.'

'That's FBI business.'

Jim pretended he hadn't heard the comment. 'According to Sloper's Corrections Officer, he and Saleh and Lazar became big buddies. No doubt Sloper knew the Feds were closing in on him and Lazar arranged to get him out of the country. Remember the guy snatched off the street in Sana'a? The media called him William Lampeter. It wasn't William Lampeter – William Lampeter was a soldier who died in the First World War – the man they kidnapped was Cy Sloper. And that was followed by a staged execution of Sloper. Except it wasn't Sloper, it was some poor wretch they probably pulled out at random. Sloper is now safely embedded with the Sons of the Caliphate, and the entire operation was almost certainly masterminded by Lazar.'

'Oh come on.' Abadi sat back. 'I couldn't control everything Lazar got up to.'

'Maybe you couldn't. But one thing's for certain. You've been trying to prevent a possible cyber attack from the jihadis. But you know what? You've added two highly skilled cyber practitioners to their ranks. You, Agent Abadi, have made the situation incomparably worse.'

Abadi grimaced but said nothing.

'Okay,' Jim said. 'So now we know. Lazar is no use to you and he's of considerable value to them. Would it be a good thing or a bad thing if someone took him out?'

Abadi pursed his lips. 'It'd be a good thing, I guess. But he'd be hard to find.'

'Maybe not that hard – if you level with me about what really happened in that US Embassy attack.'

There was a heavy silence. Then Abadi said slowly, 'You heard already. One of our drones crash-landed, they refurbished it, and used it to target the Embassy.'

Jim decided to push a little harder. 'Bullshit. The drone crashed. It was a total write-off. Even we wouldn't have tried to rebuild it and you know damned well they couldn't.'

Abadi chewed his lip. Then he said, 'Wait here,' and left the room.

After a few minutes Jim began to fidget and glance at his watch. Obviously the intel he'd been guessing at was highly classified. Had he gone too far? Was he about to be carted off somewhere for enhanced interrogation?

Ten minutes later he was just wondering what would happen if he simply got up and left when Abadi appeared at the door. Jim relaxed; there was no one with him.

'You've put a lot together,' Abadi said. 'I've persuaded someone it would be a good idea to have you completely in the picture, so you don't go stumbling around screwing everything up. You're on the Special Activities Division selection list so you're not considered a security threat.'

'That's nice.'

Abadi ignored it. 'A meeting's being convened downstairs about the Embassy attack. They're just waiting for some people to get in from Nevada. If you want to be present you can be there – as an observer. That means you keep your mouth shut. Deal?'

Jim shrugged. 'Deal.'

'Come with me.'

Abadi led him to an elevator. He used his ID card on a scanner, and they rode it to the lower ground floor. Here he walked over to a blast-proof door, opened it with a handprint reader, and they descended a staircase to an even lower level. Jim could guess the reason. Meetings like this involved high-ranking people, and these below-ground levels would be secure in the event of hostile action, including a bomb attack. Abadi opened a conventional door and they went in.

The meeting room was much longer than it was wide. It was thickly carpeted and dominated by a polished wood table that extended for much of its length. Many of the twenty or so generously upholstered chairs around the table were already filled by men and women, some in business suits, others in Army, Marine Corps, Navy, or Air Force uniforms. There were a lot of medal ribbons. A large screen occupied one end wall. As they came in some of those present gave them curious looks. They took two chairs towards the end of the table.

Abadi leaned towards Jim and pointed discreetly. 'That's Joseph Templeton. He's my boss, Director of the CIA and the Commander of JSOC. And the man over there is Admiral Mike Randall, Director of the NSA. He's also

Commander of USCYBERCOM, the US Cyber Command.'

That was as far as he got, but Jim already knew by now that he was in very, very senior company. The door opened and three men wearing Air Force uniforms entered the room. The aide accompanying them addressed Templeton, who would presumably be chairing the meeting.

'Sir, may I introduce Colonel Douglas Baxter, Commander of the Drone Control Center, Nevada, and pilots Major Todd Harper and Major Hank Allshaw.'

Templeton acknowledged them with a brief nod. 'Gentlemen, thank you for coming.' He waved them to the remaining chairs. As soon as they were seated he said, 'Right, let's get started.'

Jim studied the CIA Director with interest. Joseph Templeton was lightly built, clean-shaven, and although he was probably in his fifties he had a pink, fresh-out-of-a-hot-shower complexion. The dark-grey suit was immaculate. He leaned forward and looked round the table with gimlet eyes to make sure he had everyone's attention. The room went completely silent. The man gave Jim the uneasy sensation that anyone here, including him, could be challenged with a question out of the blue.

Templeton began, 'No need to express our revulsion at this devastating attack on our Embassy personnel in the Yemen. I want to focus first on how it was managed. I asked Colonel Baxter and his team here to let us have a first-hand account of the actual events. Colonel: you've brought the record of that mission as I requested?'

Jim blinked. *This was one of our own missions?*

'Yes sir, I have,' Baxter said, standing now with a memory tile in his hand. He looked around for the reader.

Another aide hurried forward, took it from him and plugged it into a console at the back of the room.

Baxter stood near the wall screen. He said, 'The mission objective was an identified jihadi target about 200 km east of Sana'a. It was conducted out of the Code 80 airbase, with a Damocles drone equipped with six Radius bombs.'

There was a swift intake of breath from some of those present.

'The recording starts during the final bombing run. At your request the recording has not been edited. Please bear in mind that this was a stressful situation.'

The screen came alive with a view from the drone's forward ground observation camera. Desert terrain below the craft flowed rapidly by. Sound came on.

'Target minus two. I have a visual.'

The camera zoomed in on a cluster of buildings in a ruined village.

'Arm weapons.'

'Weapons armed.'

'Commencing bombing run.'

The buildings grew larger… larger…

The screen went blank.

'What the fuck…?'

'What happened?'

'No comms.' A thump. *'It chose one hell of a time.'*

The picture changed to a large map, with the drone icon trailing a white line in a curling path.

Baxter's voice. *'You've turned away. Did you deliver the payload?'*

'No, sir. We lost the link.'

'Nonsense, it's turned south. No airfields there.'

'Well, it's not responding, sir. Maybe ground took back control.'

'We'll see about that.'

Footfalls, then silence. More footfalls.

Baxter's voice again: *'They did not assume control, and they somewhat resented the suggestion.'*

'Look at that turn, Colonel. This is no wild bird. It's being controlled from somewhere.'

'Well not from here.'

Baxter: *'And not from ground.'*

It went quiet for a while. Jim's attention was riveted to the wall screen.

'Seems to have settled on one heading now, sir.'

Baxter (loudly): *'With me.'*

Baxter again: *'If it maintains this course it'll be over the eastern part of Sana'a in about ten minutes.'*

'San'a...?'

'Can we scramble jets?'

'No time for that. My God... Get me the US Embassy in Sana'a. Now!'

Pause.

'On the line now, sir.'

'All our operatives are busy at the moment. Please hold. Your call is important to us...'

'Christ Almighty! Not that number. Direct line to the Ambassador!'

Pause.

'Sorry, sir... Line's engaged.'

'Interrupt the call.'

Pause.

'I'm on a call right now. Is this urgent?'

'Code Florida! Get your staff to the bomb shelters immediately!'

'Code Fl... Who is this?'

'This is Colonel Baxter, Director of Drone Operations Center, Nevada. Repeat, this is not a drill. Get your... Hallo? Hallo?'

The screen went blank.

The room was as still and quiet as a graveyard. Templeton broke the silence.

'We believe at least four of those Radius bombs exploded on impact. The Embassy was reduced to rubble, trapping those working inside. We're still looking for unexploded ordnance and that's obviously slowing the rescue effort.' He looked around the table again. 'Any questions for Colonel Baxter or his operatives?' No one spoke. 'All right, thank you, Colonel.'

Colonel Baxter returned to his seat.

'So,' Templeton continued, 'how did this disaster happen? Mike, you have something for us?'

Jim followed Templeton's gaze to the man who Abadi had identified as the Director the NSA. Admiral Mike Randall had a tanned, lined face and a stubble of silver-grey hair. The medal ribbons on his Service Dress Blues covered half his chest.

'I think we have, Joe.' The voice was deep and resonant, with a faintly Southern tinge to the accent. 'Our initial guess was that hostile elements had somehow hacked into the satellite, the one that relays the commands from Nevada. There is no evidence of that. The satellites are very secure, and the transmission logs show that correct commands were being issued. But they were not received by the drone.'

'You have some other explanation?' Templeton asked.

'Yes, I believe I do. It's likely that the commands were swamped by a powerful broadband noise signal transmitted on the same range of wavelengths as our own. When that happens the receiver automatically seeks another channel that's strong enough not to be affected by the interference. If it can't find one the craft defaults to landing in the nearest suitable airfield. But it did find one, a signal from a North Korean satellite.'

Templeton's eyes narrowed. 'That satellite is run by the Reconnaissance General Bureau, North Korea's spy agency.'

'Correct. I think most people here are aware that North Korea is conducting a proxy war against us. They evidently have a functioning drone control centre either in the Yemen or in their own country. It's probably not that sophisticated – which would explain why they crashed the drone into the Embassy rather than just releasing the bombs. Of course, that made it look more like one of our drones had gone rogue.'

'You're discounting that possibility, then? That our drone went rogue?' Templeton asked.

'Yes we are. There were plenty of safeguards in that craft which would deploy if it lost the command transmissions. They didn't because it thought it was still under control from us.'

A man lifted a finger for Templeton's attention, and got it. 'Joe, the White House wants to know who was responsible for the attack. You're pointing the finger at NK, but couldn't the jihadis have managed this on their own?'

Templeton said, 'Mike?'

The Admiral shook his head. 'The jihadis do have technical expertise, Nathan, no question. But do they have that kind of drone control capability? I don't think so. Does North Korea have it? They most certainly do. And we know they support the jihadis.'

A woman in a business suit said, 'Excuse me, but who are these jihadis you're referring to?'

Templeton glanced at her and said brusquely, 'There's only one group of any significance left in Yemen. They call themselves the Sons of the Caliphate.'

'Oh, them.' The woman sat back.

A man raised his hand. The uniform was that of a Lieutenant-General in the US Army, and as he was here Jim assumed he was the Commander of Army Cyber Command. He asked, 'What was the original mission objective? All I could make out were ruined buildings.'

Templeton said, 'Reconnaissance drones had followed three vehicles, believed to be a jihadi convoy, into that village. The vehicles were hidden inside some of those damaged buildings. We concluded that they were preparing for an attack of some sort. That's why we initiated the approval process for taking action.'

'Was it deliberate, do you think?' the one-star General asked. 'Did they lure us into attacking that village just so they could do this?'

'Highly unlikely. The convoy was spotted by a Rotofan returning through a mountain pass after a training exercise. Three vehicles were on their way through the pass, two of them big all-terrains, and the third something they described as either a troop carrier or a large camper. It was almost dark and all three were well camo'd but the Rotofan was flying low, so it couldn't miss them. It spotted them by pure chance.'

The General sat back and Templeton looked round the table. He said, 'All right, we've heard how this exploit could have been managed. We're laying it at North Korea's door, but clearly we don't have sufficient evidence to mount a kinetic response. So the next question is: what do we do about it?'

27

Templeton started to look round the table but a hand was already half-raised. 'General Seaman?'

'Flatten that village.' The speaker was a florid man in the uniform of a USAF Major General.

Commander of 24th Air Force, Jim thought. *That's the most likely in this context.*

The man continued, 'See here, to pull off a stunt like those folk did, you need a big dish and a powerful transmitter. That means it's a fixed installation. So we pound that village 'til no two bricks are standing one on top of th'other. Use conventional manned bombers – we have some within range.'

'But are the insurgents still there?' the woman in a business suit asked.

Templeton pointed to Baxter. 'Colonel?'

'I can't answer that, sir. Until we can counter this new threat I cancelled all future drone operations, reconnaissance included. The insurgents could have left by now but we don't know that.'

'Makes no odds if they're there or if they're not,' the USAF General said. 'We need a demonstration here. We need to show these people if they pull our tail we gonna turn around and bite them real hard.'

'It may be an underground installation,' Templeton said.

'Then we use bunker-bustin' bombs,' the General replied.

The US Army man said, 'We might learn more from a ground operation.'

'No case for that!' the Air Force General exclaimed. 'That village is a ruin, the non-combatants cleared out years ago. There's no possibility of collateral damage, none at all. You put boots on the ground, you got to get them out there and they got to go in slow and careful.' He waved a hand dismissively. 'All that takes too damned long. We need an immediate response here.'

'A gesture,' the woman in a business suit said, Jim thought with a touch of sarcasm.

'Yeah, if you like to call it that. A gesture. A nice big one.'

Templeton looked round the table again. 'Any other suggestions?'

Baxter said, 'Sir, I would like to make the Drone Control Center operational again as soon as possible.'

'Of course, that goes without saying. Mike?'

The NSA Director responded, 'My people are on it as we speak. Based on the exploit we believe they used we can modify the software to remove that vulnerability. As soon as we've done that we'll pass the fix to you so you can reprogram all existing drones.'

'Very good. Anything else?' Again Templeton looked around quickly, and this time it was too perfunctory to invite a response. 'All right, I think we've got as far as we can. General Seaman, you have the green light for a bombing raid. Meanwhile Mike's people and mine will work on fixing the drone software. Thank you, ladies and gentlemen. Any other suggestions, bring them to me.'

People got up and began to file out of the room.

Jim shook his head. They'd been handed an opportunity on a plate and it had totally passed them by.

*

Abadi must have picked up Jim's reaction because as soon as they sat down again in his office he said, 'You don't look too happy about what went on in there.'

'I'm not,' Jim said.

'Nor am I.'

For a moment Jim thought he'd misheard. 'You're not?'

'No,' Abadi said. 'Why didn't you speak up?'

'You told me to keep my mouth shut. That was the deal. Why didn't *you* speak up?'

'Look, Colonel...' He paused. 'Do I have to keeping calling you Colonel?'

'Depends what you're going to say. If you're going to be friendly you can call me Jim. If you're going to be a patronizing tightass you can call me Colonel.'

The half-smile was back. 'Then I'll call you Jim. I'm John.'

'Okay.'

He took a breath. 'Look Jim, I'm going to level with you. The Lazar thing's gone bad, I admit it. I made a mistake. He seemed like the dream candidate for this one. I had a lot of contact with him during the training sessions – that was eight years ago, before I headed up this Directorate. Quiet guy, but very smart, very quick on the uptake. I would have liked to keep him on then and there in some capacity but of course I couldn't. Then he got involved in that Baghdad incident. I let him stew in Leavenworth for five years, but he was always in the back of my mind. It took patience, I can tell you. Finally I decided the time was right and I went down there. I thought he might remember me, and he did. We got on well, I had it all set up. But, like I say, I made a mistake. Maybe Saleh convinced him he really would be better off with Sons of the Caliphate.'

'Did you check on him after the transfer to the penitentiary, you know, to see how things were going?'

Abadi shook his head. 'That would have been a very bad idea. If Saleh had gotten the slightest hint Lazar was meeting someone all bets would have been off. Worse still he could have sent him into a trap.' He shrugged. 'Maybe it was never Lazar's intention to cooperate, maybe he changed his mind – I don't know. Either way it's an awkward situation. That's why I stonewalled you to start with, and that's why I didn't speak up just now, not in front of a high-powered gathering like that. I'd like to put this whole thing right somehow before it starts to come out.'

Jim said, 'And how do you propose to do that?'

'You want Lazar, too, don't you?'

'Yes.'

'Then maybe we can work on it together.'

Jim gave him a guarded nod. This was more like it. 'We can see how it goes.'

For several seconds the only sound in the room was the hiss of traffic on the highways below. An aircraft passed overhead, and the noise died slowly away.

Abadi broke the silence. 'So tell me why you weren't happy in there.'

Jim straightened up. 'Lazar was attached to a jihadi cyber unit. Do we agree on that?'

'Absolutely. Lazar has military experience but that's nothing special – they probably have more than enough people for combat training. In any case, Lazar's idea of military strategy wouldn't count for much with people who send women or children in as suicide bombers. But military experience *and* knowledge of cyber techniques – now that's a harder combination to come by. So you have to be right, Jim, they'd put him in with the cyber warriors. And with his background he'd probably be in charge of them.'

'All right, let's take it from there. This drone strike on the Embassy. Makes no sense at all.'

'Go on.'

'Suppose it's like that Air Force guy was saying: this was a fixed installation in or under that ruined village, and it was done with a big antenna and a powerful transmitter. The last thing the jihadis would do is turn the damned drone around and bomb the Embassy with it. That'd be like erecting a signpost saying "Look, everyone, we're over here". They'd know the US would retaliate by destroying that entire target area. Which is exactly what's going to happen. Except the enemy won't be there. They'll be miles away by now.'

Abadi frowned. 'You can't be sure—'

'John, Special Forces personnel have a different mindset to the people in that committee room. Lazar has it, but so do I, and I can see his fingerprints all over this. He knows the value of mobility. No way would he hole up in one place and make himself a stationary target. Think about what arrived there: a camper – or whatever the biggest vehicle in the convoy was – and two large all-terrains. What does that say to you?'

'A mobile headquarters?'

'Exactly. And no ordinary insurgent convoy would have a defensive set-up as sophisticated as that. It's a crack jihadi cyber unit, I'm convinced of it.'

'Well if you're right how did they take over that drone? Like Seaman said, you'd need a big antenna and a powerful transmitter.'

Jim smiled. 'You'd get the same result with three smaller antennas and transmitters, all pointing in the same direction. You can do that if you've got three good sized vehicles. Which is what they do have.'

Abadi nodded slowly. 'The US drone that crashed a year ago. You think they were responsible for that, too?'

'Possibly. Or...' Jim's eyes narrowed. 'Maybe that's how they found out how to do it. I take it the drone didn't burst into flames.'

'No. It was badly damaged, though.'

'The electronics package probably survived that. They could have salvaged it from the wreckage, worked on it and passed the results to their North Korean friends. Or they gave them the whole package and let them work on it.'

'It's a possibility. We know there's cooperation. The Korean People's Army has given them access to some channels on their military satellite.'

Jim waved a hand. 'There you go. So from the jihadis' point of view, the strategy would go like this. Their cyber unit moves at night and it's concealed by day, and it doesn't stay in one place for more than a few days. In the very unlikely event they're spotted and an attack drone comes in they swamp the control transmission, the KPA takes over, and they crash it. Job done – makes it look like the drone malfunctioned. While the US is scratching its head they move quietly to some place else and no one is the wiser.'

'But that's not what happened.'

'No. I think someone at the KPA got a little excited and decided it wasn't enough for them. So they turned the drone around and crashed it into the US Embassy.'

Abadi nodded. 'It's the sort of thing their Joint Chiefs Cyber Warfare Unit could manage.'

'I suspect Lazar is none too happy about it either, not because the Embassy was destroyed with a serious loss of life – he could care less about that – but because activating that defensive manoeuvre revealed too much about them.'

'Jim, you say they move at night. But that convoy was spotted at dusk.'

'They were going through a mountain pass. Maybe they decided it would be too tricky in total darkness. That's why this was such a break. It was right in front of their noses, but the people in that meeting just couldn't see it. Especially that gung-ho Air Force General. He was angry. He wanted something to bomb.'

Abadi sat back, chewing his lip thoughtfully. 'How dangerous do you think Lazar is?'

Jim responded without hesitation. 'Very. Not just for setting up cyber offensives – they could probably manage that without him. But he can identify the critical infrastructures they could hit. They'd be hard to hack into but, as you said before, there's always a weakness somewhere. And there's more. In that mobile home of his he can use the satellite channel to connect with jihadi groups elsewhere. I think he was behind the ambush in the Cameroon that got my guy killed.'

Abadi frowned. 'What makes you think he was behind it?'

'He knew the type of mission that would bring us in and he set it up in a subtle way that went by a believable route. By the time it came to us it looked like a standard operation. Then he told the local hotheads how we'd tackle it – or they got that part from his book – and my squad walked into a trap. I'd want to nail Lazar for that alone.'

'Any idea how?'

'I need to engage that mobile unit on the ground. But to do that I have to know where it is. Lazar will be aware of the danger of a retaliatory strike, so he'll pull out quickly. Even if he doesn't get going until nightfall there'll be heat trails from the engines or the exhausts or the ventilation on that camper. What we need is a lot of sweeps with a high-altitude drone fitted with sensitive infra-red cameras—'

'They won't send up drones while there's still a risk of them being used against us.'

'There wouldn't be a risk. That trick of theirs is only going to be effective with an identified target at low altitude. We need to move fast, though. Right now there's a limit to how far they could have gone, which gives you a smaller radius to search. You've got your JSOC people in the building and Colonel Baxter's probably still here, too. Now's your chance. It's an ideal opportunity. See if you can convince them of that.'

Abadi got to his feet. 'Okay. Do you want to come with me? This was your idea.'

'Be my guest. The way things are, you might need to stack up some credit with them.'

Abadi gave his half-smile. 'Thanks, Jim. Where will you be?'

'I'm going back to Fort Piper. You can reach me there. I'll give you my secure phone.'

They linked cell phones and exchanged contact information.

The meeting was over. Jim walked out of the building and caught a cab to the airport.

*

Jim's flight landed at Raleigh-Durham, and one of the pool cars was waiting to drive him back to Fort Piper. He'd not long arrived at the base when he received a call on his secure phone.

'Yes John?'

'No go, I'm afraid. The Director took the view that the measures we're taking are enough for the moment. As for the rest, he said it's pure speculation. And Colonel Baxter didn't want to risk sending in drones – even high altitude ones – until Cyber Command and the NSA have sorted out the vulnerability. Sorry, Jim.'

He sighed. 'That's it, then, those guys will get clean away. Well, when your Director realizes his mistake perhaps he'll remember who warned him. Thanks, John.'

'What for?'

'For trying.'

He clicked off.

So according to the Director of the CIA, Conrad Lazar and Cy Sloper will shortly be lying under a ton of rubble.

He is so, so wrong.

28

The pilot of the lead F38 glanced across at the four who were off his port wing. They were flying fast, five hundred feet above the desert landscape. Outcrops of rock raced towards them, then whisked away beneath. The target crept onto the Flight Display and moved downwards.

He radioed, 'Target ahead. Attack formation.'

The other four aircraft took stations, each one above and behind the other.

The ruined village with its dilapidated buildings came into view. The lead pilot said, 'I have a visual. Going in.'

He activated the head-up display, eased the nose down until the target floated up into the centre of the sight, and his thumb came down on the button.

Three Wotan rockets rushed out from each wing, converging on the buildings. He lifted off and banked sharply up and to starboard, the desert tilting below him. Circling back he saw the second aircraft drop its payload of Radius bombs. Then that F38 banked in its turn and the third aircraft dropped its payload further on, then the fourth and fifth with bunker-busting bombs.

'Mission complete. Return to base.'

The five aircraft formed up again and headed back.

Behind them a column of dust and smoke rose into the sky. It was visible for fifty miles.

*

The camper rocked and juddered over the rough terrain. This far out in the desert there were no roads, just unsurfaced paths of packed sand, and even these were littered with small rocks and flinty stones. By now the sun had sunk low on the western horizon, turning the desert pink and streaming long shadows from every tiny irregularity.

Conrad Lazar walked through the camper to the cabin and spoke to the driver in Arabic. Moments later the camper slowed and came to a halt. The two large all-terrains pulled up behind them.

Cy Sloper looked up as Lazar came back. 'Where are we, Conrad?'

Lazar grunted. 'Nowhere.'

'So why'd we stop?'

'No villages on this route, so here's as good as anywhere.'

'Out here? You don't usually stop in the open.'

'Yeah,' Lazar snapped, 'and I don't usually have to haul ass in an all-fired fucking hurry, either. That,' he added with heavy emphasis, 'is not my style.'

Cy smirked. 'What's style got to do with it?'

'My style,' Lazar said, his face darkening, 'is what keeps you and your nerdy friends alive.'

Cy enjoyed baiting Conrad from time to time, but he knew where to draw the line. It wasn't a good idea to get into an argument with the big man. Conrad contained was threatening enough; Conrad unleashed was something none of them wanted to face.

'Come on,' Cy said, in a more placatory tone, 'you saw the newsfeeds, you saw what that drone did to the Embassy. It would have been us if we hadn't activated the defence.'

'I know that, but they were supposed to make the thing crash and burn. They could've dumped it in open desert, or on a village somewhere. But no, they've got to dump it on the fucking US Embassy! Jesus, why not just pick up a phone to Washington? Best intelligence they've had for years.'

'You think they'll come after us?'

Lazar flung a hand out. 'Of course they'll come after us! From now on we have to be twice as careful.' He took a breath. 'Well, we've got a couple of days before they start sending out drones again. We're safe enough for the moment.'

'You sure?' Cy licked his lips. 'They could send manned flights, couldn't they? Right now we're sitting ducks.'

Lazar shook his head. 'F38s and F42s don't have the endurance for find-and-destroy missions; they'll only send them to identified targets. Which they don't have. So move your butt. We're going to eat.'

In the short time it took them to gather outside for a meal the sun had set. The moon, which had been a pale challenger in the sky for the past hour, was now in full possession, casting a silvery light over the scene. There were three groups. The eight jihadi escorts clustered in one group, their black robes merging with the darkness. Four young men in T-shirts and jeans huddled together in another group. Cy sat with Conrad slightly apart from the others. Conrad never allowed cooking fires when they were in enemy territory, so it was a simple meal: cold, spicy vegetable stew, scooped up with flatbread and eaten with salad. There was fruit to follow.

For a while they ate in silence. It was Cy who broke it. 'Where're we going next?'

'Just another stopover.'

'I hope it's better than the last one. No fun to be had in a deserted village. Can't we go somewhere with a bit of life? Somewhere like the town we came from, up in the Sons territory. Shit, that even had a proper harem. That's what we need, Conrad, fresh meat. The two girls we brought with us are worn out. They haven't even come out here to eat.'

'I know. We'll be back there in a day or two. Make the most of it.'

They lapsed into silence again. Then Lazar's satellite phone buzzed. He got up without a word and walked away to take the call. He returned a few minutes later.

'Abd al-Matin?' Cy asked.

'Yeah. He's pleased about the Embassy strike. It's all right for him, he's not out here.' He paused. 'He's got his doubts about you, though, Cy. Thinks we should execute you, just in case.'

Cy Sloper's eyes widened. 'Jesus, Conrad, you said you'd vouch for me.'

'I did vouch for you. I never said it would be enough. You better think of something good to convince him.'

He strolled over to the jihadi group to talk to the driver. The four young men he'd referred to as Cy's nerdy friends shrank a little as he passed.

Cy watched him go, his mind blank with terror. He struggled to collect his scattered thoughts.

If Abd al-Matin gives the order, the jihadis over there'll top me without pausing to draw breath. What can I do that'll impress him? What's quick and dirty?

Then he remembered something, and a sly smile crossed his face. He got up and headed straight for the camper.

29

Ranger Airways flight RGA127 out of San Francisco was at cruise altitude, destination Cincinnati. In the cockpit, Captain Sam Marshall had reclined fully in the left seat, his feet up on the bar below the control panel. He'd swapped his uniform for a T-shirt and shorts soon after they'd taken off from San Francisco, put a pillow behind his head, and he was sleeping peacefully. In the right seat First Officer Ewen 'Mac' McKenzie was flying the sector. The aircraft was autoreporting waypoints and there was nothing for him to do but look the instruments over once in a while. Thousands of feet below them a blanket of cloud moved slowly by, the fluffy tops dazzlingly bright in the sun. He glanced at his watch. Half an hour since the last routine call to cabin crew. Mac lifted the interphone and kept his voice low.

'Hi, Monica. Just letting you know we're still alive and conscious up here. At least, I am. I think Sam's dreaming of a beach in Hawaii.'

'Sounds nice,' the Purser said. 'You need anything, Mac?'

'No, we're good. I'll call you in a half-hour. Maybe time for a coffee then.'

'Okay.'

He shot a glance at Sam, scanned the instruments briefly, then settled back.

Ten minutes later there was an insistent *beep...beep...beep.*

Sam opened one eye but didn't move. Audible cautions like this weren't uncommon, and the issues were generally very minor.

This one wasn't.

The Engine Indication and Crew Alerting system displayed a message in amber:

Insufficient fuel.

Mac cancelled the sound. 'That's bizarre.'

Sam shifted his position slightly. 'Problem?'

Mac wrinkled his nose. 'Not sure. We've got a fuel message for some reason. We're still flying and we've got twenty odd tons left, so we're not coming down any time soon. I can figure it if you want to go back to sleep.'

Sam grunted, 'Nah, I'll take a look.' He struggled into a seated position, and the pillow dropped to the floor.

'Okay,' Mac said. 'I've got the plane, and I've got left radio.'

Sam reached for his headset and put it on. 'We'll start with your admin,' he said, picking up the touchpad. 'What does the board say? Nope, looks good, last refuelling we were two tons over. Port wing tank... good. Starboard wing tank... good. Flows out and between... all good. Did we hit headwinds or something?'

Mac said, 'No.'

'Can't believe there's a leak, but let's just see if fuel's streaming from somewhere.'

He pushed buttons and visuals came up from the on-board cameras.

Meanwhile on the Traffic Collision Avoidance System display an open diamond, representing an aircraft in their vicinity, went solid white. Proximate traffic like this was routine enough not to demand attention.

Ping-pong.

A message appeared on the alerting screen:

CABIN CALL

Mac lifted the interphone. 'Mac.'

'Sorry to disturb you,' the Purser said, 'but one of the Grade 2's pressed the button before I could remind her you're on rest. It's just that the trash compactor in the forward galley has hung up. Any objection to resetting?'

Sam muttered, 'For Christ's sake...' but Mac said, 'No, go right ahead.'

On the navigational display the white diamond became a yellow circle, coming in quickly at the bottom of the display and the warning sounded:

Traffic, traffic!

Sam jerked his head up and viewed the display. 'Jesus, look at that. Must be a supersonic.'

Mac passed his tongue over his lips.

The yellow circle became a red square and now the two aircraft were on a collision course, closing at a probable combined speed of 1400 mph. Mac's hands were poised on the controls, ready to react.

The Resolution Advisory came promptly over the speaker:

Descend, descend!

Mac double pressed the autopilot disconnect and pushed the control column sharply forward. Sam grabbed the arm rests of his chair. 'Easy, dude, easy. We got a whole twenty seconds before it hits us.'

A red bar had appeared on the Primary Flight Display. Mac moistened his lips and drew gently back on the column until the aircraft had attained the new pitch. At that moment there was a blur of movement and a slender aircraft flashed overhead.

Mac ducked instinctively, although in another part of his brain he knew the other pilot would have received a 'Climb, climb' advisory, ensuring an adequate separation for the pass.

He took a breath as the aircraft receded. 'Sorry, Sam,' he said, 'had plenty of those in the sim, but that's the first I've had for real.'

But Sam was already talking calmly to Air Traffic Control.

'Ranger one twenty-seven. TCAS RA. Resuming flight level 360.'

The reply came: 'RA acknowledged Ranger one twenty-seven. What were you doing? You have to advise if you're avoiding weather.'

'We weren't avoiding weather,' Sam said patiently. 'We were following the flight plan.'

'Check your flight plan Ranger 127. You are not routed via India Romeo Kilo. Rejoin airway J80 prior to point BAYLI immediately.'

'J80 before BAYLI, roger. Ranger one twenty-seven.'

Sam leaned forward and did a quick route copy into RTE-2. Then he reprogrammed the autopilot. 'Done.' He looked at Mac. 'Confirm?'

Mac said, 'Execute.' Then, 'Hey, look at that! The fuel message went off. It must have been the routing…'

'What were we doing?' Sam said. He pressed RTE-2 to bring back the routing they'd just left. Mac heard an intake of breath. 'We were on J26 to Bravo Delta Foxtrot! It didn't even have us going to Cincinnati. Did we get a re-route while I was snoozing?'

'No...'

Sam shook his head. 'Things don't just change by themselves.' He looked round at Mac. 'You playing straight with me?'

Mac's mouth dropped open. 'I didn't touch it, boss.'

'Well how the freak does something like that happen? No wonder we got a shout for insufficient fuel. God alone knows where it was trying to take us.'

There was a buzz from the other side of the cockpit door. They glanced at the monitor. It was the Purser. Sam released the lock and she came in. She looked pale.

'What happened back there?' she asked.

'Sorry, Monica,' Sam said cheerfully, 'Had to avoid another aircraft. Drinks get spilled?'

Monica shook her head. 'We have a medical emergency. An old lady was coming out of the toilet when it happened. She was thrown up and down. She's in a lot of pain. I think she may have broken her leg.'

Sam winced. 'Is she stable?'

'I think so. She just keeps saying how much it hurts.'

'Look, I'd sooner not divert. We've passed St Louis, Cincinnati is a straight-in approach and we're set up for it. I'll radio ahead to get the paramedics on board as soon as we're parked up. You okay with that?'

'Yeah, I guess so,' Monica said. 'We'll make her as comfortable as we can. I can take her vital signs. If things do start to go downhill we may have to consult on Medlink.'

'Sure. Any change let me know.'

As Monica left the flight deck Sam said, 'Mac, basic modes and radar vectors, I don't trust these damned electronics. I'll do the talking and you can handfly us in.'

30

George Walski emitted his usual bad-tempered grumble when the cell phone on his desk buzzed. He snatched it up and looked at it. Voice only, caller withheld. He tapped to connect anyway. Not everyone had this number.

'Walski.'

'George, this is Naomi – Naomi Fine.'

'Oh, right.' Walski straightened up subconsciously, and adjusted the phone properly to his ear. Naomi Fine was a senior Network Vulnerability Analyst at the National Security Agency. They'd worked together once before. Naomi was a good person to have on your side. She was emphatically not a good person to have on any opposing side. 'What can I do for you, Naomi?'

'I need to call on a company. It's an aviation issue, high priority. Could be arrests involved. I'd like to have a couple of Federal Agents with me.'

Walski winced at the pile of work on his desk, opened his mouth to mention it, then thought better of it.

'Where we going?' he said.

'Seattle.'

He inclined his head. Seattle was nice. But if they were on a scheduled flight he couldn't take his usual sidearm. An FBI shield wouldn't get you past the security check-ins these days – you could buy the damn things on eBay. He'd have to draw a plastic Glock and some copolymer ammunition and even they didn't get through unless you put them in hold baggage, which meant delays. Not good.

'Where d'you want to meet up?' he said.

'I have a government Slipstream waiting at Andrews, so you can bring your usual hardware.'

Walski smiled. She'd read his mind. 'Andrews' was Joint Base Andrews Naval Air Facility Washington, and a Slipstream was a small business jet. Seemed like she wasn't joking about the urgency.

'Meet me there in an hour,' she said. 'I'll brief you on the flight.'

'Will do.'

He tapped off, but not before she had. He buzzed a number, a desk on the ground floor.

'Henderson? You wanna make an arrest out in Seattle?'

Agent Henderson said, 'Nah, sorry. Gotta meet someone in ten minutes.'

Walski buzzed another number. 'Westbury? You free right now?'

'Negative, George. On a big case.'

Shit.

Then he grinned as an idea came to him. He hurried out of his office and ascended the short flight of stairs to a room on the fourth floor.

'Grieg, you wanna come with me out to Seattle? Got some NSA business to do out there.'

*

As soon as the Slipstream had reached operational height the three moved to the back, where Naomi Fine could face the two agents across a small table.

Tony Grieg had been interested to meet the analyst. He'd just had time to look at her biog before leaving for the air base. It was impressive: electrical engineering at MIT and a PhD in computer sciences at Stanford. She then served on Stanford's faculty for four years, got married, had two children, and joined the NSA ten years ago. That put her in her mid-forties. Presumably she still had domestic commitments, despite which she'd soared through the grades.

At the base he found a trim woman with a brisk manner, dark, curly hair and a smooth, pale complexion. There was a touch of lipstick but no other make-up that he could see, and he usually could see. Her black trouser suit was well cut, and worn with a high-necked blouse. She carried a large shoulder bag whose contents almost certainly included a lap top or tablet.

Walski said, 'This here is Senior Agent Tony Grieg.'

Tony dipped his head politely and said, 'Ma'am.'

She didn't shake hands. Her eyes flicked up and down him, evidently more interested at this stage in his bulk rather than his brain. Then she just said 'Good' and jerked her head towards the waiting Slipstream. There were no further exchanges until they were airborne.

When they were settled around the table a flight attendant placed coffees in front of each of them but she ignored hers. As soon as he'd withdrawn she said, 'There's been a spate of resolution advisories.' Perhaps perceiving their blank expressions, she added, 'Actions pilots have to follow to avoid mid-air collisions. If it was a one-off it could be an isolated accident, but five within twenty-four hours, all of them in US airspace, and it's no accident. And all on the same type of aircraft: the Lightspeed 444.'

Tony nodded. Lightspeed was a spin-off from a much larger company, tasked with making aircraft for medium-haul flights. The LS444 was a popular choice for airlines that ran domestic services. He'd flown on them a number of times.

'Not just that,' she continued. 'All the incidents had the same pattern, a departure from the flight plan that set the aircraft on an unauthorized course. Air space is crowded, gentlemen, it's crammed full of airways. The chances such a rogue aircraft would encounter one at the same altitude, travelling in the same or opposite direction are extremely high. We could easily have had a disaster on our hands, so thank God for on-board collision avoidance systems. The pilots were debriefed, of course. All of them insisted they'd made no changes to the flight management computer. The traffic controllers were interviewed, too, and their reports are consistent. In each case the aircraft adjusted its course on busy airlanes without clearance. The aircraft were into a conflict before they spotted what was going on. Ordinarily we'd assume human error, but the events are so similar it has to be something else. The FAA has stepped in and grounded all LS444s until the issue's been dealt with. Civil Aviation Administrations in a dozen other countries have been notified, and they've done the same.'

Tony whistled softly.

'Exactly,' she said with a grim smile. 'The airlines are up in arms. They've had to cancel hundreds of flights – not just here in the US, but all over the world – and they have aircraft parked up in all the wrong airports. They're losing millions of dollars a day. Hence the urgency.'

She seemed to notice the coffee for the first time, took a sip, and winced.

Walski said, 'So we're going to the manufacturers in Seattle. Why there?'

She sat back, interlacing her fingers. 'The nose of a modern airliner is stacked with banks of computers that manage every system on the aircraft. The software for those computers is written in-house. It should be immune to penetration, but the company's convinced this is a cyber attack. They may or may not be right. Either way that's where we have to start. And I need to cover the possibility that one of their employees is guilty of terrorist activities.' She smiled. 'In which event, it will be comforting to have you two with me.'

Tony said, 'Won't the company's programmers be trying to sort this out, ma'am?'

'Don't call me ma'am, Tony,' she said, surprising him with the use of his name, 'I'm not the President. Naomi will do. The answer is: maybe. But even if they are they'll need some help. These programs could have about a billion lines of code. I've got some experience of the programming language they're written in, which is why I've been assigned to this job.'

Walski drained his cup of coffee. 'They expecting us?' he asked.

'Well, they're expecting me.'

31

They landed at Boeing Field, an international airport five miles south of downtown Seattle. There they were met by a uniformed company chauffeur who drove them the short distance to the Lightspeed HQ. Their presence appeared to be an embarrassment to the company, because they were quickly whisked out of the reception area into an elevator and up to the top floor, where they were taken through to the Chief Operations Officer.

The COO rose from behind his desk, his gaze darting from Naomi to the two agents. Then he came forward, a smile carefully pasted on his face and a hand extended. He was slightly overweight, with a pink complexion. He wore an immaculate blue suit, a pale blue shirt with a darker stripe, and a blue silk tie. Tony caught a whiff of aftershave.

The COO said, 'Welcome to Lightspeed, lady and gentlemen. I'm Charles Redbanks.'

The hand Tony shook was large and dry. The COO shook hands with Walski, and Naomi offered him her fingertips. A leather-upholstered chair had been placed for her, but Redbanks now drew up two more, gestured to them, and resumed his seat on the other side of the desk.

He leaned back comfortably, his arms firmly planted on the rests, gesticulating from the wrist. 'Maybe I should tell you a little about myself,' he said. 'I've been in aviation all my life. I flew combat aircraft when I was with the Navy and then I joined the parent company and worked my way right from the bottom up. When Lightspeed was formed I came to it as COO. So I know the aviation industry inside out, and never in my experience have I come across an aircraft as reliable as the 444. We write all the software here. It's as good as we can get it – and let me tell you, that's pretty darned good. The triple-4 has flown hundreds of thousands of miles without incident. We have a clean slate—'

Naomi interrupted. 'Excuse me, Mr Redbanks, you do not have a clean slate. You have five near misses inside a space of twenty-four hours, several passengers with badly scalded arms and one with a broken leg, thanks to the evasive manoeuvres. Your aircraft are grounded all over the world. You need to cooperate with us or your company's reputation and that aircraft's record will be trashed.'

It was impressive, Tony thought. She'd barely raised the pitch or volume of her voice from a conversational tone, but it couldn't have been more effective if she'd put a gun to his head.

The COO held up both hands. 'We'll be glad to cooperate with you, Mrs Fine, no question about that. All I'm saying is, that aircraft has been in service for years without a problem. If there was a serious bug or glitch in the software – the flight management system, especially – it would have surfaced long before this. Then out of the blue we get five resolution advisories! Five! How do we explain that? It's got to be a cyber attack. That's what I told the FAA when they contacted us. I said we needed expert help on it, and I'm real glad you're here to give us that help, Mrs Fine. What I don't understand is why you brought two federal agents with you.'

Naomi ignored the implied question. She asked, 'Are you confident of your staff, Mr Redbanks?'

He slapped the arm of his chair with the flat of his hand. 'One hundred per cent. When it comes to our programmers, they're vetted at the highest standards of security. They undergo psychological profiling at that stage and it's repeated at six-monthly intervals. We have regular lectures and inspections by cyber experts. We're aware of the need for cyber security, Mrs Fine – we have to be. Every day thousands of passengers rely on us to deliver them safely to their destinations, and we take that responsibility very, very seriously.'

'And your programming environment is independent of the internet?'

'Absolutely. We operate on an intranet, and it's air-gapped from any public network – my God, even the air gaps are air-gapped!'

She said, 'Well, Mr Redbanks, your diligence in that area should help us to isolate the problem. It does, however, place it right *here*.' She jabbed a forefinger downwards.

He heaved a sigh, and said, 'Who would you like to talk to?'

'We'll start with your chief of software development.'

He got to his feet. 'Okay, I'll take you down there now. Unless I can offer you some refreshment first?' He scanned them, eyebrows raised. 'We have a fine canteen here, and they'll still be serving lunches.'

'Sounds good to me,' Walski said. He glanced hopefully at Naomi.

She half-closed her eyes. 'I'll buzz you if I need you, George.'

Walski brightened. 'How about you, Tony?'

Tony smothered a smile. Walski had a sparring kind of friendship with him that never extended to using his first name, but he must have realized how odd it would sound to outsiders.

'I'll pass, George. I'm interested to know what's downstairs.'

'Okay. Maybe I'll join you later.'

They left through a PA's office, where they shed Walski, and walked along a corridor to a different elevator. Redbanks showed his ID to the reader and punched B. They emerged into a large open-plan area full of people sitting at work stations. It was, Tony thought, not unlike the ground floor at the Hoover building, except for the rooms glassed off at the end. Redbanks entered one of these and they followed.

He introduced them to Glen Olson, a tall, gangly guy who looked like he wasn't yet out of his twenties. He was wearing an open-necked shirt which hung outside his jeans.

'Glen,' Redbanks said. 'I'm trying to convey to our visitors here that this place is air-tight, cyber-wise. All our programs are written in-house by carefully vetted personnel. Right?'

Glen gave a one-sided smile. 'Right. Well, yeah, pretty much all in-house.'

Naomi pounced on it. 'What do you mean "pretty much"?'

'Well, just occasionally we're under a lot of pressure to produce the next block point—'

'Block point?'

'Er, you can think of it as a software update. These are big programs. You can get the odd bug – minor irritations, nothing more. Or some on-board equipment is due for upgrade and the software has to be revised at the same time. So we issue a new block point and they gradually update all the aircraft with it.'

'So you *have* outsourced work. When?' Naomi asked.

'Doesn't happen often. I can look it up.'

Naomi smiled thinly. 'Yes, why don't you do that?'

Glen sat down at his desk terminal and tapped for a while. 'Yeah, here are the Minutes for the Review Board meeting, December 2056. I remember it now. There was a deadline to get the block point out before the end of the year. It really pushed us to the limit here, so we outsourced some of the grunt work. Nothing much, certainly nothing important, just the IFE.'

'In-Flight Entertainment,' Naomi said.

'Yup.' He turned to the COO. 'You remember this, Charles?'

Redbanks looked at the screen over Glen's shoulder. 'Yes... but we've used that company before and they operate strict security standards, similar to ours.' He turned to the others, chuckling. 'The IFE,' he said. 'At worst the passengers would get the wrong film.'

Naomi ignored it. 'Has that been updated since?'

'No.' Glen shrugged. 'No need, that part works fine.'

'We'll take a look at it,' Naomi said.

Redbanks raised his eyebrows and smiled. 'As you wish. Look I have things to do. I'll leave you people to your w—' He was probably about to say 'wild goose chase' but a steely glance from Naomi stopped him in his tracks.

'Er, work. Glen, you'll let me know if you need me again.'

'Sure.'

They left the office and went onto the main floor, with Redbanks' figure receding in one direction and Glen leading the way in the other.

Tony bent over to murmur to Naomi, 'Why are you interested in this, Naomi?'

She turned her head to catch his eye and whispered, 'You'll see.'

Formidable though this woman was, Tony felt a flash of warmth. He'd met people like this before. There was an indefinable charisma about them.

Glen stopped at a huge wall screen, which displayed a pattern of coloured boxes, each one labelled and joined to others by a network of lines.

'This here's a schematic of the whole operating system,' Glen said. He traced a finger over it and stopped at a box marked IFE. It had a series of numbers and letters on it. He copied them to his cell phone, then they followed him to an unoccupied work station and he entered the information. The screen filled with code.

'Here's the code for the IFE.' He glanced up at Naomi. 'The language is pretty low-level – that's why it runs so fast. It'd take us quite a while to work through it line by line.'

Naomi opened her bag and took out a lap top. 'Which is why I brought this. Could you port it over?'

Glen's face fell. 'Gee, ma'am, you know we're not allowed to take code outside of this room.'

'It's not going outside this room. We'll delete it when we're finished.'

He hesitated. 'Er, maybe I should okay this with Charles.'

'Glen,' she said, her tone light, yet strangely insistent, 'your company has triple-4s grounded all over the world. I do think Charles expects you to cooperate fully with the NSA.'

He swallowed. 'I guess you're right.' He pointed to the lap top. 'That's not connected to the internet, is it?'

She gave him a patient look and he subsided. 'Okay, okay, go ahead.'

Naomi booted up the lap top and handed him a cable, which he connected to the console. When the transfer was complete she entered some instructions, hit a key, and the lines began to scroll. She looked up.

'Gentlemen,' she said. 'I believe we have time for some coffee.'

They didn't go to the canteen. Two machines in a corner of the room served up the coffee, hot and strong, and they took the paper cups to Glen's office. They chatted about other things for ten minutes, then Naomi said 'Good' and got up. They followed her to the work station, hurrying to keep up. The display had stopped scrolling, and six long lines of code were flashing in red, alternating with the message 'SUSPICIOUS CODING'. She sat down, cancelled the message, and examined them, line by line. They waited for fifteen minutes, watching her but saying nothing. Then she pointed to the screen.

'There it is. This program scans specifically for code sequences of that type. This one sure took some finding,' she added, shaking her head. 'Whoever put it there buried it in apparently normal instructions.'

'What is it?' Tony asked. For all the sense it made to him, he could have been looking at a page of Sanskrit.

'A nice little trap door,' she said. 'Sitting there, waiting for someone to use it.'

Glen craned his neck forward. 'Well, I'll be...' He reached across with an 'excuse me' and scrolled up a few lines to a comment. 'It's in the subroutine, the one we outsourced.'

'That part is evidence, so I'm afraid it *will* be going out of this room,' she said. She selected the lines and part of the adjacent code and moved them to another file. 'Okay, you can watch me delete the rest.' When it was done she straightened up and said, 'Now Glen, are you absolutely sure this was the only part of the software you outsourced?'

'Oh yes. We don't do it unless we have to. This was exceptional, because of getting that block point out on time.'

'All right, then. What you have to do now is rewrite that subroutine and get your COO to issue another block point. Our job's just started, though. I need the details of that company.'

'Sure, I'll get them for you.' As they walked back to his office he said, 'Say, that program you used is real cool.'

She smiled. 'I'm glad you like it. I wrote most of it myself.'

'Can I get a copy?'

'I'm afraid not, It's NSA property.'

Glen found the company quickly on his office lap top. Naomi photographed the screen with her cell phone, and exported the converted text to her contacts list. The company was LG Data Management Consultants, located in Silicon Valley, not far from San José.

She said, 'We left someone in the canteen, Glen. Where is it?'

'First floor. You want me to take you there?'

'No, we'll find it.'

As they rode the elevator Naomi said, 'If your friend George has quite finished his lunch we'll collect him and go straight to that company. And this time there won't be any warning.'

Tony scratched the back of his neck. 'I don't get it,' he said. 'This is part of the in-flight entertainment suite. How can that put a plane on a collision course?'

'The point is, Tony, it bypasses the firewall and gives an intruder entry to the wifi system. Whoever uses it gets access to the entire on-board network – *including* the avionics. Mr Redbanks should have known that. Let's go.'

32

George Walski spent much of the two-hour flight from Boeing Field to San José asleep, only to wake up when they were already on the descent.

'Sorry,' he said, rubbing his eyes. 'Was working late last night.'

Working your way through a crate of beer while you watched the game, Tony thought, but said nothing.

Naomi Fine put away her lap top, on which she'd been studying the lines of code she'd extracted at Lightspeed. She said to Tony, 'Whoever wrote that code is very smart. The way it was phrased made it look like part of the subroutine. Without my help I doubt they'd have found it.'

When they'd disembarked at San José International they hired a taxi and it drove them to the company. Tony and George went in first, their ID wallets open to show the FBI badges, and in the ensuing confusion someone called the CEO, who came down himself to see what the fuss was about. Naomi explained why they were there.

'I hope you're wrong,' the young CEO said. 'Lightspeed is a good account. Come with me.'

He left them with a senior manager, older than the CEO but still fresh-faced and casually dressed. He looked up orders in December 2056.

'Yes, here it is. A subroutine from the In-Flight Entertainment system. I gave it to... Ranny.' He looked round at them, his face troubled. 'He's a quiet kind of guy, very conscientious. Doesn't strike me as a terrorist.'

'They never do,' Walski said. 'You got a room where we can interview him?'

'You can use my room. There's a table and chairs in it.'

'Thanks,' Walski said, beginning a yawn. 'What's this guy's full name?'

'Randolph Walker.'

Walski stopped in mid-yawn. 'Randolph Walker?' He looked at Tony. 'We've heard that name before.'

Tony said, 'Yes, we have.'

*

As expected, Randolph Walker put up no physical resistance, merely protesting his innocence, which he continued to do all the way to the Senior Manager's room. They directed him to a chair at the table with Walski next to him. Tony and Naomi Fine sat opposite. At this point Randolph lapsed into a sullen silence.

Tony studied the young programmer across the table from him. He was in his late twenties, maybe early thirties, slightly built and a head shorter than Walski. His straw-blond hair was long and gathered in a ponytail, and his cheeks and chin carried a feeble growth of blond beard. He wore a T-shirt and jeans, an outfit that had seemed to be almost universal among the programmers they'd seen at both Lightspeed and LG Data Management Consultants. Tony had to agree with the Senior Manager, though: Randolph Walker did not look like a terrorist to him either.

Tony broke the silence. 'Randolph,' he said. 'Anyone you want to notify about what's going on?'

Randolph moved his eyes to him without moving his head. 'I want a lawyer.'

'You'll get a lawyer.' Tony took a deep breath. 'Thing is, we're kinda pushed for time here. We read you your Mirandas, you don't have to say anything. But maybe it would be easier if you did.'

'Easier for who?'

Tony grimaced. 'Look. Code was found in a subroutine that shouldn't have been there. That code's caused some close encounters in the airways, and it's something of a miracle no one's been killed.'

'I told you, I didn't put it there. It's not the kind of thing I'd do. Ever.'

'Randolph,' Tony said. 'This incident is going to cost the airlines and the aircraft company millions of dollars. People are looking for someone to punish. Lightspeed will certainly pull their account with your employers, and you are now out of a job – that's for sure. And terrorist activities are serious. If you don't cooperate you could be inside for a long spell.'

Randolph set his jaw doggedly. 'I didn't write that code.'

'So who did, Randolph? Who put it there?'

Randolph looked at him, and suddenly, unexpectedly, his eyes welled with tears. He let them course down his pale cheeks, where they meandered into the wispy beard. Then he planted his fists on the table and his cry came right from the lungs. 'This shouldn't be happening to me!'

'Who was it, Randolph?' Tony repeated.

The programmer looked down, and when he spoke again his voice was small and weary.

'It was a real tough assignment. The pressure was on, and the code's written in a low-level language without a compiler. I was struggling and I knew it. No way was I going to make the deadline. I asked one or two of the other guys for help, but they were pushed for time on their own work.' He sniffed.

'Go on,' Tony said gently.

'I thought of this friend of mine, real smart with code like this. I took the job home and he worked on it for me.' He buried his face in his hands. 'I knew it was against the rules, but I had no choice. Programmers are two-a-penny in these parts. If I hadn't made the deadline I could've been fired. I guess... I guess he must've put those lines in. I sure as hell didn't.'

Walski said, 'You're talking about your friend Cy Sloper.'

'Yeah, Cy.'

Walski shook his head at the others.

'I know the Feds have been after him,' Randolph said, 'because two of your guys came round a while back and interviewed me, wanted to know where he was. I didn't know. I still don't know.'

'It didn't occur to you that he might tamper with the code he wrote for you?' Tony asked.

'Hell no. I had a quick look through it but it seemed clean to me. Listen, the kind of things he got up to, I'm not surprised he's in trouble now. But when he helped me out – that was more than two years ago, man. I was his friend. I never thought he'd do something as shitty as this to me.'

He was almost choking now. 'Bastard. If I find him I'll wring his lousy neck.'

'Join the line, Randolph,' Walski said. 'Join the line.'

33

Jim Slater answered the phone and was surprised to hear Tony's voice.

'Tony?' he said. 'I thought…'

'Yeah, yeah, I know. Nothing's changed. Only I stumbled across something that'll interest you.'

He outlined the visit to Lightspeed and the arrest at LG Data Management Consultants.

'No question,' Tony concluded. 'Cy Sloper's active all right. He's the only one who'd know about those lines of code he'd planted, and how to use them.'

'Something I don't understand here, Tony. You say it was more than two years ago when he helped Walker out with that coding. He hadn't served time at that stage, so Lazar was still in the future for him. Why did he insert the trap door?'

'You know what? I think this guy is just an inveterate hacker. He couldn't resist the opportunity to leave a calling card, just in case he ever wanted to get back in.'

Jim gritted his teeth. 'What'll happen to Walker?'

'Hard to say. Way I see it, all he's really guilty of is disregarding the company's security regulations. He's lost his job for that alone. If he can convince the court there was no intention to commit terrorist acts he may not have to serve a jail term as well.'

Jim paused a beat, thinking about the implications. Then he said, 'Have you told John Abadi about this?'

'Yeah. I don't know the guy but I thought I'd better bite the bullet. Cooperation between agencies, and all that. I reminded him of your conversation and then told him what went down. He said "Thank you".'

'That's it? That's all he said? Thank you?'

'Oh, coming from a CIA man that's quite something.'

Jim huffed a laugh. 'Okay, Tony. Thanks for the heads-up.'

'No problem. You take care now.'

Jim ended the call.

Five potential mid-air collisions, endangering the lives of how many passengers? – two thousand, at least, probably twice that many. Maybe now Abadi can persuade his Director that Cy Sloper and Conrad Lazar and their jihadi friends are a real and present danger, not bodies under the rubble of that village.

He shook his head and sighed.

After a few moments he got to his feet and glanced at his watch. Some of the guys would be in the gym right now, practising hand-to-hand combat. In his present mood it would be just the thing.

*

The gym was a long, high room, equipped with weights apparatus, parallel bars, ropes, vaulting horses, and other paraphernalia for strength and circuit training. The far end, however, was set out as a dojo. Four men were on the mat, practising in pairs, when Jim entered. Like Jim, their feet were bare and they were dressed in Judo Gi. Four were watching and waiting their turn. He noticed that Holly was among them.

Jim moved quietly up to Ned Howells, who was directing the exercises. 'Thought I'd join you for a bit,' he said.

'Sure. You can go on next. Why don't I put you with Holly? The other guys are getting pissed off with being trounced by someone half their weight.'

'She's that good?'

'You'll find out.'

There were several slaps as bodies hit the mat and the men got up, nodded to each other, and walked off. Ned went over to the others and Jim walked onto the mat. Holly came out to join him. She didn't smile or greet him in any way, but her eyes roved quickly over him, and he guessed she was already sizing him up as an opponent. He was a lot taller than her and a good deal heavier but then so were the other guys. Two more men had taken the mat but Jim was aware that they weren't engaging, just watching him.

They bowed briefly, he gripped her jacket and she gripped his, and they began to pull and push each other tentatively. He was quickly aware of the strength and balance in that lithe body. The movements became more exaggerated and turned into a kind of waltz. Then she pulled upwards and towards her to get him off balance. Her weight was on her bent right leg, freeing the left for the sweeping ankle throw he could see coming. It came in very fast, but he lifted his own leg out of the way, then contacted the side of her calf and followed it through. It should have put her on her back, but in an extraordinary show of gymnastic agility she used her momentum to rise up, and now she was above and behind him, her legs locked around his neck in a strangle hold. Her weight was pulling him back, and he knew that if he fell with that strangle hold on it would be all over. So he didn't fall; instead he launched himself upwards and backwards, and landed heavily on top of her.

His neck was free and he rolled to one side and got up quickly. Holly hadn't moved. He stepped forward, heart pounding. She was out cold. He knew what he had to do. Some time ago he'd learned a resuscitation technique from a Japanese black belt and he applied it now without even thinking about it. He sat her up, hooked his fingers under her pectorals, which in this case also meant her breasts, put his knee in her back, and jerked. She gasped, blinked, and shook her head.

He heard intakes of breath from the men who'd gathered on the mat to watch.

Ned was standing in front of them now. 'Is she all right? Holly, you okay?'

She blinked again, then nodded slowly. 'I guess.'

Jim helped her to her feet and led her off the mat.

She put a hand to her head.

'Holly, I'm sorry. I shouldn't have done that to you.'

Her grey eyes came round to him. She was frowning. 'I remember the moves till I put you in a neck lock. Then what?'

'I jumped backwards. It was like a body slam. I'm really sorry. Just did it instinctively.'

'Guess I shouldn't have gone for the neck lock. Left me vulnerable.'

'It would have been easier on you to take the fall from the ankle throw. But you don't take the easy way do you?'

She met his eyes and gave him a wry grin. 'No. Never did. Never will.' She began to walk, but stopped abruptly, putting her hand to her back and wincing.

Jim's eyes narrowed. 'Come on, we'll have the physio look you over. If he's got any concerns I'll drive you to the military hospital myself.'

'It's only—'

He looked at her, raising his eyebrows.

She shrugged. 'Okay, okay.'

He turned to Ned, who was watching them anxiously. 'Ned, you carry on. I'll deal with this.'

As they were leaving Jim heard Ned clap his hands for attention. 'Okay, never mind the acrobatics, what you just saw was a sweeping ankle throw and the counter. Let's just practise that for a bit.'

34

Jim had time to change back into uniform while Graham Campbell, the physiotherapist, was examining Holly. Then, as he'd promised, he drove her to the military hospital.

For a while they drove in silence. Then she asked:

'What did the physio say?'

'He thought it could just be a pulled muscle, but it could also be a minor back injury. That's why he strapped you up. It certainly needs to be looked at.'

'Yeah, that's more or less what he told me. Well, I'm certainly getting the VIP treatment. You could have had a corporal out of the pool drive me.'

'I'm responsible for your injury, so I feel better doing it myself.'

She looked across at him. 'You shouldn't feel bad. I overreached myself, is all. I didn't think you could fight that well. You saw that ankle throw coming. Most guys fall for it.'

'I guess I read the movements. I didn't expect the strangle hold, though. I don't know how you got up there.'

'Little speciality of mine. I won't be using it again—' she gasped with pain as he turned a corner. 'There's no rush, you know. It's not life-threatening.'

'Sorry, I'll try to drive more smoothly.'

She blew out a breath. Then she said, 'You know, aside from Ned you're the first one in that gym to get the better of me.'

'I've had a lot of experience. Training, retraining, different instructors, different techniques. Then I became an instructor myself, both here and with the 22 SAS. And I've had to use those techniques in the field – in fact it's the only reason I'm still here.'

'I guess that was the take-home lesson for me,' she said. 'You've got it, the killer instinct. In that moment you felt your life was in danger and the rest was pretty much reflex. If it was for real you'd have followed up and I'd be dead.' She paused. 'I've seen action but I've never killed a man in close combat.'

'You have the skills. If your life depends on it you'll use them. Here we are.'

He parked the car, helped her out, and walked her slowly into the Emergency Department.

*

No one was around in the hospital waiting area, which was just as well. He wondered what people would have made of a colonel being there – they'd expect someone of that rank to have better things to do. He could have delegated this job, but he was still glad he hadn't. And actually there was nothing vital he should be dealing with at the moment. Unless the CIA changed their mind about locating that mobile cyber unit he had little hope of finding Lazar. And

SAF operations in general had ground to a halt while they devised new procedures.

The building was air-conditioned but a trace of disinfectant hung in the room – probably something they used to clean the pale-green, non-slip composite on the floor. The padded seats were upholstered in a scuffed dark-green imitation leather, and there was a selection of magazines on the low table in front of him, which he ignored.

He got up, went over to a machine in the corner and dispensed a beaker of black coffee. Then he stood there, sipping it. What would he say to Bob Cressington? It was one thing for a soldier to be injured in a combat situation but quite another to have it happen during training. Being personally responsible made it that much worse. Holly was probably right: it was pure reflex, but that was no excuse. He was there as an instructor, he should be able to suppress reactions like that. Was it foolish pride, a determination not to be beaten by anyone, especially a woman half his size? He didn't think so – and he certainly hoped not – but it worried him all the same. Suppose it had been a karate session? Would he have stopped a lethal blow short? It didn't bear thinking about.

He glanced at his watch. She'd been gone nearly an hour. Was it more serious than they thought?

The incredible thing was that she'd treated it as a learning experience. She could have been really angry – she was entitled to be angry – but she understood what he'd done and why, probably better than he did himself. She really was a remarkable girl.

The beaker was empty. He was thinking of refilling it when he heard footsteps. He put it down and turned to see a very tall African-American doctor holding the door open for Holly, who came in, walking a little better but holding herself stiffly. She had a large envelope in one hand. Jim went over to them. He glanced at the doctor's name tag: Dr J. Jackson.

'Hello, sir,' Dr Jackson began. 'You a relative?'

'I'm her CO.'

'Oh.' His eyebrows made a brief excursion. Then he said, 'Well, we examined her and did a CT scan. She's fractured a spinous process. I saw a few like this when I was in emergency services. You get it in earthquake victims when a building falls on them.'

'Yeah,' Holly said, with a meaningful glance at Jim. 'It was something like that.'

'Medically speaking,' the doctor continued, 'it's a minor fracture.' He smiled. 'Doesn't mean it don't hurt none.'

Holly grunted.

'It's stable, no need for any intervention, but we strapped her up again real tight, and she's got some painkillers. Should heal inside six weeks, if she keeps to the rules.'

'Which are…?' Jim asked.

'Spinous processes don't stick out for fun, they provide an attachment for muscles.' He was speaking half to Jim and half to Holly. 'You don't want those muscles pulling on this one while it's trying to mend. So bed rest initially. Gradually introduce a little walking. Take the painkillers as needed. Increase the walking later, but nothing strenuous. Limit the sitting – puts more strain on the spine. Got all that?'

They both nodded. 'Thanks, doc,' Jim said.

'Sure thing. In future, you be careful what you get up to in those hand-to-hand combat classes.'

Jim grimaced. 'We'll do our best.'

*

Jim drove back. 'How are you feeling?' he asked.

'More comfortable but a bit bombed. Must be those painkillers he gave me.'

'What's in the envelope?'

'Dr Jackson's report, including the CT scan. Considered a legal document, so it's printed out. Standard procedure, apparently, to give to bosses or COs who think you're goofing off.'

'Well, I'm not one of them. You've got at least six weeks sick leave. You're welcome to spend the time at the base or you can go back home. Your call.'

'I don't know. What do you think?'

'I think you should spend a few days in the medical centre. We've got beds there for recovery and rehab. After that? You might find it a bit frustrating, especially when everyone else is taking part in exercises and training. I can get someone to take you home.'

She nodded. 'Sounds good. Dad's got a little place out in Maryland. Nice walking. I could spend some time there.'

'Okay. but don't overdo it. I want you back in six weeks to start training again.' His attempt to sound severe didn't convince him and it evidently didn't convince her, because she responded with a grin and an emphatic 'Yes, sir!'

He smiled. 'What about your father? Should I let him know what's happening?'

'Hell, no,' she said, 'I'll tell him myself when I feel up to it.'

They drove on in silence for a bit. Then he said, 'Er, is there anyone you'd like to visit you while you're laid up? One of the women, one of the men?' He was surprised to feel a tightening in the chest as he said 'one of the men'. He realized he was secretly hoping she hadn't got that close to any of them.

'I don't think so,' she said, and he breathed more easily.

'But maybe...'

Again he felt that tension.

'Maybe Sally. She knows what it's all about, because she's been through it herself – actually a lot worse than this. Also I like her.'

He relaxed. 'Okay, I'll tell her. And maybe she'll go with you when you feel ready to make the move.'

They entered Fort Piper and he pulled up as close to the medical centre as he could. She was about to go in when she turned to him.

'That resuscitation technique you used. Not exactly designed for women is it?'

He felt the heat in his face. She'd come round very fast, and she was aware of what he'd done.

'I guess I should apologize for that, too. Seemed like the right thing to do at the time.'

Her lips quirked, suppressing a smile. 'Don't beat yourself up about it, Jim. See you later.'

He held the door open for her and watched as she made her way carefully inside.

He let the door swing to and stood still for a moment. It was the first time she'd called him Jim.

35

The SAF squads came in, carefully disabling claymores and avoiding laser sentries. Then, on a signal, they made a coordinated entry into the low dwellings. Men in black robes ran out yelling, but they were quickly rounded up and left lying on the ground, hands and feet tied. The squads made a final check from house to house. It was all over in a few minutes.

'Good operation,' Jim said to Tommy Geiger. 'Combine that with the other strategy and it should work really well.'

'Okay, guys,' Tommy shouted. 'Well done. Let the "jihadis" loose and we'll go back for debriefing.' He turned to Jim. 'We'll have a post-mortem, see if anyone picked up a snag or something we could have done better.'

'I'll come with you.' They turned and made their way back from the practice ground. 'Why were you taking captives, Tommy?'

'That's the toughest scenario. Normally we wouldn't bother.'

Jim nodded. *Damn right we wouldn't.*

A group of grinning soldiers in long black robes jogged past, chatting. As Jim was watching them go his phone sounded.

'Oh-oh.' He stopped and clicked on. 'Yes, Bagley?'

'Agent Abadi is trying to contact you, sir. He said he'd phone on the secure line in ten minutes.'

'Okay, I'll be right there.'

He looked at Tommy and shrugged. 'Sorry, I'm wanted. You go on without me.'

*

John Abadi got straight to the point.

'Jim, as soon as all the drones have been modified the Director's going to authorize high-altitude reconnaissance flights, night and day.'

'Oh, really? What made him change his mind? Those near-misses in US airspace?'

'Yeah. The Air Force bombed the original target but with this fresh cyber attack – well, a mobile jihadi unit in Yemen is beginning to look more credible as the source. He's not entirely convinced but the Director of National Intelligence and the White House Chief of Staff are pressuring him to do something about it.'

'Wonderful. And if you pick up that mobile unit I suppose your Air Force General will blow it to atoms with a strike.'

'Er, not exactly. That's why I wanted to speak with you. Jim, it'd be much better if we could capture it. We'd round up some of the hackers, see how sophisticated their equipment is, what their plans are, find out if there are any other units, that kind of thing.'

Jim could see something coming. 'Right...'

'Best of all, I'd get Lazar back to face the music. You wanted that, too.'

'I'd be just as happy to bring him back in a body bag, but I take your point. So what are you saying?'

'The CIA can authorize action through its Special Activities Division. Yours is one of the Special Operations Forces we can call on. Do you think you could have a force out there in the Yemen, on standby?'

Jim thought for a moment, then sucked in a breath. 'Not immediately. Our new operating procedures call for some specialized equipment. It's on order, but not all of it's arrived.'

'Okay, but when it comes?'

'The request would have to be made through my line of command, John.'

'Sure, I just wanted to see if it's feasible.'

'It's feasible but it's expensive to keep a force on standby like that. I'll have to discuss it with General Harken. And no doubt he'll be talking to your Director about who foots the bill.'

'Okay. I'll leave it with you. Can you get back to me?'

'Sure.'

'Oh, and Jim…'

'Yes?'

'Remember what you said to me about the mind set of Special Forces personnel? You said you know how Lazar thinks. The other side of that coin is, Lazar knows how *you* think. If you do go out there it's not going to be easy. Don't underestimate Lazar. He's real smart.'

'Well I'll just have to be smarter, won't I?'

36

Holly was lying in bed viewing a holoscreen above her head when he came in. She saw him and reached for the switch to extinguish the screen.

She gave him a wan smile. 'Hallo, Jim.'

'Hi. How are you?'

'Bored stiff,' she said. 'When our wonderful medical staff saw what was in the envelope they confined me to bed for a week. It's only four days and I'm already stir-crazy. They won't even let me sit up, except for meals.'

'You should enjoy it. You're living the life of Riley.'

'Riley's welcome to it – whoever he is.'

'Think of it this way: one week of bed rest now is going to give you two weeks off the total recovery time.'

'There is that, I suppose.'

She fiddled with the bed sheet. He noticed that her hair seemed longer. She was probably letting it grow in preparation for her trip home.

He cleared his throat. 'Holly, I wanted to say something to you about your mission, the one I aborted.'

'You don't have to, Jim. You explained it already.'

'I did, but I know a lot more now. Look, this isn't for general consumption. Keep it to yourself, okay?'

'Okay...'

'The kidnap thing was staged.'

She blinked and her eyes widened. 'What?'

'Yes, the whole thing. The US citizen in question was defecting to the jihadis, and it was made to look like a kidnap. Later they filmed the execution, except the man being executed wasn't him.'

'Who was it?'

'We don't know. A Yemeni, probably. Some luckless civilian they'd captured.'

'Just as bad. Somebody still lost his life.'

He grimaced. 'True. All I'm saying is, it wasn't the person you were sent to rescue.'

She nodded slowly. 'Why are you telling me?'

'I felt I owed it to you. You led a team out there to rescue someone who turned out not to be what he seemed. And... I thought it'd make you feel better about it.'

'Right.'

For a while neither of them spoke. She resumed fiddling with the bed sheet. Then she turned her head to look at him.

'They could have moved him on straight away but they didn't, did they? They had a US citizen. They knew we'd mount a rescue attempt. It's like you said, they waited there deliberately to lure us in and I would have fallen for it. You saved my life, not just mine but the whole squad's.'

Jim winced. 'That's putting it a bit strongly, but I wasn't taking chances.'

'It's that survival instinct of yours – isn't it, Jim? – the reflex response that put me in here, and the ability to sniff danger in the field.' She paused. 'How come it didn't work for Brian Murdoch?'

'I tried to pull the squad but I did it too late, they'd already gone in. The damage was done.' He sighed. 'The survival instinct you talk about – I think it's there, but it's not that reliable.'

'I was watching you at the funeral in Arlington. You had tears in your eyes.'

'I liked him a lot. And I wish to hell I'd acted sooner.'

The silence fell again, and again she was the one who broke it.

'Does it change anything, this information you have now?'

'It makes me even more determined to find the people responsible for planning it – the trap they set for Brian and the one that almost succeeded with you.'

'How are you going to do that?'

'We're making progress. I think we could be deploying in the Yemen before long.'

She let out a long breath. 'And I'm going to miss all the fun.'

'Don't be too sure of that. We're in this for the long haul. That guy you used as a driver out there, was he reliable?'

'Youssef? Yes, completely.'

'And he knows the terrain?'

'Seems to. The people I spoke to said he knew the country real well, including the danger spots.'

'We may be able to use him again. Do you still have his contact details?'

'I'm sure I have, I'll look them up for you.'

'Thanks.' He got to his feet. 'You have everything you need at the moment?'

'I think so.' As he turned to go, she said, 'Jim?'

He turned back.

'I'm glad you told me.'

He nodded, then left the medical centre to walk to his office. It was curious the way she stirred him up inside…

He was still thinking about it when he opened the door to his office and found General Wendell Harken waiting there.

'Wendell! What brings you this way?'

'I gather Holly Cressington's in the medical centre.'

Jim nodded. 'Bad news travels fast.'

'She phoned Bob yesterday. He wanted to visit her but he'll be in California and Oregon the next few days, seeing various defence contractors. I told him I'd look in on her.' He frowned. 'I gather it was a training accident. She wouldn't say more than that. What the hell happened to her, Jim?'

Jim grimaced. 'My fault entirely, I'm afraid. We were practising unarmed combat moves and I dumped her too hard. She has a minor fracture of a spinous process. Should heal in six weeks or so, given adequate rest. She's in reasonable spirits but she's finding it hard: "rest" isn't a word you'd normally find in her vocabulary. I'm sure she'll be grateful you've come. I take it she knows you.'

'Bob and I go back a long way, and Holly and I have known each other for much of that time. I have a high regard for her.'

'Me too.' Seeing the suddenly alert expression in Wendell's eyes, Jim added, 'She's a fine soldier.'

Wendell held his eyes for a moment longer. Then he said, 'Well, coming here gives me a chance to go over the latest developments with you. You haven't been updating me.'

'I'm sorry about that. So much has been going on. Do you want to see Holly first?'

'Yes, I've got a little present for her. Then I'll come back here.' He got to his feet.

'I'll take you over there.'

Wendell half closed his eyes and smiled. 'I know where it is, Jim.'

*

Wendell returned half an hour later and Jim pulled out a chair for him.

'She's bored. I gave her a military computer game she can play on that screen above her head.'

Jim smiled. 'I should have thought of something like that.'

'I talked to her about the injury. She doesn't blame you, Jim. Said something about your survival instinct. I think she's being generous.'

'She is, I feel really bad about it.'

'Well, well, let's talk about your progress with the FBI.'

Jim brought him up to date with what he'd found with Tony and then from John Abadi. Wendell interrupted only occasionally for clarification or further information. Finally Jim said:

'In short, Conrad Lazar's a danger as long as he's out there. I'm pretty sure he's responsible for setting up the trap that killed Brian Murdoch. He'd have caught Holly and her squad as well if I hadn't aborted that hostage extraction. And this guy Cy Sloper we were supposed to rescue is part of a cyber warfare group that's almost certainly behind the destruction of the Embassy in Sana'a and this recent cyber attack on passenger aircraft.'

'The near-misses. Yes, Joseph Templeton's been on to me about that. When they've modified all the drones he'll be setting up reconnaissance flights to find this group while they're on the move. He was in favour of an air strike but Agent Abadi persuaded him it would be better to capture them. He wants us to have SAF units on the ground so we can move as soon as they've got a target.' Wendell gave him the familiar under-the-eyebrows look. 'What do you think of that?'

Jim said, 'I'd be happy to see the whole damned bunch blown sky high, but Abadi thinks we'd get more useful intel if we captured them. I guess it depends on who pays the bill.'

'Not everyone's convinced this group is responsible but right now they're a logical target. After the Embassy business and these near-disasters in the air the President wants action. They're still arguing about who's going to pay for it but the bottom line is, the money won't come from us. So it's approved. Are you good to go?'

'We're still waiting for some of the new equipment to arrive. Apart from that I think we're ready. The exercises have gone well. The guys are dying to try them out for real.'

'All right, then.' He got to his feet.

'Do you have to get back tonight?' Jim asked. 'You could have dinner here and we can find you a room.'

'No, thanks. Stuff to do.' He glanced at his watch. 'There's a flight in about an hour. Can someone run me to the airport?'

'No problem. Thanks for coming down, Wendell. Bob doesn't really need to see Holly here. I think she'll be well enough to go home in a few days, and she can rest up there.'

'Okay, I'll tell him. Jim, you're not thinking of going out to the Yemen yourself, are you?'

'That's exactly what I am thinking. I have to see how these new operating procedures work in the field, and you can only do that at first hand.'

'Well, you be damned careful.'

'Aren't I always?'

'Frankly? No.'

37

The camper and the two big all-terrains had stopped in another ruined village. They'd taken their evening meal in what was once a market square, where there was still some open space between the piles of rubble. As usual Cy Sloper sat slightly apart from the young men, who in turn distanced themselves from the eight jihadis.

Conrad strolled up.

'Did you speak to Abd al-Matin?' Cy asked.

'Yeah. He says we don't have to kill you.'

Cy grunted. 'Is he always so generous?'

'No. But he seems to be satisfied with what you did. 'Course he was disappointed there weren't any fatalities, but he was pleased with the economic disruption. Economic disruption is big with al-Matin. So that's it, you can stop dicking around with aeroplanes and do something useful for a change.'

Cy grimaced. 'You're such an inspiring leader of men, Conrad.'

Lazar ignored him. Instead he walked across to the group of young men.

'You people have the next exploit ready yet?'

Khalil Masood looked up. The direct approach was unexpected. Khalil would normally work through Cy Sloper, because Cy was close to Conrad Lazar and no one else had the slightest desire to be close to Conrad Lazar.

Khalil was a recruit from Belgium and he spoke good English, but since Lazar had addressed him in Arabic he responded in kind.

'Yes, we are ready. We are inside the Smart Grid for the Eastern Connection. Everything is prepared. You want to do it now?'

'No. It's midnight here. In one hour it'll be rush hour in the Eastern United States. We'll get maximum disruption if we do it then.'

Khalil smiled. 'Okay.'

'What comes first?'

'We take out twenty-five large generating stations.'

'You're shutting down the generators?'

'No, in this first stage we are just taking them off the grid.'

Conrad frowned. 'The other generators will compensate, won't they?'

'We have made that more difficult. It will happen, no doubt, but very slowly.'

Conrad stared hard at him. 'This going to work?'

Khalil shrugged. 'I think yes. But if it does not, no one will know. That is the beauty of cyber warfare.'

The big man nodded. 'All right, wait an hour, then get on with it.'

He went back to Cy, squatted down, and put another forkful of the cold food in his mouth. Still chewing, he said, 'When your nerds have got that exploit going, get them to bolt their stuff down and we'll hit the road again. We should reach jihadi-held territory by daybreak.'

'How long will it take our friends back home to modify the drones?'

'Not much longer. After that they'll be hoping to catch us on the move. Which is why we're not going to be on the move. We're going to go to ground up there for a bit, then they can look all they want.'

Cy nodded. 'Good idea.' He jerked a thumb over his shoulder towards the young men, 'It's working well, isn't it? This'll be the biggest thing so far.'

'It's a step along the way.'

'Along the way to what?'

Conrad continued to eat without replying.

Cy frowned. 'There's more to this than poking the US in the eye, isn't there?' He strained to see some sort of reaction from Conrad, but in the moonlight all he could make out were those bushy eyebrows, the eyes dark sockets below them.

Then Conrad raised his head. He said, 'Yeah.'

'So what are you planning next?'

Was that a smile? It was too dark to say, but the voice came back slow and hard.

'I'm going to wipe out the Special Assignment Force.'

Cy started in surprise. 'Why?'

The eyebrows came closer together and his voice was a growl. 'It's personal.'

He dropped the fork onto his plate, got to his feet, and walked off.

The conversation was evidently over, so Cy gathered up the two empty plates and took them over to the camper. He mounted the steps and switched on the light. Only then did he see that Conrad had bent the fork in half.

38

Like many people on the Eastern Seaboard, Doug Turner was late home from work. Rhonda heard the key rattle in the lock, and the front door open. She took a torch and went out from the kitchen into the darkness of the hall.

'I'm glad you're back, darling,' she said, kissing him on the cheek. 'How was the journey?'

Doug Turner stood his brief case against the wall and stretched his back. 'It's a zoo out there. Just as I'm leaving the City the traffic lights quit – all of them. There's a multiple pile-up at 9th and Franklin and everyone's trying to divert or go round it. Madness. Same all the way home. What time did it start?'

'Power's been off here for the last hour. I can't use the microwave and I don't want to open the fridge or the freezer because I don't know how long this is going to last. The kids are fed up. There's no TV and the router's out so there's no wifi and they can't play their games.'

Doug waved an arm. 'What's the matter with these people? We pay our bills, why can't we get a decent service? What's the excuse this time? A tornado in Scranton? I don't think so. I'm going to phone them.'

'Landline's not working, Doug, you'll have to use your cell phone. And remember you can't charge it if it runs low. Now don't you start getting all worked up, it's not good for you. Here, you take the torch, I've got a candle in the kitchen.'

She returned to the kitchen, leaving him to hang up his coat and dump his stuff in the study

He walked in a few minutes later, grumbling. 'Lines are all jammed. Guess all their phones are going at once. Good, serve 'em right, let them know how pissed off people are.' He looked up. 'So what are we going to do for dinner? I'm hungry.'

She gave him a bright smile. 'The barbecue will be working.'

He pistol-pointed a finger at her. 'Good thinking, Batman. Where are those big LED lamps?' He opened a cupboard, felt around, and brought them out. 'Here, you can have one and I'll take the other outside while I get the barbie fired up.' He opened the door to the patio, then said over his shoulder, 'See what you can find – burgers or hot dogs or something. And while you're at it, get a couple of beers, too.'

His cell phone sounded and he reached into a pocket. 'Yes Pete, went off about an hour ago... It sure is... See ya.'

He looked at Rhonda. 'That was Pete. Hasn't left work yet. Wanted to know if we've got an outage here.'

*

The limousine that picked up Chester Hardman, Secretary of State for Homeland Security, drove to the White House at speed. He passed quickly through the security checks to the West Wing and descended to the basement. His face was like thunder as he was met by the Situation Room's Senior Duty Officer.

'What's so important I had to be dragged out of another meeting?' he demanded.

'They're waiting for you in the break-out room, sir,' the Duty Officer replied with a polite smile, opening a door.

Hardman had indeed been summoned from another meeting. He had been enjoying dinner with a very attractive and seemingly impressionable young lady at an expensive but discreet restaurant on the outskirts of Washington. Things were going well when the room lighting, already low, went out completely. The only source of light now was the single candle on each table, which in Chester's view could only improve his prospects. The improvement was short-lived. A few minutes later the Manager emerged.

'Ladies and gentlemen, a thousand apologies. As you see, there is a power outage. You may stay but it is impossible for the kitchen to operate in such conditions. There will of course be no charge for your meals.' His voice dropped meaningfully as he added, 'The electricity company will be paying for them.' There was a scattering of polite laughter.

Chester and his young companion had just finished their starters but he was a resourceful man. He was about to suggest that they take the bottle of Château Margaux he'd ordered and finish it at his pied-à-terre when his cell phone rang. Within moments his expectations of a pleasurable evening had vanished altogether.

'Cindy, I'm so sorry,' he said. 'The Director of the National Security Agency wants me in the White House Situation Room immediately. It's a CRITIC call, which means I have to respond. After that I'll need to speak to the President.' Her eyes widened. She was clearly disappointed but he was pleased with the effect of mentioning the President. He shrugged apologetically. 'This is what it can be like.' Then he crinkled his eyes in what he hoped was a confidential manner. 'I'll get you a cab.' And he flicked his fingers imperiously at a waiter.

Now, accompanied by the Duty Officer, he passed through the main conference room and into the break-out room, a small, plain, windowless office with monitors on two walls and the same black leather armchairs as everywhere else in the suite. The Duty Officer withdrew, leaving him with the two people who'd been awaiting his arrival.

'What's the problem, Mike?' he said. He was still agitated but his tone was moderated by the presence there of the Director of the National Security Agency.

Admiral Mike Randall was in shirt and black tie, the shirt sleeves rolled back neatly. He indicated a chair, and after a moment's hesitation Hardman sat down and looked expectantly across the small round table. Randall said:

'Chester, we have a cyber attack on our hands, a bad one. It's caused a black-out in a whole slice of the Eastern Connection, from New Jersey down to D.C. There'll be a full meeting inside shortly, but I thought it would be helpful for the three of us to meet first.' He indicated the woman in the chair next to him. 'You know Laura Gianni, don't you?'

'Laura.' Hardman nodded to the Director of the Department of Energy, a stocky woman in her forties. 'What did they do?'

'Took twenty-five of the largest generating stations out of the grid,' Gianni said.

'Nuclear plants?'

'Among others.'

'Isn't that dangerous?'

Gianni shook her head. 'They weren't damaged, just taken off the grid. They've been shut down for the moment.'

'Why isn't the rest of the system responding?' Hardman asked. 'That's what Smart Grids are for, isn't it?'

'The feedback from the synchrophasers has been compromised.'

'What in the hell are synchrophasers?'

Gianni said, 'Synchrophasers monitor the grid all the time. Operators need that information to respond to abnormal situations or outages like this. And just when we need it, we haven't got it. You should see our control room. More than half the monitors are blank. No way did all this happen by accident.'

Hardman ran a hand over his thick, beautifully coiffed hair. He turned to Randall. 'This is critical infrastructure, for God's sake! How did they get in?'

'We don't know. I've put one of my top analysts on it. If she can't find out how they did it no one can.'

Hardman pointed in the direction of the Watch Floor, where he knew dozens of operatives would normally be glued to monitor screens, generating situational awareness. 'Are we all right in there?'

'Yes, the whole seat of government is on a microgrid, us included.'

Then, with sudden alarm. 'What about Wall Street?'

Gianni replied. 'New York City's unaffected, they're on a microgrid, too. You know, these precautions were put in after a series of very bad weather incidents.'

He subsided. 'Yeah, I remember now. Just as well. If the financial centres were affected...' He threw his hands up.

'This is quite bad enough, Chester,' Randall said. 'Our people are working flat out with the DoE's digital engineers, trying to regain control.'

Gianni said, 'And we've called in as many retirees as we can contact, engineers who worked the grid before the Smart set-up came in and the synchrophasers were installed. They know how to manage things manually, so it should ease the situation. She sighed. 'I'm afraid that still won't be enough. We'll bring in every station – coal, gas, oil, hydro, wind, solar – but even running them at maximum output it'll be a struggle to compensate. We can restore some sort of service, but we really need those big plants back on line.'

*

Doug Turner lay awake for a while after his wife had got up. He contemplated the thin morning light seeping through a gap in the curtains. There was, he decided, some upside to a power cut. Much to the children's disgust they'd all gone to bed early, and Doug and Rhonda had taken full advantage of it. He felt pleasantly relaxed. The house was oddly quiet without the sound of TVs and computer games. The street outside was quiet, too. Less traffic. He thought about his colleagues at the office, all swearing by their shiny new all-electric vehicles. They'd be glad to have an old hybrid like his right now.

Would anyone be going to work today? He couldn't see how his own company could function. In a while he'd phone to find out. He eased himself off the bed and went to the bathroom. The water from the hot tap was barely tepid.

He cursed under his breath; the central heating pump wouldn't be working. After a moment's thought he went and retrieved a rechargeable electric razor from a bedroom drawer. There was just enough juice left in it to shave, but unless the power came back on he'd grow a beard rather than shave in cold water. There'd be no lingering in a shower, either.

He dressed, made his phone call, and went down to the kitchen, where the children were having breakfast cereals with cold milk.

'Just spoke to the boss. He said don't go in, don't even try. City's in gridlock. Lights aren't working, there are jams at every intersection, and there's nothing we can do if we did get there. No phones, no computers.'

'I just spoke to the school. They're closed for the day, too.'

'Yay,' twelve-year-old Nigel shouted, punching the air with both fists. 'I can go on with the game.' His face fell. 'Ah, no I can't. Shit.'

'Nigel!' Rhonda said. 'You just watch your language, young man.' She turned to Doug. 'If you feel up to it, honey, you should fuel up the car and pop in to Walmart. We don't know how long this is going to last, and you know how people clean out the shelves when it happens.'

'So you want me to clean out the shelves first?' She dropped her head patiently to one side. 'No,' he added quickly, 'you're right. Give me a list of what you need. Mostly tinned stuff, I guess.'

Doug got back from the supermarket two hours later. 'Got most of it,' he said. He blew out a breath. 'Jesus, though, the line-ups at check-out were something else.'

Rhonda, who'd spent most of the morning pottering about in the garden, helped him unload the groceries.

'That's great, hon,' she said. 'You did real well. The kids are riding their bikes in the park. Do you want to get them in? Lunch is all ready.'

After their cold lunch the kids went up to their rooms. Doug fell asleep in an armchair.

At three o'clock in the afternoon his eyelids flickered and he stirred and looked around. Something had changed. Then it registered. What had roused him was a low hum from the refrigerator.

'Hon,' he called. 'I think the power's back on.'

She came in and tried a light switch. The room light came on. 'Thank God for that. I'll make some coffee. Nigel, Maddie, power's on!'

Maddie and Nigel called down together, 'Great!'

Doug sighed. They'd probably watch a film on TV. He'd shower and shave and go back to work in the morning, the kids would go to school. Rhonda would probably visit some friends.

Things were back to normal.

39

Conrad Lazar occupied the passenger seat of the lead all-terrain as they approached the town. Following behind was the camper and behind that, the other all-terrain. The lead vehicle stopped at the check point and Lazar watched from the passenger seat as his driver got out and went over to the sentry. Both were dressed in the long black robes and headdress of the Sons of the Caliphate but the sentry was a head taller. A Kalashnikov AK74 assault rifle hung in front of him. A second sentry, younger but similarly dressed and armed, stood behind him. Conrad lowered the window so that he could listen to the exchange.

The sentry pointed to the camper. The driver shook his head. The conversation became more heated. Conrad opened the door and went over.

'What's the problem?' he asked the driver.

'He wants to look inside the camper. I told him it wasn't possible.'

Conrad turned to the sentry, who returned the look, dark eyes half-closed. He spoke in Arabic. 'I am Colonel Conrad Lazar. What is in that camper is not for your eyes.'

The sentry drew back his lips, revealing uneven blackened teeth. 'If you want to go any further, *everything* is for my eyes. Otherwise,' he jerked his head in the direction they'd come, 'you can turn around now.'

For a few moments no one spoke. Then, dropping his voice, Lazar said:

'Why don't you phone Abd al-Matin and see whether he agrees with you?'

For a brief moment the sneer faltered. Then the sentry pointed at him. 'Why don't you phone him?'

'Very well.' Conrad took the satellite phone from his pocket and clicked the quick dial number. Moments later he was conducting a long conversation. Then he passed the phone to the sentry. 'He wants to speak to you.'

The sentry took the phone warily and raised it to his ear. Despite the black beard and the dark skin the man blanched and seemed to shrink.

He said, 'Yes, yes, at once' and handed back the phone. 'Okay you can go.' He winced and shrugged his shoulders. 'I didn't know.'

Conrad said nothing, just led his driver back to the all-terrain. As he sat down Cy Sloper leaned forward from the back seat. He was grinning. 'I got some of that. *Colonel* Conrad Lazar?'

Lazar answered without turning his head. 'He obviously knew I was a foreigner. Made sense to give him a high rank. Come on, let's get moving.'

The driver put the all-terrain in gear and the convoy rolled on into the small town.

An hour later the two of them were alone, relaxing with soft drinks in a room furnished with hangings and carpets. The air was warm, but comfortably so. Some chairs had been installed for people who preferred not to use the plump cushions on the floor. Cars seldom passed in the street outside, but there were occasional light motorcycles. Otherwise the only noises were transient snatches of conversation from passers-by and the distant shouts of children or vendors.

The building they'd taken over was situated at the outskirts of the town. It was known locally as 'The Palace', and had once belonged to a local Imam. He and his entourage were long gone, and the few squatters who were currently in residence moved out when Conrad and his team arrived. There was no need to show weapons or use force; Conrad simply told them he was taking over the premises for a short time. They could leave now or wait to be evicted by the jihadi soldiers. They left quickly.

'Back in a decent place at last,' Cy Sloper sighed. 'Lively markets, hot food, plenty of people, nice girls. Lot better than a ruin.'

Conrad said nothing. He suspended his tumbler from his fingertips and rotated it slowly. Ice cubes chinked against the glass.

'Matter of interest, Conrad,' Cy said. 'Why do you want to keep moving at all? A place like this is safe enough, isn't it?'

Conrad barely reacted, but under those beetling eyebrows his eyes moved to his companion. 'You trust everyone out there in the town?'

Cy recoiled slightly. 'Me? No. I mean, how could I know them all?'

'Right. So suppose one of them happens to see two all-terrains and a big camper roll in with a lot of new arrivals. And suppose there are people who pay well for information like that, especially after the Embassy business. We could become a prime target for an air strike.'

'See what you mean. Still, they won't be making any drone strikes at the moment, will they?'

'They've probably modified the drones by now. Even if they haven't they can use conventional manned aircraft or even mount a ground attack. But all that takes time. Air attacks require high-level assessment of collateral damage. Putting boots on the ground takes even longer. They have to get them out here first.'

'So how long can we stay?'

'This place is safer than most, so maybe a couple of weeks. Then we move on. We have to keep ahead of the game.'

Cy nodded. 'You're a smart guy, Conrad.'

The big man stared into his glass.

Cy looked up at the shuttered window, beyond which a group of chattering girls was hurrying by. 'The folk here don't seem to mind the town being occupied. Why's that?'

Conrad shrugged. 'The Sons spend money and they haven't crucified anyone, not yet anyway. What's not to like?'

'What about our girls?'

'They're not from here. They were captured further north.'

'Right.' He glanced at his watch. 'Speaking of which, it's bedtime. Do you want to sort out a couple for the night?'

By way of reply Conrad drained his glass, set it on a small round table, and got to his feet.

They walked down a corridor to a large room. At this time of day the ten girls who served in various roles as house slaves were assembled here for night duty. Sitting on a stool outside the door was a heavily bearded man cradling a semi-automatic rifle. He saw Cy and Conrad coming, got to his feet, and opened the door. All three went inside.

The room was plain, the windows barred. A sudden silence fell on the girls, who were seated on cushions on the floor. The bearded man signalled for them to get up and come together, and Cy and Conrad stood there for a moment, appraising them.

Conrad stepped forward and pointed to a girl of about sixteen. She backed away. He took another step, gripped the back of her neck and forced her towards the door. Her pained gasps were shut off as the door closed behind them.

Cy spent a little longer, his eyes roving to and fro. Finally he decided on a girl of similar age to Conrad's. She had the beauty typical of young girls in this region, light-brown complexion, dark hair, and dark sloe eyes. He put out a hand to her. She shrank away, and said, 'Please…'

'Ah, so you speak a little English?'

She shook her head.

'No problem,' he said. 'What we'll be doing is kind of international.'

The bearded man came forward and jerked his head. She extended a hand tentatively and Cy took it and led her out. The sentry followed them and closed the door.

As they walked away Cy looked over his shoulder and smiled at the bearded soldier. Speaking in English, without caring whether the man understood or not, he said, 'No one told me I couldn't enjoy myself.'

40

Jim had made a point of going to the sick bay to visit Holly every day. This time he found her reclining on the bed, fully dressed in her Army Service Uniform except for the boots, which were placed neatly by her locker.

'So you're all set,' he said, pulling up a chair.

'Yes. Sally should be here in a half an hour. She'll take me to the airport and arrange wheelchair boarding and debarkation. My dad will send a car to meet me at Washington.'

'Good. You'll have to be seated in the cars and the plane, so be sure to lie down when you get there.'

She gave him a rueful smile. 'Don't worry. Jed and Petra have drummed it into me.' Her expression became more serious. 'They've been great, actually.'

He nodded. It was good to know the medical staff were performing well – and that it was appreciated.

He glanced around the room. 'Well, I expect you'll be glad to see the back of this place.'

She looked at him. 'Mixed feelings. The first four days I was bored out of my skull. Then I said to myself: You've been running all your life. This is your chance to lie back and take stock. So I did.'

'And did you reach any conclusions?'

'Sort of.' She frowned. 'You're busy, Jim. You don't want to be listening to my ramblings.'

'I've got time. Go ahead.'

She took a breath. 'I always knew I wanted to join the Army, and I guess right from my teens only the SAF would do. Everything I did, all the training, all the bookwork, that was the goal I had in the back of my mind. Most of the time it seemed like it would always be beyond my reach. But look at me now, wonder of wonders, I'm here, a Captain in the SAF, my life's ambition fulfilled. So I'm thinking, okay, is this how you want to spend the rest of your life? And you know what? I'm not sure.'

Jim said, 'You can be in active service for a while, then consider your options. With your resumé you'll have plenty of choice.'

'Mmm, I guess so. Jim, you've been kind to me.'

He gave a short laugh and pointed to her, lying on the bed. 'If this is being kind to you, you must have had a hell of a rocky childhood.'

She smiled, a distant, wistful smile. 'No, I meant…'

Her voice dropped and he leaned in to hear. In a flash she cupped a hand behind his neck and kissed him full on the lips.

He jerked back, passing his tongue over his lips, tasting the waxy perfume of her lipstick. He was breathing fast. 'Holly, this didn't happen. I'm your CO. It's not—'

'Not proper?' She laughed. 'You Englishmen are so correct! Don't worry, it won't happen again.'

A silence fell between them. Then he said quietly, 'Not that I wouldn't like it to happen again.'

'I know.'

Voices outside broke the silence between them and Sally Kent breezed in. 'Oh, sorry.'

Jim leapt to his feet. 'It's okay, Sally. I was just visiting. So, Holly, see you in about six weeks?'

'Before that, I hope. I'll have a check up in Washington after about four. Maybe some physio. With luck I should be back after that.'

'All right, don't rush it, though. Thanks, Sally.' And he left the sick bay, trying to look more relaxed than he felt.

*

All the new equipment had now arrived at Fort Piper, although the soldiers had had only a limited amount of time to familiarize themselves with it.

After one more successful exercise Jim walked back to the main camp with Tommy Geiger.

'Okay, Tommy, it's going well. We've got the four most likely scenarios pretty much nailed. I'll get on with the logistics and we'll deploy out there. Three squads, two for operations and one to manage a base camp with comms links. We'll rotate some of the duties to keep them busy.'

'I don't suppose you'd let me go out with them, would you, Jim? It would be good to see some real action once in a while.'

'Sorry, Tommy. The buck stops with me, so I have to be there to see how these new operating procedures work out. I'll need you here as second-in-command.'

Tommy sighed. 'Okay. Maybe next time. You coming in for lunch?'

'No, I'll have a bite in my office. I want to get this Yemen thing set up as soon as possible. We'll be moving out in the next couple of days.'

41

The camper was parked in one of the stables at The Palace. In it Cy was watching a large transfer go on its way. He leaned back, his fingers interlaced behind his head, and smiled.

'Cy Sloper, you are an artist,' he murmured.

The initial transfer would appear to be a payment for an arms assignment. But the company had a subsidiary that required a transfer across borders, and the subsidiary had a supplier that involved funds making a further jump to Estonia. From there the transaction disappeared into the dark net and went in several directions, each making further hops. He watched the bar on the computer screen stretch across, then finish its travel and disappear. Job done. Funds transferred, the route untraceable.

Cy stretched and looked at his watch. Nearly midnight. Time to wake up one of the girls and take her to bed. He sat up, blood pulsing faster in anticipation. Then he heard a quiet tread behind him. It was Khalil. He spoke in English.

'We are ready for the second stage, Cy,' he said. 'The best part.'

Cy smothered his irritation. 'Go on.'

'They used manual control, as we expected. They increased the output from generators in other parts of the network and power was on again in twenty-two hours, which is quite good.'

'That's good?'

'Yes, good for them but also good for us. At this time of the day all the generators are working hard to compensate for the ones we took out of service. Now we wind up the missing generators in New Jersey and New York State and put all of them on line together. The grid will be too slow to respond. Pouf! Massive overload!'

'Will the generators be wrecked?' Cy asked.

'Maybe, maybe not. But for sure there will be a lot of damage. Then we switch the synchrophasers back in and disconnect. In this way it will be even harder to know where the attack came from.'

Cy smiled. 'Okay, I'll tell Conrad.' As he left the room he looked over his shoulder. 'You're a clever bunch of bastards, Khalil.'

Khalil acknowledged this by bowing his head. 'Thank you, Cy.'

42

Doug was outside checking the level of propane in the gas container when the house lit up with a series of colossal bangs followed by loud cries. He rushed inside.

Rhonda was standing in the kitchen, mouth slightly open, staring at smoke coming out of the dishwasher, the fridge, and the kettle. The hand-held homogenizer was lying on the counter top and she was rubbing her elbow.

'You okay?'

'Um, got a shock, went right up my arm.' She examined her blackened fingertips, rubbed a thumb across them, and put them under a tap. Over her shoulder she said, 'Check the kids.'

'Where are they?'

'Upstairs in their rooms.'

He took the stairs two at a time, stumbling and cursing as he missed a step.

'Everyone okay in here?' he shouted. 'Nige? Maddy?'

Nigel's voice came out of the darkness. 'My computer went bang. I've lost *everything*!'

Madeleine said. 'It's a real poo. Right in the middle of my favourite show.'

He went into her bedroom first. It reeked with the acrid smell of burnt electronics, but there was no fire. In Nigel's bedroom he noticed the same smell. A wisp of smoke trailed from the computer and twisted its way to the ceiling, catching the light from the window on its way.

He galloped downstairs and looked around the study. There was a faint smell of burning in here, too. His lap top was on the desk. It hadn't been on charge, and it looked all right. On the window sill the router had blown to pieces.

Rhonda came in behind him.

'I don't get it,' he murmured. 'There's a surge protector in the distribution board.' He peered below the desk. 'Jesus, it blew that, too.'

He turned and frowned. She was still rubbing her fingers. 'You all right?'

'My fingers are still numb. What happened?'

'Must have been a lightning strike.'

'Weather outside looks okay.'

'That's true. First the black-out, then this. Weird.'

*

In the control room an array of blank screens flickered, then came on. Red lights flashed all over the topological map of the system. The supervisor hurried over.

'What happened, Carl?'

'All twenty-five generators came back, all at once. It put a massive surge through the network. Just look at what it's taken out.' He pointed at the map.

The supervisor's phone was already in his hand. He clicked, waited, then said, 'Ma'am? We have a situation here.'

*

'What am I supposed to do, Rhonda?' Doug stood in the kitchen, palms out. 'Can't get cash – either the ATMs aren't working or they haven't got any more cash to put in them. I'm low on gas, because the gas stations were mobbed yesterday. It's even worse today. Cars backed up almost to the highway, and most of the pumps are dry already. How am I going to get to work? No bus service, no rail—'

'Why aren't the trains running?'

'Signal systems are down on every line. Any case, they need power, too.'

'Good thing you got some groceries in before.'

'Yeah, but how long's that going to last?'

*

In the White House Situation Room the three Directors – Chester Hardman, Mike Randall, and Laura Gianni – met in the break-out room again.

'The senior staff will be meeting in the Surge Room in fifteen minutes,' Randall said. 'The President's taking a close interest, and she'll be in the chair. I'd like the three of us to be situation-aware beforehand. Laura, what's the current position on the energy front?'

Laura Gianni shook her head. 'Frankly? Chaos. This surge did a lot of damage, and it's going to take time to fix. We're prioritizing.'

'Hospitals?' Hardman asked. 'How are they coping?'

'Surgical theatres can run on backup generators for a while, but only for a while. Most of that equipment runs on diesel or liquid gas, and fuel supplies are delayed because road and rail transport's a mess. Then there are people being treated in their own homes: dialysis machines, oxygen deliveries, stuff like that. The longer it goes on, the more they're at risk. Emergency services will have first call on what gets through, but it'd be best if we could restore power. Trouble is, it's so widespread – sub-stations and transformers damaged and power lines down all over New Jersey and New York State. The engineers are working 24/7.'

'How long's it going to take?'

She shrugged. 'Hard to say right now. One week? Two? Could be more.'

Hardman passed a hand round the back of his neck. 'Jesus. People will start getting desperate. There'll be civil unrest, looting... Mike, how the hell did this happen? Is this another trap door thing, like the airliners?'

'No, not this time. I spoke to my Senior Analyst, Naomi Fine, this morning. She started by looking for a trap door and there wasn't one, so they were stumped for a while. There are millions of lines of code in those programs and unless you know what you're looking for it's hopeless. But she's smart. She remembered a worm that fitted the picture. It was developed by our own people some years back and somehow got leaked into the public domain. Remember that?'

Gianni and Hardman both nodded. Randall went on:

'It spreads through computers but only has one target; the rest don't even know it's there. Anyway she searched for the sequence and found it, buried in a lot of other code that also shouldn't have been there. Clearly it gave someone total access to the control systems of the Smart

Grid. How it got in there we don't yet know, but we've extracted it now. The software's okay to use again.'

Gianni said, 'Well that's good to hear, Mike, but the problem we have right now is repairing the physical damage.'

Hardman ran the fingers of one hand through his hair, then realized what he'd done and patted it back into place. 'So who's responsible?' he asked. 'North Korea? They're the usual culprits.'

Randall shook his head. 'I put that to Naomi. She says no. The clue is in the extra code. The NKs write code in a certain style. It's taught to them in the Command Automation University in Pyongyang and we've seen it before in the work of Unit 110. It's not obvious, of course, like code written in Korean. They're wise to that these days; they write English code.'

'Pity.'

'I'm not sure it would have helped. Korean language can come from South as well as North Korea. Cyrillic doesn't nail it to Russia either. It could always be somebody someplace else, who wants to make it look like North or South Korea or Russia.'

'All right, so who?'

'We don't know,' Randall said, 'but she says it's skilfully written to merge into the existing code. It reminds her a bit of that trap door sequence she found in the aviation exploit.'

Hardman frowned. 'What happened about that? I heard they arrested someone.'

Randall said, 'They did, but he wasn't the real culprit. Far as I know that one's off the radar.'

They fell silent for a full minute. Then Hardman sighed.

'This business is costing the country billions a day,' he said. 'Dammitall, we've got a cyber warfare capability. Can't we retaliate?'

Randall said, 'Not without a clear attribution. If we got it wrong it'd be interpreted as a first strike and things could escalate quickly.' He hesitated, eyes narrowed. 'You know…'

'Yes?'

'If it was a nation state a hostile action like this wouldn't come out of the blue. There'd be some sort of run-up, a serious deterioration in international relations.'

Hardman said, 'There hasn't been anything like that recently.'

'I know, which suggests a nonstate source for this attack.'

'Islamic terrorists? A bunch of jihadi madmen couldn't have managed it, surely?'

Randall said, 'I think you're underestimating them. What hits the headlines are terrorist attacks by demented zealots and brain-washed individuals wearing suicide belts who think they're going to blow themselves to Paradise. But there's a more sophisticated side to it. They can hire the technical know-how they need. They may even have it in house, among Western-educated guys who go out to join them. Those people may or may not share their hosts' religious views, but it hardly matters. The point is, they're working for them. Right now there does seem to be a prime candidate for a unit of that sort.'

'The mobile jihadi outfit I've been hearing about?' Hardman asked.

Randall nodded slowly. 'That's exactly what I'm thinking.'

Hardman glanced at his watch. 'We'd better get inside. Will Templeton be at this meeting?'

'You bet,' Randall said. 'So will our esteemed Director of National Intelligence, breathing down his neck.'

'Good. I'll have a word with both of them.'

43

Jim had hammered home the message of surprise to his people so often that he wasn't about to forget it himself. So when more than thirty US service personnel arrived in the Yemen they weren't emerging in full view at Sana'a International Airport. Instead they disembarked from a USAF Worldmaster III at the secret Code 80 airbase. As soon as Jim had seen the men settled into temporary accommodation he asked for a driver, and an E2 from the base was assigned to drive him to Sana'a in an all-terrain.

He returned the following morning and summoned the squad leaders: Eddie Mayer, who would be leading Blue Team, and Ted Nichols, who would be leading Red Team; he'd be leading Green Team himself. They stood at a big table in the ops room and he took a rolled-up map from under his arm and spread it out for them.

'I spent quite a bit of time with this guy Youssef, Holly Cressington's driver on her mission. You were with them, Ted.'

'Seemed like an okay guy to me,' Ted Nichols said.

'My impression, too. He certainly knows the country. What's more important to us, he knows which villages are inhabited and which aren't. There was fierce fighting throughout this zone,' he drew his fingers over the map, 'driving out first al-Qaeda in the Arabian Peninsula and then the Islamists, town by town and village by village. The ones I've ringed in blue are uninhabited now, evacuated during the conflict and too damaged now for anyone to go back to.'

Ted and Eddie rolled the ends of the map back so that they could view the whole of it.

'What's the target, Jim?' Eddie asked.

'Okay, I can tell you now. The destruction of the US Embassy in Sana'a – you saw the videos. We're after a cyber warfare unit that's probably responsible.'

They jerked forward. Ted murmured, 'No shit.'

'A member of that unit, an American guy called Cy Sloper, also seems to have been interfering with the navigation systems of airliners back home. On-board collision avoidance systems prevented five disasters before the FAA closed things down.'

Eddie whistled softly.

'One of the other people in the unit,' Jim went on, 'is a former sergeant with Special Forces Reconnaissance Detachment Alpha, name of Conrad Lazar. Remember him at all? He was in a recon team with us on several missions back around 2050.'

They shook their heads.

Ted said, 'Before my time.'

Eddie said, 'Mine, too.'

'Well, this guy has a major grudge against the SAF. I'm pretty sure he masterminded the ambush that got Brian Murdoch killed. He's probably calling the shots with this cyber unit, so it won't be a pushover. The US wants their guts for garters. So do I, Lazar especially.'

'Too right,' Eddie said.

'Now,' Jim said, 'Sloper and Lazar were inserted by a jihadi they met in prison, so it's fair to assume they're aligned with the jihadis and operating to their agenda. Our problem is, they're highly mobile. We believe they've equipped a large camper of some sort, and they also have two all-terrains. JSOC has high altitude drones looking for them, and we need to move quickly when they've been spotted. Question is,' he waved spread fingers over the map, 'where's the best place to base ourselves?'

They looked blank.

'All right,' he said. 'Put it this way. You're a Special Forces Reconnaissance guy in charge of a cyber cell in Yemen. Where are you based?'

Eddie Mayer said slowly, 'Nowheres. Sounds like they're doing it right. I wouldn't want to spend more than a few days in one place either. Too dangerous.'

Jim nodded encouragingly.

Ted Nichols said, 'I'd hole up in one of those derelict villages, then move on to another one. The fewer people who know where we are, the better.'

Eddie said, 'Yeah, but sooner or later we're gonna need food, water, fuel, stuff like that.'

Ted shrugged. 'Best place to get them would be the jihadi-controlled area, up here.' He pointed to the eastern area of the country. 'Drop by, do the shopping, and go back on the move again.'

'I agree,' Jim said. 'And if you look at the distribution of these ruined villages they could do a long loop out of the jihadi-controlled area over here and back this way.' He traced an ellipse. 'So where should we plant ourselves?'

Eddie pointed to the middle of the ellipse. 'Somewhere in this area, I guess. Then you're only a couple of hundred miles from them, wherever they show up.'

Jim looked closely at the map and pointed. 'There's a derelict village in that zone. Shabwaz.' He straightened up. 'Okay, we'll head for Shabwaz. If it's suitable we'll set up camp there. Tell your squads we'll rest here overnight, but be ready to move at 0600.'

They made a move to go, but Eddie paused at the door. 'Jim?'

'Yes?'

'I'm real glad to be on this one. I mean *real* glad.'

Ted said, 'Yeah, me too.'

Jim nodded. 'The men are going to feel the same way. Let's keep that focus – all of us.'

44

The camper was still parked in one of the stables of the former palace. Inside it, spirits were high. When news of their successful disruption of the Eastern Connection reached them there'd been high-fives all round.

Despite this, and actually to no one's surprise, it had failed to lift the black cloud that was Conrad Lazar's constant companion. His beetling eyebrows remained fixed in their permanent frown and he'd already set the team to work on the next exploit. He was taking a closer interest in this one than anything that had preceded it. Cy Sloper was in the operations section with the team when he became aware of the big man standing over them.

'How far have you got?' he demanded, speaking in English to Khalil Masood.

Cy started to reply but Conrad cut him off with an impatient wave of a hand. 'Let him tell me.'

'We are inside the SCADA system – that's the Supervisory Control and Data Acquisition system.'

Lazar's face contracted with irritation. 'I know what it is, dummy.'

'You want us to cut the water supply?'

'No, I don't want you to cut the fucking water supply.' He sighed. 'There's more to cyber warfare than piddling around with lines of code. The first stage is *research*.' He prodded his chest with his middle finger. '*I've* done the research.'

All the operatives were watching him now.

He grimaced, as if explaining himself further was a painful necessity, then said:

'Look, this plant was commissioned a few years back. It supplies water to Wake County and part of Durham County. We're talking about a densely populated chunk of North Carolina – it includes cities like Raleigh-Durham and its suburbs and satellite towns. Demand for water is high, so they had to identify new sources. That's a problem, because there's a shortage of new sources.' He gave them a grim smile. 'You know what they did?'

A fierce enthusiasm seemed to surge up inside Lazar. Cy had never seen him so animated or heard him talk so much. He felt a small thrill of excitement.

This must be it. This is the exploit Conrad's been working up to all this time.

Khalil and the others waited.

'No? Well I'll tell you. They used waste water that had been condemned. Yes, foul, contaminated water. It's usually just treated lightly and sent out to sea because it carries such a high microbial burden.'

Cy cut in. 'Sorry, Conrad, but you need to explain what you mean by that.'

This time Conrad didn't seem to mind the interruption. 'I'm talking about bugs – *E. coli*, *cryptosporidium*, *giardia*, *salmonella,* and a whole bunch of unpleasant viruses and toxins. But that's okay, because this plant is the very latest in water treatment. It takes in that foul water, and after a few stages it looks clear, and it probably tastes okay, but the bugs are still there.' He held up a finger, and repeated, '*The bugs are still there.* After that they get removed in a highly effective disinfection stage.' The finger turned and pointed at Khalil's chest. 'That's the stage I want knocked out.' He shrugged. 'Of course, you'll have to lock the sensors at the same time to show the last reading. That way the company thinks they're still sending out nice pure drinking water to all their customers.'

Khalil uttered a soundless whistle. 'That will be difficult.'

'You're up to it.'

He turned on his heel and strode away. Cy scuttled after him.

'I take it the SAF is one of this company's customers?' Cy said.

'Correct.'

'So they get the runs, is that it?'

'No.'

They left the camper, stepped into the searing heat of the day and crossed the sunlit compound to the main building. At the entrance Conrad stopped and turned to him.

'To start with they'll be getting stomach cramps, throwing up, and shitting blood. But some of those bugs are lethal, especially in those concentrations, so it's going to get worse, and quickly. A lot will die, others will be invalided out with kidney damage.'

Cy nodded slowly. 'And how many civilians affected?'

'Millions.'

Cy's voice rose in pitch. 'Companies will close. There'll be lost working hours, insurance claims, class actions against the water company, the contractors, the government – this could be the biggest caper yet.'

Conrad nodded. He entered The Palace and continued down a corridor with Cy still in pursuit.

Cy said, 'I still don't understand how this affects the SAF, though. All right, you take out a few, maybe more. They can be replaced, can't they?'

Conrad shook his head, then stopped again. 'The SAF gets an appropriation from the Department of Defense. They have to defend it, year on year.'

Cy said, 'So?'

'So think about what's going to happen. There are several million people in the affected area, all ill, a lot dying. Emergency services can't cope and their staff are sick, too. What does a state do in that situation? It moves the US Army and the National Guard in to keep order, transport patients, and so on. The troops avoid the local water supply – if they have any sense – and they do a great job. And where is the SAF all this time? Fucking nowhere. The nearest military installation isn't lifting a finger to help out because they're in bed, sicking up their guts. It's a public relations disaster for them.'

'Yeah, but—'

'Shut up and let me finish. By the time it's all blown over the SAF has lost a lot of men and they need to recruit and train replacements before they can be operational again. So they apply for funding. Will they get it? Will they hell! People will start to remember that these guys, who are supposed to be supermen, weren't around when they were really needed. This and our other exploits have cost the government billions of dollars so they'll be looking at ways of saving money. Top of the list: the SAF. Bringing them up to strength will be costly, and there's no case for it, not any more. So they'll merge what's left of them with the SEALs or Delta Force. End of the fucking SAF.'

Cy said, 'Jeez, you sure figured things out, Conrad.'

Conrad nodded. 'Yeah. And the neat part is: we don't have to fire a single shot.'

45

The four big desert-going vehicles drew in to Shabwaz and came to a halt. With six balloon tyres and the curious suspension developed from Mars exploration technology they could travel at thirty or more miles an hour over the roughest terrain. Now, however, even they faced a challenge. This had once been a sizeable village but it had suffered badly from the shelling. Barely a house had escaped damage. Most had collapsed inwards, filling the space with rubble, from which pieces of ironwork, pipes, and splintered wood projected at odd angles. Others had toppled into the narrow streets, which were now littered with bricks, stones, and plaster, all streaming dust in the desert breeze. Scraps of paper floated along the streets or quivered feebly in the debris.

Jim sent in a patrol to conduct a house-to-house check but there was no sign of habitation, recent or otherwise. The patrol guided the vehicles in over the least obstructed route and they parked up in an open square that may once have been a market. The houses were too damaged to be usable, so they set up tents near the vehicles: a headquarters tent with a satellite link for communications, a large kitchen and mess tent, and a few tents as sleeping quarters. They could just as well have based themselves in open desert but there were advantages to being here. The villages were linked by rudimentary roads, little more than paths through the sand cleared of the larger rocks and low-growing shrubs. These had gradually consolidated with use, and they made both navigation and driving easier. It would be secure enough in the village, with lookouts posted day and night.

They settled down to wait.

*

Now that they knew the target everyone was poised for action, but as day after day went by, and there was still no word, the sense of urgency began to dissipate. The men were used to landing and going more or less straight into action. Waiting around like this didn't suit them. Jim organized local reconnaissance details and exercises to maintain morale but it did little to alleviate the underlying boredom. At times he wondered if the posting to the Yemen had been a gigantic mistake. And then he'd see in his mind's eye the dark, brooding countenance of Conrad Lazar, and he'd remember the book the man had written to sabotage SAF operations, the murderous ambush of Brian Murdoch's team, the disaster narrowly avoided by Holly and her squad, and now the cyber exploits directed against the US and its citizens. And Jim knew he could not leave the Yemen without facing this man and bringing him to justice.

He was in the makeshift HQ at the end of yet another day when a call came through. A corporal held out the phone to him. 'For you, sir.'

Jim took it from him quickly. 'Jim Slater.'

'Jim, it's John Abadi. Is this line secure?'

Jim looked skywards. 'John, the CIA must be subject to cyber attacks every minute of the day. You've got firewalls, packet sniffers, logic traps and God-knows-what-all, so if anyone knows the answer to that question it's you.'

'Yes, well, all right. You're not connected to anything else down there?'

'No.'

'Okay. Where are you, right now?'

Jim fought down growing irritation. 'You know darned well where we are. Fully deployed, waiting for the call. Have been for more than two weeks now.'

There was a sigh. 'Yeah. Just that the Director's hopping up and down about this latest attack.'

'Another one?'

'Yeah, power supply network this time, affected a lot of the Eastern Interconnection. It's causing massive disruption and it'll cost billions to put right. Homeland Security's giving him a sore ear, and so is everyone else. They want to know why these people haven't been stopped. He wants results.'

Jim gritted his teeth. 'Well if he wants results he'd better find us a target.'

'I know. Nothing yet, they may have gone to ground somewhere. I wanted to be able to tell him you're ready to move when we do pick up something.'

'You can tell him that, all right.'

'Okay, thanks Jim.'

Jim closed the connection. When he looked up he saw that everyone was motionless, watching him expectantly. He shook his head.

As he handed the phone back, the corporal said, 'Colonel, it's eleven o'clock. You should get some sleep.'

Jim sighed and rubbed his eyes. Even if Lazar's convoy was on the move at night the chances of reconnaissance drones being in the right sector at the right moment to spot them were slim. It was a waiting game, and unless they got some sort of break it could go on for some time yet.

He nodded to the corporal. 'You're right. What about you?'

'I'll be relieved soon. There's an all-night rota.'

'Okay. Wake me if there's a call.'

'Will do.'

46

Jim slept soundly and there were no interruptions. At The Palace, however, something was happening that would change the entire outcome of his mission.

By 4.00 am the moon had set and the compound, previously striped with pale light and deep shadow, was in total darkness. At the side of the building a door opened quietly and three figures emerged. They closed the door softly behind them, then hurried down a side passage, away from the courtyard that extended to the front.

The cool night air pierced the thin fabric of Latifa's dress but it was fear, not cold, that made her shiver. She knew – they all knew – what would be in store for them if they were caught. To the Sons of the Caliphate an escapee was no different to a lawfully married woman who was unfaithful to her husband. Everyone would be brought out to witness the cruel penalty, and it would not be a simple beheading, but crucifixion or flogging or stoning to death. She remembered little Nadia, just fourteen years old, who couldn't stand the nightly abuse any more and tried to run away. They tied her hands behind her back and placed her up to her chest in a narrow pit so that she couldn't fall over. Then the rest of the girls were forced to throw the first stones. The stones kept falling short, which enraged their captors. They shouted at the girls, slapped and punched them and finally stepped in to finish the job themselves. The one they call Mustafa, with the bad teeth, told them they would be next if they didn't watch. But they closed their eyes before Nadia's poor bloodied head dropped forward, and they condemned her brutal executioners with their silent tears. So Latifa shivered as they reached a wooden gate that marked the limit of the compound. It was padlocked but it wasn't too high to climb over.

Safiya went first, jumping for the top, then hauling herself over. They heard her drop to the other side. Nasrin had more difficulty; her foot slipped and thudded against the door. Latifa's pulse hammered and she said 'Shhh...' and glanced nervously over her shoulder. Nasrin was still struggling, so Latifa stepped up and pushed against the girl's feet until finally she tumbled over. Then it was her turn. She jumped up and brought first one foot, then the other, over the top. She knew she was going to fall awkwardly, so she pushed herself away from the door and landed heavily, but soundlessly, on the other side. Safiya helped her up and holding hands they ran and ran, paying no attention to the sharp stones that stabbed into their bare feet. Eventually they had to pause, doubled over and gasping for breath.

Latifa straightened up. 'Where are we going?' she asked, between gulps of air.

Safiya responded. 'This is an old route, so there must be villages somewhere along it.'

'Suppose the Sons are there, too? They'll take us back!'

'We will be careful. Come on.'

They joined hands and began to run again.

Above them the heavens were littered with stars but it did little to penetrate the darkness. They continued to run blindly, trying to keep to the tightly packed sand and stopping only briefly to rest from time to time. An hour and a half later the black sky began to fade to grey, and the fainter stars disappeared from view. The next time Latifa cast a backward glance a pink blush was rising all along the eastern horizon. Within minutes the sky overhead had lightened to a pale blue and the sere landscape emerged on every side. She bit her lip. It was both good and bad. Good, because the path ahead had become clearer; the packed sand now shone in the sunlight, and the small flinty stones and shells that had lacerated the soles of their feet cast shadows that made them easier to avoid. Bad, because in the full light of day they could be seen for miles. There was nowhere to hide, and their only chance was to put as much distance as possible between themselves and the Palace before their absence was discovered. But half an hour later Nasrin moaned and sank to her knees.

'I can't go any further, Safiya.'

'We can wait a few moments while you get your breath back.'

'It's not that. I hurt too much. You go on without me.'

Latifa turned to Safiya and their eyes met. She said to Nasrin, 'You know we won't do that. We swore at the start we would stick together, whatever happened to us.'

Safiya scanned ahead. She pointed at a dark shape shimmering on the horizon. 'I can see something over there. It must be a village. Can you make it just a little further, Nasrin? We will help you.'

Reluctantly, and with some sharp intakes of breath, Nasrin got to her feet. The three walked unsteadily towards the village.

As they approached they could hear the sounds of a population stirring, taking advantage of the cool early hours of the day. A dog barked and there was a faint buzz of conversation. Pans clattered in a kitchen somewhere.

Safiya said, 'We are still in Sons territory. If they're here we'll have to make for the next village.'

Nasrin shook her head slowly. 'I can't...'

'Very well,' Safiya said, 'we will just have to take a chance. We will try a house. *Imshallah* they won't send us back.'

Latifa inhaled sharply, but she said nothing.

They were approaching a dusty street at the edge of the village. The first house was a modest, stone-built dwelling. They approached cautiously and Safiya knocked on the door. A woman appeared, her eyes widened, and before they could say anything she put a finger to her lips and beckoned them in.

'You have escaped?' she asked.

'Yes,' Safiya said, her voice rising. 'Please don't send us back. They raped us every night, we can't—'

'Hush now, no one will send you back to those devils.'

Latifa gasped with relief. 'The blessings of Allah be upon you.'

Safiya said, 'Are they here, too – the Sons of the Caliphate?'

'No. Sometimes they pass through, that is all.' She turned and called, 'Sadiq! Come and see what we have here.'

The man who appeared wore a pure white cotton thawb and a black-and-white keffiyah secured with a black headband. His beard was threaded with grey and the skin of his face and hands was leathery and brown. Dark, deep-set eyes flickered quickly over the group.

'You must take them to your cousin Fayyad,' the woman said.

He nodded.

She turned back to the girls. 'Sadiq's cousin has contacts. If you have information about the jihadis the Yemeni Army will be very interested. He can arrange for them to pick you up and they will take you somewhere safe. But first you must eat and drink and we will do something about your feet, you poor creatures.'

The man spoke, his voice high and thin. 'Hurry. When they find that you are missing, this village is the first place they will look.'

'You are very kind,' Safiya said, 'but you are putting yourself in great danger.'

He gave her a half-smile. '*You* put yourselves in great danger.'

'Yes, but we had no choice.'

For a moment he was silent, then his expression softened. He said quietly, 'I, too, have no choice.'

For a fleeting moment she just looked at him. Then she took his hand and kissed it.

*

They arrived at Fayyad's house at midday. Sadiq had borrowed a small open-backed truck to bring them here. He'd urged them to crouch down among sacks of cattle feed and then he threw in empty sacks to cover them up.

'If we are stopped by the Sons,' he said, 'there is nothing I can do for you. I will swear that you crept in while I was not looking and I will shout at you, cursing you for bringing me bad luck. Do you understand?'

They were terrified but they had no choice; they had to trust this man and pray to Allah that he would not drive them back to their captors.

They did not encounter any patrols and he did deliver them to Fayyad. After that he departed immediately.

Fayyad was taller than Sadiq and looked a good deal younger. He took one look at the girls and ushered them into a back room.

'We must hide you until we are ready to move. It is not very comfortable but you will be safe if the Sons come looking for you. You understand?'

Safiya nodded. So far these people had done what they promised. She knew the risks they were taking, and she was not about to argue.

Fayyad moved a chest of drawers and lifted some floorboards. He stepped down onto a ladder and descended into a chamber below. A flickering light emerged, then he reappeared and beckoned them to go down. The space was furnished with mattresses on the floor and there was a jug of water and a glass but little else. The light came from a thick candle on an upturned wooden crate. The air was cool and tinged with wax and the sulphurous smell of the burnt match.

He put a finger to his lips. 'Rest here. Be very quiet. This may take a little while. I will bring you something to eat later.'

He ascended the ladder and replaced the floorboards. They heard the chest of drawers being dragged back into place. Then all was silent.

The girls looked at each other and Safiya felt a moment of panic. Had she led them into a trap? Was this really a safe hiding place or a temporary prison, somewhere to hold them until the Sons arrived and gave Fayyad and Sadiq generous rewards. She took a deep breath. These people seemed genuine. She just had to put her trust in Allah.

She settled wearily onto a mattress. Latifa did the same, and Nasrin dropped onto hers with a sigh.

They reached out and held each other's hands. And they waited.

47

The screen displayed the down-camera view from the drone. Major Todd Harper stretched his neck.

'God, don't you just hate these round-the-clock reconnaissance ops?' he said to Hank, who was navigating. 'Who's taking over from us?'

'Mark and Beth.'

'Well, where the hell are they?'

'Todd, there's another hour to go yet.'

'Oh yeah. Shit.'

'Come on, it's not so bad. We were lucky to pull the eight-to-four shift.'

'I know.'

'Turn coming up, Todd. You okay?'

'Yeah, here we go.'

Even with image intensification the moonlit landscape below consisted merely of shades of grey. It was the satellite navigation screen that displayed the papier-mâché relief map, the foothills of mountains in the north-east of Yemen, as if they were in daylight. They checked it from time to time, but only to ensure they were sticking to the search pattern. Their focus had to be on the vague shadows seen by the camera.

Todd sighed and settled the craft on its next sweep. Then they both sat up.

'Infra-red signature!' Hank shouted.

Even as he said it the camera steered and zoomed in automatically. The bright spot separated into three streaks.

'Three vehicles, Todd…'

But Todd was already on the line to Colonel Baxter.

*

The flap of the comms tent moved back and Jim looked up. Sergeant Allison stood in the doorway, his face illuminated by the battery-operated lights, the darkness behind him impenetrable. Allison was in charge of the mess.

'Yes, Gene?'

'Just finished making an inventory, chief. We're running low on food and water. Thought I should let you know.'

'How much is left?'

'Three or four days, is all.' He shrugged. 'Sorry, I stocked for three weeks. Didn't think we'd be out here as long as this.'

'Neither did I, Gene, neither did I. Don't worry, I'll deal with it.'

'Thanks.'

As Allison left, the phone buzzed. It was John Abadi.

He spoke quickly. 'JSOC Reconnaissance got a sighting, Jim. Three vehicles. Guess this is what you were waiting for.'

Jim's heartbeat quickened. 'Where?'

Abadi gave him the coordinates and Jim traced a finger across the large map. 'That's in jihadi-held territory.'

'Yeah, I know.'

'The Yemeni Army is operating in that whole area, John. How do we know it's not one of their patrols?'

'Well, this group is travelling at night. The Yemeni Army usually moves by day.'

'Usually.'

'Yeah.'

'Not good enough. If we ambush the wrong side it could cause an international incident. Do Yemeni soldiers stop anywhere overnight?'

'Their base near Sana'a is a lot easier to defend, so they make excursions from there. Normally they head right back to base.'

'Normally. So you want me to go in, all guns blazing, based on "usually" and "normally"?'

There was a sigh. 'If you don't, you could miss this opportunity.'

Jim thought about it. The political situation out here was still volatile. Yemen's government was an uneasy coalition, forged from a recognition that al-Qaeda in the Arabian Peninsula and the Islamist militants were the common enemy. It had resulted in the restoration of Sana'a as the capital, Saudi had called a halt to their operations, and there was an understanding that US Special Forces could assist in operations on the ground. But if he got this wrong, all that could fall apart. The CIA wouldn't own up to their part in it; they'd duck for cover and leave him to take the fall.

Jim took a deep breath. 'All right, I'll tell you what we'll do. If that convoy doesn't go straight back to the base, it tips the odds a bit more in our favour. So if they stop overnight you give me the coordinates and we'll see what we can do.'

'Okay, sounds good. Thanks, Jim. I'll get back to you.'

The line went dead. Jim looked at the phone, then put it down. He badly wanted this to be the target, but he had to be careful. They could make things worse. A whole lot worse.

The moon cast a silvery light over the encampment as he went to seek out the other two squad leaders. Some of the men were in their tents, grabbing some sleep, but he found Eddie Mayer and Ted Nichols sitting in the open, chatting quietly in the cool of the evening. He led them back to the comms tent and clicked on the light. It was one of the good things about operating in the desert: the solar-powered batteries were always fully charged.

'Just had a call,' he said. 'Reconnaissance reported a group of three vehicles a couple of hundred miles away, moving in a westerly direction.'

Eddie stirred. 'Shall we get going?'

'Not yet. I don't want to move until reconnaissance tells us they've stopped and I get the coordinates.'

He paused, lips tight.

'Something the matter, Jim?' Ted asked.

'I don't know, we're under strength for this kind of operation. I should have brought another squad. Low on supplies, too. I'll contact Tommy Geiger, ask him to fly out another squad and a small truck. They can pick up more supplies at Code 80 and bring them along – kill two birds with one stone.' He checked his watch. 'It's mid-afternoon over there. I'll phone Tommy now.' He looked up. 'Just tell your men reveille at 0400 hours. If I have the coordinates of a stop by then we'll make our move.'

'Suppose they don't stop?' Ted Nichols said. 'Suppose they just keep going?'

'If they keep going right back to Sana'a they'll be Yemeni Army. If they stop they probably aren't.'

Ted said, 'How sure is that, Jim? We don't want to be attacking a Yemeni patrol.'

'My thinking exactly. But they're travelling under cover of darkness, so chances are they're insurgents and they'll make a stop before dawn.'

'Before dawn is cutting it fine,' Eddie said. 'We need to get to them while it's still dark.'

Jim gave them a grim smile. 'If this is the gang we've been waiting for it's a fair bet they know our standard operating procedures. They'll be expecting any attack to come between two and four in the morning. So that's just what we're not going to do.'

48

No sooner had Tommy Geiger put the phone down from Jim's call when there was a light knock at the door. Sergeant Bagley's head appeared. 'Er, Captain Cressington's back, sir. She wants to see you.'

'Holly? Already?' Tommy Geiger said. 'Okay, show her in.'

Holly entered the office and hesitated. 'Hi, Tommy. I was looking for Jim.'

He gestured to the chair in front of the desk and she sat down. 'Jim's out on a mission, Holly, so I'm XO. How're you doing?'

'I'm good. I want to go back to work.'

'Bit soon, isn't it?'

'It's five weeks, Tommy, quite long enough for me. And the doctors said it's okay.'

'Right. Well, er, I expect you'll want to settle in. Maybe do some light exercise.' He looked around the paper-strewn desk and sighed.

'Is there a problem, Tommy?'

He closed and opened his eyes. 'No, yes, well... Sometimes I don't know how Jim copes with all this. Harken wanted me to send three squads to San Salvador, It's a joint exercise with their drug enforcement division. I got them away last week and now Jim wants a fourth squad with him. We're supposed to keep people on standby here in case of a crisis closer to home—'

Holly straightened up in her chair. 'Jim's in the Yemen, isn't he?'

'Well, yes...'

'And he needs another squad?' She opened her hands. 'Okay, I'm here.'

'You? You're not fit yet.'

'Fit enough. Tommy, those people Jim's after, they're the ones who staged that fake kidnap. They nearly killed me and my whole squad. I want back at them.'

She fixed him with those light grey eyes. For a few moments they stared at each other. Then the phone went.

'Secure line,' Tommy said, reaching for it.

Holly got up to go but he flapped his hand to indicate she should stay where she was.

'Fred!' he said. 'How's it going?... Already?... Good... That long?... I see... Yup...Okay.'

He closed the line and returned to Holly. 'Captain Stammers, calling from San Salvador. Job almost done. They'll be back here in three days.' His face clouded. 'Jim won't want to wait that long, and we're short of officers...'

She smiled and tilted her head expectantly.

'Well, all right. Get your people together. I'll arrange a USAF transport. And you'll be picking up supplies at the other end.'

'Thanks, Tommy.' She got to her feet and made to leave the office.

'Holly?'

She turned.

'I'm going out on a limb with this, so for God's sake be careful.'

*

Jim had spent the night in the comms tent, dozing in a chair, waiting to hear from Abadi. The call had come through at two in the morning. It was the news he'd been waiting for: the suspect convoy had stopped. Jim had noted the coordinates and now they were on their way there, the four SAF desert-going vehicles raising a cloud of dust sixty metres wide.

As they neared the village Jim slowed them down and ordered a detour that led them in behind a ridge to conceal their approach. They parked the vehicles and Jim went forward with Eddie to observe the target. The two men lay behind dunes with the rising sun at their backs, looking for personnel or the flash of sunlight from glass or metal. They had their helmet comms switched on.

'Not a big village, is it?' Eddie said.

'One main street, the north end less damaged. Let's try it from a different angle.'

They moved stealthily, keeping low, then stopped again and raised their binoculars.

'See the house one from the end?' Jim asked.

'Yeah, looks like an all-terrain in there.'

'Where's the camper?'

'I don't know but they're at home, all right.'

Jim grimaced. He'd have been happier with a more positive sighting, but it was time to make a decision.

'Okay, we'll go in. Let's brief the others.'

The three teams were waiting for them by the vehicles.

'Right,' Jim said. 'You know the drill. Take 'em captive if you can, shoot if you have to. No one gets away or they'll tell their buddies how we did it, and that has to stay a secret. Red and Blue, in the forward positions. Green, you'll do the flying. We'll use the arrow formation, straight down the main street. Any questions? Good, let's go.'

When everyone was in place, Jim gave the orders through the helmet comms.

'Respirators on. Drones, go.'

Seven small drones took off under the control of members of Green Team and headed for the village in arrowhead formation. Jim watched with approval. They'd had limited time to practise this new technique but they'd learned fast. A signal to the drones deployed the anaesthetic gas as they entered the main street, flew along its length, then split left and right to lay the gas down on the other side of the buildings. The lead drone turned and made a second pass down the main street.

'Green, land the drones. Red and Blue Teams, stand by.'

He allowed a few minutes for the gas to enter the buildings through the vacant windows, then 'Red and Blue, go.'

They mopped up quickly, just as they'd practised several times back at Fort Piper, going from house to house and cable-tying the wrists and ankles of the unconscious insurgents. Jim watched their progress through binoculars. Then a movement caught his eye. He'd glimpsed two figures as they appeared between a couple of damaged houses. They were running along the street behind.

'Ted, Eddie, two in the street behind, running to your left.'

'On it!'

He'd lost sight of them now, but moments later he heard shouts. A volley of shots echoed around the houses, then silence. Jim left Green Team gathering up the drones and hurried down to the village.

Eddie came up, breathing heavily. 'Challenged them, Jim, but they didn't stop. We had to shoot.'

'Okay, right decision.'

Ten jihadis were still alive, and Red Team had distributed them between four of the ruined houses. Most were still unconscious. A couple had worked themselves into a sitting position and were watching their captors, dark bloodshot eyes roving from one to another.

'Where's Ahmed?' Jim said. Ahmed was a second-generation American. When it came to local dialects he was the SAF's most fluent Arabic speaker.

'Here, sir,' Ahmed responded, coming up behind him.

'Ask them what they were doing here,' Jim said.

Ahmed put the question to the two who were watching them. Jim could hear the harshness in his tone. One of the men sneered. The other spat on the ground.

Ahmed turned to Jim. 'I don't think you'll get anything out of this scum, Colonel.'

Ted came in. 'Jim, Eddie, come and look at this.'

Jim said, 'Stick around, Ahmed. I may need you in a bit.'

He joined Eddie and followed Ted to the house near the end of the street where they'd seen the all-terrain parked. The vehicle was there and now the rear door was open. The loading bay was filled with rifles, ammunition boxes, and suicide belts.'

Ted pointed. 'These guys were planning a suicide attack.'

Jim frowned. 'Did you find the other vehicles?'

'Yeah, two more like this one.'

'No camper?'

'No.'

'And no Americans?'

'Sorry, no.'

'Damn.'

He walked back to the vehicles with Eddie. The big man said, 'I know these weren't the guys you really wanted, Jim, but the drones, the gas – it all worked like a charm.'

'Yeah, but our primary target is still out there, and we have no idea where.' He sighed. 'All right, I'll call in the Yemeni Army to collect this lot. You guys head back to base.'

'You don't want us to stay?'

'No. The Yemenis know there are Special Forces operating here, but they don't know who, how many, or where they are. It has to stay that way.'

'What about you?'

'I'll wait here for the Army.'

'You could come back with us, Jim. Those jihadis aren't going any place.'

'I know, but we need to hand over properly. Who's managing comms?'

'Wayne is.'

'Okay, leave him here. Carter, too. And Ahmed. We can use his language skills when the Yemeni Army gets here.'

*

The Yemeni Army turned up in quite a convoy: a jeep, an all-terrain, then a troop carrier, then another two all-terrains. Almost before the jeep had stopped, a portly officer in the front passenger seat had got down and he was walking over, arms swinging wide. As Jim went to meet him he registered the three gold stars on the man's epaulettes and extended his hand.

'Colonel James Slater. Thanks for coming, Captain. Let me show you what's here.'

He led the way over to the ruined houses where the captives were, and then showed him the vehicles with the munitions and suicide belts.

The Captain turned dark, liquid eyes on him. He spoke in heavily accented English. 'You have saved many lives, Colonel.'

'No,' Jim said, and pointed at the man's chest. '*You* have saved many lives.'

The man's brow creased.

Jim turned round. 'Ahmed, explain to the Captain that we aren't here. He must accept the credit for capturing these insurgents.'

Ahmed hurried up and spoke rapidly in Arabic. The Captain's face cleared. He nodded deeply to Jim. 'Thank you. How did you find?' He jerked a thumb over his shoulder.

Jim caught Ahmed's eye and he translated as Jim spoke. 'Luck, really – ours, not theirs. We were looking for a jihadi convoy, two large all-terrains and a big camper. Have you seen anything like that?'

The Captain's moustache drooped a little and he shook his head. 'I am sorry.'

'Okay, it was worth a try. Wayne, Carter, Ahmed, a quick check around to make sure we haven't left anything behind. Then we'll pull out.'

Ten minutes later they were back at their vehicle. Jim said Carter could drive, and they got in. Carter reached for the ignition, but Jim put a hand on his arm. He'd noticed that the Captain was holding a handset extending on a coiled lead from the jeep. He was speaking into it and glancing in their direction. He passed the handset back and walked over.

Jim jumped down. 'You have a sighting?'

Ahmed had joined them and with a glance at him the Captain responded in Arabic at some length.

Ahmed said, 'He hasn't had a sighting but he's received a report. Three girls escaped from a jihadi compound. Sounds like they were being kept there as sex slaves. They're being passed through some kind of local pipeline. The people handling them want the Yemeni Army to pick them up.'

'Could be a trap,' Jim said.

Ahmed put it to the Captain, who shook his head and replied.

'Apparently the source is reliable,' Ahmed said. 'He contacted HQ with a password, and now HQ wants the Captain to respond. The rendezvous is only 50 ks from here. He'll send our prisoners back to Sana'a with an escort, but he's going to pick these girls up. He wants to know if we're interested.'

'Why us?'

'The girls say they have information. They mentioned some Americans.'

Jim blinked, then answered quickly. 'Okay, tell the Captain we're interested. We'll follow him.'

The Captain nodded and spoke again.

Ahmed said, 'Where we're going is on the edge of the territory held by the Sons of the Caliphate. He says it's best to travel with the windows open and the rifles pointing out.'

49

Safiya woke with a start. Like the two other girls, she'd been resting on one of the mattresses in the cellar. At first she just lay there, her body still quivering with anxiety about their situation, the risk of recapture – and the dreadful consequences. Gradually her physical exhaustion overcame her and she'd fallen asleep. From above them came the noise that must have aroused her: the sound of the chest of drawers being shuffled across the floor. All three girls were sitting up now, wide awake, and Safina began to breath fast. Light streamed in as the floorboards were lifted. Then the silhouette of a head appeared in the aperture.

A voice said, 'It's me, Fayyad.'

She moistened her lips. Was there anyone with him?

He came down the ladder carrying two bags. She continued to watch the opening but he appeared to be alone.

'In here,' he said softly, pointing to one bag, 'you will find a bottle of water and some food: tajeen-bread, olives, dates, and fruit.' He pointed to the other bag. 'In here there are three headscarves. They are coloured, not black like the ones you are wearing. Put them on; you will blend more easily in a crowd. You leave in about three hours. Many women are in the street at that time, going to the market. My wife will come with you; they will be looking for three women, not four. She will lead you to another house. After it is dark a car will come for you.'

Safiya was breathing more easily. She said, 'I don't know how to thank you—'

'Don't thank me now. The danger is not yet over.' He went back up the ladder and the light from the entrance was extinguished once again as the floorboards were replaced.

The candle shivered in the slight draught. It did not look much lower. She could not have been asleep for more than an hour or two.

They ate and drank, then inspected the headscarves. Nasrin selected one with a pretty, flowery pattern, Latifa chose one in a plain light brown, and Safiya took the last, which was silver-grey. Then there was nothing to do but wait again. Finally the now familiar sounds of shifting furniture came from upstairs, the floorboards were lifted, and Fayyad beckoned to them.

They went up the ladder. A woman was standing there holding some shopping bags and baskets. She was middle-aged, stout enough to fill her robe, and her face was brown and creased. 'This is my wife, Mira,' he said. 'She will go with you.'

Mira nodded to them and handed over bags and baskets, so that each of them was carrying something. 'Do not look around you,' she said, pointing a finger at them. 'We are simply women going to the market.'

Mira led the way. At the front door Safiya hesitated and looked out. It was the first time since their escape that they would be showing themselves in public in full daylight and she felt terribly vulnerable. She exchanged glances with the other girls. There was trepidation in their eyes, too.

Mira said a brisk 'Come', and gingerly they followed her into the open street.

The sun was lower in the sky, although warmth still radiated from walls and stretches of stone paving. The street was thronged with women. They wore robes mainly of black or brown, and headscarves of a variety of colours and patterns, and all were carrying baskets or bags. Thanks to Fayyad, Safiya felt they were merging well. She resisted the temptation to swivel her head from side to side but her eyes continually roved to and fro, looking out for the black robe, headscarf, and beard of one of the hated Sons. Her mouth was bone dry and she gripped her basket tightly to stop her hand from trembling. Nasrin was very quiet. Latifa seemed more relaxed. She was chatting with Mira.

Soon they heard the rising hubbub of a busy market and the street opened into a square filled with stalls. After so many weeks of suffocating confinement in The Palace her heart lifted at the familiar sights and smells – the makeshift structures with their awnings, the hanging pots, pans, lamps and candlesticks, robes and headscarves, the counters loaded with fruit and vegetables and spices. The air was full of the shouts of the vendors and the buzz of conversation from the women. In another life, another time, she would have lingered, but they had to keep up with Mira. She weaved back and forth until they were behind the stalls, in among piles of boxes and crates. They walked quickly between them to a dark alley beyond and down a narrow, dusty street lined with tall houses. Mira entered a door on the right and they filed into a cool, dark hallway. She closed the door carefully behind them, then led them up a wooden staircase to a landing and ushered them into a room. Safiya crossed to the window and saw that it overlooked a small yard at the back of the house.

'Wait here,' Mira said. 'I will go into the market and buy a few things, then I will go home. In a couple of hours it will be dark and a car will come. The driver's name is Rafi. He will come to this room and take you to meet someone from the Yemeni Army. Allah be with you.'

The girls stepped forward and each embraced the woman and kissed her cheeks. Safiya's eyes were full of tears.

'May Allah bless you and your husband, Mira,' she said.

Then the woman was gone.

*

The Captain led the convoy in his jeep. They drove with the windows open, Jim holding his rifle and scanning the landscape on his side. There was a big Yemeni Army all-terrain in front of them and another behind them, both bristling with rifles.

Carter, who was at the wheel, grunted, 'Something up ahead.'

It looked at first sight like another village. They drove in and ahead of them the Captain's jeep came to a halt. Carter pulled their all-terrain in behind him. On either side of them was a row of long, low concrete huts.

Jim looked at Carter. 'What do you make of this?'

'Looks like it used to be a barracks,' Carter said.

'My impression, too. Let's go. Take the rifles. If this meeting has been leaked to the jihadis it's a perfect place for an ambush.'

They got out and followed the Captain and his three men to the largest hut. It wasn't locked and they went in, leaving the door open. One of the Yemeni soldiers remained outside, his rifle at the ready.

The interior of the hut was stiflingly hot. There was a table and several chairs and everything was covered in a fine layer of dust. They sat down.

The Captain folded his arms and stretched out his legs. 'Now,' he said, 'we wait.'

Jim picked at his shirt, which was sticking to him. 'What is this place?'

'It used to be a Yemeni Army base,' the Captain said, with Ahmed translating as before. 'It is abandoned now because it is too isolated and the jihadis are not far away. However it is useful as a rendezvous. We would never use the villages. There may be no jihadis but there could be informers. The villagers' lives would be put at risk.'

Jim nodded. 'Who will be coming here?'

'His name is Rafi. We have met before. He will be bringing three girls. We pay him, of course. He could get more by taking them back to the jihadis but he hates them. They killed his son.'

They fell silent. Jim got up and crossed to a window. The light outside was fading fast. One of the Yemeni soldiers left the hut and returned with a battery-operated lamp. He was just in time; the sun set quickly and soon the darkness outside was complete. The temperature began to drop to a more comfortable level.

'Not long now,' the Captain said.

Forty minutes later there were three warning knocks at the door and they got up and went outside. The rattle of an old diesel motor floated across the desert and echoed lightly from the huts. Then a car appeared, travelling on side lights alone. They dispersed quickly, keeping away from the light that spilled from the open door of the hut.

The car approached, stopped in the light, and the noise of the engine died, leaving a sudden silence. After a short pause the driver's door opened and a man got out. He shouted something and Jim caught the name Rafi.

The Captain emerged and approached him. Jim moved closer but stayed out of sight at the side of the hut. There was a brief conversation. The Captain looked inside the car, returned to the man called Rafi, and Jim saw money changing hands. Then the man opened the front and rear doors and three girls got out. He closed the doors and got back in the car. The engine coughed into life and he drove off. They waited until the noise of the motor had faded, then they all emerged from the darkness.

The girls faces were white in the light from the hut, their eyes wide and dark. Jim said to Ahmed, 'Tell them they're safe now. They're with the Yemeni Army.'

Ahmed repeated the message and one of the girls murmured *'Alhamdulillah'* and all three hugged each other, sobbing with relief. After a respectful pause, the Captain ushered them into the hut and indicated the chairs.

Jim said, 'Ahmed, you stay here, I'll need you to interpret. Everyone else outside. We don't want to crowd these kids.' Then he signed the Captain by wagging his finger between the three Yemeni soldiers. The Captain barked an order and the three went outside. Jim took a chair and sat down.

The Captain spoke softly to the girls and Jim realized he was asking them their names.

The girls responded, 'Safiya', 'Latifa,' and – with another sob – 'Nasrin'.

The Captain went on, Ahmed translating as he went. Ahmed was really very good at this, Jim thought, good enough for a job at the UN.

'He's asking them where they were first captured.'

One of the girls replied.

'He's telling them it's too dangerous to go back there. He will take them to Sana'a and they will be looked after. When the jihadis are defeated they will be able to go back home.'

The girls nodded and one said something.

Ahmed said, 'The one in the middle is Safiya. She thanked him. She seems to be speaking for the others.'

The Captain spoke again and Ahmed continued to translate, so Jim could follow the entire exchange. 'You have had a terrible experience and you are very brave girls to have escaped. But you can help us to defeat the evil men who took you. Will you do that?'

Two of the girls looked blank but Safiya sat tall and said they would.

'Where were you held?'

'We don't know the name of the town. They took us from our homes, put us in a closed vehicle, and drove us there. But it was a large building with many rooms. They called it The Palace. In front of it was a courtyard with walls all around, and there was a sentry at the gate.'

The Captain's eyes narrowed. He said something to Ahmed, who relayed it to Jim. 'He knows somewhere that fits this description. It was originally the palace of a powerful Imam. It's not too far from here.'

The Captain returned to the girls. 'Are these the clothes you wore there? You did not have to cover your faces?'

Safiya's lip curled. 'The jihadis, they told us women must dress modestly at all times except in front of their husbands. But here, they said, all of us are your husbands. They laughed a lot when he said this.'

Nasrin interjected, 'It was true. We had to lay with every one of them.' Her breath caught and she wiped a tear away with the back of her hand.

'How did you escape?'

Safiya took a deep breath. 'We had planned it for a long time, the three of us. We said if there was a night when we were left alone we would do it. Last night Latifa and I were not needed – the men had been working hard at something, I think, and they wanted only to sleep. But Nasrin was taken – by the big American.'

Jim leaned forward. With Ahmed's help he asked, 'Can you describe this man?'

Safiya started slightly on hearing his voice. Then she said slowly, 'Tall, heavy. Thick eyebrows that met in the middle. Of all the men he was the worst – every one of the girls said the same. He was brutal, he enjoyed hurting us. And when he'd finished taking his pleasure he would kick us hard, right out of the bed, and leave us to crawl away.'

Latifa added, her voice shaking, 'He made you feel like an object, nothing more than a vessel for his hateful seed.'

The Captain turned to Jim, his expression conveying both sympathy and disgust. 'They are not men, these people,' he said quietly, 'they are animals.'

Safiya said, 'He was filled with hate that one. I think he even hated himself for wanting us.'

She swallowed and looked down at her hands.

Jim asked, 'Do you know the name of this man?'

She straightened up slightly. 'The other American called him Conrad.'

Jim nodded grimly. 'The other American?'

'Pale, pimply. A weedy young man. I heard Conrad call him Cy.'

Jim nodded again. 'Thank you very much. We know both of these men.'

The Captain shot him a quizzical look, then turned back. 'Please go on,' he said.

She sighed. 'That night he took Nasrin. She's the smallest and the youngest, and he knew it would hurt her more than the others.'

A small moan escaped from Nasrin and she began to tremble. Latifa took her hand and squeezed it.

Safiya continued, 'When he kicked her out she came back to us and said we must go. She was in a lot of pain and I argued with her but she was very brave. She said she could not bear to have it happen again. And on her way back she had seen that the man they always posted outside our door had fallen asleep.'

The Captain said, 'How did you get past the sentry on the gate?'

'We could not go that way. But when I was on kitchen duty I used to take the waste outside. In the passage there I saw a heavy wooden gate leading to the back. It is secured with a padlock but it is not hard to climb over. I think many years ago they delivered things and collected the waste from there – now they just come to the front like everyone else. So that is how we went. We waited until the moon set and it was really dark outside and then we went down to the kitchen and out into the passage. We climbed over the gate and ran. Poor Nasrin was suffering badly so we stopped at the first village we saw. It was light by then and the people were already up. They were very kind. The woman bandaged our feet, because they were bleeding – the jihadis always took away our shoes at night and the stones in the desert were very sharp. We were taken to another house and then another and finally this man Rafi came in a little car and drove us here.'

She finished a little breathlessly and looked down at her hands again.

'You are safe now,' the Captain said. 'We will take you to Sana'a and you will have treatment at the hospital.'

She nodded.

'Safiya,' Jim asked. 'Can you tell us how many people were in The Palace?'

She turned to consult briefly with Latifa, counting on her fingers. Then she said, 'Before the Americans came there were just ten girls and ten jihadi soldiers. During the day the girls did the cleaning and the laundry and helped in the kitchen. Two women did the actual cooking. Whatever we did we were watched by one of the Sons. During the night – well you know what happened during the night. Then the two Americans arrived.'

Latifa took it up. 'They had eight Sons with them. The man Conrad did not want so many soldiers, so he ordered his own to go into the town.'

Safiya said, 'The Americans also brought four other men. They were not soldiers. Sometimes they took us to lie with them at night, but during the day we did not see them. They seemed to work outside the main building, perhaps in the stables.'

Jim said, 'Thank you. This information is very helpful.'

The Captain looked round at Jim, eyebrows raised, and Jim nodded that he had no further questions. He stood up.

'Come then. We will take you now to Sana'a.'

50

They travelled in convoy with the Yemeni army vehicles until they were outside jihadi-held territory, and shortly afterwards Jim gave them a wave and their paths diverged. By the time they got back to Shabwaz and their temporary base the additional squad had already arrived and were milling around. He went over to meet them.

'Welcome aboard, guys. Miguel, who's leading this squad?'

Sergeant Miguel Garzón was one of their Mexican-born recruits. Miguel had a moon face and a very wide smile. Today it was even wider than usual.

'Captain Cressington, Colonel.'

His jaw dropped. 'Captain…'

'Hello Jim.'

He turned and found himself looking into the smiling face of Holly Cressington. He felt a surge of delight at seeing her, eclipsed almost immediately by consternation.

'What are you doing here?' he said, as sternly as he ccould manage.

'You needed another squad, so Tommy sent me.'

'But you're not fit for operational duty!'

'Who says I'm not? The doctors said the bone had knitted together nicely. That was two weeks ago and since then I've been having physiotherapy and doing exercise every damned day. I'm fit. Believe it.' She drew him aside. 'Look Jim, I know who you're after and I'm after them, too. I want part of this.'

He sighed and shook his head. 'Okay, okay. Go and find Eddie and Ted and bring them to the comms tent. Ahmed? With me.'

Minutes later Holly joined him in the tent with Eddie and Ted.

He said, 'Sit down everyone. Okay, first I need to bring Captain Cressington up to speed. Holly, a convoy was spotted heading west. They stopped overnight in a ruined village and we tackled them next morning, killed two, took the rest prisoner. Unfortunately it wasn't the convoy we were after. I called in the Yemeni Army to take charge of the prisoners and I stayed on to wait for them. With me were Ahmed, Wayne, and Carter. The rest of the guys came back here.

'Eddie, Ted, this is the part you weren't around for. A Yemeni Captain turned up with about twenty of his finest. They were loading up the prisoners when he got a tip-off. Some girls had escaped from a jihadi compound. He sent some of his force back with the prisoners and we went on with him to interview the girls.'

Eddie raised his eyebrows. 'Why?'

'There was some talk of Americans.'

Eddie's eyes widened, and he slapped a fist into his palm.

'Well it didn't mean they were *our* Americans, but it was worth checking out. So we went along and spoke to the girls. Bingo! This place they escaped from? Turns out that's where our target is.'

'Jeez,' Ted said, shaking his head. 'We're waiting for drones to sight the convoy and all the time they're lying low up there.'

'It was a stroke of luck,' Jim said. 'But those girls had guts. One of them told us what went on and Ahmed here did a great job of translating. Ahmed, if I leave anything out, you speak up, okay?'

'Yes, sir.'

'The girls were being held as slaves in a place they called The Palace. During the day they did menial tasks: kitchen, laundry, cleaning. At night the jihadis took them for sex. But not just the jihadis. Six more men arrived there. She described two, even knew their names: Conrad and Cy.'

Eddie and Ted murmured.

Seeing the frown on Holly's face, Jim added, 'The fake kidnap in Sana'a, Holly? Cy Sloper was the US citizen.'

'The one who…?'

'Yeah, that one. Conrad Lazar was the guy who set it up.'

Her eyes narrowed but she said nothing.

'We didn't press them about the four others,' Jim went on, 'but it certainly sounds like they're the cyber team. She thought they worked outside the building some of the time, maybe in the stables.'

'Stables?'

'Could have been built for the original owner's horses and camels. In which case they'd be big enough to park large vehicles in. Vehicles like a camper van or motorhome.'

'So where is this place?' Eddie asked.

'From the description of The Palace the Yemeni Captain had a pretty fair idea where it was. We looked at it on the map after we finished interviewing the girls. The town he had in mind is about 25 ks south-east of where we were, and that sounds about right. He couldn't tell us much more. The girls mentioned a walled area in front of the building with a sentry at the gate. Sounds like there's a significant presence in the town so there may be a check point outside it – we don't know that, though.'

Ted frowned. 'If there's a sentry how did the girls get out?'

'There's a back door in a passage by the kitchen, probably a delivery point in the past. They climbed over it. One of our squads could do the same to get in. Another could take out the sentry and come in at the front.'

'What's the combat strength in there?' Eddie asked.

'It's not a big garrison, just ten jihadis. The cyber team had another eight when they came in, but Lazar sent them into the town, so it stays at ten. I guess they always have a sentry on the gate, and if there's a checkpoint there'll be one or two out there, so seven or eight in the building itself. You could count Conrad Lazar in, too, but I shouldn't think the others would put up much resistance. Snag is, with the town being occupied there'll be a lot more jihadi soldiers within easy reach.'

Ted asked, 'Is The Palace in the middle of the town or at the edge?'

'Yeah, that's important. If it was built first the town could have grown up around it. If not, it could be almost on the outside. We don't know, is the answer, and we need to know. So what I propose is, first we move our base. We're too far from the action here. Let's take a look.'

They got up and spread the map out on the table. Jim pointed.

'Here's the target. We need to be close, but not so close they can spot us with small drones. 10 ks minimum.' He pointed. 'What about this one? It's ringed in blue, so according to Youssef it's uninhabited.'

'How far's that from the target?' Eddie asked.

'About 20 ks.'

The big man nodded. 'That's okay. We can take the vehicles up to 10 ks and leg the rest.'

'All right, we'll go for it. If you get your people together now we can be there before nightfall and look it over. But maximum alert. We're in jihadi-controlled territory up there.'

'And after we've moved in?' Holly said. 'One thing's obvious: you need a reconnaissance before dawn to see if there's a check point, where the palace is, where that back door is, and where it leads to.'

'Yeah, that's right,' Jim said slowly.

'The other thing that's obvious is I'm doing it, with my squad.'

'Hold on just a moment. Why is that so blindingly obvious?'

She smiled brightly. 'Because your three squads have seen some action already. You said so: you intercepted a convoy and took a lot of prisoners. My people have been hanging around for weeks, thirsting for action. It's their turn.' She opened her hands. 'Agreed?'

Jim chewed his lip for a moment. Then, 'All right. But no engagement. This is strictly a reconnaissance mission.'

She inclined her head. 'Thank you, Colonel. I'll go and brief them now.'

She left the tent and Jim turned to face Eddie and Ted.

'What are you two grinning at?'

51

At 2 am Holly took her squad out in the desert-going vehicles. She was up front, with Sergeant Adam Newsom driving. Adam wore night-vision glasses and Holly navigated with GPS, but progress was slow just the same; the open desert here was strewn with rocks and they were trying to keep to the path of packed sand that served as a road. When the GPS indicated they were within 10 ks of the town they parked the vehicles.

'Okay,' Holly said. 'I'm afraid we'll have to leave two of you to guard the vehicles. Adam, Sean – that's your job.'

Sean groaned and Adam said, 'Ah, shit.'

Holly ignored the protests. 'The rest, with me. If you see anyone or anything take cover.'

'Take cover? You joking?' Miguel said. 'In this place you could see a gopher hiccup from 10 ks.'

'I don't think they have gophers here, Miguel, but I take your point – it's very exposed. There's a bit of scrub around. Just do the best you can. Let's go.'

She used her GPS to keep them on track. All the others wore night-vision glasses. Eight ks later Miguel dropped flat. They did the same and Holly crawled up to him.

'What is it, Miguel?' she said softly.

He pointed. 'Checkpoint up there.'

She drew down her night-vision binoculars. 'Quite right, two sentries. Good, first point established.' She turned slightly and hand signalled that they should deviate to the left.

The GPS went back into its pouch; the screen was too visible in the darkness and they were near enough now. They moved quietly. The weapons they'd been told to avoid using were at the ready all the same. Half an hour later they made out the rooflines of the town. A tall building seemed to be a good candidate for The Palace and they headed in that direction. Soon its sheer extent became clear, and confirmed the identification beyond doubt.

The Palace itself made up most of the rear boundary of the compound. On their right a short section of wall bridged the gap between the main building and a row of lower buildings, each of which was fitted with a heavy wooden door. The last of these formed part of the boundary wall extending forward.

She pointed. 'These must be the stables. They face the back. Meant they could take the animals in and out without disturbing anyone on the palace side.'

The compound was situated towards the edge of the town but it wasn't completely outside it.

Second point established, Holly said to herself. *Now for the gate.*

She checked her watch. This whole thing had taken much longer than she'd anticipated. Before long the sun would be up.

They moved close to the rear wall. At the other end of the main building the arrangement was similar, with a gap and a row of low buildings, but in place of the short section of bridging wall they found a gate. Kieron, who was built like an ox, lifted her effortlessly so that she could look over the top. She could make out a passage and a door, which presumably led to the kitchen. She tapped him on the shoulder and he let her down.

'Good,' she whispered. 'I can see the passage and I think that's the kitchen door. That's as much as we can do for now. We're running out of time.'

The desert was bathed in peach-coloured early morning light by the time they got back to the vehicles.

Sean and Adam were waiting. They'd already turned the vehicles around and now they were leaning on them in a clear show of boredom and frustration.

'Okay people,' she said, 'let's go.'

They climbed into the desert vehicles, and again Holly rode in the one in front with Adam at the wheel. After a few minutes they entered irregular terrain, maybe a dried up river bed. The path ahead was striped in shadows as it dipped into successive troughs. The vehicles were designed to stay level over rough ground so they'd barely noticed it on the way in. The tyre tracks from their inward journey still showed up in relief in the low sun, so it would be easy enough to navigate back. She settled into her seat. The return journey promised to be a lot quicker than the outgoing one.

And then they encountered the jihadi patrol.

52

Sean heard Holly's shout in his comms helmet – 'Deploy!' He was at the wheel of the second vehicle, so she'd have seen them before he did. The forward vehicle slewed off the path to the right and he threw his own off to the left. The doors opened and they spilled out to either side. There was no debate about not engaging now and this was one standard operating procedure that hadn't changed. A vehicle was the last place you wanted to be. The hostiles could have RPGs.

He scuttled into one of the shallow depressions in the sand and quickly put on his respirator mask, aware that the others would be doing the same. Like the body armour it wasn't comfortable, but safety came first. Then he snatched up his multi-rifle and levelled it. The jihadi patrol was much closer now: two vehicles, the one in front a light utility vehicle with a machine-gun mounted on the top, nodding and rising as it approached along the uneven path. He sucked in a short breath. Concealment was hard enough in this landscape and from up there the gunner could easily acquire targets. He quickly measured the distance in his sights and set the range of the smart grenade in the underbarrel launcher. The gunner must have spotted him, because he opened up with a continuous burst that sent fountains of sand spurting in his direction. He rolled to one side, but the vehicle had tilted into a dip and the burst stopped short. He raised the rifle, sighted, and fired. There was a deep thud from the launcher and a brilliant flash above the vehicle, followed by the explosion. A puff of white cloud hung in the air, wisps trailing from it like tentacles. The vehicle came on, but there was no longer anyone at the machine-gun. It stopped, doors opened, and three men jumped out keeping low, two to one side, one to the other.

He heard the thud of another grenade launcher from his right and an explosion lifted the light utility vehicle and dumped it back blazing fiercely. Four men leapt from the jeep behind it and deployed in both directions. They were well drilled, running about five metres before ducking down again before anyone could bring a weapon to bear. Running and ducking, they began to spread out, the clear intention being to enfilade the squad from both ends.

This was a scenario they'd practised many times back at Fort Piper; Sean knew his role and the others would know theirs. Half of them would put down suppressive fire, making it harder for the enemy to come up long enough to run any distance or take a proper aim. The other half, Sean included, were snipers. Their job was to choose their targets carefully and take them down with single taps or groups of three. By now the air was full of the noise of fire and counter-fire. A near miss sprayed sand over Sean's helmet and visor, but someone had spotted the shooter and he saw a black-robed figure throw out his arms and fall.

Sean set his rifle sight on the point where a jihadi had just disappeared, and waited. Others were bobbing up and down but he shut them out of his vision, focusing on the one spot. His target rose and he squeezed the trigger. The man went down.

One of the SAF team shouted 'Incoming!' and Sean ducked down, expecting a grenade or a mortar. There was no explosion, just a series of pops. When he looked up he saw several lines of white vapour drifting towards them. Quickly he checked that his respirator mask was well seated. The white vapour mingled with the black smoke from the burning tyres of the lead vehicle. The combination thickened rapidly and completely obscured the view. His thoughts raced.

Shit, now what? We can't see them, but they can't see us either. Is this a suicide squad? Are they going to come through the smoke firing in all directions and yelling like goddamned banshees?

He heard an engine start and the shadow of a vehicle appeared briefly, the motor howling. The sound grew to a roar, then slowly faded away.

The firing had stopped. The squad inched forward in the ominous silence, trying to get under the fog and through it.

A black shape appeared ahead of him and he jerked the rifle up, then realized the man was dead. He heard Adam shout 'One down here' and he responded, 'And here.' Another heap of black rags lay ahead of him and he called that one, too. Someone on the right – it sounded like Ellen but hard to tell through the respirator – shouted, 'One here.'

Four down, then, plus the gunner. Three left. Were they all in that vehicle?

The smoke was thinning now. The squad got to its feet and began to quarter the area cautiously. They regrouped at the vehicles.

Adam said, 'Looks like they pulled out. Anyone hit?'

They shook their heads.

Then Miguel said, 'Where's Holly?'

*

Holly sat in the back of the jeep, still a little dazed from the gas and cursing her carelessness. As a designated sniper she'd been so focused on picking her targets she hadn't noticed the jihadi creeping up behind her. Or was it two? She had no idea, but someone had ripped her respirator loose and in the struggle she'd taken a breath and that was it. Not poison gas obviously, but a short-acting anaesthetic gas like the ones they used in the good-nites. And now here she was, in the back of an enemy jeep, her wrists secured in front of her with a cable tie.

She knew several of the jihadis had been hit – she'd taken one out herself and seen a couple of others go down – but the three men in the jeep didn't seem overly concerned. Perhaps they believed their comrades had entered Paradise. More likely they were pleased to be returning with a prize of their own: an American Special Forces soldier, and – better still – a woman.

No doubt that's why they abandoned the attack. A live American soldier would be worth a lot more than a heap of dead ones.

She could smell the man next to her, the sour stench of exertion and perhaps fear. But there was no fear on his face now as he turned to look at her. It was hard to know how old he was. Where the gaunt cheeks weren't covered with that straggly black beard the skin was darkened and lined by the sun. He grinned, revealing a missing tooth, the remaining ones uneven and blackened at the base. Then he placed his right hand on her thigh and gripped it hard. She didn't hesitate. She lifted the knee and brought her fists down at the same time, smashing them into his hand. He yelped, withdrawing the hand quickly. Then he punched her hard in the stomach. She grunted but fought down the pain and nausea.

The driver laughed and said something to his companion in the front. Her understanding of the local Arabic dialect was good, and she tuned in quickly.

The driver glanced over his shoulder. 'Did she bite you, Mustafa?'

He snarled back, 'When we rape this bitch I'm going first.'

She bit her lip.

Through the windscreen she saw the checkpoint they'd spotted during the recce. The driver braked to a halt. There was a brief exchange and they rolled on, down a gentle incline into the town. The vehicle paused at a wrought-iron gate set in a high wall and a sentry swung it back. They drove up to a large building and stopped. This had to be The Palace.

The man next to her said something in Arabic to the others and as soon as they got her out they pinned her down, her hands above her head. They cut the tie, forced her hands behind her back, and fastened the wrists there. Her helmet, respirator and the belt with her semi-automatic pistol were gone – they must have been taken while she was unconscious – but now they searched her thoroughly for other weapons and removed her boots and socks. Then they dragged her to her feet and marched her inside the building and along a maze of corridors. She tried not to think about anything except where they were taking her. The floors were paved with flagstones, covered in places with threadbare carpets and cool under her bare feet. The walls and ceiling were lined with grubby whitewashed plaster. They turned and descended a stone staircase to another corridor. One of them opened a door and the others shoved her inside. The man with the bad teeth lingered there for a moment, massaging his right hand with the left. He spoke in Arabic. Unfortunately she understood.

'Soon I will be back. Then we are going to see who will hurt the most.'

He went out, a key turned in the lock, and she heard receding footsteps.

She looked around her. The room was completely empty and the stale air reeked of must and urine. Like the corridors, the floor was stone-flagged, but here it was stained darkly in places with what may have been oil or old blood. No plaster here – the stone walls were bare. Feeble scratchings low down indicated that she hadn't been the first to be confined in here – and that it hadn't gone too well for the previous occupants. There were no windows. She couldn't have reached one anyway with her wrists bound.

She gritted her teeth and tried to free her wrists but the plastic ties were too tight, biting into the skin.

Why hadn't they tied her ankles as well? Presumably it was easier to walk her in here than to carry her. And after that, why bother? After all, she was smaller than any of them, and a woman.

*

'We looked everywhere, Jim,' Kieron said. 'She's gone. The jihadis must have taken her.'

'They got away in a jeep,' Miguel added, 'but we didn't see it until the last moment on account of all the smoke and gas.'

Jim slowly closed his eyes and opened them. 'Did you take any casualties?'

Miguel responded. 'No. They were well trained, but we killed five out of eight.'

Adam said, 'There were a few bullet-holes in the desert vehicles but they weren't put out of action, so we were lucky. It would have been a pretty successful encounter if it hadn't been for this.'

This – this minor detail, Jim thought. *The daughter of the US Secretary of Defense is in the hands of the jihadis. That's all. Jesus.*

'Tell me what you learned from the recce.'

Miguel said, 'Road looks like it leads almost straight into the town, but there's a check point. Sentry box and barrier, two guys manning it.'

'Okay, go on.'

'We looped around to get to the back of The Palace.'

'How far was that, compared to straight in?'

'About twice as far, Kieron?'

'Yeah, about that.'

Jim nodded. 'Where's The Palace in relation to the rest of the town?'

'It's at the near end,' Miguel said, 'but not outside it. We didn't see the front, just the walls. The stables, too. Six each side, opening to the back.'

'And the gate the girls mentioned?'

Kieron said, 'Yeah, we found it. There's a passage between the main building and the stables on that side. Gate is quite high, solid wood. We could get over that, no problem.'

Jim said, 'Okay, muster everyone in the mess tent.'

The mess tent was the only one big enough to take four squads. Jim could see from their grim expressions that word had got around. He didn't waste time.

'We've got a hostage extraction to do, and fast. Captain Holly Cressington is inside a jihadi-held compound. We're going to get her out.'

There was a general murmur of assent.

'We'll take three squads. One squad needs to stay here to manage comms and protect our base. Red Team – that's your job.'

There was a moan of protest from Red Team.

'Sorry, someone's got to do it and you saw some action last time. Blue Team, you'll stay with the vehicles.'

More moans.

'All right, listen, it's not a holiday. We know the jihadis patrol that road, so spread out and be ready for them. The rest of you will go in. We don't want to alert the entire town garrison, so take suppressors for your weapons. Miguel, lead them to that rear entrance – it'll take longer but we can't risk being seen on the road. Go in through the kitchen door. You meet any jihadis, take them out. Search room by room, starting at the back and the lowest level – that's the most likely place they'll be holding her. Once you've found her get out of there fast, through the front and up the road.'

'Sentries?' Miguel asked.

'There won't be any. That's my job, mine and… where's the squad marksman?' A hand went up, and he registered the gangly, red-haired figure of Corporal Tom Jensen. He was the youngest soldier in the unit, and by far the best shot. 'Tom?'

'Sir?'

'You got your silenced sniper rifle here?'

'You bet, sir.'

'Good, you'll come with me. Any questions?' There were none. 'Okay. We'll take three vehicles and travel eight, eight, and seven. One place left for Holly – and it's not coming back empty. Adam, you've been there before, you drive the lead vehicle. I'll ride up front with you. Miguel, you come with us. Let's roll.'

53

They drove fast. The road to the target was easy to see in full daylight, the packed sand glazed and shining in the sun, and still bearing traces of the earlier tyre marks. Neither he nor Adam needed to consult the NavAid.

Soon they spotted the bodies, humps of black cloth on either side of the road. Two minutes later Miguel leaned forward from the back seat and said, 'Only 10 ks from the town now, Jim. Maybe we should stop here.'

Jim winced. Time was of the essence and he would have preferred to move up closer with the vehicles. On the other hand the landscape was so flat that the vehicles, or the dust raised by them, would be visible from a distance. Adam glanced his way. He closed his eyes and nodded.

The convoy came to a halt and they all got out. No one spoke.

Eddie and his squad stayed behind in charge of the vehicles while the others set off, jogging at a steady pace.

*

She paced around the cell, a sick feeling inside her. She knew what lay ahead for her if she remained here, and she tried desperately to work through various escape scenarios. She came up with nothing. In the end she'd have to play it by ear and take whatever opportunity might come her way.

How much time had passed since they dumped her here? Half an hour? At least that much. Something would surely happen soon.

Steps sounded on the corridor outside her cell. Her heart began to hammer. Was this it? Had they come for her? Would they do it here or take her somewhere else? Now, listening carefully, she could distinguish only one set of footsteps. She took up a position a metre or so away from the wall.

The lock rattled, the door opened, and the jihadi from the jeep came in. He stood there, looking at her, lips peeled back from those blackened teeth in a semblance of a smile. Above the ugly teeth a beak of a nose, and above that, dark eyes shining with vicious anticipation.

He turned the key in the lock.

*

A small access door opened at the back of the stable where the camper was parked and Conrad Lazar emerged into the heat and light of the palace compound. He blinked for a moment, adjusting to the sudden brightness. Then his eyes narrowed. A black-robed figure had come in at the gate. The man paused for a moment to speak to the sentry, then entered the compound. He was followed by five more. They all but disappeared as they followed the shadow of one wall around to The Palace.

Are they doing that to keep out of the sun or are they trying to avoid notice?

Lazar moved up quickly and intercepted him at the palace entrance. 'What's going on, Ashraf?'

The man didn't meet his gaze. 'Just came in from the town. I recruited some more men.'

'Why? I said ten soldiers were enough.'

'We lost five. We were out on a routine patrol, and we were attacked.'

Lazar frowned. 'And they took down five? After all the training I gave you? Who were they anyway – Yemeni Army?'

'I don't think so. They were in those big desert-going vehicles. The ones with six big tyres.'

'American Special Forces,' Lazar sighed. 'And you idiots engaged them.'

Ashraf gave him an uneasy smile and shrugged. 'We didn't do so badly. Mustafa and Wasif captured one of them. A woman.'

Lazar felt a surge of blood rise to his face. 'You've got a Special Forces prisoner! Why the hell didn't you tell me?'

Ashraf shrugged. 'We were going to tell you but Mustafa said he wanted to have some fun with her first.'

'Mustafa? Who runs things around here, me or Mustafa?'

'Well, you do, of course—'

'What were they doing here?'

'I don't know.'

'You don't know.' Lazar shook his head. 'Well we need to find out, don't we? I'd better have a little chat with her.'

'She may not tell you.'

Lazar gave him a patient smile. 'When I've finished with her she'll tell me. You keeping her in one of the cells?'

'Yes.'

'Okay, I've got a couple of things to do, then I'll go out to the camper to fetch some tools. I'll be along there in fifteen minutes. She won't last long. After that Mustafa and the rest of you can have your fun. Bring some friends in from the town, too, if you want.'

He turned away to hide a smile and hurried down the corridor.

An American Special Forces captive, no less. Could this be the SAF? Now that would be a bonus, wouldn't it?

*

They tabbed 8 ks with Miguel leading the way. Then he signalled and they dropped as one man.

'Check point is over there,' Miguel said, pointing.

'Okay, you guys know what to do. Get going. Tom, you stay here with me.'

Jim crawled forward and brought up his binoculars. The check point swung into view: a barrier, a sentry box, and two black-robed sentries. One was standing just outside the sentry box; the other was to his right, half-turned towards him. It looked like they were having a conversation. Beyond the barrier the road was flanked with razor wire on both sides. It sloped gently down, presumably all the way to the town. He noted the reading on the built-in infra-red rangefinder: 900 metres. He looked over his shoulder to where Tom Jensen was waiting expectantly and beckoned.

When the young soldier reached him he said, 'Tom, the two sentries at that check-point.'

Tom nodded. He stretched out and levelled his rifle, an M208 self-loader built from the ground up as a silenced sniper rifle, and put his eye to the telescopic sight.

Jim had a pretty good idea what was going on in the marksman's mind. On a calm day at the firing range he could make a shot like this, but not under these conditions. Although there was little breeze, heat was rising from the desert. There could be cross-winds between him and the target and there was no vegetation tall enough to hint at what their strength might be. He also had to allow for spindrift and bullet drop, both of which would be substantial over that distance. No doubt Tom had a heavy load in the subsonic ammunition he was using, but a bullet travelling at that speed couldn't deliver anything like the energy of a normal round. That meant he had to be spot on. If either of those guys returned fire it would bring out the entire town.

'Got to shorten the range,' Tom said, and began to crawl, alligator-style, the rifle extended in front of him.

Jim hesitated, then began to crawl after him. It was a while since he'd done this. He remembered assault courses with the paras and the SAS, struggling under a net with a full pack. When he repeated it with the SAF, Drill Sergeant Bill Wicks was there, yelling and sending live rounds over their heads to urge them on. It had saved his life once and that had lessened, though not altogether extinguished, the desire they all shared to frag the bastard. Fit as he was, the exertion now forced him to stop a hundred metres behind Tom to catch his breath.

He raised the binoculars again.

*

In the camper Conrad Lazar opened an underbench drawer and selected pliers, wire cutters, a screwdriver, and a bradawl. He considered adding a power drill, but decided what he had would be more than adequate. He moved with quiet deliberation, passing the tools to his other hand as he opened the camper door and closed it behind him. Then he opened the small access door and stepped out into the courtyard. He closed that one, too, and walked around to the entrance of The Palace.

*

The man they'd called Mustafa turned from the door and walked up to her. Holly's thoughts raced, her chest rising and falling.

I'll get just one shot at this.

He stopped in front of her, his lips curling. Then he began to unbutton her shirt.

She stood rooted to the spot. He was breathing through his mouth and she closed her eyes in disgust as his fetid breath wafted into her face. He fumbled with the buttons, one... two... three... and the shirt gaped open. Still smiling, he held up his right hand.

'This hand you hurt,' he said in Arabic. He held up the other one. 'But this one works good.'

He opened and closed the fingers forcefully to demonstrate, then dipped his hand inside her shirt and under her bra, and closed his fingers over the soft swell of her left breast.

She stepped smartly back and to her left. He was already half-turned and the move put him off balance with his weight shifted to his right foot. Her own right foot moved in a lightning arc, gathering the man's left ankle, collecting it with the other and dumping him on his back. Without pausing she jumped and dropped her knees onto him, the right one, with most of her weight on it, landing on his throat. She felt the delicate bones crumple with the impact. He gurgled, he thrashed, he struggled for air, mouth open, eyes bulging. Just to be sure, she held her weight on that knee until he went limp, the mouth still gaping wide, bloodshot eyes staring sightlessly at the ceiling.

She swallowed. This was what she'd been trained for and now she'd finally done it. She'd killed a man in unarmed combat. There was no sense of triumph, just the awful realization that she could never be the same again.

She pushed the thought to the back of her mind. This was just the start. She'd dealt with this one, but others would come soon. The door was locked and her hands were tied. Somehow she still had to get out of here and she had to do it fast.

54

Jim lowered the binoculars and looked at Tom. The marksman had settled into a dip behind a saltbush, and he was shuffling his legs into a comfortable position. He put his eye to the scope again and made some adjustments.

Jim didn't underestimate the difficulties. Tom had to fire, work the bolt action, resight, and squeeze the trigger again before the second man could react. No fancy head shots here, even from this shortened range; right now he'd be putting the cross hairs on the chest of each target in turn, then he'd make the corrections for the flight of the bullets.

Jim raised the binoculars again, brought them to bear on the sentries and waited.

*

Holly listened but she could hear no noises outside the cell. Then she sat back and moved the dead jihadi's robe with her toes. Most of these men carried a fancy dagger called a *khanjar* tucked into a waist belt. This one was no exception. She gripped the hilt with her toes and began to work the dagger out of its sheath. From the time she'd turned five she could pick things up with her toes, something her friends tried to emulate but could never manage. She was small for her age, but she remembered how she'd revelled in the feeling of superiority this one area of accomplishment gave her. It would never have crossed her mind that one day it might save her life. She manipulated the dagger free. It was fairly plain as these things went: a sharp, slightly curved blade and a hilt of carved camel bone. Now she needed some way of supporting it.

The room was completely bare, so there was only one answer. She bottom-shuffled to a better position and worked the hilt of the dagger as far inside the jihadi's gaping mouth as she could manage. She used her foot to nudge his jaw up against the hilt, then turned, found the edge of the blade with her fingers, and began to saw at the plastic ties. The dagger wobbled about but still gave her a cutting action on some of the strokes. She was already thinking ahead. If she stripped off the man's robe and head scarf and took his sandals she might just make it out of the enclave without raising suspicion. But she'd have to move fast. She worked the ties up and down more briskly.

*

Tom was taking his time and Jim didn't rush him. Crawling for that distance would make even a young man like him shaky, and he needed to settle completely. Then he'd breath easily in and out, press his cheek against the stock, take a breath and hold it, and his finger would tighten on the trigger...

There was a sharp puff of sound like compressed gas escaping, the slide of the bolt, then another puff. First one sentry then the other flew backwards, arms outstretched. Jim kept the binoculars on them but neither one stirred.

*

'What the hell's going on?'

Lazar had arrived at the cells to find a door open and several soldiers standing around.

'She's gone,' Ashraf said. 'The American prisoner has gone.'

Lazar opened his hand and the tools clattered to the floor at his feet. 'You fucking idiots! You let her go?'

'We didn't *let* her go. She killed Mustafa. Got out.'

'Then find her! She can't have gone far.'

Ashraf said, 'I'll check the back door by the kitchen. That's how those three girls got out.'

'That's pointless. They knew their way around the Palace, this woman doesn't. Check with the sentry at the front gate. Find out if he's seen anything. Now!'

A few minutes later Ashraf returned. He shrugged apologetically. 'The sentry's dead. And I phoned the two at the check point. No reply.'

Lazar narrowed his eyes. 'How'd she get up there so fast? Okay, at least we know which way she went. Get your guys together, grab a vehicle, and go after her.'

*

Holly was thinking about the check point at the top of this road. She'd managed the sentry at the gate of the compound, but there'd be two at the check point. How long would they be deceived by these clothes? The robe and headscarf were all right. The sandals had been way too big and she couldn't keep them on; she just hoped her bare feet wouldn't be noticed under the long robe. She could keep her head down and that way they wouldn't notice the absence of a beard. At least that's what she hoped.

She knew that behind her, in The Palace, they could already have found the empty cell and the dead jihadi. Her instinct was to run, but she didn't dare to in case it attracted attention. Nor could she deviate from the road, because there were coils of razor wire down both sides.

The dagger was in her hand, concealed among the folds of the robe. She gripped it tightly and continued up the road.

*

Having satisfied himself that the sentries were now out of the equation, Jim prepared to get to his feet. Before he did so he swung the binoculars to scan quickly along the road to the left – and ducked back down. He'd caught sight of a head swathed in a black scarf, rising and falling as a jihadi came up the road towards the check point.

Alarm coursed through him. Tom was in a slight dip behind that bush and he would have nothing like as good a view of the road below. He was drawing back the sniper rifle, probably about to get to his feet. He would present a clear target and even if the man missed – and it was likely at this range – the firing would bring the whole garrison out.

He tried to attract Tom's attention but the marksman was slowly picking up the ejected cartridge cases and putting them in his pocket. Jim slithered forward, doing the alligator crawl faster than he'd ever attempted before, trying to cover the ground between them. After about eighty metres he was breathing hard; his chest felt as if it had been rubbed raw by the stony sand, his heart was hammering, and his muscles were burning with fatigue. He was within ten metres of Tom before the young man looked up. Jim flapped a hand, signalling him to keep low. Tom squatted down, frowning. Jim hauled himself the remaining distance.

'Hostile... coming up...,' he gasped.

Tom regarded him with a lop-sided grin.

Jim read the look.

You're getting too old for this.

It wasn't made easier by the recognition that he was probably right. Jim felt an urge to tell him to wipe the smile off his face. Instead he hardened his voice and said:

'You'd better get back in position. You've got another kill shot to make.'

55

There are two ways a sniper can work. He can either move the sights to the target or he can fix the sights at a point where he knows the target will appear. Jim knew Tom would take the second option. For one thing that hostile would have to come through the check point, and Tom was already ranged and corrected for a target there. For another thing the line of sight was less clear further down the road and if he fired from this angle there was a risk the bullet would hit razor wire and be deflected. The only complication was the two dead men at the check point, but they'd fallen back into the sentry box, so the bodies wouldn't be visible to the one coming up the road, at least not immediately. He'd have to be taken out before he saw them.

The jihadi would reach the barrier first. It was down, of course, so he'd have to move to the side of it. At that point the inside of the sentry box would come into view; that's when Tom would make the shot. At this range it would take about two seconds for the bullet to travel the distance. He'd make a tiny correction for the target's movement and that would be it.

Tom had settled back into that slight depression in the sand. He'd adopted a comfortable firing position, the rifle extended in front of him and resting on the edge of the dip.

Jim moved the binoculars from the check point down the road and picked up the jihadi again. He frowned. Why only one of them? If it was time to relieve the sentries at the check point there should be two. He scanned further down the road but there was no one else in sight.

The target approached up the gently sloping road, visible now from scarved head to robe, which was long enough to brush the ground. He was two hundred metres or thereabouts from the barrier, the right hand tight against the robe. Presumably he was coming on duty, so why wasn't he carrying a rifle? And why was he walking head down, as if solving some colossal mathematical problem?

One hundred metres. The target turned slightly, looking behind him. That was odd, because there wasn't anyone behind him.

Fifty metres.

Forty metres.

Thirty... twenty... ten...

At the barrier now, moving to go round it.

He glanced at Tom, saw his finger taking the slack out of the trigger.

One jihadi, not two.
No rifle.
Head down.
Looking behind him.
'Hold your fire.'

Tom looked up, eyes wide. 'What? Why?'

'I want a better look. Wait till he spots the sentries. See how he reacts.'

Tom returned his eye to the sight and Jim raised the binoculars.

The figure rounded the barrier and froze, staring at the sentry box, then whirled to look round.

Tom's mouth fell open. 'Jesus!'

'Holly,' Jim breathed. He switched on his helmet mike. 'Miguel, call it off, Holly got out somehow. Get back here fast.'

'Roger that.'

'Eddie, did you hear that?'

'Sure did.'

'Okay, get your guys together and bring the vehicles up. Check point's been neutralized. Look out for us.'

'Wilco.'

He turned to the marksman. Tom was on his feet, a look of near horror on his face. It was understandable: he'd come within a whisker of killing one of his own officers.

'Tom, you go off and wait for the others. We'll all meet up at the road.'

Tom licked his lips, and nodded.

For a moment Jim watched the lanky figure jogging away, the long sniper rifle balanced in one hand. Then he ran down to the check point. Holly was nowhere in sight. She must have ducked behind the sentry box to discard the robe and scarf, which made sense. The two sentries had obviously fallen to a sniper, and she knew she was in danger of going the same way so long as she was wearing those clothes.

He called out, 'Holly! It's me, Jim.'

She appeared – barefoot and in her desert camo combat uniform now – hurried over, and they fell into a strong and urgent embrace.

'Boy,' she muttered into his chest, 'am I glad to see you!'

He held her close. Relief flooded through him: relief that she was safe, even more relief that he'd stopped Tom in time. Mingled with this was the wonderful feeling of her firm body clasped tightly to him, and embarrassment because – natural as it was – he shouldn't be standing here with his arms around a junior officer.

She pulled away. Had she sensed his unease? Those wonderful grey eyes were clear and wide, and she was breathing hard.

'Sorry, the stink of that man's clothes must still be on me.'

'No, it's not—'

She cut in. 'We need to get away from here. Any time now they'll be coming after me.'

He winced – of course she'd be pursued and the only firearm they had between them was the semi-automatic in his belt. He dodged back to the sentry box, unlooped the slings of the dead sentries' rifles from around their heads, and brought the two weapons over. He handed one to her and they ran together back to the vantage point he'd occupied a few minutes earlier. Then they looked at each other. They'd both heard it: an engine, revving hard, and it was coming from the town.

Jim pointed to a patch of low vegetation, spindly shrubs of a type he'd seen all over the desert. It was about two hundred metres from the road.

'Come on.'

The ground was rough but she made no complaint as she ran across it in her bare feet. They reached the bushes, found a place that would put the densest growth between themselves and the road, and ducked down. Almost immediately the all-terrain from the town came past at speed. Through the sparse stalks of vegetation he glimpsed rifles poking out of each open window, dark faces and black headscarves. Just the one vehicle.

She said, 'Where's your backup?'

'Should be here in ten or fifteen minutes, two squads on foot and a third in vehicles.'

'I wonder if we've got that long.'

'Well, we can't be seen from the road. Best to lie low here.'

She was chewing her lip. 'They're mad as hell,' she said. 'They've found the ones I killed.'

'What happened?'

'They put me in a cell. After a bit one of them came in to have a bit of fun with me. They'd tied my hands but not my feet.'

He suppressed a smile. 'That was a mistake.'

'Yeah, a great big one. I put his clothes on and took his knife, then I went out the front.'

'Out the front? What about the sentry at the gate?'

'Worked my way round the walls of the compound, on the side in shadow. I was wearing black, so I must have been invisible. Then… I used the knife.' Her voice faltered.

Jim realized she was holding it together. She'd told him she'd never killed a man in close combat. Well now she'd killed two. It was going to catch up with her.

He rubbed her shoulder gently. 'It's okay, Holly, you did what you had to do—'

Their heads jerked up. The all-terrain again, but the engine had a different note and it was changing pitch periodically.

Jim lifted the binoculars. He saw a plume of dust and sand coming away from the road, then turning and going back, crossing the road and out to the other side. They were smart. They'd gone out along the road as far as they figured she could get on foot, and now they'd started to look off-road. They knew she wouldn't stray too far from it in case there was a chance of rescue, so they were zig-zagging systematically back and forth, travelling more slowly because of the rough terrain. He didn't need the binoculars any more; he could see the vehicle clearly, and it was getting closer all the time. This vegetation was thin. It wouldn't conceal them if that vehicle was making a traverse anywhere nearby.

He looked back at Holly. She'd guessed from the sounds what they were doing and she was examining the rifle, checking the magazine, familiarizing herself with the action. She looked up and met his eyes. Her jaw was set.

He considered the odds. Ten jihadis in The Palace, according to the girls who'd escaped. Holly had killed two and Tom had killed two. They were in too much of a hurry to get reinforcements, so there should be just six of them – five, if they'd left someone on guard. Five to two, and they probably had grenades. Not good.

The sound grew louder. They crouched low, waiting. Jim brushed his sleeve over his face and head and it came away dark with sweat. The temperature had to be well over forty degrees.

The sound receded, then grew again as the vehicle came back on their side.

He lifted the rifle and looked it over. He'd fired an AKM once and this was pretty similar. He made sure it had a full magazine. It had, but 30 rounds wouldn't go far. He set it for single shots, took a deep breath and settled down again.

The all-terrain receded, then returned. They crouched low. It was very close, maybe 50 metres away, and now it slowed down. Had they been seen? Perhaps not – it was turning and going back to the other side. But they'd be spotted on the next sweep, no question about that – it would be almost on top of them. He glanced at Holly. She was on one knee, the rifle at her shoulder, waiting. He adopted the same posture a short distance to her left.

The vehicle started on the return sweep. This would be the one. Surprise was their only hope.

'Fire just before they spot us,' he whispered. 'Take the front, I'll take the back.'

He snuggled the rifle into his shoulder and listened to the engine note rising, rising. He frowned. It wasn't just one engine, it was two or more. Abruptly the vehicle skidded around, spraying sand in every direction and, howling in low gear, raced back along the road to the town.

Jim stood up. Three big desert-going vehicles were coming in. He turned towards Holly and smiled.

'Relax, Holly, the cavalry have arrived.'

56

Eddie was waiting with Ted at a respectful distance from Holly's tent as Jim emerged.

'I left Ellen with her,' Jim said.

'How is she?' Eddie asked. 'I saw her when you guys climbed in. She looked pretty shook up.'

'She's been through a lot. She did fantastically well but the adrenaline's worn off. It's all hitting her at once.'

Ted nodded. 'Delayed shock.'

'Yeah. Ellen gave her the usual stuff to calm her down and help her sleep.'

He led them back to the comms tent.

Eddie said, 'That jihadi patrol vehicle we saw must have been out looking for her.' He laughed. 'They sure high-tailed it out of there when they saw us coming.'

'You cut it fine. They very nearly got us both.'

They went inside and sat at the table. 'So,' Jim said, 'we know Lazar is in there, and he knows by now there are Special Forces in the area.'

'Makes our job harder,' Eddie said.

Jim said, 'Maybe.' He leaned back and looked at each of them in turn. 'But maybe not.'

*

Lazar came into the camper, his expression even more thunderous than usual.

Cy looked up. 'What was all that racket?'

'I can't believe these...these imbeciles!' Lazar shouted.

The cyber operatives were clustered around a monitor at one end of the bench. They turned to look at him.

'Call themselves a fucking army...'

Khalil came over. 'Conrad...'

Lazar turned on him. 'Will you shut the fuck up while I'm talking?'

Khalil turned away, noisily expelling a breath. Cy waited.

Lazar lowered his voice and started again. 'Our jihadi friends sent out a routine patrol,' he said. 'They ran into trouble, there was a firefight, five killed. That's five out of eight. No losses on the other side, not that they're aware of. Does that sound like Yemeni Army to you?'

It was best not to disagree with Conrad when he was like this. Cy said, 'I guess not.'

'Damned right, it's not. It's Special Forces. We know they're operating out here. So our guys get creamed. Okay, what's new? What's new is they actually take one of them prisoner. And it's a woman.'

Khalil tried again. 'Conrad...'

'I told you to shut the fuck up!'

Khalil made a throw-away gesture with his hands.

Cy frowned. 'But that's great! It's protection. They can't bomb us now, not if we have a high value hostage. We're safe.'

Lazar pointed a finger at him. 'Correct, Cy. Or you would be if the stupid bastards hadn't let her go.'

'Let her go...?'

'Yeah. She killed one of her captors and the sentry at the gate and the two at the check point. The woman was fucking Special Forces. These idiots didn't know what they were dealing with. Of course they're too macho to come to me. *I'm* fucking Special Forces! *I'm* the one they should have come to.'

It was some time since Conrad had been Special Forces, but Cy wasn't going to argue the point. 'What was she doing here?'

'Yeah, what? If she was still here I'd have found out.'

'Might have been pure coincidence they were in the area, I suppose.'

'Yeah, might have been. More likely they were doing a recce of this place.'

Khalil tried again. 'Conrad...'

Lazar heaved an obvious sigh. 'What is it, Khalil?'

For a moment Khalil's lips were clamped tight. Cy sensed the man's indignation. He was holding back the information he'd been trying to give them. Then he composed himself.

'On your instructions,' Khalil said pointedly, 'Mansur has been listening for communications. He has picked up a strong satellite telephone signal.'

Lazar was paying attention now. 'Did you get anything?'

'We did. We recorded a conversation with someone called Jim. I think you should hear it.'

'Okay.'

With Cy behind him Lazar followed Khalil to the end of the bench where the others were still clustered. They moved out to make room.

'Mansur,' Khalil said to a thin, dark young man perched in front of a bank of equipment. He had a pair of headphones draped around his neck. 'Play that conversation back for Colonel Lazar.'

Mansur clicked a few buttons and they heard first a tone, then:

'Jim? Tommy here.'

'Hi, Tommy.'

'Just checking you got the consignment okay.'

'Sure did, Tommy. Thanks.'

'You going to be there much longer?'

'No, we'll be coming back soon. If Abadi calls you can tell him we located that unit. They're in a place called The Palace. It's in jihadi-held territory, so we've set up a joint operation with a nice big contingent of the Yemeni Army.'

'Great. Let me know how it goes, won't you?'

'Sure will.'

Mansur pressed a button to stop the recording.

'Okay...' Lazar said. 'So now we know why Special Forces are here.' He registered Mansur looking expectantly at him. 'What do you want, a fucking medal?' he snapped. 'It's your neck you're saving, not just ours.'

'Colonel Lazar, sir?'

They turned. Ashraf was standing just inside the doorway, his dark face flushed. Unless they were travelling the jihadis weren't allowed in this vehicle and Cy waited for the explosion from Conrad. Before it came, the man spilled out his news.

'I'm sorry to intrude but it is urgent and I've been looking everywhere for you. We went out looking for that escaped prisoner like you said. We ran into Special Forces again, three big desert vehicles.'

Conrad's eyes narrowed. 'Did you engage?'

'No, no. We were heavily outnumbered. We came back here. I wanted to warn you.'

Lazar said, almost to himself. 'It all fits, doesn't it?' Then, loudly to Ashraf, 'We're under strength again. Go to the town and get two volunteers to join us. And I mean now.'

'Yes, Colonel. Right away.' He hurried out.

Cy said, 'Two? We're down four.'

Conrad said, 'We travel with eight, not ten.'

'We're moving?'

'Of course we're moving. Soon as we can.'

'In full daylight?'

'Yeah, in full daylight. Standard procedures say they'll attack between two and four o'clock in the morning. By that time we'll be miles away from here. They'll have to come down the road and in at the front – it's the only way to get a sizeable force like that in here fast enough. Soon as we're ready we'll open the big stable doors and head west across the desert, like those girls must have done. They'll never even see us. We stay one step ahead, Cy. Always one step ahead.'

Cy nodded and said, 'Speaking of girls, Conrad, we'd better make a selection for the trip.'

'Forget the girls, we're not taking any. They're a goddamned liability.'

And he stormed out.

Cy pulled a face, then turned to the cyber team. 'Good work, guys. Get everything tied down. We're going to move.'

57

Jim and his troops were well concealed. One or two were stretched out behind the thicker clumps of spindly vegetation; most had dug shallow holes to lie in, scooping the sand forward and then settling down behind the ridges they'd created.

Jim had briefed them as soon as they arrived. He pointed out the path of compacted sand that extended into the distance, shining a little in the sun. 'This is the route west from The Palace, and this is the way they'll come. Three vehicles, some sort of big camper with two all-terrains. They'll travel with one all-terrain in front and the other behind – from a defensive point of view that's a no-brainer. Miguel, Ted, you'll use the small grenades under the two all-terrains. It'll trap the camper fore and aft, so no need to go for that as well. Ted, you go up there. Hold your fire till the second all-terrain passes you. Miguel, you'll be down here. When Ted's grenade goes in that's the signal for you to put yours under the lead vehicle. The rest of you: I want you out of view up to a hundred metres away on either side of the path. We're not wiping this convoy out, if that was the goal it'd be one for the US Air Force, not us. But if anyone gets out with a rifle or grenade in their hands, drop them. Ahmed, you already know what you have to do. Any questions? No? Okay, let's deploy.'

So they'd dug in. Now it was an hour later and they were still lying in the heat, waiting.

Jim took a sip of water, barely enough to moisten his lips and tongue, and managed to resist the powerful urge to pour the entire contents of the water bottle down his throat. The others were, he knew, doing the same – they'd all trained in conditions like this. But it was one thing to train with plenty going on to distract you, and quite another just to lie out here with little to think about except the heat and the thirst. His body armour gripped him in a hot, damp embrace, and the helmet and visor was making his head feel heavier by the minute.

As CO he'd had to sound confident. The reality was that it was a long shot, setting things up this way. If he'd got it wrong Lazar and Sloper and their team would get clean away or maybe not move at all. But if he'd got it right they could see an end to this business.

Eddie crawled up to Jim's position. Beads of sweat were breaking through the desert camo on the big man's face. 'Hope you're right about this, Jim. We been out here over an hour and it's hotter'n hell.'

Jim said, 'Not long now, Eddie. Got to be patient.'

Eddie attempted a shrug while supported on his elbows, and returned to his position.

Jim shook his head. He had to trust his judgement. Lazar would be thinking like a Special Forces soldier, and that's just what he was counting on. He brushed an already wet shirt sleeve across his forehead, and again ran his tongue over his lips. His attention was glued to the horizon but it was coming and going and his head throbbed.

Half an hour later the still hot air that blanketed the landscape was disturbed by the distant moan of engines. Jim levelled his binoculars quickly, saw first a cloud of dust then the darker outlines of vehicles, shimmering in the heat haze. The drone of engines got louder. In the lead was a large all-terrain, behind it a camper. The bulk of the camper and the dust concealed whatever was behind that, but he was betting it was the other all-terrain. He took a final glance over one shoulder then the other. The guys had done well; there wasn't a sign of them.

The convoy came on and the vehicles grew out of the dust and the heat. There were rifles poking out of windows but there was nothing for them to aim at. The lead vehicle was 1000 metres away... 500 metres... 50... 20... Now it was passing them.

There was a loud thud from Ted's grenade launcher and Miguel's followed almost immediately. The all-terrain in the front bucked and bounced as the grenade detonated beneath it. The one at the rear jerked up, then toppled onto its side, blown over by the force of the explosion. The lead driver revved his vehicle, trying to get away. The engine screamed but the tyres were shredded; black strips of rubber flew off and the wheel rims dug deeper into the sand. The engine died and all four doors opened. At the same time the front doors of the camper flew back. Six black-clad figures leapt out, firing their rifles wildly in every direction. Their shouts and cries of *Allahu akbhar!* almost drowned the careful tap-tap of aimed shots from all around them. They went down, one after another. Two of them fired grenades from under-barrel launchers before they were hit and fell back, one to the ground, the other against the all-terrain. The grenades exploded in quick succession. Then a heavy silence.

A full minute passed. Jim's eyes darted from the camper to the all-terrain that was on its side, but nothing moved. A smell of burning rubber from the lead vehicle's tyres wafted over him. Then Ahmed's voice rang out loud and clear, calling in Arabic to the occupants of the overturned vehicle 'Leave your weapons. Come out with your hands up.'

No response.

'Do it, or we put in another grenade.'

The doors on the upper side opened and two black-clad figures crawled out, followed by what looked like a couple of teenagers wearing T-shirts and jeans. One had a cut on his forehead, which was oozing blood. No weapons, no heroics: they emerged, hands held high, and came forward uncertainly.

Ahmed shouted, 'Hands on heads, kneel down, and do not move. If you move we will shoot you.'

They did as they were told.

Jim had been keeping tally. They'd accounted for eight jihadis – six killed and two captured – and the girls who'd escaped said the convoy travelled with eight. But then there was Lazar, and he was still a danger. The two all-terrains were empty now but the door to the living quarters of the camper hadn't opened yet.

Jim gave a signal and a group of his men emerged from cover and crouched, rifles levelled at the door. Another group hurried forward and set about tying the wrists and ankles of the four kneeling men. He left them to it and ran in the opposite direction, back to where smoke was still rising from the grenade explosions. A dozen men were on their feet. Even through the camo their expressions were grim.

'Anyone hurt?'

A soldier pointed.

Jim looked round and a cold shock ran through him. Tom Jensen, squad marksman, was lying there, his helmet and shattered visor to one side, blood from savage throat wounds soaking into the sand. His head was at an unnatural angle and one arm was trapped under his body.

Jim knelt by his side and he was reaching out to feel for a pulse when a voice behind him said, 'He's gone, Jim.'

Jim took a deep breath and got up. Kieron was standing there.

Jim said, 'Anyone else?'

Kieron shook his head. 'Would have been worse still if they'd used smart grenades. These were just fused to explode on impact, so the blast went over the top of us. Except for poor Tom. The fucking thing must have landed right next to him.'

Jim nodded, lips tight, and walked with cold deliberation to the camper. Standing opposite the door he shouted, 'This is Colonel James Slater, Special Assignment Force. Get out here, Lazar, you and all your lousy friends.'

There was no reply, just a slight buzz of voices from inside.

Jim shouted again. 'Lazar, are you listening to me? Walk out now or we'll blow you out.'

A deep chuckle escaped from behind the door. 'You're not going to do that, Slater. You want us alive – don't you? – so you can take us back to the States. Me especially.'

Ted was at Jim's shoulder. 'Should we use the gas grenades, Jim?'

'It's too chancy. I think the ventilation slots are in the roof, and they're probably baffled to keep sand out. I'll shoot out the door lock. Cover me.'

He'd taken only a couple of steps towards the door when it suddenly banged open. Conrad Lazar stood there, filling the doorway. There was a fragmentation grenade in his right hand. He was holding something in the fingers of the other hand and now he tossed it out. It landed with a tinkle at Jim's feet. It was the pin of the grenade.

A loud commotion came from behind him and someone with an American accent cried, 'No, Conrad!'

'Lazar,' Jim said, keeping his voice steady, 'you make one tiny move to throw that grenade and you're dead.'

The dark eyes under those bushy eyebrows were wild, and the mouth was twisted in a curious smile. 'Not yet. First I have an important choice to make.' His right hand withdrew slowly behind his back, and six rifles jerked up in expectation. 'And as you're so fucking smart, Colonel James Slater, you have to guess what I'm going to do. Ready?'

Jim gritted his teeth. 'Go on.'

'Option one: I toss this grenade out and take you and a bunch of your soldier-boys with me.'

'You've got no beef with us, Lazar.'

'No? What about Laverne Dacey?' he snarled. 'That piece of rat shit put me away.'

'Lacey was just following his conscience and you killed him for it. Wasn't that enough for you? No? What about the innocent civilians who died in the Yemen Embassy and the death and misery your exploits have caused in the US? Still not enough?'

Lazar shook his head, eyes half closed. 'You talk a lot, Slater, but you're not playing the game. You haven't heard the second option yet.'

'Get on with it, then.'

'Your boys in the CIA and the NSA would love to know what we've been up to, wouldn't they? Oh yes, they'd love to get their hands on us.' He glanced down. 'I see you've taken two of our cyber team but you won't get much out of them – or out of the two back here. Whatever they can give you is only a small part of the big picture. On the other hand there's all the equipment, and there's Cy Sloper. Now he has a grasp of the whole enterprise. So maybe I should just drop this grenade right in here.'

The American voice came from behind him again, high and pleading. 'Conrad, what's got into you? Don't do this. You and me, we're friends.'

'Shut up, Cy,' he said. 'I don't have friends. This is my operation, and I'll finish it how I want.'

Sweat trickled down Jim's neck. His mind was racing. There'd be no warning. Lazar had put his hand behind his back so no one could see when he relaxed his grip on the safety lever. He could count the fuse down and… and then what?

The guys have their rifles levelled and ranged. If he throws it they'll fire instantly and he'll be dead before he hits the deck. But if it explodes at a little height a grenade like that would wipe out everything within a hundred metres. He'd take maybe a score of my people with him, me included. If he holds it or drops it, he'll kill everyone inside the camper and probably wreck the equipment. So which will it be? It makes no difference to Lazar; either way his life is over. Will this be the last blow in his vendetta against the SAF? Or will he take the longer view and save the secrets of their cyber enterprise?

'Come on, Slater, you have to guess.' He paused. 'You just don't know, do you?' Lazar was leering now, clearly enjoying the moment.

Jim took a deep breath, aware that his own life was hanging by a thread. He swallowed. 'This is pointless, Lazar. Give it up. I'll toss this pin back to you and you can make that grenade safe. We'll see you're dealt with fairly.'

'Fairly?' He laughed, a hard, bitter laugh. 'Was I dealt with fairly for beating up a fucking jihadi collaborator? Was I hell! Save your breath, Slater, it's too late. It's all… too… late.'

Jim watched intently, detected a slight relaxation in the man's right arm. The countdown had begun. He stood rooted to the spot, looking on as if from somewhere outside himself. In the recesses of his brain the fuse was counting down, second by second. Alarm bells were clamouring inside his head, yet still he was unable to move. Then reality crashed in and with a visceral rush of fear and panic he shouted 'Grenade!' and threw himself sideways.

Even inside his helmet the explosion was ear-splittingly loud and a hot wind stung his neck and rattled the visor with sand. Fragments of some sort were bouncing off his helmet and something stabbed into the ground in front of him. He blinked. It was a triangular piece of glass. More fragments pattered down. The shock wave chased up a line of dust that died and settled. Then everything was still.

For a few moments he waited, dazed, apparently still alive. Despite the close-fitting helmet his ears felt like they were stuffed with cotton wool. He rose to his knees and got up slowly. The ground was covered with glass. Lying amongst it were several bloody heaps, all that remained of

Conrad Lazar. Jim's gaze tracked unsteadily back to the camper, took in the empty frames of the shattered windows. His mind began to engage and he turned round.

In every direction he saw his men getting up and dusting themselves off. Eddie came over.

He pointed. 'I was over there with Tom's sniper rifle, Jim,' he said. 'Short range. A head shot would have taken the asshole down, only the grenade would have gone off inside. You said you wanted them alive.' He shrugged. 'Made no difference in the end.'

Jim blinked. 'He held on to the grenade?'

'No, he dropped it behind him. I saw him do it just before I ducked my head.' He looked at the blood-stained wreckage. 'Blew him out the doorway.'

Jim nodded, then crunched over the glass and hauled himself up into the camper.

The interior was a shambles. Smoke hung in the air and the smell of Celonite explosive pricked his nostrils. He began to walk through, making out the ragged remains of bunks on either side, then an area – once a kitchen, perhaps – that had been stripped out to make room for benches. Smashed computer monitors and other items of electronic equipment lay scattered everywhere, amid upturned chairs. He saw two bodies, young men, like the ones who'd come out of the overturned vehicle. Both were clearly dead. Near to one of them a pair of headphones dangled by its cord over the edge of a bench, swinging gently. Seeing the cord it occurred to Jim that everything here would be connected by wire; that way there'd be no danger of picking up stray transmissions, short-range or otherwise. The cord was still plugged into a rack of equipment. Despite the damage Jim identified it as a bank of radiofrequency receivers. But where the hell was Cy Sloper?

He found him under a bench at the end of the cabin. He must have dived for cover, but there was no shelter from a grenade at such close range, especially in such a confined space. He had burns on his face and arms and dark stains were spreading over his T-shirt from multiple shrapnel wounds in his chest. He coughed a spray of bright red blood.

Jim kneeled at his side and put an arm around his shoulders to raise him a little. 'Cy,' he said.

Watery grey eyes rolled up at him.

'Hang in there, Cy.' It was all Jim could think of. Cy Sloper clearly wasn't going to make it.

Sloper tried to say something but his voice was barely a whisper. Jim bent his head closer and waited. Cy tried again.

'Tell John... I did it.'

Jim blinked. 'John? John who?'

Sloper's chest heaved a couple of times. Then, with an enormous effort, he took a deep breath. A single word bubbled between his lips, mingled with one long, last exhalation:

'Abadi.'

Jim laid the limp body back and stared at it.

And a lot fell into place.

58

'You bastard!'

Jim was standing in the middle of John Abadi's office, arms folded across his chest, feet firmly planted. His face, darkened by the desert sun, was darkened still further by rage.

'You lousy bastard! You didn't want those hackers or their equipment at all! You didn't even want Lazar! It was Cy Sloper you were after. *He* was your undercover man.'

Abadi gestured to a chair. 'Take a seat, Jim.'

'You told me Templeton turned down those reconnaissance flights. I'll bet you never even asked him! You'd gone out on a limb with this. You needed time for it to work through, get a positive result before you told your Director what was really going on. You couldn't risk having your protegé spotted and intercepted too early.'

Abadi didn't deny it, just said,'Calm down, Jim.'

But Jim was not about to calm down. 'No wonder you said "thank you" to Tony Grieg when he told you it was Sloper setting up those mid-air collisions. You'd have had egg all over your face if it had gone any higher.'

'Do sit down, Jim. All this can be explained.'

'Oh yes? How about explaining the young soldier I lost in that operation? Or the female soldier who was captured and would have been gang-raped and tortured to death if she hadn't managed to escape? Just so you could retrieve that… that…'

Again Abadi indicated the chair. 'Why don't you come here and tell me exactly what happened?'

For a moment Jim didn't reply. Then he snorted a deep breath in through his nostrils and blew it through his lips. He snatched the chair and sat down.

'We ambushed the convoy. We were well concealed, so I wasn't expecting them to pop off grenades but they did. Lazar's training, no doubt. The squad marksman was killed. He was only in his twenties and he was a damn fine young soldier.'

He paused, feeling yet again the mixture of guilt, anger, and sorrow for Tom's death. There was no reaction from Abadi.

Jim breathed in again and went on, 'We killed six, took four prisoners. But two of their cyber team and Lazar and Sloper were still in the camper. Lazar appeared in the doorway with a hand grenade. He dicked around with me for a while, then let it explode behind him. Killed himself and the other three with him.'

Abadi nodded, lips tight. 'How did you know about… Cy Sloper?'

'He was dying but he managed to say, "Tell John I did it." What did he do, John? What was it that was worth all that sacrifice?'

Abadi clasped his hands and leaned forward.

'Look, Jim. Cy Slater is – was – good with computers. He had a particular talent for money-laundering. He was so good at it that a couple of big crime syndicates made use of his services. This much you knew already.'

'Yes, I did.'

'The FBI got him on a minor count but they were closing in on him for the bigger stuff – and we're talking millions of dollars here. He could have been put away for a very long time – we knew that and he knew that. It was an opportunity. I approached him in prison and offered him a deal. If he cooperated we'd help him to lie low until we could get him out of the US.'

Jim shook his head. That explained how Sloper managed to keep his head down after he was released, despite a concerted effort by the FBI to track him down. He'd been kept in a CIA safe house.

'Once he'd done what we asked,' Abadi continued, 'we'd bring him back and make sure the charges against him were dropped. It was a good deal, and he was on board. But getting him embedded would be difficult and dangerous. That's where Lazar came in. I had him and Saleh transferred to the same prison. Cy got friendly with Lazar, did him a favour when he got out.'

'Yeah,' Jim said sourly. 'Helped him publish a book that notched up another of my men.'

Abadi grimaced. 'Believe me, I wasn't a party to that – I didn't even know about it until you told me. I recruited Lazar, it's true, but I wasn't banking on him to do anything except get Cy Sloper in with the jihadis. That much he did.'

'So it was your idea to make it look like a kidnap.'

'No, I left the method to him. I expected him to do it quietly. The shooting of those two bodyguards and the rest of it was Lazar's idea.'

'Designed to provoke us into mounting a rescue. Which was actually a trap. We almost fell for it, too.'

'I didn't know about that, either.'

'And then we had the FBI's concocted identity of a "William Lampeter" and the staged execution. All that played right into your hands didn't it? Sloper had vanished off the map.'

'It was convenient, yes.' Abadi licked his lips. 'But look, I had no control over Lazar. It seems he had his own agenda.'

'He sure did, and it included organizing cyber exploits that cost our country a lot of lives and billions of dollars.'

'Not many lives, I think. There was a financial hit, it's true, much of it borne by private industry.' Abadi sighed. 'Think of it as collateral damage. And like collateral damage, some of it you can anticipate, but most of it you can't. I couldn't know how quickly he'd take charge of that cyber team, or how effectively.'

Jim gritted his teeth. 'You put the nasty ingredients in the pot and stirred it. I don't think you can dodge responsibility as easily as that.'

He shrugged. 'Have it your own way.'

'I don't suppose you let the FBI in on what you were doing.'

He didn't answer, just tilted his head and gave that half-smile.

'Don't tell me,' Jim said, his voice rising. 'Questions of national security.'

He leaned forward. 'Look, Jim, I have nothing against the FBI. They're perfectly good at what they do, bringing individual felons to justice. In the Agency we have to look at the bigger picture. And the overall outcome of this operation was very satisfactory. You knocked out the cyber warfare team, and Cy Sloper did exactly what we asked him to do.'

'Which was…?'

'The Sons of the Caliphate had billions of dollars, mainly donations from sympathetic regimes. Cy laundered it into prearranged bank accounts all over the world, using multiple hops. Not even their cyber experts are going to find out where it's gone – in fact thanks to you they don't even have the computer he worked with. Even if, by some miracle, they cracked it, it wouldn't help them, because we've been monitoring those accounts. As soon as each deposit was made we withdrew the money and closed the account. Their coffers are empty. They won't be able to pay their recruits or buy arms and explosives, even buy fuel for their vehicles. Cy Sloper has struck them a blow from which they may never recover.'

'Come on, you're saying they couldn't simply replenish their coffers from the same sources as before?'

'Oh, they could, but it would take time. Meanwhile they're in a weakened state, and the Yemeni Army can mop them up.'

Jim shook his head. 'Well, well, Cy Sloper died a hero. Congratulations. Why couldn't you have told me?'

'That's not the way we work, Jim. When an agent goes under cover the fewer people who know, the better. Someone could inadvertently drop a hint or be captured, tortured. We had a duty to keep him safe.'

'You didn't have a duty to keep me and my troop safe, though, did you?'

He shrugged. 'You're the US Army. Your duty is to serve the United States of America, in whatever shape or form that service comes.'

'Thanks.' Jim got up. 'Cy Sloper.' He shook his head. 'The poor bastard probably even believed you. He thought you'd get him out of there alive when he'd done what you asked.'

Abadi said nothing.

Jim said, 'Tony Grieg and his FBI colleagues have a right to be told what happened to him.'

'That's not for you to do, he can come and see me. I'll tell him what he needs to know. By the way, were you right about their use of multiple antennas?'

'I'l be making a full report to General Harken and he'll inform your Director. No doubt he'll tell you what you need to know.'

Jim walked to the door, then turned. 'We won't be meeting again, Agent Abadi.'

'I expect not, Colonel Slater.'

59

Jim went straight from Langley to the Pentagon and headed on up to Wendell Harken's office. He was still bristling from the encounter with Abadi, so he paused outside for a moment to collect himself. Then he straightened his uniform and tie, lifted his chin, knocked and went in. Wendell rose to shake hands.

'Jim! Quite a coup you pulled off out there. Should make it easier next time the bean counters are debating our appropriation. Take a seat, tell me all about it.'

He listened without interruption as Jim gave him a detailed account: the waiting around in the ruined Yemeni village, the abortive interception of a jihadi convoy, the lucky break that led him and the Yemeni captain to interview the escaped girls, Holly's capture and escape, the ambush of the convoy, and finally the revelation about Cy Sloper.

When he'd finished, Jim added, 'It would have been a whole lot harder if Holly hadn't escaped.'

Wendell said, 'She's a remarkable girl.'

Something surged inside Jim. 'She certainly is.' Wendell looked up and Jim quickly extracted the warmth from his tone. 'Capable and resourceful.'

'I think we'll leave it to her what she chooses to tell her father. How is she now?'

'She put a brave face on it but she's pretty traumatized. I arranged counselling as soon as we got back. I haven't seen her since. Something she said will interest you, Wendell. Remember the part of the induction course you devised in case any of us was taken hostage? The one where you're hooded and taken somewhere by a complicated route and afterwards you have to point it out on a map?'

'They always find that tough,' Wendell said.

'Yes they do, and she was no exception, but it worked for her. When she escaped from that cell inside The Palace she was able to find her way back through a whole maze of corridors to the outside. She said I should tell you. It saved her life.'

Wendell smiled. 'She's the first one ever to thank me for it.'

'Exactly what I told her.'

There was a pause. Wendell heaved a sigh. 'Well, it's a relief you put a stop to that cyber cell's activities. They created absolute havoc over here. No doubt they had more mischief in store, too. How big a part do you think Lazar played in all that?'

'I'm sure he took a lot of credit for himself but I think they could have done it without him. My guess is what he did was identify the targets, told them where to look for weaknesses. And it was smart the way he protected the team, keeping them on the move and then going to ground in that town. We'd still be looking if it wasn't for those three girls.'

'I hope they're being well looked after?'

'Yes, I contacted that Yemeni Captain when we were in Sana'a on our way back. He said they've found them suitable accommodation. I don't know what they're doing now but anything would be better than what they had to do before.'

Wendell nodded. 'What about the attack on the US Embassy when they turned the drone. Did you get to the bottom of that?'

'We examined the vehicles in Lazar's little convoy. It was like I said: large collapsible antennas in the two all-terrains and the camper, with powerful transmitters to drive them. It was their ultimate line of defence and when they came under attack they used it.'

'What happened to all that equipment?'

'We brought it back with us. The computers are pretty badly damaged, but the NSA may be able to do something with whatever's in the drives. It'll be more tricky if they encrypted it and uploaded it to the Cloud.'

Wendell sat back, apparently pondering something. He returned his gaze to Jim. 'Something's still not clear to me. How come you were in the right place at the right time to ambush Lazar's convoy?'

'It was a calculated gamble,' Jim said. 'Lazar knew there were Special Forces in the area, so an attack had to be imminent. It was sure to come from the main entrance to the town, so he led his people out at the rear of the stables and took the route west – the one those three girls used.' He grinned. 'Just to make sure he was thinking along the right lines, I got Tommy Geiger to phone me on an unencrypted line. During the call I told Tommy we were mounting a joint operation with the Yemeni Army, targeting The Palace.'

'How did you know they'd intercept it?'

'I was pretty sure they would. I figured an outfit like that would be sweeping every available wavelength, listening out for comms. I think I was right – the camper was certainly equipped for it. Lazar thought we'd attack in the early hours because it was standard procedure, so they cleared out fast in broad daylight. We were waiting for them.'

Wendell smiled. 'A certain poetic justice in that, Jim.'

'That's what I thought.'

'It was a major problem but you were the one who solved it. In a way you saved Abadi's neck.'

Jim shrugged. 'Shame about that but you can't win 'em all.'

Wendell laughed, then got to his feet and Jim did the same. 'You'll let me have a full written report, won't you, Jim? And I'll pass it to the Director of the CIA. He's going to be very pleased.'

'You need to tell him something else, Wendell, and that'll make him less pleased.'

Wendell's face fell. 'What's that?'

'There's at least one other cyber cell working for the Sons of the Caliphate.'

'Good God, how do you know that?'

'Think about it. Lazar hated the SAF. Nothing would have given him greater pleasure than to take me out together with maybe twenty of my guys. But he didn't. Instead he did his best to destroy the equipment and anyone who could shed light on what they'd been doing. Why? There can only be one reason. They were exploiting vulnerabilities in the US's digital infrastructure, and they must have been sharing them with another group or groups. If US operatives got hold of that information they could identify the weaknesses and close them up. Then the others would have to start all over again. Lazar didn't want that to happen. Much as he hated the SAF, he wanted to inflict damage on the US even more, and what he did meant it would go on after his death. That was his legacy.'

'But thanks to Cy Sloper the jihadis won't have any money to pay them.'

'Cyber warfare's not expensive, Wendell. And we know they have other ways of making things enjoyable for their young recruits.'

Wendell sighed. 'Thanks, Jim. That's important. I'll make sure the Director knows.'

They shook hands. Minutes later Jim was in a cab, heading for the airport.

60

Jim decided not to order up a car from the motor pool at Fort Piper but took a cab from Raleigh-Durham instead. It dropped him off at the gate. As he passed through the outer office Bagley said, 'Captain Cressington said she'd like to see you, sir.'

'She's here?' He felt a stirring of expectation. 'Right. Tell her I'm back, would you?'

'Sir.'

He was at his desk when Holly knocked and came in. He stood up. 'Come and sit down, Holly. How are you feeling?'

'All right, I guess. Well...' She took the chair he was indicating and he returned to his desk. 'I wanted to tell you... I'm resigning my commission. Leaving the Army.'

He caught his breath. 'Holly, no – look you've had a dreadful experience and you're still in shock. This isn't the time to be making decisions like that. You have to give yourself time—'

'I've thought it through, Jim. This is the way I want it.'

'But for God's sake why? It was your life's ambition to join this outfit and you achieved it!'

'That's true. I've loved the whole journey, the demands it placed on me – physically and mentally, the skills I've learnt – every bit of it. But it's gone sour. I know what you were doing when I got to that check point. You and the whole troop were going to try to rescue me. Because of my bad judgement I put all of you at risk.'

Jim thought quickly. He didn't want her to go and he was trying, not too successfully, to persuade himself that he was only thinking of the good of the SAF. It was hard to know what to say, how to turn this around.

'Holly, you're not being fair to yourself. First off, there was nothing exceptional about mounting that rescue mission – we'd have done it for any one of our number who'd been captured. And second, what you're viewing as a failure was really a triumph.'

'Oh, come on!. How could it possibly be a triumph?'

'Listen to me. I fed Lazar and his friends disinformation. I let them know an attack was imminent, a joint operation with the Yemeni Army. Lazar was suspicious by nature, so he may or may not have fallen for it. But when they took a US Special Forces officer prisoner and she escaped, and the jihadis went looking for her and ran into three of our desert-going vehicles – well, all that confirmed it for him. So Lazar cleared out with his team as soon as he could, and we were in place, ready to give them a warm reception.'

She still looked dubious, so he went on, 'How tough would it have been to take over The Palace?'

'Very,' she said. 'The place is a warren.'

'There you are. We could have lost a lot of men in an attack like that. But it was you who made it possible for us to ambush the convoy instead. You saved lives, Holly.'

She smiled. 'You're very persuasive, Jim, but it won't work. A few days ago I killed two men and I did it at close quarters. Popping off a target with a rifle – well, that's almost impersonal. Crushing one man's throat and sinking a knife into another man's kidneys – that's one hell of a different ball game. We'd trained for it, of course, but this was the first time I ever had to do it for real. It's had an effect on me, I know it has. If the situation ever arose again I'd hesitate, and that could put my comrades' lives in danger as well as my own. They can't rely on me. You can't rely on me. I'm sorry, Jim, a burden like that isn't one I can carry.'

Jim swallowed. 'Holly, I'm not going to mince words. You're one of the most gifted officers we've had through here. You have the skills, you can use your initiative, and you've already gained the loyalty of your non-comms. Please don't throw all that away. If not for the sake of the SAF,' his voice dropped abruptly, 'do it for me.'

For a long moment they looked at each other and something indefinable passed between them. The atmosphere in the room had changed.

She said softly, 'I'm sorry Jim, I can't.'

He sighed. 'Suppose you did leave the Army, what would you do?'

'I could start up a gym. Teach survival skills.'

'Well no one could have better credentials.'

'Jim…' She fixed him with those astonishing light-grey eyes. 'You'd be good at that: instructing on survival skills – you've done it all before.' She looked down at her hands.

'What I'm trying to say is, you could… you could come in with me.'

He blinked rapidly. He knew this was much more than a business proposal. He also knew what it must have cost her even to make the suggestion. Nor could he dismiss the idea. It was no longer any use denying how drawn he was to her. He felt it as an ache, a longing that dragged somewhere deep inside him. Now she was saying she felt the same way. She must realize he'd done his best to act professionally towards a more junior officer and she was offering him a way out. If both of them quit the Army it would remove all obstacles, put the relationship on an entirely different footing.

Thoughts flashed through his head. What would life with her be like? Wonderful, fresh, physical, constantly changing? Almost certainly. Turbulent? Almost certainly, too, because of her indomitable and independent spirit, but that was what had attracted him to her in the first place. He could love her. He *would* love her. But…

'Holly.' He spoke as gently as he could. 'It's a tempting prospect, don't think it isn't. It might even work for a while – but only for a while. I'd start to miss my old life. I'd probably become miserable as hell and bad-tempered. We need to be realistic. It's too late for me to change. The Army's part of me, we've been together for so long now we're joined at the hip.'

She looked up again, lips twisted in a rueful smile. 'I thought you'd say that.'

They stood and he came around the desk. 'Since you're not in the Army any more…' he said, opening his arms.

She hugged him hard against her, then held him at arm's length. Her eyes were moist. 'Goodbye, Jim.'

She pulled away and left the office quickly.

After a moment or two he followed. He passed Bagley, whose disappointed bloodhound expression had been replaced by one of blank surprise, emerged into the open air and stood there, watching her receding figure. This was the turning point: Holly was walking out of his life. For a while he fought an impulse to chase after her, tell her he'd changed his mind. Even as the thought presented itself he knew he wouldn't, he couldn't. He took a deep breath and his feet led him back to the outer office, his mind on another plane entirely, whirling with a kaleidoscope of images:

A resolute young woman who wanted to be accepted on her own merits. A fiercely indignant Captain pulled prematurely from a mission. A soldier working the mechanism of an unfamiliar rifle, preparing to face death in a last, defiant stand. That bright, irresistible smile. The warmth of the unexpected kiss when she was lying in the sick bay. The feel of her body against him when she hugged him. And, through it all, those light-grey eyes, like windows into another world...

Bagley looked up. 'Colonel? General Harken just called. There's an urgent assignment for you, sir. Holoconference in ten minutes.'

He paused, looking at his ADC, and the images fell away.

'Thank you, Bagley.'

He turned and made his way to the holoconference suite.

ACKNOWLEDGEMENTS

I'm grateful to my wife Paula, sons Graham and Daniel, and daughter Debby for their feedback and suggestions. Graham deserves special mention for his invaluable help with aviation issues. I'm also grateful to my friends in the Liverpool-based writers' group 'Wordsmiths' – Neville Krasner, John Clarke, Mary Gillie, Emma Mackley, and Rachel Sayle – who listened to successive chapters and provided invaluable critical comments.

For authors like myself the internet is a superb research resource. All the same there is no substitute for an authoritative text, and in writing this book I had the benefit of two: *Cyber War* by Richard A. Clarke and Robert K. Knake (Ecco; Reprinted 2012), and *Cybersecurity and Cyberwar* by P.W. Singer and Allan Friedman (Oxford University Press, 2014). Both these accounts stress the vulnerability of developed nations to cyber threats, and perhaps my novel, although a work of fiction, will help in a modest way to reinforce the message.

Printed in Great Britain
by Amazon